FIREBIRD

ALSO BY TONY ROTHMAN

Fiction

The Course of Fortune
Censored Tales
The World is Round

Nonfiction

Sacred Mathematics: Japanese Temple
Geometry (with Fukagawa Hidetoshi)
Everything's Relative and Other Fables from Science and Technology
Doubt and Certainty (with George Sudarshan)
Instant Physics
A Physicist on Madison Avenue
Science à la Mode
Frontiers of Modern Physics

FIREBIRD

TONY ROTHMAN

WILDSIDE PRESS

*To the memory of my father, Milton Rothman,
with gratitude for the scientific life.*

Published by Wildside Press LLC.
www.wildsidebooks.com

ZERO

"You know this is mad." That's how it began. That is how Nathaniel Machuzak remembered it began. With the wind blowing into the Texas hill country and the convoy snaking after it toward folly. With his half-incredulous, half-angry challenge to the bearded Russian sitting beside him in the jeep.

"Yes, it's mad." The parched gulches the procession crossed each moment were hardly drier than the Russian's reply; his distant gaze, trained on a Brahman steer munching grass behind a barbed-wire fence, shrouded his desiccated response with fatality.

"Borisovich, there's not a snowball's chance in hell of it working. And if something fucks up...*Jesus*..."

"Machine is conditioned. Should be okay."

Nathaniel scowled ferociously at Yaroslav Borisovich Archangelsky, but that one only continued to stare out the window, bearded chin resting on knuckles. Worthy of Rasputin, the great beard provided its pint-sized wearer with effective camouflage and his bedraggled hair lent Archangelsky more than a passing resemblance to the crazy monk, but Machuzak had known this Russian too long to be fooled. Slava was crazy, foxlike, and the barely perceptible purse of his lips assured Machuzak that he was far from blind.

"Y–you've misunderstood something, Slava," Nathaniel persisted to the march-past of scrub and rock. "This was supposed to be the dedication. The plan was to give them the c–cook's tour, show them a routine pulse. That's all."

"Plans change, *moi drug*."

"I—wasn't told."

For an instant the conversation lapsed; then Archangelsky chuckled with an unearthly rumble an octave lower than could possibly emerge from such a shrimp. "Nat Edward'ich, you think we've been killing ourselves day and night for cook's tour? Who was Cook anyway?"

Managing a faint smile at the Archangelsky-ism, Machuzak did not at once reply. He recognized that he was slow in speech, to the point of hesitation, and he flattered himself that this was because he thought before he opened his mouth. But at this moment the welling anger soon overcame hesitation. "What the hell does Rasmussen think he's doing?" he hit the steering wheel with the flat of his hand, even as he knew exactly what Slava would say:

"Giving fire to the world."

* * * *

Machuzak's jeep insisted on its own judgment. The video was off, permanently, but no one could mistake the voice: Leonard Rasmussen himself, CFRC's director, online from the lab. Urgency shaded the famously boisterous tenor, one that had of late grown gravelly, but even in poor health Rasmussen did all to sound confident, sanguine. "Mac," he said, "I smell trouble brewing at the gate. Be prepared, like a good scout. What's your ETA?"

"N–no problem, Len. Give us twenty minutes."

"Thumbs up," Rasmussen said, and signed off.

A long sigh escaped Machuzak's lips. His slowness, he conceded, was not limited to speech alone.

"Be glad we don't have implants," Slava remarked.

Machuzak nodded grimly. With forty the next milestone, both men were too old to want to have anything to do with the Apple Brainwave, which wired you to the Internet once and for all. Auto fatalities for 24/7 chatterers already exceeded deaths by GPS distraction. Smart cars could take over the thinking, but drive-thru Texans hadn't exactly gone into paroxysms of ecstasy at the thought of handing over the sacred wheel to a superior intellect.

The world had changed, Machuzak shook his head with the now-permanent wonder, the geography no less. As the procession trailed the buzzards west and south out of Austin, Machuzak numbered the ranches covered with solar panels, some the older silicon and copper, more with photovoltaic nanopaint. He convinced himself that the lazy whoosh of blades turning in the wind made itself heard above the road noise.

Some things are frozen in time. A beet-red farmer perched atop his tractor stared down Machuzak and Archangelsky as the motorcade passed, leveled at them imaginary shotgun sights. The locals blamed the lab for the worsening of the water, for the annual freak snowstorms and any time their TV signal got lost. St. Cecilia and her talk-show cronies insisted that CFRC scientists were space aliens.

"We're all aliens in this *place*," Slava spat out the window.

It was true. They all spoke with accents, hardly any of them Texas twangs.

The caravan snaked up and down more kilometers, past oak trees dripping with moss, clumps of prickly pears, more ranches, down, up and—suddenly it lay before them. Machuzak pulled off the road to give the dignitaries an opportunity to gaze upon it for the first time. But whether you came over this rise once in a lifetime or every morning for a decade, you remained unprepared. There below, sprawled over three or four square kilometers, the great complex—the water towers, cooling towers, the giant structures you'd mistake for aircraft hangars, the satellite dishes, the swans gliding over the artificial lake—each time it seemed less planned than dropped. From an alien planet.

The congress members and tycoons shielding their eyes in the Texas light made astonished noises. Aye they should, Machuzak nodded. The vista confronting you from this rise is so unexpected, so irreconcilable with the eyescape, that you cannot but be drawn toward it, downward, into the valley. And they descended.

* * * *

The scene at the gate was worse than Rasmussen had foreseen. "What the—?" Machuzak exclaimed, seeing the way blocked by a mass of cameramen and bots pointing headsets in every direction and, worst of all—"Slava," he said, as he jammed on the brakes and the motorcade ground to a halt, "who the hell's been talking to the press?"

Archangelsky didn't need to say, "I told you so" as the journalists stampeded toward them.

Nathaniel's perplexity was rising by the instant. On a normal day nothing much distinguished CFRC's main gate from the entrance to the Ruby or L-Bar Ranch, nothing except the nearly invisible eyes that surmounted the modest brick fence and the buffalo roaming in the vast fields beyond. On a normal—Before him, several dozen protestors had braved the afternoon heat to prevent…what? Nathaniel shook his head; there hadn't been a protest since the lab opened. The college students—well, that anyone could understand… The Buddhists surprised him and the hermits and dropouts of all sorts interspersed among the rest, people who had simply removed themselves from the pace of the current century. More than the numbers it was the agitation, the genuine fear written on their faces, that seized Nathaniel's attention. As he stepped out of the jeep they pushed toward him angrily waving their placards. "No radiation!"

"No bombs!" a bearded twenty-year-old shouted silently in his face by flashing his phone screen at Machuzak. "This place is hit and we all go up!"

"Whoa," said Machuzak, raising his hands. "No one's building bombs here."

"What about the tritium?" the kid insisted belligerently, punching his keys.

"I've got to shoot you," Machuzak answered with a smile, which to the surprise of both of them disarmed his opponent.

At that moment, a portly businessman on the far side of fifty, shaded by a full-sized Stetson, stepped out of his long-horn-graced limo and waded into the fray. Nathaniel knew him by sight, of course, but their handshake at Bergstrom airport had been his first and only introduction to Richard Garrett, the billionaire chair of CFRC's board of governors.

"Excuse me, sir, just what is going on here?"

Despite the confrontation unfolding about them, and that he towered over Garrett by a head, Machuzak deferred to the tone of voice of a man who not only expected to be, but was, listened to. "M–Mr. Garrett, I suspect you know better than I. Rumor has it—" he glanced at Archangelsky in the jeep—"that Leonard has decided to use Prometheus to fire up the lab's power grid."

"First I've heard about it, er…Dr.—"

"—Machuzak, Nathaniel Machuzak."

"And what's wrong with that?"

"Nothing…everything."

Garrett looked up quizzically at the lanky, perturbed, perplexed scientist. "These people seem to think it's dangerous. Is it?"

Nathaniel hesitated, glanced at the fevered crowd surrounding this surreal exchange. "Hmm, probably not to us, if that's what you mean. But Mr. Garrett, believe me, that machine was not ready, is not ready—"

"Ah," Garrett shrugged jovially, considering. "Dr. Machuzak, where's your sense of adventure? I say we give it a go. If it fizzles, well…"

In spite of himself Machuzak was fast working up a sweat. They'd always known that the second-worst thing that could happen to the program was a fizzled demonstration and the worst thing was an accident. Today they were risking both. For what? He only dimly perceived the implications. On the verge of losing his temper altogether, Machuzak half spit out, "It's insane!" but confronted by his own lack of imagination, he swallowed his tongue and faced the crowd. "Why don't you come watch?" he announced to the protestors, badging open the gate.

For only an instant, shocked silence and baffled glances met the unexpected invitation, then one by one the young people nodded and moved toward the retreating fence.

"Good move," remarked Garrett.

"Welcome to the Controlled Fusion Research Center," Machuzak said, and the crowd streamed in.

The motley *guignol* of grizzled recluses munching on home-baked pies, saffron-robed monks banging drums and Energy Star moms pushing their phone-charging strollers quickly engulfed the motorcade, and the limo-bound dignitaries might have walked the final kilometer to the guardhouse. Metalized balloons bobbed above everything.

"That boy at the gate is like my daughter," observed Slava. "She won't speak to me except by texting."

Aye, the world was new. Machuzak vividly recollected that day nearly two decades ago when Americans awoke to pictures of cuddly polar bears drowning in the former Arctic ice cap. By now green had turned black. His "jeep" usually ran on algae, and long ago those fourteen-mpg Urban Assault Vehicles, which Texans believed were guaranteed them by the Second Amendment, had met the same fate as the dinosaurs, except in Crawford.

The one word you never heard amidst *solar, wind* and *bio* was *fusion.* The energy source of stars. If fusioneers, physicists like him and Slava, could do it, they would hand the world a new, virtually limitless supply of energy. The first problem, Machuzak conceded heavily, was that after eighty years of effort, the ultimate goal still lay just beyond their fingertips. The second problem was that to people like the kid at the gate, fusion meant bombs of the worst sort. Then there was the third problem: the future never had much of a constituency.

Leonard Rasmussen, CFRC's director, was determined that their endeavor should succeed. Ten years after he'd rebuilt the old Austin National Fusion Research Laboratory into the Controlled Fusion Research Center, his troops had yet to produce a self-sustaining reaction, which would alter the history of the world, but if Slava was right, they were going to try today.

＊ ＊ ＊ ＊

Machuzak waved the crowd past the perplexed duty guard, who raised the boom in spite of himself, and everyone passed through the crumbling concrete barriers that had been ordained after 9/11. Nathaniel figured the odds of a terrorist attack on CFRC were about the same as a hit against the nearest Taco Bell, but when even university students thought they were building bombs…

The crowd passed along the wide arc of the lake until at last everyone stood before the main building, gawking, giggling at the majestic fountain that rose from the water and enveloped them all in a fine spray. Their childlike wonder prompted Machuzak to see the sculpture for the first time in years. Once, those irregular, artfully corroded bronze sheets soaring heavenward through rainbow mists had reminded him of angel wings, and now he remembered that. Afresh he contemplated the small sphere surmounting the whole, bronze, brass, intricately carved away such that inner labyrinths were suggested.

"What do you suppose that sphere means?" a guest asked.

"The sun," Nathaniel answered and ducked inside, the crowd after him.

Each and every person was instantly transported outside again by the lobby, which had been designed with light. Once more transfixed, hermits and dignitaries stood together, smiling at the vaulting arches that touched skylights open to the heavens. For a second moment, the throng's admiration of a visionary creation briefly rekindled in Nathaniel a cinder of boyhood wonder. In those two moments, he discovered again what his profession was about, what it should be about, and resolved to act.

Setting off, he ignored the exhibits and memorabilia and mountains of food, determined to confront Rasmussen. The director was nowhere to be found, but his eyes lit on Leonard's wife, Theresa, surrounded by admirers. Machuzak took two steps toward that charmed circle and suddenly halted, lassoed by his damned indecision, and he foolishly stood frozen in the middle of the great lobby as Slava looked on with amusement.

Luckily, Theresa herself caught sight of him and motioned him over. "What's wrong, Mac?" she said. "You look troubled."

He'd bypass the obligatory pleasantries: "Theresa, is Len up to anything?"

"Shh," she smiled. "It's supposed to be a secret."

Christ, Slava was exactly right. For a moment Nathaniel stared blankly at Theresa. They'd known each other a decade, since he'd first set foot in this miraculous space. A handsome woman, a strong one, Theresa sometimes remarked that she read history to "be reminded of the beauty of ephemeral things," and with her husband's health in decline, she had well crossed the threshold where life's transitoriness ceases to be a surprise. "Believe me, Mac," she said, casting on Nathaniel the indulgent gaze a mother reserves for the runt of the litter, "everything will be fine. Leonard knows what he's doing."

Nathaniel scowled. As splendid as Theresa was, she wasn't a scientist.

"Theresa, this isn't the sort of thing you try in public. It's *arrogant*—" He suddenly halted, seeing. "This has something to do with ITER, doesn't it?"

Theresa's silence instantly told Nathaniel he'd hit the mark. ITER, the colossal twenty-billion-euro device that the EU and a half dozen other countries had built in southern France, had finally completed its shakedown last week.

Leonard would never allow the International Thermonuclear Experimental Reactor to beat CFRC in the race for fusion. When ITER's construction was announced, years before climate change went mainstream, the United States' first move was to pull out of the endeavor. In, out... America's endless vacillations handed Leonard Rasmussen his opening. With legendary charm, boundless vigor, infinite patience, he sweet-talked and cajoled. "I want ten billion dollars and fifteen years," he leveled his gaze on high-tech magnates and secretaries of energy. Eventually he got what he wanted, the Manhattan Project for energy.

From the ashes of the decaying Austin lab rose a glittering new entity, the Controlled Fusion Research Center. Construction began immediately on the consortium's centerpiece, christened ASSET for Advanced Steady State Experimental Tokamak. Few words, Machuzak knew, could be more meaningless to outsiders. To insiders, it meant one thing: the future, and lab hands soon christened the device Prometheus, bringer of fire. Not fully ITER's size, ASSET's design was—they hoped—smarter, and with luck it would trump its rival. Today the competition had stepped out of the shadows.

Nathaniel walked away from Theresa and found Archangelsky hovering over the hors d'oeuvres. "A tsar's table," Slava mused, only obliquely glancing at Machuzak. Then he raised his beard, grinning. "You look tortured, my friend," he said, thrusting a sparkling glass into the other's hand.

"You were right, friend," Machuzak answered, glancing at the improbable, expectant crowd now milling everywhere about them. "They're going to turn on the lights today—they're going to try."

"Of course I was right. I said it before. You think we've been busting our balls for a month now on cook's tour?"

Nathaniel nodded, belatedly as usual, he thought. When fully operational ASSET was meant to supply electricity for the entire laboratory. When. If. It had never been connected to the turbine. They'd been slowly putting the machine through its paces when suddenly the board decreed a commissioning, apparently more, and they threw Prometheus together with sealing wax and string. Oh, it was sputtering along all right—not with a torch but a match—and they'd have to dismantle the beast and spend weeks righting what they'd made wrong. Even with ITER suddenly breathing down their necks, something here did not add up. The idiots couldn't believe that they'd turn on the lights in front of an audience.

"Let them make fools of us all. Game isn't worth candle. The higher-ups will get blame."

"We all will. Tell me, Slava, weren't scientists at one time supposed to be honest, dedicated to the truth? Wasn't that the oath we took when we became physicists?"

Archangelsky threw a bewildered expression at Machuzak. "Nat Edward'ich, tell me on what strange and wonderful planet you grew up."

* * * *

With a resignation to futility, Nathaniel Machuzak again resolved to stop this lunacy. He took a step toward the lobby's center and the lab's deputy director, Cyrus Krieg-Zuber. "Into whose hard hat were the alleged feces defecated?" Zuber snarled as if offended by his phone itself. "Yes, we shall investigate at once."

"Cy, what are you on about?" Machuzak said the moment Krieg-Zuber had signed off. "I saw it myself this morning in the rf heating area. A tech was so stressed that he took a crap into his hard hat, that's all. You would too if you had any idea of what was going on around here. Put an end to it."

The blond Krieg-Zuber, accent purposely falling on the final syllable, trained his laser stare momentarily on Nathaniel, stroked his chin. Then he turned without a word, straightened the trimmed lapels of his jacket and edged toward the cameras. For a moment Machuzak stared after him, openmouthed.

Nathaniel ducked into the men's room only to be brought up short by Leonard Rasmussen turning toward him. The director hadn't been much visible around the lab for a year, not since the day when that terrible thing happened. Until that day, he'd been a compact, vigorous fifty-five, with silvering hair, ruddy skin and a sly grin, and then he stumbled. Machuzak hadn't set eyes on him at all for three months and the change was almost too much to endure. Leonard Rasmussen in a wheelchair.

The moment Rasmussen caught sight of him, he struggled to his feet.

"L—Leonard," Nathaniel stuttered simultaneously, moving to help.

Rasmussen waved him off. "It's fine," he said with the effort of one whose muscles refuse to obey. "I can make it. We have a demo to perform, don't we, Mac?"

"Len," Nathaniel pressed, "you can't do this. How far is ITER from ignition? They can't be close—"

"One day ahead is too close, Mac."

"To hell with them. You know as well as I do what you're risking. Overloads, disruptions, equipment damage—"

"ASSET was behaving during the pre-ops—"

"—reputation. What you're planning isn't a pre-op. Don't do it."

For an instant Rasmussen glanced at Nathaniel with pleading eyes and steadied himself. In that space the last piece of the day's puzzle fell into place. ITER may be breathing down our necks, but Leonard Rasmussen is determined to see Prometheus'torch set ablaze before he dies.

Machuzak fell silent and helped Leonard into the lobby.

* * * *

Cyrus Krieg-Zuber had reappeared and already begun herding the crowd across the three hundred meters of asphalt and grass that separated the main building from the great tokamak complex at CFRC. Cyrus the Great, striving with his corporate physique for every air of an acting director, if not presidential candidate, had invited the entire planet to watch. What a spectacle it would be, he assured the press, his sartorial splendor no less than his unplaceable accent convincing them that history itself was today in the making. For an instant Machuzak caught his eye, but the adder's glare Zuber shot at him before he turned again to the cameras said one thing: don't.

There was nothing for it. He passed Leonard on to Theresa and filed out with Slava and a hundred others toward what they called the pentagon. Not quite "twice five miles of fertile ground," but six stories high, the immense complex consisted of five connected subunits arrayed around a central hub. Within that hub sat Prometheus. All told, the pentagon covered the area of two or three football fields. The size of the place alone filled visitors with a certain awe, and as they approached, Nathaniel could not doubt it, each one of them was wondering what on Earth could be inside.

What is inside is not quite on Earth.

Krieg-Zuber had stationed a few smiling bots at the nearest entrance to distribute hard hats, say, "Have a wonderful day" and break-dance. Flashing his badge and teeth to the crowd, he waved it over the electronic lock, a gesture that told everyone they were about to enter forbidden domains. With nearly comical bows, he ushered in the dignitaries, then the rest, and when Machuzak and Archangelsky passed him, his expression soured.

Inside, Nathaniel and Slava found themselves shoved up against Garrett again. Soon Machuzak became conscious of a hush descending on the crowd, the same hush that descended every time visitors entered the motor-generator room and understood they are dwarfed.

"Size does matter," Archangelsky remarked.

Garrett looked askance at the Russian, not knowing what to make of him, but Slava was right. Above the persistent whir of the flywheels,

Nathaniel explained that beneath their feet spun the four huge motor-generators that power CFRC's experiments. Without them, every time they started up Prometheus they'd be in danger of draining greater Austin of electricity. He led Garrett to a chain surrounding one of the wells and the chairman caught his breath when he gazed onto the 700-ton giant resting in a pit the size of a small house. Two generators remained idle—spares—but for short periods the primaries alone could supply 700 megawatts of power: seven million lightbulbs, 700,000 microwave ovens, enough electricity for a small city. On the other hand, the purpose of these beasts was merely to put a match to Prometheus.

"That's hard to believe," remarked Garrett.

Machuzak lowered his gaze at the chairman and recounted how during their installation, a great crane was lowering one of the flywheels' outer casing into the pit. Suddenly cables began straining, snapping. Within seconds the entire crane collapsed and the stator fell into place. Four hundred tons of steel crashed down around the workmen standing atop the flywheel. A cable whipped up, smashed through the crane-cabin window and broke the operator's arm. Seismometers in Dallas and Houston registered the tremor, but no one died of a heart attack. One of the workmen did take the week off.

"Dr. Machuzak!" exclaimed Garrett, now in outright disbelief, "surely you are making this all up."

"In the realm of the gods, Mr. Garrett," Machuzak replied pointedly, "even the extraordinary is ordinary." Nathaniel regretted the words even as they escaped his lips. He was attempting to make a perhaps-too-subtle hint and was certain that Garrett would hold the remark against him as a sign of the arrogance of physicists, but the businessman appeared oblivious, shrouded by the sense of personal insignificance the motor-generators produce.

Hurrying on, Zuber led the crowd directly to the tokamak test cell. He received voice and visual authorization from the guard to enter and ordered the massive door open. Soon the onlookers were rimming the central bay, streaming videos to friends worldwide. A hush fell, more palpable than the one that had come before.

Prometheus was the ultimate plumber's nightmare and no matter how often Machuzak tried to describe it, he failed. His failure was not a matter of words, he reassured himself; the eye is simply incapable of taking in everything that confronts it. The device, all fifty thousand tons, stands nearly four stories high, but is buried by the hundreds of cables and microwave guides feeding it from all directions, by the diagnostic equipment that sprout from every crevice, by the massive particle accelerators that heat the fuel. You glimpse a ladder here, a girder there, two flags flying from the impossibly massive crane above, but Prometheus is too complex to allow you to make it into a sensible whole.

Peel away the cables and plumbing and girders and you discover a great cylindrical vessel, the full height of the machine, which contains a vacuum nearly as perfect as you'd find in deep space. Dismantle this cryostat and you reveal sixteen superconducting magnet coils cooled to 268 degrees below zero by the liquid helium flowing through their veins. Each coil reminds you of a pearish D, except this D is eight or nine meters tall, and all sixteen are arrayed around in the form of a giant doughnut. When pulsed, the magnets attempt to lurch toward each other with a force, well, several hundred thousand times what a hefty horseshoe magnet produces—but they don't lurch; their superalloy casings and the machine's massive titanium superstructure hold them fast. Finally, strip away the magnets and you peer into the heart of the tokamak itself: a D-shaped superalloy chamber, three times the height of a person, wrapped around in the shape of a doughnut.

Tokamak, Slava once explained, is a Russian acronym meaning "toroidal chamber with magnetic coils." That says pretty much what a tokamak is: a giant doughnut wrapped with magnetic coils. What it doesn't say is that inside this doughnut, fusioneers intended to create the center of the sun.

The naked eye is incapable of assembling Prometheus into a sensible whole because Prometheus was, barring perhaps ITER, the most complex device ever constructed. The product of fifteen thousand man-years of work, it was altogether too complicated. And now, Machuzak thought, as much as I am protesting, we are going to turn it on.

* * * *

By the time Krieg-Zuber steered everyone to the control room, located in a kind of underground bunker attached to the main building, 4:00 p.m. had come and gone. He directed the overflow crowd to spread out around the glass-walled visitors' gallery while inviting a select few to take their places on the "captain's deck" overlooking the command center floor.

Leonard merely waved to everyone and Zuber made his announcement. "*Mesdames et messieurs*," he said with his most sparkling affectation while running his finger along the scar of unknown provenance he wore with pride on his right cheek, "Prometheus is the prototype of machines that will someday provide humankind with clean and virtually inexhaustible energy from ordinary water. This no person can doubt. The more modest goal of Prometheus itself is to bring fusion power to our lab. Although over the past months we have been testing the machine, we have yet to connect it CFRC's grid. On the occasion of Prometheus' commissioning, it seems fitting to make the experiment."

Machuzak fumed. The great goal of ignition—a self-sustaining reaction—yes, that was the dream, but no one knew whether ASSET—or ITER—would ever achieve it. One thing was certain: with the machine in its thrown-together condition they weren't going to get it today.

"Let us now dim the lights and wait for Prometheus to turn them back on." The room went dark, leaving the onlookers bathed only in the star-glow of panel lights and monitors. With a nod Krieg-Zuber signals the COE to commence. Chief Operating Engineer Larissa Davidson sits before the controls; she has trained two years for this moment. All safety interlocks are engaged; around the room the scientists take their stations at a few of the hundreds of terminals, one poised to measure temperature, another pressure…x-rays, optical radiation…dirt.

"Two minutes, forty seconds," announces the electronic voice and the countdown has begun. Instinctively, everyone turns toward the steady tick of the clock, but then they catch sight of the flashing digits on the big screen. The collective breathing slows.

"Magnet temperature, four-point-two degrees absolute," Larissa says over the intercom. "Poloidal field magnetization commencing."

Even at that point the whine is audible, not the protest of the flywheels spinning down as the tokamak saps their energy, but a screeching from the machine itself caused by rapidly changing magnetic fields.

"Ninety seconds…eighty-nine…eighty-eight…"

Today, Cyrus announces, they are counting down toward full power; launch will be at t-minus-sixty. It makes sense. No roar of engines will greet them, no majestic liftoff of a giant spacecraft. Only a blaze of light, a miniature sun created in their midst, then…

"Prepare for DT injection and current ramp-up."

"Sixty-three…sixty-two…sixty-one…"

Liftoff. A crack resounds throughout the room as the screen monitoring the interior of the tokamak flashes red. The guests are transfixed by that flickering, incandescent glow, displayed for all in the gallery to see. At the same time the loudspeakers pipe in a great metallic wrenching as Prometheus groans under the immense magnetic forces attempting to tear it apart. From the audience there is oohing and aahing, but the scientists remain silent. Liftoff is not what counts in this game. How hot. How long. How much power…

"Beginning current ramp-up."

Nothing has fucked up. Ten seconds into the pulse and they're still sailing. Slava turns to Nathaniel with astonishment written across his face. "*Bozhe moi*," he crosses himself, "the thing may work."

My God, Nathaniel thinks, he may be right. As images fly to the corners of the world, he finds caution slipping away.

"Tap thirteen. One hundred fifty thousand volts. Rf heating, lower-hybrid drives engaged." Larissa has begun walking the taps of the high-voltage transformers, engaging some of the auxiliary heating systems. "Thirty seconds to full-power injection."

"Tap fourteen. Three hundred thousand volts."

"Twenty-five seconds…twenty-four…"

Machuzak and Archangelsky both glance over to the display wall. Five million amps of electric current are circulating in that doughnut, some fusion reactions have begun. The main beams are on the ready, prepared to bring the process to fruition. God, let us not disrupt. The two men find themselves clenching their fists and urging Prometheus on. Theresa on the captain's deck holds her hands to her face as she watches the digits mutate. "Preparing for full-power injection at tap fifteen."

"Ten, nine, eight…"

"Go! Go!" Krieg-Zuber shouts while Leonard beams.

The audience is counting: "Six, five, four…"

"Go!" Nathaniel and Slava shout with the others. "Go!" the cry fills the air.

"…zero."

Zuber jumps and punches the air in triumph. "Yes!" he cries, slapping Leonard on the back. The room explodes in wild, hysterical applause. But what's this? Ten, twenty seconds go by and Nathaniel sees no lights, fails to hear the speakers broadcasting the roar of the turbine. From the corner of his eye he glances at the display wall and sees zero helium pressure in the heat exchanger. An operator's finger points at a terminal and a flashing red bar. Indeed, anticipation has overtaken reality and everyone is cheering the emperor's new clothes. Nathaniel and Slava finally nod to each other; something has indeed fucked up. As a minute passes without a spark or flicker, the applause turns to tweeting and the world is alerted that all is not right.

"Ladies and gentlemen," Cy at last announces, "there appears to be a difficulty. We will track it down presently." He turns and snarls something to Andy Lipman, one of the technicians, who runs out of the room. Machuzak sighs.

* * * *

Despite Leonard's halting attempts to distract the crowd by explaining tokamak operations, before long everyone was back to video games. A half hour crept by. Finally Lipman reappeared and whispered something to the deputy director. As Rasmussen made another apology for the delay, assuring everyone "the problem will be solved within minutes," Krieg-Zuber angrily stormed out of the room.

"They forget first pancake is always flat," quipped Slava. "Now Cy will prove he can do more than talk on phone." Nathaniel nodded. Cyrus the Great intended to show everyone that he could fix tokamaks.

"What do you think's wrong, Mac?" asked Theresa, stepping down from the captain's deck. "You must be gloating, 'I told you so.'"

Hardly. "Theresa, probably close to a million things needed to go right for this to work. I'm sorry, it must be embarrassing for you."

She shook her head and touched Nathaniel's arm. "We'll survive."

Lipman seemed to be hesitating and Machuzak managed to catch him before he left the control room. "What's up, Lip?"

The tech answered with a shrug of resignation. "Dunno, Mac. Got a level-three fault in the neutral-beam system. Something down in the surge rooms. Maybe an old switch... You know how it is." With another shrug he ran out after Krieg-Zuber.

"I wish we had a computer from 2020, even," one of the diagnostic team was growling as he pounded on a terminal.

Another fifteen minutes crawled by as the caterers began distributing refreshments and the visitors complained that ASSET operations lacked a music track. Suddenly an agitated Lipman reappeared and whispered to Leonard, who went wide-eyed and attempted to rise, only to collapse back onto his chair. Only after a few minutes did he manage to grope for the microphone, drop it, then, when his wife handed it to him, find enough composure to speak.

"Ladies and gentlemen," he said slowly, "there a...appears to have been—" he stopped—"an accident. The...ceremony is canceled."

As everyone rushed to the captain's deck, Lipman waved Slava and Machuzak after him. Followed by others, they sprinted three hundred meters through the big tunnel to the neutral-beam power system. The safety door to one of the surge rooms was open. There on the floor amidst the maze of electrical equipment lay Cyrus Krieg-Zuber. Nathaniel guessed that he had accidentally hit one of the capacitor terminals, which sent his heart into fibrillation.

A technician straddled Zuber and was pumping his chest while another administered mouth-to-mouth through a pocket mask. Machuzak snapped on a mask as he and Slava relieved the other pair. The belated wail of the lab emergency medical team siren grew higher, louder.

"I've never seen The Terminator so angry," Lipman was saying. "When he opened the door the safety interlock should've discharged the capacitors. He must have slipped or something. Jesus..."

"Do you mean this stuff is still hot?" Machuzak asked in disbelief, rows of high-voltage capacitor terminals not a foot from his head. "What the hell!"

"Interlock failed?" asked Slava, staring at Nathaniel for a moment before resuming mouth-to-mouth.

"Screaming like a madman but he didn't jump it," answered one of the techs. "We even racked out the breakers."

"You did?" This was impossible.

In that breath the EMT arrived and took over with its defibrillator. Nathaniel got up, feeling dizzy and nauseated, and stumbled out of the surge room. To the incessant ring of phones, he made his way to his office and fell back into his chair. Mail was coming through.

ONE

Forty-five minutes after they'd left an inert deputy director in the surge room, Slava Archangelsky, hair bedraggled, eyes bloodshot, staggered through the labyrinthine corridors of CFRC toward Nathaniel's office to see that half the lab's thousand employees had beaten him there. No thought confusing his mind, he shoved his way to the door to find his colleague inside under journalistic siege.

"Do you know what happened, Dr. Machuzak?" "N…no I don't." "Are you sure?" "Cyrus Krieg-Zuber seems to have been electrocuted in an accident." "Do you know what caused it?" "Current."

"Would you care to—"

"—speculate? No!"

Resembling the mad Rasputin more than ever, Archangelsky grabbed the nearest reporter by the shoulders and herded him toward the door, just as that one huffed, "Jesus, what a fool."

"Go to hell," Slava said and booted him out. God, he needed a cigarette. What kind of country is this where it's illegal to kill yourself? Riffling his pockets, he shoved a tattered stick into his mouth, took it out when he saw Machuzak painfully staring into the reporter's wake. Slava cast at him a sympathetic glance. Like most Americans, Nat lacked a ready wit, but no scientist deserves to be called a fool because he says he doesn't know. "I don't know" is honest, more honorable by far than saying you know when you don't. In an instantaneous world, Nat's problem was that he was an old-fashioned romantic. He remembered that *PhD* meant doctor of philosophy. "Forget it," Slava tried to beat it into his brain often enough. "We are not natural philosophers pondering workings of the universe. We are here to build the tokamak. Save world from itself."

Now, having been sucked dry by parasites, Mac to most, Nat to Archangelsky, sat before the Russian with hazel eyes staring blankly ahead. "You look like hell," Archangelsky offered, puffing on the unlit cigarette. Machuzak usually came across as young for his years. Wrinkles hadn't intruded much yet, but tonight his face was all creases. "You need a drink?"

"How could this have happened?" was the physicist's only reply.

"Stupidity. Idiot plays with high-voltage system he doesn't know shit about. What do you expect? He saves *Enterprise*? Look, you predicted it yourself. Nobody listened."

"Did the local emergency people show up?" Nathaniel asked dumbly, still frozen.

"*Da*, everybody. The devil would break a leg over there."

Finally Nat exhaled and he scratched his gray-streaked temples as he did when stumped. "So, friend, we've just had the most public accident in fusion history. Christ, half the world was watching. It's already all over...everything." With one motion he brushed aside a mop of his lazy brown hair and waved across the images leaping from the monitor. "Protestors, board members, reporters... We couldn't have set it up better if we tried."

Seated on the edge of the desk, Archangelsky nodded heavily and they fell silent. He liked Nat because, unlike most CFRC grunts, he thought beyond physics. He didn't need to say that today's events had put the entire program in jeopardy; that was written all over his face. *Pravda*, Nat was a little slow. Slava briefly recollected their first meeting, six years ago when he'd come to CFRC after a previous existence at Dubna and the Kurchatov Institute. Maybe he was testing his new colleague—after all, the tokamak was invented by Andrei Sakharov himself. These Americans? Within a minute, the two had gotten into a heated argument, which required some calculations. Machuzak's math was clumsy—he'd obviously never been through enough Olympiads—and after an hour Archangelsky spat, "You can teach me nothing."

The American went white like a ghost and walked slowly away. A week later, though, Nathaniel caught him in a stupid mistake and Archangelsky laughed, "So you can teach me something after all." They hooked their arms and drank to brotherhood with a bottle of French cognac Slava had stuffed into his pocket and they'd been putting up with each other ever since. No, Nat wasn't much of a mathematician, but he had an experimental nose like a razor. Somehow his career had been derailed. He'd gotten his PhD at the Princeton Plasma Physics Lab, once America's leading fusion research center, now little more than some half-empty buildings standing in a New Jersey meadow. Leonard recruited him just as he transformed the Austin National Fusion Research Laboratory into CFRC. Recently he'd been made a division head, but everyone knew the reason for that.

The momentary silence was cut short by Andy Lipman, who appeared at the door with three emergency people. "Uh, Mac," the tech said, "they wanted to ask you a couple questions for their report." Slava got to his feet and ushered them in with a silent frown. The last thing either physicist was interested in was answering more of the same.

Neither did the emergency people appear in a hurry to ask. "Can we get this over with?" Archangelsky said, but something about Machuzak's office amused them; they clucked in mock admiration at the shelves of texts, the stacks of printouts heaped up everywhere, the blackboard, the wall charts. All the while a fire-truck beacon flashed through the window, painting everyone with pallid Christmas colors as the low rumble of the engine sent concussions through the air. In that weird twilight zone Archangelsky fidgeted with his cigarette, waiting. The fireman made a bad joke about smoking regulations, to which Slava replied with a ferocious stare. The intruder swallowed; they got down to it.

Machuzak repeated what he'd said to the reporters: At the surge room, they found Krieg-Zuber receiving CPR on the floor. He'd evidently backed into a charged capacitor and, as they'd learned, a couple hundred milliamps is just right for the heart of an acting director.

The paramedic checked his notes. "Isn't there supposed to be a safety interlock or something that discharges those capacitators when you open the door?"

Machuzak nodded wearily, glancing at Slava.

"But it failed?"

"Yes," Machuzak said, "it failed. We don't know why. There's a lot of old equipment down there. We use parts from previous machines."

"Got it. Anything else you can add, Dr. Machuzak?"

"No," he sighed again, "I really can't."

"I can," interrupted Slava, throwing down his cigarette. "Terminator shouldn't have been there in the first place. The man didn't know what he was doing. That's all there is to it."

"Slava, take it easy," Machuzak interrupted.

Archangelsky immediately caught himself, gazed forlornly at the cigarette on the floor, raised his hand in a peace salute. His nerves were more on edge than he'd realized. "Sorry."

The apology didn't seem to appease the police sergeant, who was showing more interest in the "Miss Fusion" calendar pinned above Nat's desk than in an EMT report. She turned to the Russian and said, "I'm sorry, sir, I didn't catch your name."

"Yaroslav Archangelsky," Slava replied without expression.

"*Yaa*roslaave Arch*ange*lsky?" she repeated with a serious Texas twang, obliterating his name.

"*Yah*roslav Arkh*ahn*gelsky," Slava said as if correcting a schoolchild.

The fair-haired policewoman didn't perceive the menace in Slava's voice. "You descend from high places," she said cheerfully enough, intending to alter the mood or at least show that she understood his name even if she couldn't pronounce it.

Now Archangelsky answered at absolute zero. "Just old name from old country. You need history lesson?"

"Sorry," she said, seeing that things were going from bad to worse, "just curious. You know, it's quite a place y'all have. I've always wanted to visit. Never been too clear about what you do here—"

"Build bombs," cracked the fireman, having remained in a private bubble throughout.

Archangelsky wouldn't let the remark pass. "Energy," he said severely, punching out the words. "No bombs, no secrets. We want to give the world energy. Understand?"

"Oil's pricey for sure, but we got plenty o' sun and wind in Texas. Don't need no radiation."

"Why you ignorant sonofabitch!" Slava leapt toward the fireman.

"Slava!" Machuzak shouted, at once on his feet, fully interposing himself between the two men.

"Sorry," the policewoman said in the same instant, pinning the fireman to the wall with an evil eye. "Sorry," she repeated. "You know how gung-ho we Texans can be. Anyway, I hope you can give me the cook's tour once this is sorted out. What d'ya do now?"

Machuzak accepted the peace offering and eased Slava into his chair. "Serious accidents almost never happen, but there'll be an internal investigation."

Despite the last minute's drama, the cop continued to prowl around the room in a slightly distracted manner, as if the business at hand only half captured her attention. "Seems straightforward," she said after a pause so long that both Archangelsky and Machuzak were caught off guard. "Who'll be in charge for the interim?"

The two physicists exchanged glances. "I…it's difficult to say. Our director Leonard Rasmussen is seriously ill—"

"Well, maybe this Krieg-Zoober will pull through."

"Huh?" Both Nathaniel and the Russian started. "Zuber isn't dead?"

The officer shrugged. "He was, but the EMT crew finally jumpstarted his ticker. They said he's pretty fried inside and it'll be touch 'n' go for a day or two. Anyway, we'd best be on our way. Sorry about what happened." The sergeant ushered the others out and had half disappeared herself when she took a step closer to the large wall chart outlining the principles of fusion. "Plasma physics… Yeah, people use that word a lot when they talk about this lab. Everybody who doesn't think you're building bombs thinks y'all are doing blood research and—that ain't what's goin on here."

"No…" Machuzak smiled faintly, "… it ain't."

The young woman continued to ponder the chart, eerily discolored by the flashing fire-truck beacon, and scratched her head. "This really isn't too clear. D'ya think you could tell me what a plasma is?" At a glance at the scientists' ashen faces, she retreated. "Well, maybe another time." Again she prepared to depart but instead moved closer to a cluster of photographs on the wall. "Hmm, Durham Cathedral," she said, peering closely at the first. Then she touched two fingers to her forehead in a salute, said, "Good evening, sirs," and vanished.

* * * *

Slava lifted his phone to make a call only to find that not only could he not get a signal, but his address book had been erased. Machuzak tried an outside landline but it was dead. *"Eb tvoiu mat',"* Slava muttered. Leaving Nat with a perplexed look on his face, he stepped into the corridor and ran downstairs to the lobby. John Henderson, CFRC's security chief, motioned for him to wait as he frantically tried to deal with the internal calls lighting up his board.

"What the hell's going on, John?" Slava finally interrupted.

Henderson looked up at Slava in a desperate bafflement. "W…wireless is jammed and outgoing Internet seems to have been cut."

"How?" asked Archangelsky.

Removing his cap Henderson scratched his head. "Cyrus installed some equipment in the back room last year. H…he didn't tell me what it does."

"This isn't goddamned NSA!" cursed Archangelsky. Maybe it was. This is exactly how things were going at CFRC. Four years ago Krieg-Zuber had silently put in place a routing system: all scientific papers bound for publication were siphoned to his office and secretly vetted. Nat Edward'ich himself uncovered the scheme and protested to Leonard until it was shut down.

"Why cut signals now?" Slava continued. "World knew what happened hours ago. Fucking amateurs…"

"Must be automatic. Don't ask me how."

"That miserable sack of shit… He got this from his CIA trainers at Cryotech…" Waving his arm in disgust, Archangelsky returned to Machuzak's office to explain what had happened. He switched on the light and found Nat looking more exhausted than he'd left him, brooding over the unfiltered incoming broadcasts.

"It's worse than we imagined," Machuzak said before Slava could open his mouth. Every news organization in the state was broadcasting from the environs of CFRC, and blogs—divided equally among those claiming Krieg-Zuber was alive and those claiming he was toast—already saturated the Web. Cut to Washington. Whatever coffee-infused staffers journalists can uncover at this ungodly hour are eager to assure viewers that an investigation is called for.

"Government no longer funds science," Slava talked back to the screen. "Those off-course whores can't call for anything."

"They can and they will," Nathaniel corrected him wearily. "We still get enough federal bucks that Congress can sink this ship." One or two maybe.

Slava snorted as he squashed a big roach with his foot. "The bastard isn't even dead yet."

"The bastard isn't the point, Slava; the accident is. Mark my words: the politicians will be on us within a week."

"Another prediction, Cassandra? Look at them," Archangelsky pointed to a smirking senatorial aide. "It's as if they were waiting for this to happen, ignorant sons of bitches."

"Slava," Machuzak said, suddenly turning, "what got into you before, calling that fireman an ignorant son of a bitch? Were you out of your mind? Why do you think ignorant sons of bitches want to shut us down?" Aye, you didn't need to be a Cassandra to see that in more ways than today fusioneers had themselves to blame for what was taking place before their eyes. For too many decades the bigwigs had insisted that a commercial reactor was "just over the next machine," a claim that would ring ever more hollow as Nature slowly revealed the awesome difficulty of the endeavor. Tonight that arrogance was coming to roost.

"Sorry," answered Slava with as much contrition as he was capable of. "Nerves… Anyway, public will get investigation. Too bad they won't investigate the way that *svoloch'* has been running lab." He went on to explain what had just taken place.

"Well, at least we can forget about The Terminator for a while."

"Not before the crayfish whistles on the hill."

Nathaniel chuckled morosely, swiveling away to answer incoming mail.

"Don't." Slava stayed his hand.

For a moment Machuzak stared blankly at the Russian until Slava launched a new window and pointed to the message that for years had appeared on their screens:… *Individuals using this system expressly consent to having all their activities monitored and recorded by system personnel…*

Why the implications of the advisory had never sunk in before this moment entirely eluded Machuzak and he mumbled only, "You've got to be kidding." Then he remembered Krieg-Zuber's paper-vetting scheme.

There was nothing for it. Nathaniel silently got to his feet and switched off the lights. Outside, the parking lot was deserted; phones functioned but memories were gone. The two men breathed heavily. At this hour here was only one thing to do—head to town and the Yellow Rose, where Slava would bargain with the dancers for their G-strings, and hope that tomorrow would not prove worse.

TWO

Early next morning Nathaniel Machuzak, looking no better than the fits and starts of sleep he'd had, abandoned attempts to dream and headed south. The radio did nothing to untie the knot that twisted his stomach. Over night, every media host had flocked unswervingly to the call for an investigation. The single thought running through his mind was a mordant "What next?" Dread quickly crystallized when a sunrise eco-pundit warned that CFRC's tritium supply was a sure target for terrorists. The words hit Machuzak with such force that he nearly swerved into a ditch. At once yesterday's student came back to him and he vowed that someday he'd collar the kid and explain tritium. Machuzak switched stations: yet another suicide bomber had attacked Verizon in a last-ditch effort to communicate with a human being. He flipped to the surviving Austin classical music station. Tchaikovsky, as usual.

The sight of media vans lying in wait beyond the guard booth triggered evasive action. Veering off the main drive, Machuzak skirted the pentagon and drove directly to Site Alpha on the lab's periphery. To the aging structures of Alpha Site, the original complex of the Austin National Fusion Research Laboratory, were relegated some of CFRC's secondary experiments, including the Materials Test Facility, of which he, Nathaniel Machuzak, was head.

At the parking lot Nathaniel granted himself a breath in the deep morning shadows to gaze eastward. The thought was unavoidable: No wonder the public finds us so inscrutable. What could one make of this Lego-set city? Apart from the showcase main building, the rest of the sprawl was entirely utilitarian, great shells meant only to keep the rain off the tumult below. Strangers invariably found the lab ugly and unnavigable. Machuzak had always found a certain beauty in the haphazardness of CFRC. The unrestrained growth of offices, machine shops, temporary structures that took root to become labyrinths of the mindscape. The high-tension towers, hum of the transformers, silicon panels tracking the sun, satellite dishes linking them to supercomputers worldwide. CFRC was an improvisation, an improvisation crackling with energy.

Not, he understood, today. Machuzak badged himself into the water-stained test facility and threw the light switch. The archaeological fluorescents that functioned sputtered on and produced an irritating sixty-cycle hum. He'd call maintenance, but they'd probably RIFfed the electrician.

His laboratory greeted him and for the first time in twenty-four hours he felt a space of peace. People like him could hardly escape it, really. They were born tinkerers. Nothing gave them so much pleasure as making something work, unless it was the pleasure of making something work that nobody thought possible. When he described his workplace, Slava chided him for sounding like the futurists of old, with their songs of electricity and locomotion. No, it is not progress, it is sensation. I relish the cement floors, smooth with age, the smell of oils, ozone when the capacitors spark, the glint of steel and brass atop the workbenches. The polished vacuum chambers, the test cells sprouting wires and hoses. The clacking of the forepumps, the microwave plumbing running from floor to ceiling. This is my world. Here I am in charge.

Dream on. Though he hadn't set foot here in nearly a month, to work proved impossible and he managed only to fidget and wander aimlessly through the rooms. He paused briefly at his desk and lifted his cold-fusion apparatus. The great cold-fusion scare of 1989 and the extraordinary hoopla surrounding it was beyond his memory, but he later tested the claims himself. There was nothing to the apparatus: a beaker of heavy water and two electrodes. It was madness to think that such a thing could work, but it was understandable madness. Inexhaustible energy on a benchtop. No great tokamaks, no billions of dollars, no decades lost, no high voltage, no…accidents. The Fountain of Youth. Understandable, misguided madness.

Unable to concentrate, Machuzak was about to head over to his office in the main building when the lab phone rang. Andy Lipman. Machuzak didn't like the sound of the tech's voice and Lipman wouldn't talk online. Nathaniel told him to meet at his office in ten minutes.

Archangelsky was waiting. "Have you heard about the tritium?" Nathaniel asked before Slava could speak.

"Ahh, tritium…" the Russian scoffed. "It is as harmless as radioactive materials come. They should be more concerned with radium in coal smoke."

"Tell that to CNN—"

Lipman appeared then with an uncertain rap on the doorframe and glanced uneasily at Archangelsky.

"It's all right," Machuzak assured him. "No secrets among friends."

The tech hesitated, waved the pair after him down the back stairwell, past junked computers, improbable numbers of crickets and the stagnant smell of concrete; they left the main building and made their way across to the pentagon. Years ago, in homage to Peter Max, someone ordered the pentagon units painted tan, yellow and blue. The result was considerably less than psychedelic. During the walk, a grackle cawed from Toshi Matsushima's geometry tree, where ceremonial plaques rattled like bamboo chimes, but Lipman said not a word. By the time the tech badged them in, they'd already guessed their destination: the surge room where Krieg-Zuber had glimpsed immortality.

The accident site was as they'd left it the previous day, except for the yellow DANGER DO NOT ENTER tape the police, probably, had put around the area. The truth is always too late.

"So what is it, Lip?" Machuzak said at last.

The tech yet hesitated. "Well, I figured I'd be appointed to the investigation, so I thought I'd get a head start." Motioning the physicists forward, Lipman ducked under the tape and stopped at the door to the surge room. "Look here."

Nathaniel followed Lipman's finger to the interlock at the top of the orange door. It was a simple magnetic switch like the ones you find on alarmed doors. Open the door, a relay trips, alarm sounds. Here, open the door, a relay trips the capacitors are mechanically grounded, discharging them. To Machuzak it seemed okay.

"Yep, Cy didn't touch it and I don't believe anybody else did either."

But if the interlock was intact—how? And the safety was just the first line of defense. After the fault light, the techs had also racked out the breakers—literally rolled out the circuit breakers from their cradles, disconnecting them from the circuit. There the monsters sat. In the open. What could have failed?

Now Lipman opened the door to the brightly colored room. The great power supplies at CFRC were divided into dozens of these smaller units to isolate the subsystems and make it more difficult to electrocute yourself everywhere at once. Machuzak listened for the discharging mechanism to connect. It did.

"Come on...nothin's charged now. I checked." Lipman pointed to the lightning rod in the corner—the time-honored, mandatory way of grounding a capacitor. That rule Zuber had evidently ignored.

Machuzak cast his eye over the tower of metal rings looming above them. Straight out of *Frankenstein,* these unearthly "ignitrons," two or three times as tall as he was, protected equipment down the line. A fault is detected, the ignitrons fire, the circuit is "crowbarred." A dead short in two microseconds. Toss a crowbar across the terminals of the nearest high-tension tower and watch.

Near one end of the alcove, amidst all the plumbing, Lipman pointed to a short section of busbar. "I noticed this when I came in," he said, indicating the heavy piece of copper used to conduct large currents.

"What's wrong?" Nathaniel asked, unable to see clearly in his own shadow.

Lipman waved them closer and Nathaniel saw immediately what he was getting at. The busbar, perhaps once thirty centimeters long, was now two. It seemed to have melted in the middle, leaving a gap of a few centimeters. A gap.

"This takes out the circuit protection," Nathaniel guessed, "and the capacitor discharge switch?"

Lipman nodded.

Slava also instantly understood. "Open circuit—capacitors didn't discharge when they should have."

It was not too difficult to infer what had taken place: Circuit protection goes, some component in machine fries, fault light appears in control room, Krieg-Zuber fries.

The three stood for a moment in silence. "When was the last inspection?"

"Five days ago," Lip answered. "I walked through myself. Here." He handed Machuzak a touch pad. "I suppose I could've missed something."

Nathaniel stared at the screen. The implications of Lipman's words weren't hard to divine, but his every instinct resisted them. Finally, he forced himself to look at the tech. "Are you saying," he asked, holding his breath, "that someone deliberately cut the busbar?"

"Ain't hard. Two minutes with a hacksaw—done. On the other hand, this looks it was cut by a torch. Maybe it melted under the load. I dunno. We were pressing the machine pretty hard. Some of this stuff's museum quality and I've known one or two of these to go in my time. You guys got the PhDs. Tell me."

Nathaniel paused long, glanced at Yaroslav Borisovich, stared at the electrical equipment surrounding them, listened to the distant hum of a generator. At last, exhausting every possible diversion, he whispered the word in the world he wanted least to hear: "Sabotage?"

Lipman only shrugged again. "You guys got the PhDs."

"Hmm." Nathaniel stood there, head completely empty. "Who would sabotage the machine?"

The tech didn't reply, realizing that the physicist was merely drafting thoughts, but Slava whistled softly as if to say, "How many possibilities would you like?" Then he too fell silent.

"Lip," Nathaniel asked, staring at Slava, "why did you come to me about this?"

The tech shrugged with a glance of Archangelsky. "Gotta go to somebody. Who's in charge of this place anyway?"

"Well, maybe The Terminator when he's recovered."

"That's the point, Mac," Lipman said with another glance at Slava. "Last year we found a penny in a motor-generator and Zuber's roaring sabotage. Cooling pumps break down—sabotage. Yesterday it's shit in hard hats—all my addresses have been wiped. That guy thinks he's J. Edgar but his screws are a little loose, you know. Time's ripe."

Before Machuzak could respond, Archangelsky cut in. "If the press has gone loco with the accident, can you imagine what they will do with sabotage? They'll go ballistic. Orbital."

No denying it.

"Not to mention lab itself," Slava added, almost as an afterthought. "We should keep this quiet."

"Are *you* loco?" Machuzak exclaimed in amazement. "How are we going to keep this quiet?"

"We merely don't tell anyone. Nat Edward'ich, I am of course not suggesting we ignore what has happened: we must in fact quickly determine what is down here."

"Up," Nathaniel muttered. Machuzak felt his hesitation surging forth. Again. God, where are my principles? The sound of passing footsteps argued for a quick decision. "How many people knew about this?" Machuzak asked Lipman.

He had yet to tell anyone.

"Don't."

"The bar?" pressed Slava.

Machuzak felt himself shaking internally. "No," he put his foot down, "we can't do it." Machuzak left the surge room and the other two staring at each other. After a moment, Slava ran out after him, and the two walked back to the office together. The open space between the giant forms of the pentagon and the administration building seemed larger than ever and every two paces, or three, Nathaniel found himself glancing over his shoulder. Archangelsky was fuming.

"*Brat*, are you a holy fool or just plain idiot? They'll discover that bar within hours. The instant they do…" Slava muttered something in Russian that Machuzak couldn't understand.

"Maybe we're making too much of this," Machuzak responded, more to himself than to Archangelsky. "If you were going to sabotage the machine, why not blow it up and be done with it?"

Slava did not calm down for some time. When he did, he turned to Machuzak and said, "My naive friend, remember Andreyev's play, *The Black Maskers*." The Archangelsky-ism, referring with familiarity to a play no one had ever heard of before, might under other circumstance have been amusing, but Slava's voice was fully laced with warning. "A rich duke, Lorenzo, holds ball. More and more guests arrive, wearing fantastic, grotesque masks. He asks each, 'Who are you?' but his question goes unanswered. Finally, they set fire to palace and Lorenzo goes up in smoke."

Although with the rest of humanity Machuzak hadn't read it, he vividly recollected the music Roger Sessions had written for the play. Disturbing, to say the least.

"Remember Lorenzo's question, my friend."

Archangelsky's words chilled Machuzak to the bone. "Slava, enough," he finally said, paranoia quickly rising. They entered the back courtyard of the main building and once more passed the geometry tree. At sunup and sundown when the temperature shifted and the wind picked up, the grackles there lost their minds, as if the end of the world was upon them. Now it was silent but for an occasional caw and the rattle of the plaques.

"What will you do now?" Archangelsky asked.

"We're going to have to call the police."

"What will you tell them?"

"I have no idea."

Slava walked off shaking his head and Machuzak barricaded himself in his office. It was just eight in the morning.

THREE

Not sixty seconds later, while Machuzak dredged his memory for the name of the police officer from last night, the phone rang. Nathaniel stared long without moving. When he at last answered, the voice on the other end didn't wait for a greeting.

"Hello, Machuzak?"

"Yes, who is this?"

"Not Jesse James. Richard Garrett here."

"Mr. Garrett, w…why—?"

"I'll tell you why. With Leonard and Krieg-Zuber in the state they're in, I'm gonna have to get more involved with the day-to-day here, and I'm callin the division heads for a meeting."

"W…what's happened?" What else could have happened?

"Well, Mac—or should I call you Cassandra—?" The nickname was going to stick, Nathaniel realized as the knot in his stomach twisted again. "You weren't spittin in the wind yesterday. That accident's got a lot of people spooked, real spooked. The board's gone loco overnight— Hold on a second… Mac, can you get up here? On the double."

After staring at the dead phone in his hand for one second, Nathaniel bounded up to the third floor where he collided with Garrett as he waddled into the conference room. "Moravec, the thief who runs GlobeTex, wants an explanation—now. He's threatening to pull out."

Texas Global, one of the world's largest renewable energy concerns and CFRC's largest investor. Machuzak suddenly felt hit from every side. This was no coincidence. Sabotage the program, pull out. Eliminate the competition. What should he tell Garrett? "They're not spooked. They're trying to shut us down." He stopped there.

"What's the point, Mac?" the chairman rejoined. "Why join the consortium to begin with?"

It had been a question since the day Rasmussen and Garrett, this plump maverick who'd made billions in oil and poured millions back into pet energy projects, had founded CFRC. GlobeTex was a leader in wind, solar, bio. Fusion made sense for them at the same level solar had once made sense for BP. Evidently not. Stop, Zuber talks like this. About to blurt out to Garrett the discovery of the busbar, Slava's warning came to him: "Who are you?"

"This way's a more permanent death," Nathaniel said to the chairman. "The people who hold the purse strings are waiting for the right moment to kill off the competition." The moment could always be engineered.

Garrett didn't answer, only switched on the big screen. A second later a tall, suited, androgynous figure jumped out at them in poor 3-D.

"Who is this person?" asked Moravec, who appeared more female than male, with so little intonation that he, she or it might have been an advanced bot.

"This is Dr. Machuzak, one of our physicists. I was on the phone with him when you called. He can explain what happened better than I."

"Explain?" Machuzak erupted, suddenly crossing into overload. "Damn it, Richard, who can explain any of this? Prometheus' predecessor worked. Prometheus itself was behaving okay during the pre-ops." He ran his hand through his hair, taken aback at his own outburst but unable to control it. "Christ, I told you it was fucking nuts to connect it to the grid. That's five years away—if we can get the damned thing to ignite."

The faintest glimmer of a smile spread across the remote Moravec's lips. "I'll give you six months."

"Huh?" Machuzak swiveled. What could he possibly—

"Our contract is up in six months, from today, as it happens. In six months we pull out—unless you ignite your machine."

Machuzak found himself staring openmouthed at the screen. Ignition. A self-sustaining fusion reaction. The stuff that powers stars.

"It…it can't be done," he managed to stammer.

"I'm sorry, the matter is out of my hands."

"It's…it's impossible, I tell you."

"In that case, good-bye."

The image vanished but Machuzak continued to stare. "It's impossible," he stammered again. Even as he uttered his disbelief, he saw that more than the fate of a single lab was at stake. In its gargantuan magnificence, Prometheus was the last vestige of the American fusion program. If the lab went, ITER remained. Alone.

Suddenly, Nathaniel felt himself peering downward into a vast abyss. From a great distance, Garrett's voice penetrated. "We'd better call a general meeting, Mac."

* * * *

Rumors had gone viral by 9:00 a.m., and the weary lab personnel gathering in the main auditorium sensed that something unprecedented was about to take place. That much is true, Machuzak thought. In the crush he found himself seated next to Toshifume Matsushima, the lab's great thinker, who remarked in that Eastern way of his, "The accident has spurred the regime to new heights of watchfulness and vigor." Watchfulness and vigor, Nathaniel agreed, skeptical that the "accident" designation would survive 'til the end of the day. At the same moment, a pair of workmen slid closed the big doors at the back of the stage, doors that were normally open to reveal the friendly hills beyond. Soon the room overflowed with five hundred shell-shocked people bracing themselves for the worst. In the commotion Leonard Rasmussen hobbled down to the stage on crutches and seated himself with Richard Garrett.

When the ringtones finally died away and the pall settled, Leonard took the microphone. No, he does not look well, worse than yesterday. Nathaniel felt a great pity for the director. "Friends," Rasmussen said, voice unusually hoarse, "all of you know that for ten years I have pushed this laboratory toward the goal of infinite energy. Hotter, denser, longer, I always said…" A few in the audience chuckled nervously as Leonard coughed. "We have survived indifferent and hostile governments, economic crises; we have surmounted every obstacle thrown in our path except Nature's own. Today we have suddenly been called to face our greatest challenge. We will rise to the occasion, but I shall let Richard Garrett, chairman of our board, explain what has taken place."

Garrett, all two hundred thirty pounds now on display, took the microphone. "Ladies and gentlemen," he said to the restless sea, "we indeed face a crisis. You folks know I've supported this lab's work since Leonard and I set up the consortium. And I mean through hell and high water. A lot a people think fusion is a pie-in-the-sky pipedream. If any of you still have doubts, take a look at this mornin's sites. You gotta understand that yesterday's accident…" Virtually without prologue he then dropped the last hour's bombshell: GlobeTex, CFRC's principal investor, would pull out unless within six months from today the lab achieved, "as you folks call it, ignition."

Machuzak was certain a riot would break out. Shouts of "Impossible!" rose from all sides, echoing his own first outburst. What Moravec was demanding was that they achieve the most difficult technological feat ever attempted by the human race, a task so intractable that it had eluded fusioneers worldwide for eighty years—and that they do it in six months with a machine that might not be capable of it. With a loose saboteur thrown in for good measure.

The shouts abated, only to be replaced by angry accusations that Moravec had planned this from the moment he, she or it joined the consortium. "We've been set up!" one voice cried louder than the rest. Truer than you imagine, Machuzak nodded, truer than you imagine. Toshi glanced at his neighbor in a forlorn way. "It is truly impossible, Nathaniel," his expression said before he cast his gaze to the floor.

Garrett remained on stage as Leonard struggled to his feet. "Friends," he said with difficulty, above the noise. "We have no choice. Can we do it?"

"No!" was the unanimous reply.

"Can we do it?"

Leonard's valiant exhortations were drowned out and a general strike appeared to be in the making as the sick director looked on despairingly. To Nathaniel's amazement, Krieg-Zuber himself suddenly appeared on the big screen, larger than life. Nat's first thought was that he'd been resurrected; only belatedly did he realize that Cyrus the Great must have taped the bit twenty-four hours ago at the ceremony. "Monsieurs et mesdames," Zuber was saying with his practiced smile to a circle of journalists. "Our success will be a significant moment in the history of mankind. Failure is not an option."

The ploy backfired, and as Garrett announced a meeting of the division heads for 11:00 a.m. at the ASSET conference room, the rumble of disbelief welled up again and the crowd stormed out without waiting. In the lobby Toshi turned again to Nathaniel. You always listened when Toshi spoke, but this time he said something other than what Machuzak had read in his face. "So, Nathaniel, it seems that our *kairos* is suddenly at hand, the moment of grace and opportunity. May we use it well."

"Kairos—we should all remember that," an administrator said, exiting the auditorium.

More like a perfect storm, Machuzak was thinking as Slava passed by. "Maybe we should all take our heads out of our asses," the Russian quipped loudly enough for everyone to hear and continued on his way. Machuzak slowly made his way upstairs to the ASSET conference room.

FOUR

Machuzak stood in the doorway of the ASSET conference room, the same space where less than three hours ago he and Garrett had received Moravec's ultimatum. Now, thoughts a-tumult, barely cognizant of his surroundings, he is grasping at solutions, resisting the most likely, rejecting them all as unsatisfactory or unpalatable. Nothing made sense. Nathaniel lifted his eyes, they fell on the clock and remained riveted. A morning so quickly lost toward ignition. A morning stolen? Stop. He sat down, staring blankly while the others drifted in. At the stroke of eleven, Leonard and Garrett appeared and for an instant Machuzak again considered revealing Lipman's discovery, but as his gaze swept the room Lorenzo's infernal question, "Who are you?" once more muted him.

The dozen division heads took their places around the big table, surrounded by smartboards, blackboards, antique bulletin boards posted with data, ancient overhead projectors. In this room all eyes were invariably drawn first and last to the huge chrome letters *ASSET,* which protruded cyberlike from the front wall, reminding each and every onlooker of the corporate dollars mingling with scientific blood. But now, this moment, no one could avoid the startling image of Cyrus Krieg-Zuber, who unlike an hour ago now appeared live, swathed, wired and beeping as he hovered weirdly above the proceedings from his hospital bed and surreptitiously broadcast himself to the undoubted ignorance of his nurses.

Nathaniel abruptly realized he was becoming hyperaware of everything around him. One rubbing his nose, another puckering his lips, a third fingering her hair, each wearing a downcast expression. Garrett has taken up his position at the table's head, beatified by the gleaming ASSET letters, which form a sort of halo behind him. Leonard sits to his left in the wheelchair... Who are these people?

At that moment Rasmussen opened his mouth, preparing to speak, but to his own surprise Machuzak interrupted. "Leonard, I want to know what that electronic craziness was about last night. Whoever heard of such a thing at a scientific laboratory?"

A murmur of approval at Nathaniel's words circled the table at which Fred Abbuhl, ASSET's chief engineer, added in his lazy Georgian drawl, "Yeah, Len, what was that about?"

The question caught Rasmussen off guard but the general reaction required a response. "Uh, after numerous bomb threats and worse, Cyrus authorized the plan last year," he said with a glance toward Krieg-Zuber.

The patient nodded decisively, if wearily, as his monitors bleeped. Cyrus the Great's heart was stronger than he'd supposed, Machuzak sighed as everyone glanced toward the safety posters: SAFETY HAS NO QUITTING TIME. "Yes," Zuber said with surprising force, "unsubstantiated rumors can never be allowed to damage the Mission. Wiping phones is standard procedure. In anticipation of an emergency, yesterday the system was set to trigger automatically if I did not check in. Henceforth, proceed with the utmost caution in dealing with outsiders..."

Machuzak seethed as others texted. Yes, we've had bomb threats, several a year. Why today such measures? Machuzak perceived the flaccid grumble of impotence about him now.

"In this regard," Zuber unexpectedly went on, "in order to repair the public damage, we must urgently convene an investigation of yesterday's accident—if accident it was."

The last words elicited a sharp glance from Garrett, while Machuzak ceased breathing, waited.

"We shall spare no effort in this matter," Cyrus continued. "However, in light of today's dramatic turn of events, my attention shall be occupied with overseeing the ignition campaign—"

At that Garrett interrupted, perturbation overcoming civility to the wounded. "Excuse me, Dr. Krieg-Zuber," he said, managing to correctly put the accent on the last syllable, "you're in no shape to oversee anything. Take a rest and enjoy it. We'll have to appoint an interim director today, right, Len?"

Although Leonard appeared distracted, elsewhere, he nodded with a sudden, incomprehensible irritability. "That's correct—we'll have to make a decision."

Krieg-Zuber fell silent, only the hospital noises and his heavy breathing constituting a reply, but after a prolonged and awkward suspension of all debate, just at the moment Garrett was moving to switch off the broadcast, he surprised Machuzak again by attempting a comeback. "Leonard, we *cannot* let the great challenge handed us go unanswered."

"*You've* got to do it, Len," Tom Kettering called out. "If anyone can..."

Nathaniel glanced over at Tom, who sat as usual with cowboy boots propped up on the table. Is Kettering supporting this madness or Krieg-Zuber or...? Kettering, the beefy head of the tritium division, is just an ex-marine who once worked at the government's Savannah River tritium extraction site and acts as if he were a member of the SWAT team there. Can do, shoot the fuckers. His truck sports a rifle rack and he once detailed for all within earshot how a terrorist would go about stealing CFRC's tritium supply. This is a typical Kettering pose.

Is it?

Machuzak snapped-to to see Leonard cast a pained and painful look around the table. Finally, "Thank you. I d–don't know…"

It was the first time Nathaniel had heard Leonard Rasmussen express doubt about anything, but with Kettering's interjection the course of the meeting began to veer toward the main business, the greater trial.

Fred Abbuhl leaned over to Garrett with a theatrical, conspiratorial wink intended to lighten the atmosphere and said, "Why don't you tell them the truth, Mr. Garrett? You're just continuing Len's April Fool's tradition, a few months late."

Garrett chuckled, forced himself to. "I wish that were the case, Mr.—"

"Abbuhl—"

"Yes, were that the case, but Moravec is dead serious. Dr. Machuzak heard him. Six months. From today." Garrett struck the table with his knuckle and this time all eyes turned to the clock.

"My, my," replied Fred, shaking his head in less-than-mock disbelief as he leaned back. "Mr. Garrett, sir, let me tell you, before that ill-considered demo we were getting pretty good temperatures and confinement times. A plasma is the world's most ornery beast, but I'd say in six months we might be able to show them a four-minute pulse at low power—"

We might, Nathaniel nodded. If we can show them anything at all.

"I'm sorry, Mr. Abbuhl," Garrett interrupted, "I don't understand all this tech-speak. I'm a simple man…"

The chief engineer smiled, shaking his head softly. "Sir, the bottom line is that this picayune request of Moravec's is, well, to find the right word, I don't know, I think you may have heard it downstairs… How's *impossible* sound?"

At this moment more than ever Machuzak yearned to rev Fred up—his speech, his innate tempo—but even news of sabotage would have failed to do it. The blond Abbuhl, graying as retirement loomed, was, thank God, the archetypal Southern gentleman, incapable of yielding to pressure or deadlines. All of which is required if you are going to head ASSET operations. With its hundreds of subsystems, each composed of ten thousand parts, each prone to failure, if you tend to hysteria don't apply.

And yet, what do I truly know of this man? Nathaniel felt his guts twist again.

"Mesdames et messieurs," Krieg-Zuber interjected with unexpected persistence, raising his hand slowly from his bed, "what Moravec is demanding is only what we should have done long ago. Nothing will capture the imagination of the world like ignition, the creation of a star on Earth, which will lead to an inexhaustible supply of energy for mankind. We can do this. We must do this. Our day of judgment is at hand. Our kairos, as I believe our Toshi Matsushima put it just an hour ago."

Despite Krieg-Zuber's condition, Machuzak shook his head sourly.

"What is it, Dr. Machuzak?" Garrett asked, seeing his expression.

Aye, what? How could he allow an ignition campaign to proceed...? Nathaniel chose his words carefully. "I... If I recall the remark Dr. Matsushima made after the general meeting," he said, throwing a disgusted look at Zuber, "kairos is not only the moment of opportunity but the moment of grace... Mr. Garrett, I've told you that that demonstration was not merely premature but...insane. The machine was not ready, is not ready. Before we even begin an ignition campaign, we'll have to dismantle it to recheck everything. That alone will take weeks."

"Mac is correct, Mr. Chairman," Thaddeus Hasschler put in from the far end of the table. "Our tokamak is a machine, much like the engine of a car, except with perhaps one thousand times as many parts. And we are conceivably subjecting it to the most extreme environment in the solar system outside the sun's core. First we must create a vacuum such as the one in deep space in order to get rid of everything that might interfere with the reactions."

Nathaniel watched Hasschler speak and caught himself: Thad, Tadeusz, and I are not close friends. Head of Prometheus'experimental group, his love is the machine. He occasionally attempts to be pleasant, but can't help exuding a certain European aristocracy, an effect amplified by his thoroughly bald head. Thad is a tough commander. I sometimes get mail from him sent at 3:00 a.m. Had he lived in the eighteenth century, Thaddeus could only have been a Prussian drill master with a sabre scar slicing his cheek, a distinction Krieg-Zuber somehow wears in real life. No, inconceivable...

"And once we create that vacuum," added Fred, "we gotta be sure it stays that way. Just leak checking is no job for amateurs. Mr. Chairman, sir, all that equipment to heat the fuel, those massive generators—"

"Hell," Diana Cochran, head of the cryoplant division, interrupted, joining in for the first time, "it'll take a couple weeks just to get down to operating temperatures," 4.2 degrees above absolute zero, helium's boiling point.

And now Nathaniel squinted at her. What did he know of Diana other than she was his own age, blond hair streaked with the first strands of middle years, an engineer with kids who'd somehow gotten into refrigerators? Nothing...

"Mr. Garrett," Machuzak raised his head, resolving to put an end to this folly here and now. "To create fusion you first have to heat the hydrogen fuel—this plasma—to twenty times the temperature of the center of the sun, high enough so that nuclear reactions begin—"

"This is the easy part," put in Hasschler.

"True," Nathaniel nodded in Thad's direction. "The hard part is holding it long enough to get a decent amount of energy out of it. That's the purpose of those enormous magnets. In principle they can do it, but I tell you, trapping a plasma in a magnetic cage long enough to produce a sustained reaction is probably the hardest thing ever tried. Period. No qualifiers. You think building an atomic bomb was difficult? A hydrogen bomb? If controlled fusion were that easy, it would have been done a lifetime ago."

At hearing those words Garrett's face darkened, and Nathaniel at last felt some satisfaction for producing an effect. The difficulty in confining the plasma was the main reason fusioneers had failed to build a working reactor despite the better part of a century of trying.

"So what are you saying, Machuzak?"

What he was saying is that we could heat the damn fuel to 400 million degrees. Before that fatal ceremony, Prometheus was even holding it for a few minutes before it crapped out. Old AUSTOR, Prometheus' predecessor, could produce twice as much energy as they used to heat it—two times "breakeven." Forty years ago skeptics said breakeven was impossible.

Yet.

For all that, the reaction was not self-sustaining. Prometheus was still a fireplace full of damp logs; turn off all the external heating sources and the reaction stops. That's why yesterday was such a fraud. "But," he continued to Garrett, "even if the fire catches, it could flame out in two seconds, which won't do anybody a helluva lot of good. For commercial power you need both ignition and a reaction that goes on for hours—days. Mr. Garrett, ASSET's initials stand for Advanced Steady State Experimental Tokamak. It was designed primarily to see if we can hold a plasma for days. We're not even sure it will reach ignition..."

The chairman puckered his lips, as if about to whistle, and ran a finger around the rim of his famous Stetson. For a moment it seemed as if the mists had finally dispersed and he perceived with clarity the unscalable cliff towering above them. "Leonard, ASSET is your baby. Is what Dr. Machuzak says true?"

"Richard," said Leonard with his earlier sharpness, his head now twisted into a strange position, "what Mac says is true, but I have devoted my entire life to making it untrue. I designed ASSET to achieve ignition. It can be done. It will be done. No one will ask the victor what is true."

"Ignition is within the design parameters," Hasschler affirmed. "After all, we have incorporated a simple heat exchanger and turbine—"

"Right," put in Kettering.

"—although we may have been infected by optimism."

"Dr. Machuzak's conservatism in these matters is well known," Krieg-Zuber suddenly interrupted from his bed, gathering all his strength. "That is why he is not a regular member of the ASSET team and confines himself to less significant research."

A guillotine of silence fell. For a moment Nathaniel chewed his lip. In that unaided space he felt more alone than he had in his entire life. He passed his eyes slowly over his colleagues, imagining them guests at a doomed ball, all wearing fabulous, grotesque masks. For an instant the image became so vivid that he thought he must be hallucinating. With a few breaths he forced it to pass and gained control over himself. What Krieg-Zuber had said was painfully true: until his conscription for the ceremony's preparation, he'd been living in exile as division head at the neglected Materials Test Facility. The only recourse is to quit; Machuzak pushed his chair back to arm's length, staring at the floor.

At that moment one of the group who had been elsewhere surfing looked up and said, "ITER's director just announced that they will push forward their experimental timetable."

Krieg-Zuber raised his arm heavily. "Initiate triple shifts," he breathed the command. "Immediately." The inevitable round-the-clock operations. "Monsieur Abbuhl, begin organizing the shifts at once. This is destiny, kairos."

"Triple shifts?" returned Fred with as much umbrage as he was capable of, making a last stand, "after the run-up to that ceremony? The guys'll mutiny... And you know what? It won't make any difference. We can't do it."

Forgotten, Nathaniel stood on the verge of walking out but he could not abandon the old engineer. "Fred's right, Mr. Garrett," he said, putting Krieg-Zuber aside. "We've been pulling triple shifts for over a month. Everyone's exhausted. An ignition push would be worse, a dozen times worse."

"You know, I kinda like this kairos concept," Kettering jumped in again, scratching his chin. "Maybe if we'd gotten a swift kick in the ass years ago we'd have the problem licked."

"Precisely!" wheezed Krieg-Zuber in his sepulchral baritone.

Machuzak shook his head, sighing in disbelief, and moved toward the door. No surprise that Tom embraced the ass-kicking solution. Only surprise is that he hasn't suggested bringing in the military.

"I don't know that the helium factory can keep up," Diana was mumbling to no one in particular.

"Thaddeus," Leonard told the ASSET head wearily, "assemble your team immediately and start planning ignition experiments. Not a minute to lose, remember?"

At that Machuzak closed his eyes. Yeah, blow up the machine and be done with it. The next time he blinked, the meeting had adjourned. Once more he surveyed the room. The boards, the photos of the Austin tokamaks. We had pride in them once. Chen, the large armadillo mascot standing in the corner, CFRC emblazoned on the saddle thrown over his armored back. There was something welcome in Chen's deflationary humor and even at this moment the sight of him elicited a faint chuckle from Machuzak.

Fred was standing at his side. "You all right, Mac?"

"I suppose," he lied. Yet how could he abandon his companions at their kairos? He would not. "Well, let's make the best of this. No more slacker days."

Outside, the two stood on the balcony above the building's great central atrium, filled with its palms and banana trees below and the tentlike glass ceiling above, which might have come from the hand of Le Corbusier. As majestic as it was, the lab's scale was dwarfed by the magnitude of the endeavor they were suddenly, unexpectedly preparing to undertake. Nathaniel perceived only a castle going up in flames. Garrett sidled up to them then, breaking the silent commiseration, and remarked that he didn't have the impression their task was impossible, just "difficult."

"Let's put it this way, Richard," Machuzak answered pointedly. "The EU, Japan, China, India...have poured twenty billion euros into ITER, which is designed to reach ignition. Would you bet on it, Fred?"

The senior engineer shook his head.

"The thing is, Richard, the world has seen a few tokamaks. A few have worked better than they were designed, most have worked worse; none—ever—has worked the way it was supposed to. We can kill ourselves day and night, we can be ingenious and even brilliant, but as that deadline nears, what's going to be most important is sheer, dumb luck. If you were asking me to bet, I'd bet that Moravec has signed our death warrant."

Garrett frowned and nodded silently. Then he said, "Hmm," and ambled off.

"Well, *Herr Doktor* Professor," said Fred, watching Garrett, now truly The Chairman, depart, "I don't know who or what's behind this, and God knows we can't beat the deadline, but at least now we have a chance to beat ITER."

Machuzak perceived that what he took for "this" was not what Fred meant by "this," but he only looked at Abbuhl and said, "Do we deserve to?"

FIVE

Before an hour ticked by, every phone on Nathaniel or within his reach went off simultaneously and Lise, Leonard's secretary, asked him to come up to the octagon immediately. She wouldn't say more. He took the stairs, flinched so visibly as he passed Diana Cochran that she recoiled with a snarl, and arrived moments later. The meeting's tension remained fully with him, so too the knowledge that in a few hours, an accident would become sabotage. Without delay Lise ushered him into the famous, erudite space that had once been so familiar.

Sunlight streaming through two sides of the octagon immediately drew his eyes to the luxurious semicircular desk occupying the room's center and illuminated the wrinkles on Leonard Rasmussen's face as he peered up from behind a 360-degree monitor. The same light fell onto the thousand books and Oriental art that covered another three walls; a single ray brightened a Japanese Daruma doll, which blessed the lab with good fortune and whose second eye would be painted in when the great task was accomplished. The big blue bottle atop the water cooler standing at the entrance to the private bath sparkled as always.

Even after ten years Nathaniel felt a certain reverence when stepping into this office, and as he had since he'd set eyes on Leonard yesterday, he fought back tears, but before he could wallow in the lost past, Richard Garrett's voice interrupted.

"Machuzak," Garrett said, rising from the conference table off to the side, "we've got some good news for you."

Nathaniel had hardly noticed him sitting at the table, drumming his fingers impatiently. At the big man's words, Nathaniel caught his breath. Good news no longer existed, by definition.

"The board of governors," Garrett put his arms around his shoulder, "of which I am chair, has authorized the executive committee to appoint you acting director."

For a moment Nathaniel blinked at the chairman, then nearly spit up his lunch as he attempted to prevent himself from bursting out in caustic laughter. He glanced distractedly at the medals and citations decorating the octagon's remaining walls, the photographs of Leonard with presidents of the United States, the leaders of the European Union, Korea. None of those luminaries offered advice.

"What's the matter, son, cat got your tongue?"

Nathaniel now merely stared at the chairman in full disbelief. "I...I don't understand," he said at last, just to make certain he'd heard correctly.

"Mac," Garrett replied after recovering from a sharp cough, "at the meeting you weren't exactly grinnin like a skunk eatin cabbage at midnight. Admit it, you wouldn't prefer the alternatives."

Machuzak left it to The Chairman to read his expression.

Seeing the resistance that faced him, Garrett pressed forward in a more conciliatory tone, attempting to win the reluctant physicist over to his preposterous plan. Cassandra, he rolled out the epithet again, Machuzak was the only one who showed good sense about the demonstration; everybody else was wrong. "What can I say?" the Texan concluded. "We're gonna need a level head around here in the comin months."

Nathaniel couldn't discern exactly what had been taking place behind the scenes, but his reaction was simple and firm: "I decline."

"Come on, Mac, duty calls."

"You're asking me to oversee the ignition campaign, aren't you?"

Cocking his head The Chairman said, "I'd say that about sums it up."

"Why don't you offer me the Astor suite on the *Titanic*? Look, the whole thing is crazy." Crazier, much, than Garrett knew. "You heard me before. It can't be done."

"It's gotta be done. We gotta try."

Machuzak suddenly felt trapped, set up, and every instinct told him to escape. "What about Krieg-Zuber? He won't take this lying down."

"He will, exactly, lyin down. Doctors say there's been internal injuries. Two months, at least."

Funny, Cyrus the Great didn't seem to know that.

"With respect," Nathaniel said with an increasing desperation, "I'm a scientist, not an administrator. I don't have the interest, I don't have the force of personality. Anyone at the lab can tell you that."

"You don't see yourself, son."

"Really it's absurd," Machuzak answered, voice acidic, diplomacy ended. At that, he and Garrett simultaneously turned toward Rasmussen, who had remained silent. "Leonard," said Nathaniel, knowing his words were self-serving, but betraying none of the uncertainty he felt, "you can do this. You above anyone."

With a visible reluctance, the director shook his head. "I'll stand behind you, Nathaniel, but the time..." He didn't finish his sentence. "You must take this on. I ask you."

Not that. Nathaniel could refuse anything but that. "How long? Six months, no—"

"Two months, max," said Garrett, "or until Krieg-Zuber's recovered. I give you my word."

With a sigh of resignation, of the damned, Nathaniel agreed to think it over.

"I'll expect a positive reply tomorrow," The Chairman answered. "It's time to cowboy up. Realm of the gods, remember?"

Too well. "Would you mind if I spoke to Leonard alone?" Nathaniel asked.

The rich Texan nodded, picked up his hat from the table and with a marked, bowlegged lope waddled out of the office.

* * * *

Machuzak remained standing, looking at Rasmussen in his wheelchair, deciding whether to reveal the sabotage, but it was Leonard who spoke. "I'm sorry to put this on you, Mac," he said, expression noticeably contorted, "but we have so little choice. We cannot afford to fail in our great endeavor. I have devoted my life to this project…"

"Yes, you have," Nathaniel replied with difficulty. How far this shrunken man from the dazzling father who, legend told, went to bed at midnight and awoke for calisthenics at 5:00 a.m. Yet, half immobilized as he was, Leonard insisted on wearing a jacket, today with open collar. There'd always been that slight formality, a precision in his entire manner that put one on one's mettle and was all the more unsettling because he was unfailingly polite.

As he was at this moment. "You'll have to come by for dinner with Theresa and me," he said. "You'll need real fuel during the coming trial, not bachelor noodles."

"I'm honored." That was genuine. The Rasmussens regularly invited lab hands to their spectacular home for afternoon cookouts; to be invited for dinner…

"Don't be honored. Be prepared to eat—and to think."

"Is that your idea of a bribe?" Nathaniel smiled, shaking his head.

"Of course it's a bribe. The definition of a scientist is an unscrupulous opportunist, you know that. If the Indian ambassador is in town, I'll ask you to wear a tie."

This time Nathaniel laughed. How as a freshly minted PhD he'd longed for one of those coveted invitations! How Leonard's dazzling aura of elegance and achievement had put him at a far distance. He might have been Christ on the Mount. Several years passed before Leonard became more human than god, and then Nathaniel began to see his formality as an accoutrement of office. Leonard spent his days on the phone with congressmen or at august gatherings where the planet's future was decided. He was quoted and therefore needed to be precise; he was photographed and therefore needed to appear precise.

"Tell me your plans for ignition," Rasmussen said.

Nathaniel shook himself into the present. "L–Leonard, you've asked me this minute to take charge of an impossible project that I'm not usually attached to—"

"Do not use the word *impossible* in my presence! Nathaniel, I think a walk would do you good. What do you say?"

That was more like the Rasmussen of old, Machuzak smiled. "Are you sure…?" he asked.

"Of course! Get those crutches!"

As Nathaniel grabbed the crutches propped up against the wall, Leonard struggled to his feet, helping himself to a drink from the cooler. They slowly made their way out of the building to the lake, where Leonard sat down again.

"Now," he said as the fountain spray refreshed them, "give me your ideas."

My idea is the single idea I have had for five hours—someone has sabotaged the machine. Someone may do it again.

"Mac, attention! This *is* the most important task the world has seen!"

Nathaniel chuckled ruefully and recollected those weekends when the formal director would appear at the lab in shirtsleeves and a straw hat, clutching a can of beer. He'd prowl far and wide, corner you at your bench and grill you. If you reported an insight, he'd punch the air with his fist and make you feel like the most important person in the world. Today he may have meant it. Needing to talk over an idea, he'd say, "Let's go for a walk" and off you went. Leonard was not exceptionally tall, but every stride was taken with purpose and you'd soon find yourself breathing hard beside him.

This afternoon, Machuzak was hardly breathing at all. "I think," he said, "we must heed the old Roman motto, *festina lente—*"

"—make haste slowly—"

"—or we risk making a terrible situation worse. *If* I take this on, I'll ask Abbuhl to dismantle the machine as far as possible."

"Is that necessary?"

Yes, Leonard, it is necessary. "I need to think about the triple shifts."

"Don't think. Do it," said Leonard. Rasmussen, as far as anyone could tell, had never wasted a moment of his life.

"Len," Nathaniel answered, glancing at the sun-sphere surmounting the fountain, "the important thing is to convince the gang that we are not acting desperately and that this task is achievable, even when both aren't true. I don't know how to do that."

"If ITER can do it, we can do it."

"Leonard, forget ITER. They cannot be close."

"ITER will not forget us, Nathaniel. You heard the announcement; they're already redoubling their efforts. I know those people well. I trained half of them. Maybe we need a slogan. 'Prometheus—Lighting the Way…'"

Machuzak couldn't help but sigh. "Leonard, somehow we've already gotten ourselves into a race with ITER, but we can't win. Of that I am certain."

"Why are you certain, Mac?"

"Because Prometheus has been sabotaged."

Both men stopped short. Finally Rasmussen stuttered, "W–what do you mean?"

Nathaniel told him everything. When he finished, he thought he had killed Rasmussen and was waiting for the older man to die. After a long silence, Leonard spoke again, "This can't be."

"I am afraid it is. How serious it is, I don't yet know. Maybe it was a prank."

"You *mustn't* say a word. Morale would be crushed."

"It would. How can we go forward?"

"We…you will find the saboteur. Yes, it is probably no more than a bad joke or a grudge. Mac, we are on the cusp of history. This is the moment at which we steer mankind away from three hundred years of folly. You would not let that moment slip through our grasp, would you?"

Kairos again? Machuzak saw in Leonard's remark the dying of dreams.

After another silence Leonard gazed up at Nathaniel with the same plea in his eye that he had cast at him in his office. "ASSET is my epitaph, Nathaniel, remember that."

Nathaniel helped Leonard Rasmussen to his feet and they walked back to the main building. He sprinted over to the pentagon, found Lipman and asked if it was too late. When the tech shook his head, he ordered him to replace the busbar at once.

* * * *

When Nathaniel found Slava in his office and told him that the chiefs wanted to appoint him acting director, but that he hadn't yet agreed, Archangelsky's reaction was swift and merciless: "Has a fly bit your balls? This is best thing that could have happened. Now we can control the situation."

Machuzak didn't reply directly, but thinking the news would pacify Archangelsky, he added that Rasmussen knew about the sabotage and authorized him to replace the busbar. To the contrary, the Russian's eyes grew wide, he grabbed Machuzak by the arm and marched him outside to the lake again.

"W–why are we here?" was Machuzak's confused reaction.

"Put on your brain, Edward'ich! Who knows who's listening? This is the opt-out century, remember."

Machuzak didn't get it; The Terminator was out of commission. But yes, here was the boy who had spent his childhood in Russia, Machuzak realized. Archangelsky, though, seeing his friend staring at him in horror, with equal exasperation threw up his hands. "Akh, spilling beans to Leonard may have been right thing or worst mistake of your life, but I tell you reason for this. After Time of Troubles in Russia, this stretch in seventeenth century when country was in chaos, one tsar after other until *pfft!*—nobody. Finally nobles get together and who do they crown? Little Mikhail Romanov, a teenager, a total wimp." Slava cast about for a cigarette, found one, and thrust it into his mouth. "That's why Rasmussen chose you."

"Don't you dare call me a wimp," Machuzak said angrily, turning back to the main building. With a glance at the real sun in the sky and at his watch he growled, "Excuse me, it's time to call the police."

SIX

When late in the day T. J. D'Abro at the Austin Sheriff's Department got a call from one of the physicists she'd met at CFRC not twenty-four hours earlier, she was already half out the door—for good. In her half-belligerent mood she verged on telling the guy to fuck off. Nah, she'd put him on hold. You know, why not celebrate? She puckered her lips and told him to meet her at Scholz's Beer Garten.

She would have missed him stumbling in if she hadn't glanced up from one of the picnic tables out back at the exact moment, scowling at the "game over" that blinked obnoxiously from her wrist. From a distance, he seemed tense, fatigued, distracted—she couldn't tell what—surely no more festive than the voice over the phone. She could tell he didn't come here often. That was dead obvious from the way he scrutinized the banners strung up all around proclaiming "Hook 'Em Horns" and Coors. Maybe he was worried about droppings from the trees. But hell, that was Scholz's trademark—bird shit in the beer. "Dr. Machuzak!" she called out and waved. He turned. Yup, as far as he was concerned she might have been Sally Skull or Calamity Jane walkin the streets of the Old West.

It was something like that, Machuzak conceded. The chaos of the day was tumbling through his head and before him stood cowgirl crystallized—half a cowgirl. As she unplugged an ear bud and they shook hands, she reacted with a faint, ironic smile, as if she got the joke. With what attention he could muster, he stood openmouthed in shock and admiration, victim to that streak of self-parody among Texans that makes it difficult to tell whether they are serious and dangerous to guess. D'Abro's designer jeans were smartly tucked into boots that were embroidered more tastefully than most in these parts, with scarlet stitching. He would have found her black hat—one of those flat, Mexican-style hats rimmed by silver bangles—attractive if he could have struck sabotage from his mind and if it hadn't been for the green-blond ponytail peeking out the back, but the white silk shirt and brown bandana matched it well anyway. Her earpiece, stylishly disguised as a silver-and-lapis earring, provided a nice touch. What penetrated most through the haze, though, was her distant, ironic smile, entirely uncharacteristic of the locals, which set a course for places unknown.

"Sir, you sure look like you could use a drink," she said as they sat down, amused more than she expected by the scientist's disorientation. She laid her hat on the table and poured him a beer, peering at his drawn face, observing him wince at all the "likes," "I means," "you knows," and "absolutelys" assaulting his ears. "Hey, it's not as bad as it used to be."

True enough, Machuzak concurred absently. The noise level in the Old World had significantly receded as virtual life's population swelled, in particular around the waistline. "I'm sorry, Officer D'Abro, I didn't recognize you without your uniform. It's been a..."

"... tough day?"

The physicist replied with a morbid chuckle, raised his glass as if were made of lead, and drank. Despite her Gallic-flavored surname, over the rim of his glass D'Abro appeared to be of German descent, unusual these days as Mexico reconquered the Southwest: tall enough to be within striking distance, about eight years more idealistic than he, fair, blond when not green, features soft. If it hadn't been for the smile and the hair, he might have labeled her wholesome. Back East she would have turned heads, but this was Texas.

"Remember what all those Miss Americas from Denton used to say," she pronounced as if reading his mind. "The only thing worse than being ugly in Denton is being dead."

"Are you sure that wasn't vice versa?" Machuzak managed with effort.

D'Abro granted a smile to the fellow's faltering attempts to enter the here and now and then asked with abrupt seriousness, "Anyway, Doc, your call sounded urgent. What is it?" Before he could reply, she interrupted herself with a glance at her wrist and turned away. "I...I probably can't help," she apologized.

"Why's that?" Machuzak asked.

"I've been promoted to detective today."

"Congratulations," Nathaniel answered, thinking to clink her glass, which stood ignored on the table. "That could be useful."

But D'Abro barely responded. "I resigned. Well, I took a leave," she eventually replied.

Nathaniel glanced toward the German-style bar inside, where more laws—no doubt—had been enacted than any place outside the Capitol, then peered at D'Abro again with a perplexed shake of his head.

"Don't ask. I don't know why. I'm just not good at stickin around too long. You know that."

Did he? By now entirely bewildered, Machuzak straightened. "Sorry, are you on the phone?" This time she didn't respond at all. "Look, I'll find someone else," he said and got to his feet.

At that D'Abro swiveled back and waved him down. "My fault, Doc, sorry. Why don't you tell me what's up."

"What's the point?" Machuzak said, exhausted of more than energy. "You've resigned...taken leave?"

"Yeah, I do have trouble stickin around. Attention deficit disorder or somethin." She regarded the weary physicist with some sympathy, if not understanding. "Look, tell me what's up, Doc, and I'll refer you. The news says your director friend will probably survive his heart attack."

"The question is whether the lab's heart will survive his recovery," he said humorlessly. "And don't call me Doc, please."

"Will do." D'Abro turned to salting her beer, murmuring that she liked to watch the bubbles.

Machuzak exhaled deeply, already convinced that to reveal anything to this strange woman was an exercise in futility. "I didn't call about Krieg-Zuber," he offered finally, reluctantly. "This morning one of the techs found something. I think..." She prodded him with a glance, he considered and went on. "... I think the machine's been sabotaged."

D'Abro didn't react at once. Nathaniel was certain another call had come through until she said with a wrinkled nose and intensity, "So, the professor getting zapped wasn't an accident?"

Who this T. J. D'Abro was, Machuzak hadn't decided, but he had decided that to talk was more important than to sleep. "Depends on what you mean by accident," he said, seeing himself in the surge room not twelve hours ago. "No one could've known that The Terminator would run into the power area like a madman. I doubt he'd been down there in years. When he's not bugging phones he's on a plane. Zuber was an accident, but that the demo failed wasn't—not in the way it failed." Having begun, it was easier to continue and Nathaniel went on to describe everything: the safety systems, the inspections, the surge rooms, Lipman's morning discovery. "It looks...it looks like someone cut the damned busbar in half."

When he'd finished, D'Abro only wrinkled her nose again. "Wouldn't a brick of C-4 do a better job?"

Exactly. "If you want to destroy the machine, not if you want to destroy the program. A pebble is all you need. A pebble may be what we have."

"Doc—uh, sorry—" She suddenly halted, blushing, just as she jerked upright and put a finger to her earpiece. "Nobody calls you that?"

Machuzak comprehended then that he was as far from T. J. D'Abro's world as she was from his. Two space aliens meeting in no-man's land. "That's movie talk," he replied, dismissively or wearily she couldn't say. "If you're a physicist you have a PhD, period. It's just a hunting license. The only thing that counts in our game is brains. Anyway, we're all on a first-name basis at the lab. Call me Nat or Mac, as you prefer."

"Will do." D'Abro glanced again at her screen. He'd witnessed the same continuous distraction yesterday in his office, but a minute part of her brain, evidently, was engaged. "So, Doc," she looked up abruptly, "you don't sound one hundred percent convinced this is sabotage."

"Don't call me Doc. No, I'm not, one hundred percent. Machine parts often fail in strange ways."

"Then to state the obvious," D'Abro said, cocking her head with an eyebrow raised, "you're not one hundred percent sure a crime has been committed."

Machuzak couldn't read her expression, which sat somewhere to the left of scorn but to the right of neutrality. "The only thing I'm certain of," he said, "is that we've suddenly gotten ourselves in a race with ITER to achieve ignition, a race we can't win in six months, and that a saboteur may be determined to stop us."

D'Abro's sharp shake of her head revealed complete bafflement. "What's ITER?" she asked and the question caught Nathaniel off guard. ITER was front-page news all over Europe, evidently not in Texas. Still, he would have taken the detective's tone as one of genuine curiosity if in the next instant she hadn't jumped again. "Sorry, Doc, d'ya think you could genetically engineer a spam filter...?"

He doubted it. "ITER," he explained, calling for a real beer from a waitress passing by the cheerful alpine scene painted on a small stage, "is the huge reactor several dozen countries have built in southern France. The initials originally stood for International Thermonuclear Experimental Reactor, but the greens didn't go for the 'nuclear' part—." D'Abro craned her neck in mock surprise, even as she fact-checked Nathaniel's assertion. "There were a lot of protests from Greenpeace and so on. Then some alert scholar informed the administrators that ITER is also Latin for 'the way,' and they greened the name without even changing the acronym. There are still protests. ITER was originally budgeted at about five billion euros, now it's twenty and years behind schedule. It's the largest technological project ever attempted and its director, Jules César Balard, is not about to let CFRC win a race for fusion."

"Or the reverse."

"Or the reverse." Machuzak suddenly realized that Leonard's slogan of the afternoon, "Prometheus—Lighting the Way," might be misconstrued.

"And ignition, what's that?"

Again Machuzak was surprised, as much by the abrupt sincerity in the woman's voice as by the question itself. "Ignition is the dream of all fusioneers. Our bid to save civilization. Ignition is a self-sustaining fusion reaction, a fire that catches and gives you a lot more energy out than you put in to get it started. Until now no reactor has achieved ignition, but if you can't do it, commercial power is just..." He trailed off, shaking his head.

Examining the scientist's weary face over her own glass, D'Abro began to sense a man who believed in what he did, or at least tried. "You know, Doc, there's lots here I don't understand. All the people we talked to last night were grumbling that the demo was way premature, but nobody had the guts to say so except you. Why the hell would a lab full of pure geniuses try such a thing?"

Machuzak chuckled, weakly. "Officer—Detective?—in the 1970s, Princeton beat out Oak Ridge for a contract worth several hundred million dollars. Oak Ridge had proposed a giant ignition machine, almost as big as Prometheus—fifty years ahead of its time. There's no chance, none, it ever could have worked. Ignition." Now he managed an outright laugh. "You find a premature demo surprising? I don't."

"The Oak Ridge tomahawk was a fraud?" D'Abro exclaimed with astonishment but was answered only by the face of the sphinx. "You know, I was actually researching this ignition on the drive over. Six hundred videos today say you guys are swindlers and what you just told me proves it."

"No, it doesn't."

Her voice shifted instantly from antagonism to wonder. "But can you really do this—provide Earth with a star?"

For an instant the physicist hesitated and D'Abro was poised to pounce again, but then he said simply, "We know we can do it someday, not in six months. Minus a day." Absently he traced a large *1* on the table amid the bird droppings.

"That's the second time you said six months. Why?"

"Because this morning Moravec called." Before she could ask, he filled her in on the consortium, the morning's unexpected call from GlobeTex's strange CEO, the ultimatum. "Six months. From today."

D'Abro listened with widening mouth. "And Moravec made this ultimatum before sunrise after the accident!" she exclaimed when Nathaniel was finished, loudly enough for the people at the next table to turn.

He nodded.

"And it didn't occur to you that the two are connected?"

"Don't tell me you're a conspiracy theorist," Machuzak said with a gaze no less severe than hers was incredulous, but she didn't react. "What's the point of sabotaging the machine if you can pull out the moment your contract's expired?"

"Certain amount of logic in that," D'Abro conceded unhappily.

"Look, the accident's scared everybody. GlobeTex may be simply spooked, as The Chairman says, but I had the strangest feeling that Moravec was being forced to do it... I can't explain why. And *don't* ask." Actually, he couldn't blame D'Abro for weaving conspiracies; against his instincts he'd been weaving all day.

D'Abro didn't ask. She took a gulp and then said as if the last exchange hadn't occurred, "I don't understand what GlobeTex's doing in your consortium to begin with. Aren't they into wind, solar, biofuels?"

"They *are* an energy company," Machuzak replied, accepting a Brau-Weisse from the waitress.

"I really don't get it," D'Abro objected. "I mean, the point. Wind and solar are here. I don't know anything about nukular fusion, but if you can't even make it work, how's it going to compete?"

As the faint smell of urine wafted over him from the toilets, or the Capitol, Machuzak conceded she had a point. The case for fusion was hardly straightforward. "Maybe you've noticed that CO_2 hasn't always decreased in the past twenty years. Solar's not cheap, we're using as much fossil fuel as ever, legislation goes nowhere in Congress, Texas ignores every regulation and every time someone grows a biofuel in one place, the price of food goes up somewhere else. Not every country is bathed in sunlight, the wind doesn't blow all the time. An intelligent grid design helps but you still need a backbone power supply. It takes energy to charge plug-ins. Where does that come from? Where do the emissions go? You think the price of beef and silicon chips is an accident? We've got to start using less energy."

Suddenly the physicist was more animated than he'd been since he arrived, gesticulating like an Italian. D'Abro couldn't stop herself from bursting out in laughter. "I'm sorry," she apologized. "You came in here like a cat walkin in mud, and suddenly you seem alive. It's kinda cute, actually."

Machuzak laughed—at both of them. He *was* finding it difficult to understand this woman. Discounting earpiece and thought processes— hell, she remained perpetually mobile. She'd lean forward on her elbow, fiddling with her bracelet or wrist screen, then suddenly sit knee up along the bench, long, manicured fingers wrapped around her chin. Whether it was swagger or sass, God knows he couldn't say.

"I'm flattered," he eventually replied, "but I often think the greatest evil in the world is the idea that you can get something for nothing. You gotta refine silicon and copper for solar collectors, making fertilizer takes energy—lots. There's no free lunch."

"Yes," she said with the rising Texas diphthong that makes it sound like *yee-ass*, "seems I heard that once upon a time. Conservation of energy you physicists call it, if I'm not mistaken."

"Good girl," said Machuzak,

She let the borderline condescension pass. Maybe this physicist was a bit crabby after his strange, trying day, but he did seem sort of human, as if he'd always been wrestling with…questions. He looked to be finding his way, groping. "All I can say is that you folks sure don't have a lot of friends. Energy companies don't like you, greens don't like you and you don't like each other. The question is, who hates you enough to sabotage your program?"

Machuzak could manage only a perplexed shake of the head and the two at last fell silent. Finally, after a pause long enough to give birth to a militiaman, he said, "So where does that leave us, with you having resigned?"

"Let's say I've taken indefinite leave. Look, the feds won't be interested in this—no sex, no money, no drugs, no publicity. Even the sheriff's department won't give a dang unless you convince them a crime has been committed. So…why don't we go have a look at the scene of the *incident* and see if there's anything you missed."

"Now?"

"The sooner the better. Then you can use your rocket-scientist's imagination and figure out why somebody would spike your machine."

"I am not a rocket scientist," Nathaniel mouthed silently as a fistfight broke out behind them. They walked into the bar, where a cantankerous health inspector was threatening to shut the place down, settled up and for the second time this day Machuzak headed south.

SEVEN

Seeing the physicist's exhaustion, D'Abro offered to take the wheel of his jeep and met no resistance. She grabbed an aluminum box from the trunk of her own car nearby, but now, sitting before the unfamiliar controls, she asked what sort of jeep this was. "It runs on algae," Machuzak told her.

"Where do you tank up on that?"

"One of our guys built a pond at the lab. Algae produces biofuels ten, a hundred times more efficiently than grasses, so we're trying to grow it in the car's tank itself—but yeah, still no pump at the local station. Infrastructure takes time. No instant fixes."

"No Mr. Fusion?" D'Abro smirked as she decoded the dashboard and they took off.

Machuzak was not only exhausted but famished. South of town, on the infinite field of fast-food and biodiesel signs that rise pikelike high above the plain to impale civilization, D'Abro stopped long enough for him to grab a burger from the car window. Before he finished a bite she was fiddling impatiently with the radio and caught a talk-show pundit in midflight:

"—After all, the laboratory's tritium supply makes it too likely a target for terrorists."

Machuzak nearly choked on his fries, but D'Abro merely snatched a sip from his soda, put her foot to the accelerator and pressed him. "What about that tritium, Doc? Everyone's talkin about it."

"Talkin," Nathaniel nodded, "not understandin." Usually he told people tokamak fuel is hydrogen, which was true, but it isn't ordinary hydrogen. "We use two isotopes: deuterium—heavy hydrogen—and tritium, extra-heavy hydrogen. Tritium is mildly radioactive."

"Why would terrorists want it?" D'Abro asked with sudden interest.

The scientist, feeling but partly revived as the caffeine began its work, sighed heavily. "The military uses it in hydrogen bombs. If a terrorist got enough, he could add it to a fission bomb as a sort of booster, making a crude hydrogen bomb." That's why the tritium safeguards at CFRC border on the supernatural. That's why at Savannah River, SWAT teams guard the country's tritium stockpile.

"How much you need?" D'Abro pressed as they turned off Route 290.

"You get shot if you ask," Machuzak replied. "It's not a lot—grams —but we don't have a lot at CFRC. You'd have to steal virtually the entire supply."

"This must be connected—"

"*No.*" He put his foot down. "Ockham's Razor, detective, prime directive in science: find the simplest solution. Terrorists... Sheesh..."

"You shave with Ockham's Razor every day, Doc?" D'Abro retorted and, not waiting for his response, pushed another preset.

Machuzak nodded after one second, two. "Tchaikovsky. Third Orchestral Suite, fourth movement, sixth variation."

"Wow," said D'Abro, "you oughtta be on a quiz show. Is your memory that good for everything?"

"Not quite," he equivocated, biting into his sandwich, "but musically I've always been able to identify nearly anything. The world's most useless talent."

"Glad to hear you don't spend all your time thinkin about tomahawks." She helped herself to his remaining fries.

Machuzak didn't react and they continued southward. Twilight was descending. As they crested the final rise and the lab came into view below, D'Abro said, "There's a whole lot here I still don't understand. Like where that Miss Fusion calendar in your office came from. Seems about as likely as an armadillo with brains."

"No more unlikely than anything else connected with fusion," Nathaniel chuckled. "Christ, the whole US program started because the *New York Times* screamed that Argentina had fusion in 1950. Ever heard of Bob Guccione?"

"*Penthouse*? *He* was before my time. *Playboy* asked me to pose for them once. 'Girls of South by Southwest' or somethin. Mighta been a hoot. I was a wild undergrad-thang then, but I said nope. I did dance at Sugar's once or twice to pay the rent."

D'Abro spoke offhandedly, but having put up with her now for two hours, Nathaniel was somehow already certain that Sugar's would have been merely another of life's distractions for the strange woman. Why not? This *is* the Republic of Texas, where bumper stickers proclaiming *Secede* mean it. "Guccione thought fusion would save the world. He poured sixteen million out of his own pocket to build an economical miniature tokamak—"

"Sixteen million?" D'Abro whistled. "No shit?"

"No shit. He even created a subsidiary of the magazine to oversee the project: Penthouse Energy and Technology Systems." Nathaniel paused, sure D'Abro would get the joke, but her face remained a perfect blank. "PETS."

Now she smiles. "T, A and fusion—now there's an angle I hadn't considered. My, my, the world *is* full of interesting connections."

They soon reached the main gate and Machuzak passed the detective his badge for scanning. As the fence swung open, she quipped, "You short on biometrics around here?"

"You've been watching too many movies," he said, before admitting to D'Abro that Guccione had lost every cent. Down the drive the guard booth was already empty for the night. After D'Abro grudgingly accepted Machuzak's badge again and the gate lifted, they drove on to the main building. She grabbed her box and they walked inside.

* * * *

At once T. J. D'Abro's expression changed as she was transfixed by the expansiveness of the lobby and she began prowling about. Moments hadn't gone by before she homed in on a glass case that housed a bird, as large as a peacock and certainly no less colorful, but one wholly unnatural. Whatever mad artisan created it had fashioned the eyes from emeralds, or what might pass for them, the beak from gold. Rising above the head, a crest of diamonds and sapphires. A train of ruby and gold feathers trails away to curl around the bird's silver feet. The wings, spread above the head like a ballerina, have been fashioned from the same fabric of ruby and gold. This crystalline bird, glittering, dazzling, would be more at home in a museum than a laboratory. At the same time, its very luminescence, as overdone as the Dallas skyline, telegraphed its kinship to a rhinestone cowboy.

"Why, that's as pretty a sight as I've ever seen," D'Abro exclaimed of the gaudy creature, shooting a video. "What could it be?"

"The firebird," Nathaniel replied. "Do you know the ballet?"

D'Abro had never heard of it.

The jeweled bird had been presented to the laboratory by a Russian visitor long ago, he told her. The firebird is a symbol of dreams and hope; according to legend, anyone who catches one of its feathers is assured of realizing his heart's desire.

"Whoever gave you this gift was an optimist," said a voice from behind them. "If you read the original fairy tales, she is not so nice."

For an instant, Machuzak caught his breath, until he recognized the accent as Archangelsky's. "Working late?" he asked, and as Slava sullenly turned up his lips, said, "I believe you two have met. Dr. *Yah*roslav Arkh*ahn*gelsky, T. J. D'Abro, occasional detective." Puzzled, Slava gingerly took her hand and D'Abro forewent the pronunciation of his name.

"Slava is, uh…informed. You might as well come with us, Slava. Do you think the nb supply area is clear?"

"Should be okay. No *acting director* has authorized triple shifts." He stared at Machuzak significantly. "Tired bots have gone home." Seeing that D'Abro's attention was still fixed on the bird, Archangelsky shook his great beard like an ancient bard. "This firebird causes a lot of trouble," he sighed mournfully, "a lot of trouble."

The three of them cut through the atrium to the back door and walked out toward the pentagon.

EIGHT

A few minutes later Machuzak badged them into the central hub. No one was in evidence at this hour. Nathaniel removed a safety key from the interlock, pocketed it, and at the push of a button the heavy door to the tokamak bay swung open.

From their brief acquaintanceship, Nathaniel would have guessed that nothing could silence T. J. D'Abro. But standing on the test-cell floor, gazing up at the colossus covered with its cables and plumbing, at the monstrous crane hanging above it, all on a scale more appropriate to Vulcan's forge than to a human workshop, she frames no questions, no witty remarks escape her lips. For himself there is: six months, saboteur.

After a few moments of stillness, the young woman shook her head and gulped. "Why don't we have a look at that whatever-you-called-it—surge room—and see what we got?"

They descended to the bowels of the power-supply area, completely deserted but for the overpowering gloom of a medieval dungeon, ducked under the DO NOT ENTER tape and opened the door to the surge room, which appeared undisturbed.

"I'm gonna check for latents, fibers, you know..." D'Abro said, craning her neck at the science-fiction setting around her. "Normally the crime-scene techies would take care of it, but since this is an unofficial visit..."

This time Archangelsky could not restrain his own bafflement at the woman. "What do you mean, 'unofficial'? You are detective or aren't you?"

Reluctantly, D'Abro fessed up to Slava that on this day of her promotion she'd taken indefinite leave. The Russian rolled his eyes in Machuzak's direction and the latter answered with already proficient exasperation. D'Abro snapped. "You docs think you're bein saddled with a greenhorn amateur who doesn't know shit about tomahawks, don't you?"

"Look, Bedbug," Machuzak replied, by now more than fed up with the woman's continued judgments and imputations. "Every scientist I know is a professional amateur. We're amateurs because everything we try, we're trying for the first time. We're professionals because we have the sense to know that whatever it is, we're going to have a helluva time with it. Every one of us is a greenhorn." Now more than ever. "Got it?"

"Got it," D'Abro swallowed, red faced.

As she opened her aluminum case, Slava flipped on the light and pointed out the fateful busbar, half hidden in the maze of electrical plumbing. D'Abro took one look before she snapped a picture: "I thought there was a gap." No embarrassment in her voice now.

Slava and Nathaniel glanced at each other. "There was," Nathaniel said. "I told you, didn't I? Our director is worried about panic—he authorized me to have it replaced."

As she slipped on a pair of gloves, D'Abro shook her head with an expression no less sour than Slava's had been. "Cover-up's worse than the crime, boys."

Machuzak understood that no good deed goes unpunished, but his irritation only mounted. "Bedbug, if you think the last thirty hours around here have been normal…! I've told you everything I know, damnit, and remember, we can't absolutely rule out that the thing just melted."

D'Abro scowled but wasn't as concerned as her reproach had made her sound. "Calm down, Doc. I know you've had a rough day." Her physicist was holding up better than most people she met on duty, actually. She flipped off the light, playing over the equipment with her own special light source, dusted.

"You'll probably find our prints all over here," Slava said.

"I expect to," she replied dryly. At that D'Abro noticed something, crawled past the ignitrons and capacitors toward a far corner. The other two saw only the camera flash before she backed out of the maze again and stood up with palm held open. "What d' y'all make of this?"

"May I?" Machuzak asked with his eyes, and D'Abro handed him a pair of gloves. She'd found two thin pieces of copper—what was left of them. Each piece was five or six centimeters long and largely melted, but Nathaniel imagined that they had originally formed two halves of a rectangular sleeve, which might have easily slid over a busbar. He and Slava exchanged glances and Machuzak told him to see if he could find the original busbar.

D'Abro's fiery gaze was now unambiguous. "You mean you may have thrown it away?"

"No. It's on my desk in the main building." Slava was gone.

Machuzak and D'Abro stood facing each other. He understood in that moment that D'Abro must be asking, "Who is this reticent fellow who sought out the law but has not exactly acted this day with the strength of a comic-book hero?"

The detective didn't put to him Lorenzo's question. She took a hand vac, ducked down behind a capacitor bank and just before she turned it on said, "Now, as I understand it, that there plasma is some sort of hot gas."

Nathaniel perceived no escape. "A plasma is nothing mysterious," he answered reluctantly. Most of the visible universe is plasma: stars, the northern lights...the neon signs that trim Austin skyscrapers. "It's just a gas that's been heated to at least about ten thousand degrees, enough so that the electrons have boiled off from the nuclei. We say you've ionized it. *Plasma* is a synonym for ionized gas. That's all."

"Why do you need to heat it?" She switched off the vac just long enough to pose her question.

Machuzak's fatigue was fast returning, but the surreal quality of this conversation with a lithe woman, who in the semidarkness resembled nothing more or less than a Halloween cat, inexplicably increased his willingness to go along. "You get energy when you slam those deuterium and tritium nuclei together so that they fuse, but since they're both positively charged, you've got to get them moving fast enough to overcome their electrical repulsion—that requires heating them to, oh, four hundred million degrees."

D'Abro nodded but was missing something. "What are the magnets for?"

"Nature is generous. The secret of the tokamak is that magnetic fields deflect charged particles. You've heard of the Van Allen belts?" D'Abro played her light up and down over Nathaniel's face. "Cosmic rays fly in from deep space and end up spiraling around the Earth's magnetic field. The Earth wears a magnetic shield. The thing is, you can't confine a plasma by any material. It's so hot that enough of it would vaporize the tokamak. As it stands, inside Prometheus there is so little—it's almost a deep-space vacuum—that the walls act like a freezer and cool the plasma way below the temperature needed for nuclear reactions."

D'Abro had been on the verge of accusing the physicist of being in love with facts, but she began to perceive that he wasn't in love with facts; he was in love with facts in motion, facts that led somewhere. "Seems simple enough," she said anyway, feeling contrarian. "Hardly string theory."

"The devil's in the details," Machuzak scoffed. "The other important thing about plasmas is that they conduct electricity, like wire. Probably in grade school you connected a battery to a wire and watched it deflect a compass needle." D'Abro nodded her light again. "The current's generating its own magnetic field. Sakharov's idea for the tokamak was that you zap a few million amps of current through the plasma and it generates a magnetic field; the field squeezes the plasma and heats it. Squeeze hard enough and fusion begins."

"So what's the problem?" she wants to know.

"Squeeze a water balloon in one place—"

"—it goes gaflooey somewhere else."

"Precisely. Now try holding a beer with a glass made of rubber bands."

"Come on, Doc, it's impossible."

"Yup, that's about how hard it is to cage a plasma. At least it's the hardest technological feat ever tried, period."

D'Abro extinguished her light source and for a moment became silent. Suddenly her disembodied voice rose archly, "Tell me, Doc, are y'all doin this because it's worth it or because it's hard?"

Machuzak wished he were less weary and could anger, but he conceded that her implied accusation was not completely off target. The challenge was part of fusion's allure, the temptation of the "technically sweet." Glory would shower a few, but he had nothing to be ashamed of. "Bedbug, most people don't think it's worth it. Technically, it boils down to one thing: fusion is about a million times more efficient than burning fossil fuels. There's more energy in the top two inches of Lake Erie than in all the world's known oil reserves."

"Really?" Even the distraction of silencing her phone could not mask D'Abro's surprise. "Y'all just slurp up that water in Lake Erie and burn it?"

"Nature may be generous but she's not straightforward. We need deuterium, which we get from heavy water, D_2O. Ordinary hydrogen, from H_2O, doesn't react well enough. Only about one out of every five thousand water molecules is heavy, but even that tiny fraction in the top two inches of Lake Erie would be enough. For millions of years."

At that D'Abro finally got to her feet with her tapes and bags of dust. "Now, Mac, let's whoa a bit. Where's the catch?"

The main one was that they hadn't achieved a sustained fusion reaction, let alone a commercially viable reactor.

D'Abro's stance, arms akimbo, showed she wasn't buying. "Now wait a minute. What about the tritium? You said it's radioactive. Aren't you risking another Chernobyl or Three Mile Island?"

The inevitable had arrived. Like everyone, D'Abro was confusing fusion with fission, when about the only thing they had in common was "nuclear." "Look, Bedbug," Machuzak replied after a sigh, "I'll say it again—there are no free lunches. We would have done better if we'd just explained fusion's problems to the public. A deuterium-tritium reaction produces four times more energy than a deuterium-deuterium reaction and is much easier to get going. That's why weaponeers use tritium in hydrogen bombs, and that's why fusioneers use it in tokamaks. Yes, tritium is mildly radioactive."

"Ah," said D'Abro, firing a finger pistol at his eyes.

"But its half-life is only twelve years, as opposed to twenty-five thousand for plutonium, and a meltdown is physically impossible in a tokamak."

"Why is that?" D'Abro asked, now fully facing him again.

Luckily, at that moment Archangelsky returned and Machuzak was able to say, "Bedbug, if we're still speaking to each other in forty-eight hours and you haven't figured it out, ask again." His voice had almost left him.

"Have you found anything?" Slava asked as he handed over a plastic bag containing the remains of the original busbar.

"I'm actually surprised how clean the place is," D'Abro said. The physicists weren't; you didn't want junk floating around a surge room. "No one's been whacking off here, for sure. Nothin obvious except some grease and prints." While D'Abro opened the bag, the two men pressed nearer. She held up the two halves of the original busbar and Nathaniel tried to slide the pieces she'd found over the melted end. Yes, they appeared to fit. Little imagination was necessary to see that the two new pieces formed a sleeve that bridged the gap cut in the busbar, except that the thin sleeve had melted—more likely exploded—under the high currents. The sleeve's only purpose could have been to camouflage the gap. At that moment any uncertainty that they'd been dealing with sabotage evaporated without trace.

"My money's down that someone is determined that your tomahawk won't ignite—ever." D'Abro's tone was flat as she reached into her pocket and offered Machuzak a hundred.

Only the night sounds of a giant laboratory broke the silence as the full implications set in. Finally Machuzak said, ignoring the bill, "Will you turn over what you've found to the Sheriff's Department?"

"I suppose I could," D'Abro nodded, "but I'm not sure there's anything on the DNA side, and even if I got usable prints, I somehow doubt they'd show up in the FBI database."

"They might show up in ours." D'Abro flicked on her light again and trained it directly into Slava's eyes. "The Terminator recently installed fingerprint identification system. Will go online soon."

"So you do have biometrics," D'Abro interjected with the same dryness as before.

Machuzak wasn't amused. "Bedbug, if you still haven't gotten it, this is a civilian lab, not Los Alamos. Security has never been a priority."

"I've noticed." This time her voice was fully desiccated. "Well, boys, let's have a look at your fingerprint database."

"I'm not authorized."

"You could be," interjected Slava. At D'Abro's raised eyebrow he explained: "This afternoon powers-that-be requested Nat to become acting director."

D'Abro squinted at Machuzak. "You didn't tell me, Doc."

"I haven't decided."

The detective looked to the floor, sighed, then shook her head decisively. "I think you have. Bein that I find myself on leave, Doc, you're going to take the job, hire me as a security guard and"—she flicked Nathaniel's badge slung on a lanyard around his neck—"we're gonna have a look at everyone who's been in this surge room recently. Damn, and I was looking forward to a little quiet meditation."

They ascended to the tokamak bay in silence and out to the parking lot. Past midnight, stars were bright. Regarding the physicist's upward gaze, D'Abro said, "You know, Doc, I'll bet when you were a boy scientist blowin up rockets, you never thought you'd end up here."

"That is for sure, Bedbug. That is for sure." This was indeed not the future that a youngster thirty years past had beheld in the wintry stars.

"And tomorrow when you become director and have to decide between going for ignition and riskin your machine, whatta y'all do?"

Machuzak continued to stare heavenward. "'For we are bound where mariner has not yet dared to go... '"

"Huh?" D'Abro wrinkled her nose.

"'And we will risk the ship, ourselves and all. O daring joy but safe! are they not all the seas of God?'"

"You'll go for it then?"

The physicist brought his gaze down to her eyes, sucked in his breath and exhaled long. "Let's say I'll pray that we find the saboteur before he gets nervous."

NINE

The next morning Nathaniel Machuzak, expunging the weariness from his bones, awoke before dawn, swilled a standing cup of coffee, and drove south. The temperature swings, severe this time of year in the semi-desert, sent him shuddering in the jeep, whose top he'd left open. By the time he reached the outer gate, the landscape had turned purple and he began to shake off the cold. The chill mounted.

Down the road he badged himself in at the guard booth and noticed the sign hung to the left of the boom:

Remember:
Turn in Your Radiation Badges
Today

Only the tritium handlers and the techs who spent their days on the machine would remember. For everybody else, radiation doses were no greater than the Austin background and they would do only one thing with the monthly reminder: ignore it.

The guard was the tall, angular and silent one. As he asked himself who the fellow staring across the space was, Machuzak thought he sensed a fugitive veil of compassion soften the hard features. About to drive off, he noticed for the first time in years the sign on the booth listing the materials forbidden to bring on-site: explosives, benzene, hydrofluoric acid, radioactive substances... "Do you check every vehicle daily for those materials?" he asked. The granite face scowled and asked whether he was carrying any firearms. "Would you expect anyone to say 'yes' to that question?" Nathaniel retorted. Realizing that empathy had been imagined, he flashed his badge across the reader and the gate opened.

At the main building Nathaniel yanked open the lobby doors to see that someone had posted a big Hollywood calendar on one of the columns, the kind whose leaves fall off one by one to ever-so-gracefully mark the passage of time. It showed the number of days to ignition, six months' worth. A photo of Bill Balustradi's bearded, smiling face was taped up beneath it, but no smile crossed Machuzak's lips as he tore off the day they had left behind.

He took two steps at a time up to the third floor to find he'd beaten both director and secretary. For a few minutes he paced, the elevator doors opened and Lise stepped into the foyer, irradiating the space. Lise might have been one of the German beer maids painted on the walls at Scholz's: tall, buxom, boisterous and fabulously blond. Her Teutonic efficiency was no less authentic and before she sat down the coffee was brewing. "They're expecting you, Mac," she said with her radiantly lip-sticked smile. "Leonard and Mr. Garrett will any moment be here."

They showed half an hour later. When The Chairman stepped out of the elevator and saw Nathaniel pacing before him, he beamed like he'd eaten the canary, but when he perceived the physicist's expression, something closer to fright seized him. "This way, Mac," he said, ushering him after Leonard into the octagon. For an instant Nathaniel felt in free fall as he gazed through the floor-to-ceiling glass wall overlooking the atrium. Garrett closed the blinds and sat down at the conference table. "What'll it be, Mac?" he said gravely.

"I'll do it—," said Nathaniel.

Garrett slapped his hand on the table. "I knew we could count on you."

"I have conditions."

"Name them," said Leonard from his wheelchair as Garrett sobered again.

Nathaniel turned first to The Chairman. "Two months, as promised."

Garrett crossed himself.

"Cell-phone wiping and email blocking shall cease."

"I didn't authorize that," Garrett and Rasmussen responded simultaneously.

Now Machuzak faced Leonard and leveled his gaze to the great man's eyes. "That I don't answer to you, Leonard, to Richard or to Krieg-Zuber. That I'm director and you are not my shadow."

The older man nodded softly, with difficulty. "As you wish, Nathaniel. I trust you will not be above taking advice."

"A wise man once told me that an adult is someone willing to take advice—even when it's the right thing to do."

Both Leonard and The Chairman smiled. "Your first directive, sir?"

"My first question: Have you spoken to Moravec since yesterday?"

The Chairman nodded, shook his head. "I didn't see any slippage. Whatever he is gives me icicles. That guy could eat the devil with his horns on."

"Then let's get the division heads together, right away. And get me an appointment with Moravec, *now*."

* * * *

The meeting began well. With Leonard and The Chairman flanking him, Machuzak stood at the head of the table before the ASSET letters and told the dozen people gathered there that an hour ago he'd taken the job of acting director. To his surprise, applause greeted him all around. For an instant he stared blankly as the words "You people don't know it, but the machine's been sabotaged" verged on escaping his lips. He blinked and said, "Thank you. Now let's get to work."

He announced triple shifts, seven days a week with overtime. "Fred, organize them today, and take the beast apart."

"Will do, sir," Fred saluted.

The division heads took the announcement of twenty-four/seven operations without grumbling more than a roomful of freshmen. When Machuzak declared that they'd meet daily at 8:00 a.m., beginning tomorrow, they grumbled more. Abbuhl mentioned that rain had leaked into pentagon unit 4, shorting out some components. At that, Tom Kettering, boots propped up, put in that even with the recycling plant going full blast, an ignition campaign meant they'd have to import extra tritium from Savannah River. "Do it now," Machuzak replied and caught Kettering off guard. Diana Cochran reported that a nitrogen shipment scheduled for the morning would be delayed because the tractor-trailer had jackknifed on the way to CFRC. Her factual remark sent Thaddeus Hasschler into orbit, roaring that he couldn't work surrounded by such incompetents and that they might as well give up now.

A shouting match erupted before his eyes and Nathaniel remembered the Austin lab's push to build ASSET's predecessor, AUSTOR. After a cutthroat competition, ANFRL had killed General Atomics and Oak Ridge for a $700 million government contract on the basis of a deadline. The staff worked like madmen to beat it. More dead than alive they got their "first plasma" at one minute to. "Pink glow," it's sometimes called—the tokamak lights up like a neon sign. For $700 million they'd built a fucking neon sign. Then they stripped it down and started over.

Now we will do it again, for ten billion dollars.

As Hasschler and Cochran railed at each other, the sensation that had gripped him since yesterday tightened: These people are shards of personality, I know nothing of them—nothing. Jesus, stop. Looking up from his wrist he raised his hand and read aloud the morning release from ITER: director Pierre Jules César Balard had ordered a review of their DD timetable. ITER had planned to use the low-yield deuterium-deuterium reaction for several years before switching to the high-octane deuterium-tritium mix. The news release could mean only: That was going to change.

As the room fell silent, Machuzak walked over to Hasschler, put his arm around his shoulder and asked if since yesterday he'd gotten a team together to begin planning the experiments. Glancing at the list Hasschler handed him, Nathaniel told him to add Toshi Matsushima and Slava Archangelsky. Thad balked; neither would agree. Machuzak met his sullen stare and assured him they would.

He adjourned the meeting then, asking Fred Abbuhl to stay behind. When the two of them were finally alone he whispered, "Check everything, Fred, and I mean everything in the biblical sense."

"Sir," Abbuhl saluted.

"And Fred, how is the mood today?"

"Everyone's still in shock, of course. It's only been twenty-four hours since Moravec's ultimatum. We'll live without The Terminator at the helm, if that's what you mean."

"I suppose we will."

Fred said he'd get the machine up to atmosphere at once and disappeared. As Machuzak opened the door, Theresa Rasmussen, walking from her husband's office, caught sight of him and stepped into the conference room. "The whole thing is terrible, isn't it, Mac?" she offered, touching his arm. "This ignition deadline. It seems so impossible... And Cyrus..." She lapsed into a momentary silence, then said as if somewhere else, "*Il n'y a pas de morts*. That was Maeterlinck, wasn't it." And that was Theresa's signature habit. She'd sometimes leave off a conversation but continue the dialogue internally with herself. When she surfaced, leagues away, those stranded ashore were more than a little bewildered about how she'd gotten there. "Leonard says he invited you to dinner, Director sir. Why not tomorrow, if you can spare a few hours?"

How infinitely far tomorrow seemed from the now. "That would be nice. I'll do my best."

Theresa squeezed his hand and continued on her way.

Once again Nathaniel made ready to depart, but just then the big screen blinked on. He half expected to see Moravec, laughing, but no, it was the white-swathed Cyrus Krieg-Zuber, broadcasting again from his hospital bed. Machuzak involuntarily stiffened.

"So, Mac, old boy," the sick man said, "you have your revenge. Very clever becoming director, as temporary as that will prove to be."

"You were listening?"

Krieg-Zuber didn't reply.

"Big Brother had nothing on the average twenty-first-century consumer. What do you want?"

"Merely to advise you, I intend to step in when the doctors permit and you'd be wise not to attempt anything I would not authorize."

"What would that be? More jamming? More firings because some-one has sent mail you disapprove of? More exiles to remove people whose ideas you've filched?"

Krieg-Zuber smiled wearily and benevolently. "Put aside ancient quarrels, Mac, old boy. The fate of the Mission is at stake. We require iron discipline from the troops. Have a punch clock installed—"

Machuzak cut him off. "Shut up, Cy. I'm not listening. The stress on the crew during the insanity that got us into this fix was unbelievable and is going to get worse. Morale is what needs to be in fighting form. As of today your measures are going to cease. Why do you want a punch clock anyway? You already monitor entrances and exits to time lunch breaks. Why all that skullduggery the other night surprised me, I don't know. Maybe you think everyone around here is so desperate to hang on to their jobs that they'll put up with anything, or that they've forgotten ol' Ben—those who give up essential liberty for security deserve neither liberty nor security. I haven't forgotten, Cyrus."

"This is your problem, Machuzak," Krieg-Zuber answered, weakly raising a finger. "We are engaged in a great struggle for survival, the Manhattan Project for energy, and you think we are at a decadent univer-sity. The Manhattan Project—the most successful scientific endeavor in history. Secret, secure and aimed at one goal alone. No loafers permitted, old boy, no hobbyists."

Machuzak pondered the slightly older man hovering larger than life above him. One of them was fighting the wrong war, in the wrong cen-tury. "The odds are that in six months this lab will cease to exist," he eventually said, "but we'll go down as a scientific laboratory, that I swear on my grave—and yours."

"You have never understood what we are about, old boy. Admit it, you are a second-rate hack who confines himself to problems of no sig-nificance."

"True, I have never understood what *your* lab was about," Nathaniel returned, suddenly losing his anger, "but if you, Cy, ever knew what science is about, you forgot long ago. And take it from me, being second-rate is a notch above being third-rate. There's only one thing I want to know from you: did you feel dizzy in the surge room?"

Caught off guard, Krieg-Zuber merely replied, "Uh, yes. How did you know?"

"I didn't. Now, either recognize the fact that I'm in charge or die. I don't care which. Good-bye."

Once more about to leave, Machuzak turned when he heard a lone pair of hands applauding behind him. Slava, having snuck in, sat in the corner. "'I perceive you now, beginning of high and turbulent days.' It's about time you put that motherfucker in his place."

"What are you doing here?"

Slava put his finger to his lips, motioned Mac into the corridor. "Heard you accepted inevitable. Instructions, Boss?"

"Get on Hasschler's team and start planning experiments."

"That's not what I meant. I felt dizzy in surge room too. What were you talking about?"

"Meet me at my lab, late."

He left Slava standing in the corridor alone and stopped in Lise's office, two steps away. Moravec in Copenhagen was, but agreed to meet him in three days. Set it up. He declined her offer of a spare office up here, near Leonard's, and disappeared down the stairwell. At the security office he informed Henderson that they were moving to triple shifts and needed to bring on a new security guard. The chief readily agreed. Machuzak said he had a qualified candidate in mind and he'd send her around ASAP.

Another thing: Did Henderson know where The Terminator had installed the phone jammer? John took him into a back room and pointed to the equipment. Machuzak yanked the plug. What about wiping software and email blocking? Henderson shrugged. Well, we'll know if it doesn't stay turned off. At that moment Machuzak noticed in the corner a fiber-optics junction box that serviced the lab. Somebody had installed a simple splitter on the cable, a splitter that bled off every byte of Internet traffic into or out of CFRC.

"Where does this go?" Machuzak asked severely, vividly seeing the advisory on his computer screen.

"To my computer." Henderson shrugged. "Don't know where else."

Machuzak knelt to disconnect the splitter, halted and stood up. "Let's leave it."

One more thing. He was assigning Lipman and a few others to write up the accident report. They'd need the access records for the past days. Without further prompting, Henderson sat himself at a terminal and brought up the week's records.

Nathaniel nodded. He'd foreseen the dozens if not hundreds of entrances to the nb supply area. Lipman, Faberman...half the technicians at the lab. Himself. What's more, the system was an electronic sieve. If anyone tailgates, like Slava and D'Abro last night, that one is invisible. When Nathaniel arrived ten years ago, Henderson himself asked what areas he needed access to and programmed him in then and there.

Ten minutes after Henderson handed him hard copies, Nathaniel authorized Lipman to enlist two others to write the report and ten minutes after that he was on the phone with D'Abro, telling her to get her ass down to CFRC.

TEN

T. J. D'Abro arrived two hours later and smiled slyly at Machuzak's unintentional snap of his head. Jettisoned were yesterday's stylish accoutrements and beauty-queen persona. Overnight she'd transformed herself into an Austin slacker, an authentic biker chick arrayed from top to bottom in leather and studs. Only the swath of green hair identified her as the same woman he'd met at Scholz's. No, after barely taking his extended hand, distraction seized her and she swooped in on the infernal bird, then followed her curious nose toward the other lobby exhibits.

Machuzak watched, wishing to touch her naïveté. Nevermore. She lacks his sense of premature obsolescence. She does not know that what the exhibitors have forgotten to reveal is that many of the projects on display were long ago canceled, never built or never will be. With the rise and fall of our endeavor, the vagaries of our fortunes, the precariousness of our survival, no one thinks to remove what has been lost, to erase the future, which is already past.

"Director, sir," she said, saluting, "T. J. D'Abro reporting for duty."

With a glance at two nearby technicians shouldering an electrical ladder and cable, Nathaniel said, "Come," and introduced her to Henderson, who welcomed her aboard. "At the lab, security means equipment more than intruders," he informed her. "You'll be checkin that the cooling systems are on. Has water flooded a laboratory? That sort of thing." Right, D'Abro glanced at Machuzak. "You'll need to take a basic safety test to get badged, and a short radiation course to be cleared for the machine area."

"Will do," D'Abro said and Machuzak left her to her studies, reminding her that the word when fighting a fire is *PASS*: *P*ull the plug, *A*im the nozzle, *S*queeze the trigger, *S*wing the extinguisher.

"Wouldn't *PISS* be more like it?" she replied and he told her to come to his lab when the day was done.

* * * *

After twilight, D'Abro appeared at the Materials Test Facility in Alpha Site, bitching that one required GPS to navigate CFRC.

"A test," Machuzak replied dryly, looking up from his desk, which sat to one side of a cluttered laboratory dominated by a big metal cylinder two meters long. D'Abro wrinkled her nose at an oily smell permeating the space and cocked her head at a persistent clacking that reminded her of an antique gasoline lawn mower. The physicist paid no attention any of it and instead asked, "How did yours go—the tests, I mean?"

"PASSed with flying colors," she smiled. "I memorized the emergency phone numbers, so I aced the safety test, and the radiation course is all ALARA—As Low As Reasonably Attainable—or is that Achievable? Damn, what were those phone numbers?" She lifted a copy of the Bhagavad Gita amidst the piles of technical papers on the scientist's desk, put it down. "Where are we, Doc?"

Nathaniel got to his feet, peered into the corridor and locked the door. "I don't know," he said. "We do know ITER will be pulling something soon… I've ordered triple shifts…" He shook his head to himself, baffled, disgusted and walked over to a workbench where he'd spread out some hard copies. "I also got the access records, everyone who was down in the nb supply area for the past two weeks. I don't see anything funny. Every name's authorized, no one vanished into thin air."

"I meant, where are we—this place?" D'Abro said, craning her head as she joined him at the bench.

"The covert op was your idea, Bedbug," he said, for the first time noting her blue CFRC uniform. "This is the Materials Test Facility. There's no traffic here except for my two colleagues who like half the lab have disappeared since the accident."

Standing beside him, D'Abro ran her finger down the records. "Slava and I tailgated on your badge last night, didn't we?" she remarked. "I know, this ain't Los Alamos." She pointed out Machuzak and Slava's names several times, most recently three days ago. "We were down there a lot second shift, checking out equipment. Deadlines, you know… Everyone on this list had good reasons to be in the dungeons."

"Doc, just because the badges were there doesn't mean the names attached to the badges were there. Tell your techs to interview these people for the accident report and find out what *bodies* were there." There'd be nearly a hundred, Nathaniel thought. The detective sighed. "Okay, let's check the surveillance videos. Where are the cameras positioned?"

With a puzzlement that lay between real and feigned, Machuzak glanced around the space. "You see any? There are a couple in the main lobby, a few at the pentagon entrances and every centimeter in the tritium vault. I doubt there are any at all in the power areas. Who'd walk off with an ignitron?"

"Somebody sabotaged Prometheus, Doc. All right, Henderson'll show me. Motion detectors?"

Now Machuzak choked. "You really are kidding. The only thing that's ever been stolen from this lab were some radiation badges by a group of Korean tourists who wanted souvenirs."

"Okay," D'Abro sighed in an exasperation that equaled Machuzak's own. "That leaves the fingerprints." Henderson had already walked her through the new system and all she needed was time alone. "I'll wait on the DNA. Bein that I'm no longer official, it may take some strings... The problem is, Doc, your system is so leaky, there's hardly any evidence to believe that anyone *was* down there."

Even as Machuzak wondered whether he'd torpedoed this investigation from the start by recruiting a neophyte detective on indefinite sabbatical, D'Abro got to her feet and began to wander around the lab, peering at the tarnished gas cylinders shoved to the room's perimeter, turning from one thing to another with abrupt, sharp movements. She reminded Nathaniel of a bird, perhaps the firebird herself.

D'Abro stopped before a map taped to one of the gray storage cabinets. It appeared to be the United States—sort of. The coasts had federated with Canada, the Southwest had allied with Mexico, the Midwest was a religious autocracy, Texas a born-again republic. The legend read, "Post-Civil War 2.0." D'Abro about laughed, but the laugh stuck in her throat. Texas had been negotiating with the feds for autonomy.

"One reason Rasmussen created the consortium here," Machuzak said, this time as if reading her mind, "is that it's the most powerful state. Fusion won't stop the country from splitting up, but with the climate changing, people worldwide are migrating, fighting over resources. If they were more equitably distributed, conflict would go way down."

"Hmm," was D'Abro's only reply, then she swiveled around to the big test chamber in the room's center, which stood on a stainless-steel stand reaching to her shoulders.

Nathaniel didn't wait. "Basically, all this stuff is to test materials under bombardment of a plasma," he said, running his hand over the two-meter-long cylinder. "In a tokamak you've got particles at four hundred million degrees slamming into the walls. In a commercial reactor the plasma is producing so much heat that it's approaching the power radiated by every square meter of the sun. That's the environment we're creating. You better damn well know how the walls react, what materials can survive and how to cool them. Believe it or not, the problem has been constantly avoided and remains unsolved. No one is sure how long ITER—or ASSET—will last under real conditions. What we do here is important."

D'Abro nodded pensively, thinking that her physicist was trying hard to convince himself. "Wouldn't you have more fun goin to a football game?" she asked, maybe half joking. D'Abro didn't wait for a reply, glanced at her wrist screen and said, "What this?" pointing to a little hooded flame that had been rigged up on the side of the big cylinder.

"That?" he snorted. "That, Bedbug, is my concession to the environmentalists. My still. People are afraid of what goes on here"—D'Abro flinched uncomfortably at the gaze he leveled at her—"so instead of venting all the deuterium gas after I run it through the chamber, I burn it in this here distillation tube like the flames you see at oil refineries. It makes heavy water. Sometimes we give batches to local labs. Some oddballs still use it for cold fusion experiments. Mostly," he said, pointing to the tube running through a little hole he'd made in the wall, "I just let it drain outside."

D'Abro opened the small spigot and gave it a taste. "A little flat," she said, flashing her smile. A pause and then, "You know, you're a strange fellow."

"How so?" replied Machuzak, puzzled. She was staring at him almost angrily now, and he hadn't the faintest idea why.

"I just can't figure you out," she said with visible, audible frustration. "You dress casual, on the surface no one would call you pretentious. But there's somethin real internal about you—"

"I suppose so," Nathaniel conceded. "The life of the mind *is* internal."

"You got the Bhagavad Gita on your desk like some damned philosopher," she went on heedless, voice sharply rising, "and when you start explainin this stuff you can't help soundin superior, like your shit's a different color up—"

D'Abro's sudden hostility left Machuzak stunned, but today, this moment, he felt no urge to respond in kind. "Bedbug, I'm not going to defend myself to you. God knows we're not track stars around here and we're sure not as glamorous as movie stars, but damnit, we are scientists. We're athletes of the mind. What we're good at, on a fair day, is thinking. If you ask me a scientific question, you're going to get the best answer this scientist can give you. I don't know who you think builds tokamaks or solar cells, but it sure as hell ain't Madame Sososstris down at the local tarot parlor."

"Sorry," D'Abro apologized suddenly and looked away, bit her nail.

"Remember," said Machuzak, cocking his head, "we're all greenhorns here."

A brief silence ensued, but D'Abro's flash of bitterness had spent itself as quickly as it had flared. "Sorry," she repeated, lowering her head contritely, "I guess I've always been pissed off that I never became a scientist—or anything else. I can't do math and I can't stick."

"You aren't alone," Machuzak answered sympathetically. The disease was endemic by now. Online life had decimated concentration to the extent that almost no one had the skills to do research.

"As it stands," D'Abro went on with the barest hint of a smile, "I'm sort of a physics groupie."

At that Nathaniel stared with openmouthed disbelief. Movie stars had groupies, rock stars... Physicists? Dream on.

"It's true," she said, now visibly blushing. T. J. D'Abro then revealed herself to be a born-and-bred Austinite, daddy a bona fide oilman. She'd naturally gone to UT, The University, which Nathaniel had guessed at Scholz's from the ring girdling her finger. "I tried reading a few books about string theory and a couple about physics and synchronicity, but never got too clear on the connection, ya know. I just didn't know what I was good for. Detective work sort of interested me for a while. It's not too different from science, don't you think? We're both trying to find the answer."

"Yes," reflected Machuzak, "but in science you aren't always presented with the question." By now he was truly convinced of a broad provincialism blanketing D'Abro's entire outlook. "Tell me, Bedbug," he asked her, "have you ever left the republic?" Many Texans hadn't.

She nodded shyly. "I spent a year in England."

"Ah," said Nathaniel. "Durham Cathedral. Why England? Seems unlikely for a gal like you."

"Unlikely for sure, but the Rhodes people thought to give me a scholarship, so I went to Oxford... I know what you're thinking."

"No, you don't," he said even as he shut his gaping mouth. "And I've already gotten tired of your mind-reading."

"Sorry, it's a bad habit... Hell, I wasn't even sure where Oxford was. I applied for that Rhodes on a lark and was damn sure there'd been a big mix-up when I got it. But, Doc, I never really got into the dang City of Spires. Swilled beer on Tuesdays at the King's Arms, didn't do much else, never finished my scholarship, came back to Austin after a year. England's sort of a luke country, ya know, luke weather, luke food, luke people..."

As far as Machuzak could make out from her circumspect, even embarrassed account, D'Abro knocked about for several years, sneezing in an archaeological lab or living high on Daddy's credit card, then somewhere in her jumbled odyssey she met a UT professor who taught forensic anthropology and ended up auditing the course. That's when she decided to try detective work. "But I still don't know what I'm good for."

"Is that why you quit yesterday?"

She nodded, almost sheepishly. "It's more than that, Doc. I look around this lab—it's so…unreal. I mean, it's not on a screen, ya know? You guys actually build things, tighten bolts. How does having five thousand friends help you learn to do that?"

"It doesn't," Machuzak replied honestly. "It doesn't." The young woman seemed genuinely afraid, afraid of the world she was living in, afraid of the world she'd today entered. For a moment he almost felt sorry for her.

"Well," she said, checking her networking site, "it's already late. I'd like to see the tomahawk area again. Maybe we can figure out how someone can get down there undetected, if that's what happened."

Machuzak nodded. Fred Abbuhl was still organizing the triple shifts and the machine area should be clear. They set off. As they walked across the fields toward the pentagon, D'Abro unexpectedly asked, "What's between you and Krieg-Zuber?"

"What do you mean?"

"To be honest, Doc, you and Slava don't exactly show a lot of commiseration when his name comes up. 'Cyrus the Great.' 'Terminator.' What happened?"

"Let's just say I came to this lab to do science."

They gained the pentagon and he was about to badge them in when D'Abro stayed his hand and flashed her own badge across the reader. Entering, she said, "You'll tell me some other time."

"Yeah." At the door to the tokamak bay, Machuzak took out the safety key from the interlock, as he had last night, and pocketed it.

This time D'Abro asked.

"Another puzzle. To gain entry to the test cell you need to remove one of these keys from the interlock. It's not that they allow you in. Once you remove the key, the machine can't operate. Not to mention all the backup switches that shut down Prometheus should a door so much as jiggle. ASSET couldn't have even begun to function if anyone was in the vicinity at the time."

"Hate to tell you, Doc, but nothin we know at the moment, which ain't much, indicates that anyone *was* down there."

The heavy door swung open and once more they faced Prometheus. Already Abbuhl has begun the disassembly and a few giant parts lie scattered around the floor. Once more the sight of the colossus silences D'Abro, but Nathaniel knows what the place will look like in the coming weeks and he turns to the stairwell leading down to the neutral beam power area.

Halfway to the underbelly he realized she was not with him. "D'Abro!" he called. No answer. He climbed up the stairs but didn't see her. "D'Abro!" he called again.

He walked toward the tokamak, noticing now that one of the access ports had been opened during the day. Then he jogged, fearing the worst. He ducked through the port, making his way through the great cryostat toward the torus itself. Between two giant magnet coils a pair of legs stretched out toward him. "D'Abro!" His cry echoed in the tank, but—no answer. Moving forward he saw that the detective's head lay at an inner port and that she was unconscious.

"T. J!" he shouted, nearly passing out himself. He fell against the cryostat floor, shook his head, forcing himself not to breathe. With a desperate pull, he got her loose and dragged her out to the main floor. After a few slaps on her back, she sputtered to life.

"Whew," she said. "What hit me?"

"Are you out of your fucking mind!" Machuzak shouted, glancing at a poster, A BEATING HEART IS A SAFE HEART. "This is no goddamned amusement park! That machine was filled with nitrogen gas. Jesus, you're lucky to be alive."

"Nitrogen?" was all she said. "Why?"

"Why?" Machuzak could hardly believe it and pointed to a "Confined Space" warning. "To kill idiots like you... To keep the machine clean, for Chrissake... They've opened it up today..."

A few minutes passed before they recovered legs and sanity. Brushing herself off, D'Abro said meekly, "I'm sorry, sir; it won't happen again."

"If it does, you'll be dead."

D'Abro's expression showed that she wanted to make amends, but Machuzak's cold fury left her at a loss. Finally she said softly, "Thanks, Mac. You saved my life."

"You're welcome, T. J.," he replied, nothing else coming to mind.

They walked back toward the Materials Test Facility in silence. "You know, it's the first time you've called me T. J.," she said.

"No, I called you T. J. when you were knocked out in the machine, but probably you didn't hear me."

"I guess I didn't." She smiled and held out her hand.

Before he could take it, Slava emerged from the MTF, wanting to know where they'd been. Machuzak didn't reply, waved the two toward the building, but Slava shook his head and suggested they meet on Sixth Street instead. Agreed. As Machuzak drove into town, he remained unsettled by D'Abro's harebrained misadventure, but it might have proved useful. They still had no better idea of who had spiked the machine or why, but at the end of this day, again fighting off the urge to sleep, he become convinced he knew why Krieg-Zuber had nearly met his maker.

ELEVEN

By the time they converged on Sixth Street, it was well into the a.m. The music, focused by hard walls and deep enclosures, shot laserlike onto the streets. When they opened the door to Maggie Mae's and dissolved in sound, they searched farther for a safe haven. The trio walked a block or two past the massage parlors, bearded cowboys, studs and leather, tongue rattles and nose rings. "If it protrudes, I'll pierce it," the sign flashed. T. J., again in her biker duds, urged Slava to yield to an earring; he declined, pushing on through the throngs of fourth-generation hippies and automutilators. He stumbled against the eight-hundred-pound gorilla, accoutered in red hat and tie, looked up to see the birdman proffering his echnicolor assortment of parrots, macaws and cockatoos. Behind him the dwarfish paraplegic draped in a KKK shroud sat high in her hydraulic wheelchair, embroidering.

Austin's archaeology normally cheered him, but Nathaniel frowned when a Bible thumper, dressed nattily in a gray suit and tie, thrust a tract into his hand. "As it is written, there is none righteous, no, not one." The three pushed on harder but could not avoid the reconquistas, demanding the formal receding of the Southwest to Mexico. Nor could they shun the hordes of the destitute lining up outside the *Medecins sans Frontiers* emergency clinic or the echo of a well-known dance club, where young customers sat in silent rows, plugged in and staring blankly. At last they holed up at the Driskill, the once grand, then dilapidated, then re-grand hotel marking the end of the amusement district.

Nathaniel began without prologue under the stare of a giant steer head above the fireplace. "Slava, when we went down to find Zuber, did you notice anything unusual?"

"You're talking about dizziness, not Terminator lying unconscious on the floor? Yes, I said so this afternoon. I thought it was nausea."

"So did I. But I had the same sensation an hour ago when I went into the tokamak after D'Abro."

"Are you sure it wasn't nausea again?" T. J. asked, smiling faintly. Even on Sixth Street, she'd been unusually reticent, chastened.

Chastened or not, it was exactly the wrong thing to say. "If that had been a pure nitrogen atmosphere, you would have been dead within one breath." The physicist snapped his fingers. "One. You were lucky it was just residual gas that hadn't been purged. A visiting Japanese scientist pulled the same stunt once and bought it."

"I'm sorry," she said with the same reserve, "I've already apologized."

Machuzak sighed. "No, I'm sorry. One shouldn't tally these things. One should just do what is right and forget the rest..." The two glanced at each other with determined smiles and he turned again to Slava. "Is it possible that the surge room was filled with gas? For all his excitement, the bastard doesn't seem to have tried anything. Suppose there was nitrogen down there, he got dizzy, backed into a capacitor."

"It's conceivable," Archangelsky agreed. After deuterium, nitrogen was probably the most common substance at the lab. They used it everywhere: liquid nitrogen surrounded liquid helium coolant as an insulator. If the machine went down for maintenance, they usually filled it with nitrogen until technicians or ex-detectives needed to enter. "Perhaps sulfur hexafluoride," Slava speculated. SF_6, an inert insulating gas, prevented electrical arcing between high-voltage components. The ancient switches in the surge rooms were filled with it. SF_6, six times heavier than air, would have sunk to the floor where they were administering CPR, but neither of them recollected sounding like Darth Vader.

A glass of cognac, two of wine arrived. T. J. lifted hers and said quietly, "Seems to me y'all tryin to make this more complicated. Ya know, cops have an expression: 'If it looks like a horse and has hooves like a horse, then it's probably not a zebra.' Police version of Ockham's razor."

"Bedbug, who sees vast conspiracies everywhere, talks about complications," Machuzak said. "I did not imagine my dizziness, neither did Slava... You know, Bedbug, in science you may proceed by logic but you begin with a hunch. The access sheets don't seem promising. Is there any way we could detect nitrogen or SF_6 in the surge room?"

"Two, three days after the event?" Slava wrinkled his nose, downing his cognac. "This is unlikely."

In an enclosed area it might be barely possible, Nathaniel suggested. If not, could there be any reaction between nitrogen or SF_6 and the components down there that might have left a trace?

Archangelsky shook his head and ordered another cognac. Nitrogen was not highly reactive; SF_6 not at all.

"Too bad Cy didn't die—then we could exhume the body."

In spite of herself, T. J. spit out her wine and put a hand to her mouth while the guests at the next sofa threw a merry glance their way. At that moment Nathaniel was acutely aware of her physical presence, her sparkling eyes, which might have been filled with stage glitter. She looked at him over her hand, lowered it the slightest amount and bit the knuckle of her forefinger.

Changing course, Nathaniel recounted his conversation with Krieg-Zuber that afternoon. "I don't know how long he's going to be out of commission, but…" He trailed off, shaking his head. "You don't need to be Cassandra to see that when he gets back on his feet…"

"I thought you didn't want to be director," responded T. J.

"Only a madman would, but Krieg-Zuber has always run the lab day to day, more so since Rasmussen fell ill. He led the push to cancel everything but ASSET. You'd think a lab was a place for investigation, but no. 'Our Mission, old boy, is to drop ten bombs into the same hole, as the general said.'"

"This is true," added Slava, downing a second glass as the waitress handed it to him. He was beginning to show effects. "Pompous ass has done everything to change lab from scientific organization to military-industrial complex. Remember day when he puffs up chest and announces that everything but Prometheus is canceled? I tell him: this is science, you do not explore alternatives? Someday your tokamak will look like elephant. Other machines will prove better. Other countries will build them. Worst thing you can do is lock yourself into this design, I told him. That is risk we are prepared to take, it is best bet. Fuck you, I said."

"My, my," T. J. smiled wanly, "have I fallen into a scientific laboratory or a pit of vipers?"

"You see, T. J.," said Nathaniel, "movie stars may fight over publicity; we fight over immortality. Slava is right, Zuber's gotten rid of everybody who's ever had an idea he couldn't steal—"

"Four years ago he started going *pazzo*," Archangelsky interrupted, drilling a finger into his temple. 'Into whose hard hat were the alleged feces defecated?' There is no way we could let him be director again. Time was perfect—"

"So that's it!" exclaimed Machuzak, rising fully to his feet. Suddenly he understood the chain of events. "Y—you had me appointed."

Slava lifted his hands in feigned surprise. "Brother, I am not so powerful to do anything."

Amazement at how fast Archangelsky acted is one hundred percent. "You must have talked to Garrett within hours after we discovered the busbar."

Slava raised his glass in a salute, which only prompted Machuzak to raise his fist to strike him. T. J. looked on in genuine alarm until Machuzak sighed and lowered his hand, chuckling. "Well, somebody needed to take this on."

"Thank you," was all that Slava said and Nathaniel sat.

D'Abro puckered her lips, considering all she'd heard. Her discomfort, which Machuzak had taken for penitence, had become more evident with each word of the conversation. "I need to ask…" she said, deciding. "What were you two doing down in the power supplies? You guys are PhDs and all, but surge rooms are engineers' territory."

After a glance between them, Slava talked. "You think you are at a fabulous installation, rich and gleaming, but after we became 'dedicated lab' everyone became multifunctional. Last days were nuts getting ready for so-called commissioning. And physicists do talk to engineers, you know. It is good to know experiments can run."

D'Abro cast an unsatisfied look at Machuzak, but when he frowned, her expression immediately dissolved into one more contrite. She did not comprehend much about this strange place and its inhabitants, but the man sitting opposite her had this morning, largely at her behest, taken on an impossible task. And two hours ago he'd risked his life to save hers. "Where do we go from here?" she said.

Machuzak's wrist prodded him. "Huh? The Real World is calling."

D'Abro sat upright, puzzled. "You guys have avatars?"

"We sometimes hold meetings there." Machuzak told Slava to log on.

A moment later the pair was standing on the rim of an erupting volcano facing a genuine fire-breathing dragon, complete with scaly wings and flaring nostrils. When the monster spied the two avatars facing him, he took flight and headed out over an expansive sea, whose surface shifted from a dark opalescence riven with flashing tongues of red, to a gleaming diamond lattice, to a golden fretwork studded with varicolored gems. Machuzak and Archangelsky were after him. It was a strange duo, a winged horse and a furry black hat with chicken legs and beady eyes.

Nathaniel and Slava followed the dragon until it suddenly dove toward an island and alighted on the plaza of a grand conference center; then before the physicists' eyes it morphed into a huge armadillo, which scurried under the eaves of the wood and stone complex built in Japanese-Karelian style. Machuzak and Archangelsky likewise set down and rushed into the center. The avatars glanced at each other even as their owners did in the Driskill lounge; both had been to ITER's Real World conference center before.

At a meeting under way, colleagues, mostly in human form with nametags, milled about the lobby. The sudden appearance of Machuzak's horse and Archangelsky's hat, racing through the hall, interrogating everyone with whom they collided about whether they'd just seen a dragon or a giant armadillo, drew raised eyebrows but no answers. The two sped through lecture halls, lounges, bars purveying virtual alcohol; their quarry eluded them.

At last one of Slava's Russian colleagues said that he'd seen an armadillo scamper into the video parlor. The winged horse and chicken-footed hat ran in to see find a number of avatars heatedly arguing—what to do about CFRC?—but no armadillo was in sight. As Pegasus and Hat nervously circled the room, their alter egos at the Driskill carefully recited aloud the names of everyone present. D'Abro had thought to log on to ITER's website and was simultaneously checking the online personnel list; all were genuine ITER physicists.

The pair searched further. A minute later, on a broad terrace overlooking the sea, they glimpsed the armadillo rounding a corner. Machuzak went directly after it, while Archangelsky cut through the nearest room and emerged on the other side. They'd trapped the beast. Pegasus and Hat pounced on the animal, which stood as tall as they did, but it promptly blinked out of existence. The avatars got to their feet, puzzled. On the ground lay a large chess piece. Hat picked it up: a queen with a shot glass for a crown.

"What's that?" asked Nathaniel.

"A trophy from a visit I made to ITER," said Slava. "We had little chess tournament—you take the shot of vodka before each move. I won." D'Abro wrinkled her nose at the strange form of Russian roulette while Slava paused, continued. "Not many people were there. Armadillo was."

"Sure sounds like an invitation to me," T.J. whistled and peered closely at Machuzak. "You don't think ITER's in on your problem?"

Nathaniel ran his tongue over his lips. "I think you two deserve a vacation in Provence. Be on a plane in the morning—if you can, tonight."

"Not bad idea," said Slava, considering.

"I've never been there," said T. J., getting up. "I'll need to check whether my passport's expired…"

Machuzak shook his head sadly. "A person should always carry two things in this world: a valid passport and a sweater."

"You're not comin, Doc?" she blushed.

Again he shook his head. "I need to sit down with Moravec."

TWELVE

By eight the next morning, Slava and T. J. were at Bergstrom scrambling for a flight to Houston, and an hour later they were searching at Houston for a flight toward Marseilles. Archangelsky's skeletal plan was no more than to surprise the dragon and learn the meaning of its prophecy.

"Let's hope it doesn't turn out to be a wild-armadillo chase," remarked D'Abro, who sometime after having stowed her sweater and jacket, accepted a beer from the flight attendant. Slava only tugged at his beard, bought a new supply of cognac and the two settled back for the long leg to Europe.

"I don't think I've ever known a Russian, Dr. Archangelsky," T. J. offered, mutilating his name as always. "I'll get that right sooner or later. What part are you from?"

"Why don't you just call me Slava; it's easier. I grew up in Moscow, the Big Onion, but that was a long time ago."

"You wouldn't go back?" she asked, sensing a certain sadness in his reply.

Yaroslav Borisovich Archangelsky shook his disheveled head. "There is nothing to go back to. For the decade after the Soviet Union collapsed, there was spasm of democracy, but the place has reverted to time-honored Russia. It is country that can't shake off its past. But this is like all countries. In America you are so bloody individualistic, you can't take one step in any direction—to sign climate-change treaty, initiate carbon tax. You have a right to live as you please and destroy everything else. Second Amendment."

D'Abro let that go. Slava didn't wear a ring but she asked anyway whether he was married or had children.

"Sometimes married," he said after a pause, rubbing the crease on his finger. "Dostoevsky, you know, did not write out of vacuum. In Russia everything is drama. Everything. My daughter is American—well, virtual. Can't talk face-to-face, has five billion friends she's never met."

Slava downed what was left of the too-small bottle, and as the United States fell away, D'Abro could see that he was staring across vast seas and into times long gone by. "You know," he said at last without prompting, "they built tokamak at my institute, the Kurchatov, one of world's first superconducting machines. It was before my time. They ran it precisely once." He held up a solitary finger to D'Abro's skeptical eyes. "Oh, tokamak worked okay, but at that moment Soviet Union slipped out of existence and liquid helium supply went with it. They sold machine to Chinese for one ruble. What was that worth then? A penny? A hundredth of cent? The Chinese ran it for long time. If Prometheus fails and ITER, they will do it. Chinese have two billion people thirsting for energy. I doubt it will be with tokamak, though."

T. J. didn't follow his meaning. The Russian opened another bottle.

"Tokamaks are big, complicated, expensive, prone to failure and inherently not meant for steady-state operation. You need all kinds of fixes to make them run long enough for fusion. It is inconceivable that anyone would want to use a tokamak for commercial reactor. Its cousins, stellarators, mirror machines will prove better, but at CFRC we are glued to doughnuts. This is what happens when wagon bands get rolling. Like I said to Krieg-Zuber, worst thing to do is lock yourself into one design. But whole world put twenty billions of eggs into ITER. Texas put ten billions into ASSET. Science can always progress if you have infinite amounts of money. If you don't, you become like hammer hitting one nail."

At this moment T. J. felt like Slava's daughter, suppressing an urge to text the man beside her. "I didn't really get what you were saying about Krieg-Zuber last night, that he's been in charge. Doesn't Rasmussen approve everything?"

Slava snorted and took another drink. "Being director of big lab does not mean you are in charge. You know Golden Rule: 'He who has gold makes rules.' Until he got sick, Leonard was always running around, begging for gold. When he wasn't begging he was on plane to Korea, Japan, China. Asians treat him like master, god even. He will be remembered as father of fusion. Day to day Terminator ran lab. But he likes power more than science. A few people who love science, Nat, me, fought back."

"Hmm," D'Abro said, lapsing into silence again. After some time she went on. "By the way, Slava, Nat said you couldn't have a meltdown in a tomahawk and that if I couldn't figure out why, I should ask." Her time limit hadn't expired but her patience had.

"He is correct," replied Slava, chuckling. "In fission reactor, cooling system fails, uranium becomes so hot that it destroys reactor. Meltdown. In the tokamak we need big magnetic fields to keep reaction running. Magnets fail or machine ruptures, plasma escapes, gas cools down in blink of an eye and reactions stop. *Pffft*. That's all."

"You leak out tritium into the atmosphere, though, right?"

"*Nu da*, but a tiny amount of tritium is no big deal. And it ain't melt-down… You know, there is something I miss about Russia."

"What's that?"

"The word for *clever* is not an insult. I wish public would once in a while credit scientists for having some idea of what they are doing… How are you finding your first case, or whatever you call this?"

T. J. shook her head in a baffled way. She already doubted her days tracking down stolen credit cards were going to help with five million amps, tritium and tokamak sabotage. "If I ever write up a report when this is over," T. J. said, gazing into her beer, "I can't imagine what it will be."

"Do what scientists do when they write budget proposals," Slava shrugged. "Invent."

* * * *

At Marseilles the next morning, Slava refused to wait "three hours for a bus into the mountains"; they rented a car and followed the GPS to-ward Cadarache, sixty kilometers northeast, home of the French Atomic Energy Commission.

"You think we're just going to walk into a nukular establishment?"

"That is exactly what we are going to do. Surprise is best weapon." He pronounced the last with gravity and handed her a forged ITER badge.

"Where did you get these?" she started, but Slava merely frowned.

Well before the gate, T. J. perceived that the Cadarache facility matched or exceeded CFRC in size, housing not only ITER in a huge tomblike complex, gypsum white, but an older tokamak in a smaller building, as well as a dozen fission research reactors. The facility lacked the artistic merits of CFRC's showcase main building, but she grudg-ingly conceded that the Provençal hills, nearby castle and river held advantages over the scrubland of southwest Austin.

The ITER complex sat outside the security fence and D'Abro abruptly understood why Slava foresaw no serious difficulty getting past the elderly guard who turned away from a soccer match, pulled a cigarette from his lips and asked with no apparent interest the reason for their visit. They were here for the tour, Slava said, and were told where to park. At the lot, Slava handed T. J. her badge and headed toward the front entrance of the low-lying administration building. The mistral was blowing and T. J. slipped on her jacket.

The whole place had the feel and smell of a giant construction site, which was the truth of the matter, for ITER had been completed only a year or two earlier, and loose gravel still got underfoot. But granting no time for T. J. to gawk at the monumental and characterless shed that faced them, Slava headed straight for the front door and sought out Dima Sazhin.

Sazhin started at the unexpected rap on his spartan office's door, and at catching sight of Slava, he leapt to his feet and embraced his old friend, kissing him soundly on the lips. At once the blond Dima began gesturing wildly and the two launched into an animated conversation. Sazhin appeared to be a few years younger than Slava and, disconcertedly, wearing a thick walrus moustache he reminded T. J. of Captain Kangaroo. She couldn't follow a thing, except "Slava!" "Hell!" "business" and "vodka," the last just as Sazhin slid open his desk drawer and poured three glasses. Without a blink Slava downed the shot; T. J. tried, failed. Then, in English: "It's urgent." Dima's round face dropped into a puzzled frown.

"We've got trouble at CFRC," said Slava, glancing about the office, shutting the door behind him.

"We know," deadpanned Sazhin. "Too bad about Krieg-Zuber. What a crazy accident."

"Dima," Slava said, taking his arm, "it wasn't an accident."

Sazhin didn't catch Slava's meaning and continued waving. "Well, it was damned stupid going straight for ignition on opening day—but we know how these things snowball. Ceremonies, deadlines, money, deadlines, pride, deadlines..." He paused long enough to smile toothily at the beautiful stranger in his presence. "You think you have bureaucracy over there... Now we'll pull the same stunt here just because you guys tried it—and we'll have our own accidents."

"Dima," Archangelsky finally cut him off. "That's not what I mean. I mean it wasn't an accident."

Sazhin peered at his compatriot, twirling his moustache. "What was it then?"

"I can't tell, Dima, and if you breathe word to anyone, I swear to Almighty God that I'll string you up by your eggs on Nikolsky Gate." Dima crossed himself in the Orthodox manner. "Do you remember that little chess tournament we had when I visited about five years ago?"

Sazhin wrinkled his nose. "You flew across Atlantic to ask me about a vodka-laced chess tournament?"

"Dima, who was there? There weren't many—five...ten...?"

"Hmm, so small event, such a long time ago. You, me, Misha Klebanov, Alessandro Marietti... Will Marlow... I can't remember."

"Dima, remember! Somebody who was at tournament contacted us—probably warning us not to go for ignition."

Slava's chum jerked his head up and smiled crookedly. "I am to be surprised at this? Half of ITER staff is ready to blow you to hell. Who do you robbers think you are, trying to steal ignition from us?"

"This is science," Archangelsky shrugged "Open thievery. What do you expect?"

"Expect?" Dima stared with wide, then narrow eyes. "Do you have any idea of what your foolish prank has started? We were planning to spend years on low-power experiments before going for real burn, but since Monday, everyone here is determined to squash you. You don't believe me when I tell you ITERniks must now try the same stunt. You think EU has sunk twenty billions of euros into The Way to let a bunch of cowboys show us The Way Out? You can't understand how dangerous this situation has become."

Dima's anger-laden outburst forced Slava to understand that CFRC truly had a race on its hands, a race with the most formidable opponent conceivable, the most formidable even had the playing field been level. "Dima, are you trying to stop us?"

"Me?" He put his arm around his friend's shoulder. "I want CFRC and you to survive so that when ITER fails, I have waiting job."

"Dr. Sazhin," T. J. interrupted firmly, "were you in the Real World two days ago?"

After a startled pause, Dima made a motion of his head to Slava in the direction of the woman. "Go ahead," Slava said.

"Yes, I was at the ITER conference center early. I told Slava's hat I saw armadillo."

T. J. glanced at the list she'd made in the Driskill lounge, though she couldn't imagine anyone inventing such a story. "Yeah, Dima Sazhin, that's you all right. The others aren't on the list." She faced Sazhin. "Sir, can we talk to Marietti, Klebanov and Marlow?"

"Well, they still work here," the baffled Dima shrugged.

"Let's find them," said Slava.

THIRTEEN

They hadn't gone five steps down the corridor when the last person in the world Slava wanted to see saw them: Pierre Jules César Balard, the director general of ITER himself. Slava turned away too late.

"Dr. Archangelsky," the nearly two-meter-tall Balard greeted him with a heavy French accent. "No one told me you were visiting."

Slava accepted the extended hand, which fully engulfed his own. "Was in area. Just thought I'd drop in to see Dima."

The bald Balard's reputation was of a brusque, intransigent tyrant who'd been inspired by his own name. It might be necessary if you are coordinating a project involving thirty countries, Slava conceded. Inevitably, Balard brought up events at CFRC.

"Give my best to Krieg-Zuber." From the way Balard frowned and rebuttoned his jacket, Slava could see the director was about to say more. He did. "Zis was, of course, not unexpected when you attempt something so foolish. What did Leonard think he was doing, Dr. Archangelsky? Trying to beat us? By what moral authority does Leonard think he has ze right to attain fusion, to challenge *moi—moi*?" He thumped his vast chest. "The civilized world has invested in ITER—in CFRC? *Pfff*. Listen carefully, Dr. Archangelsky. I will never—never—allow zat son of a bitch Rasmussen to win zis race against me. I will show you what we can do here and by the time I am finished, there will be nothing left of him but a *pip*, a laughingstock on every continent. No, that is too good. He will be forgotten, completely forgotten. That is what ze bastard deserves…"

Dima took Slava's arm, intending to spirit him out of harm's way, but Archangelsky shook himself loose. There he stood, in an unbuttoned sports jacket, resembling today if not exactly Rasputin then a rock musician, drawing himself up to his full height, which put the top of his head somewhere short of Balard's shoulders. He raised his chin to the starched figure towering over him and pointed his finger straight at the director's nose. "You, sir, think you have moral authority to achieve fusion. You with your lowballing of costs and billions of euros of overruns, not to mention years lost with magnet problems and overstuffed claims for baby ITER. You know as well as I do the thing will never do what you advertise. You call this moral authority? Maybe others can make it happen quicker, cheaper. Maybe we Texans will do it. You stand here telling me you will crush us and call yourself moral authority. Hah. I spit on it." Slava paused, almost surprised at himself, and literally spat at Balard's feet. But he wasn't quite done. "Tell me when in science does anyone have moral right to breakthrough? In some long-lost fairyland, gentlemen scientists grant moral authority to rivals, but you are neither moral nor have authority anywhere but in ITER-land. Come on, pussyfoot"—Slava suddenly put up his fists, began to dance like a boxer—"show us what you've got. We're ready for anything."

Fully enraged, Balard raised two clenched hands over his head, as if about to squash the pint-sized Russian with a sledgehammer, but Dima again grabbed Slava and this time dragged him away. Balard screamed after them, "I will crush you like insect! You have no chance, none!"

"Bring it on!" Slava shouted back with raised fists as Sazhin hustled him into the nearest elevator. The doors closed.

T. J. let out a long whistle. "Whoa."

"*Eb tvoiu mat'*," both Dima and Slava breathed simultaneously, undoubtedly for different reasons.

"You weren't kidding," T. J. said after she'd finally caught her breath. "He really hates Rasmussen." Dima nodded. "And Slava, what a performance." She held him by the shoulders at arm's length, then kissed him smack on the lips.

"You may regret that," Slava said.

On the third floor the doors opened and T. J. asked, "Does he hate Rasmussen enough to do anything?"

Dima shrugged as they exited. "Two months from now I show you the scars on my back from director's cracking whip. That much he will do. The rest?" He shrugged again. "I told you, half of ITER staff is ready to blow you to hell. After what just happened, Balard would light match."

* * * *

T. J. was soon convinced he was right. "You remember Slava Archangelsky?" Dima said to Alessandro Marietti as they cornered him in his office.

"Of course," the Italian replied, shaking hands. "The best drunken chess player on two continents."

"This is why we need to talk, Alessandro," Slava said to the handsome young Latin, whose black hair and chiseled face could have belonged to a movie star who'd intentionally forgotten to shave that day. "Do you remember who was at that chess match?"

Marietti produced the names Dima had, plus Sabine Warzel, a German. He thought there were some others, but it had been four years ago, maybe five. Slava pressed him to ignite his memory.

"Sir," T. J. interrupted, glancing at the picture of stray cats on the Campo dei Fiori that Marietti had taped above his desk. "Were you in the Real World this Saturday?"

"No," Marietti replied, suspicions rising. "What is this about?"

"A matter of urgency," Slava said.

Before Marietti could respond, T. J. asked if he had a Real World account. The young man nodded and reluctantly logged on, offering his account information and IP address only because he knew Slava. T. J. hadn't learned much from her computer security courses, but enough to know that an IP address meant little.

"Eh, what is this about, really?" Marietti said finally, getting to his feet. "This has something to do with that happened at CFRC? You know what we think about that, don't you, Slava? You deserved it—"

"Some of us think so too—"

"You are like a *putanna* who gives the clap to the whole village, no? You endanger everybody—"

"I've already told him," put in Dima.

"In three days the whole world program has gone *pazzo*. Everybody is infected. You should read Machiavelli, why do states go to war with each other when they don't want to—"

By now Marietta was making wild gesticulations and Dima was already on his phone to Marlow. "He's in the test cell," he said to Slava and T. J. "Come."

* * * *

A few minutes later they reached the tokamak bay. The machine was down for maintenance. Dima got authorization to enter and the door opened.

"Behold," said the Russian.

Suddenly, without warning, ITER stood before them. T. J. gulped as her hand went to her neck and her knees nearly gave out. The device confronting them was unlike anything she'd ever seen. Half again as large as Prometheus, the machine stood, she guessed, fifteen times as tall as she did. The tokamak bay was far cleaner than at CFRC, all the scientists wearing ties tucked into their shirts. The innards of the machine were entirely obscured by the great cylindrical cryostat that housed it, of the same sort that surrounded Prometheus, whose purpose was to provide a vacuum barrier between the superconducting magnets and room temperature. Immense blocklike devices protruding from the cryostat were covered with heavy cables that ran on metal trays through the walls and out of the test cell altogether. Slava was commenting to Dima on neutral beams, a term T. J. had already heard several times without comprehension at CFRC.

The feeling of insignificance she'd experienced while standing before Prometheus was magnified here over and again. Mere humans no longer had any say in the course of events, and their fate was in the hands of giant, alien devices with a life of their own—impersonal, inscrutable, implacable.

"This is the machine that the civilized world is counting on to prove that limitless energy is possible," said Dima.

"Some of the civilized world," Slava corrected.

Will Marlow was a big American who spoke with a flat Californian accent. Like Marietti, he volunteered his Real World account and avatar. Nothing. "Who was at that chess match?" Slava put to him the question.

Marlow scratched his head, racking his memory. "You, me, Alessandro, Misha, Sabine, some post-docs and grad students, I think…"

"*Pravil'no*," recollected Slava through half a decade and vodka, "there were some younglings. Who? You've got to remember."

"Oh, those transients never stick around for long—you know that, Slava. Jesus, they're anonymous."

"There must be records," T. J. interrupted with annoyance. "If they were students, somebody knew they were here—like their professors, maybe."

They made for the exit and agreed to split up, Slava and T. J. going after Sabine Warzel and Misha Klebanov, Dima saying that he'd try to find some records, but it was like searching for bank account numbers without knowing the customers. T. J. asked Marlow why he was here instead of in Texas.

"Originally it was because I like Europe and thought the job would be more stable. But with the economy for the past decades… ITER was a giant gamble from the beginning and almost never got finished. Now that stunt you idiots pulled has put the entire world program in jeopardy. The race is on. We'll rush years ahead, do something stupid and ITER will fail. Governments won't forgive us and that will be the end of fusion for the next century, mark my words. Damn you all." Marlow walked away.

"Don't say I didn't warn you," Dima said and was off.

* * * *

Misha Klebanov was abroad for a week. Sabine Warzel, a dark-haired, pretty German from Munich, had been at the Real World conference and was on T. J.'s list. Her avatar matched the one they'd seen.

Sabine also dimly remembered some post-docs and grad students hanging around the chess tournament, but couldn't produce names. "I believe there were a couple French, a Spaniard, a Japanese or a Korean, I'm not sure…maybe a Chinese or two."

"Japanese or Koreans would've been shooting videos," T. J. said. "And posting them."

"Good point," agreed Slava and Sabine simultaneously and they logged on. Sabine's office was hardly distinguishable from the others—computer, a white board, papers. T. J. began to think that though she'd fallen in with the most international bunch of characters imaginable, the laws of nature required all physicists to be identical, regardless of sex. "Bosons," quipped Slava to her mystification. Sabine remembered that one of the Chinese was a woman. There never were many in physics, she smiled.

"For sure," D'Abro said, thinking she'd seen two female physicists at CFRC. "You don't get lonely?"

"That would depend on what you're hunting for," Sabine smiled again.

Soon, their search coughed up a short video of a pink-eyed, red-nosed Archangelsky, surrounded by, indeed, some Europeans and Asians, one a woman, but neither he nor Sabine could identify anybody in the picture. "Do you have facial recognition software?" T. J. asked.

"Bedbug, as you said, somebody around here should have records," answered Slava, wrinkling his nose. "Why don't we check personnel office first." As T. J. protested that online would probably be faster, they forwarded the video to Dima. Thanking Warzel, and hoping to evade a diatribe about CFRC, they were half out the door when T. J. thought to ask whether she'd ever been in at CFRC.

"Sure. Several times,"

"Do a lot of ITER physicists spend time in the States?" T. J. continued, curiosity aroused. Ah, something distinguished Sabine's office after all: a large beer stein standing on the windowsill, open, with a plastic flower stuck in it.

"Nowadays, it's mostly the reverse," the German laughed broadly. "The American labs are almost nothing now, and ITER is such a gigantic project. You know, contracts are spread over sixty countries. They tested magnets in Japan, Germany, Korea, Switzerland… Chinese peasants wound coils for a dollar a day. We ended up with more administrators than physicists. This is modern science."

"Thank you, that's very interesting." T. J. remarked and she and Slava were into the corridor.

"By the way," Sabine called out, "may a tornado wipe CFRC off the face of the Earth."

* * * *

T. J. and Slava were momentarily alone. It was late in the day, nearing five o'clock, and although Klebanov was missing, T. J. didn't feel the trip had been wasted. They had a better idea of who had been at the chess tournament, and she was now absolutely convinced that the ITER folks had it in for CFRC.

"Find Dima and hunt down those records," she ordered. "In the meantime, I'm gonna visit with M. Pierre Jules César Balard."

She mangled his name almost as badly as she did "Archangelsky," but Slava started anyway. "You think he will speak to you now? And why would you possibly want to talk to that *svoloch'*?"

"I don't know exactly what you just said, Slava, but leave it to me. One thing, though—stay out of sight." She smiled radiantly.

He led her to the director's office; she smoothed out her hair in the big window's reflection, brushed off her suede jacket and abandoned the Russian. Shrugging, Slava tracked down Dima, who'd been trying to explain to the staff who they were looking for. The video on Dima's handset helped them identify three of the Europeans, while several others remained anonymous. But now the day had trickled away and everyone abruptly vanished. It would have to wait until tomorrow. Slava made his friend swear that he'd continue working on it.

Archangelsky paced for an hour when T. J. phoned and they met out front. "We need to find a place to stay for the night," he said, glancing at the sun, which nearly touched the hills. The only facilities in the immediate area were a gas station. "I doubt we will be welcome in dormitory."

"Don't worry about it," T. J. replied. "We're staying in the castle, courtesy of the director." Archangelsky shook his head with disbelief, but she shook her head right back. "You've been married too long, Slava. As someone once said: boobs, Doc, boobs."

"But did you get anything out of him?" Archangelsky answered, once he'd recovered.

"Yeah. I'll tell you after I've gotten back from dinner."

FOURTEEN

At eight o'clock the morning after Sixth Street, while Slava and T. J. made their way to Europe, Nathaniel entered the lobby of the main building and tore off the top page of the deadline calendar. He crumpled up the paper and tossed it into the nearest basket, watching another day slip uselessly from their grasp.

Ripping off the sheet had not been his first act this day. Two hours earlier, he'd badged himself into the test cell, where one of those stand-up balloons of Edvard Munch's *Scream* with Bill Balustradi's face pasted over it now guarded the entrance. Although it was hardly dawn, skies yet gray, the lab was alive. An undermanned first shift had just gotten under way, and clean-suited technicians were disappearing into the tokamak to begin the task of washing the inside of Prometheus' great toroid by hand. Under Abbuhl's eye, techs were all over the area, checking everything... but what needed to be checked for. One of their first tasks would be to make certain all safety interlock systems functioned properly, short-circuiting the possibility that Lipman's accident investigation would uncover anything.

The chief engineer walked up to him and tossed Machuzak a bolt the size of a rolling pin. "We've been finding some of these, Director, sir," he said. "Counterfeit bolts."

"*Counterfeit?*" Machuzak sucked in his breath, catching the monstrous object. His was thinking: *explosive*.

"I mean substandard. Chinese. We should be able to identify them."

"Neutron spectroscopy?"

"Labels."

"Do it." With a small relief, Mac slapped Fred on the back; the engineer was gone.

* * * *

Machuzak had not come to the test cell to watch. The suspicion that The Terminator had succumbed to gas would not free him, and he desperately needed to disprove it. If his hunch was right, it might snag this saboteur before a second strike, but Nathaniel couldn't deny that what captured his imagination was the intrigue of an idea. D'Abro had missed the mark when she suggested that detectives and scientists were twins. Detectives are paid to find; scientists are paid to seek. There is no other profession paid to be confused. It is a great privilege—had been.

Machuzak knew his plan was harebrained, but he clambered down to the neutral-beam supply area and, waiting until the coast was clear, sucked a sample of surge-room air into a little evacuated cylinder. Thief-like, he stole back to the Material Test Facility where he kept an old quadrupole mass spectrometer, not much different he supposed from the ones they were always mentioning on crime shows that identify the atomic constituents of samples of unknown substances. His obsolete machine was capable only of detecting parts per million, which would more than do.

Nathaniel cranked up the voltage and ran tests on the surge-room air and controls from lab corridors. When he finished, the cracking charts lay before him on the bench. There the telltale spikes at mass number 14 for nitrogen, but on both test sample and corridor control—the same height. There oxygen 16, argon, neon, carbon dioxide… He could see no significant difference between them. No, here: The surge-room air shows minute traces of SF_6, which slowly leaks out of the high-voltage switches and must be periodically replenished. Seek and ye shall seek.

Nathaniel felt certain he was blind. The idea *must* be true. I felt the gas, damnit. Nevertheless, Machuzak was now forced to concede that the idea was no more than one of those clever conjectures relinquished by their creators only under extreme duress, and ultimately lead nowhere.

He was about to depart for the main building when his assistant, Jerry Wilson, unexpectedly appeared, glancing shyly about the clutter, and asked if they might speak. Nathaniel hadn't set eyes on him since the accident; only a short message had informed him that Jerry was taking a few days off.

Wilson was endearingly bashful, rarely able to bear the weight of another's gaze. "Umm," he said, looking toward the floor, "last time I talked to Cy, he was threatening to shut down the MTF and scrub Toshi's experiment. I was kinda wondering…"

Machuzak puckered his lips, nodded. Krieg-Zuber had only weeks ago threatened to close down the MTF, and Wilson's concern for self-preservation was understandable. Formerly, Jerry had been a diagnostician who measured the properties of a tokamak plasma. For a few years, he'd worked happily on ASSET's predecessor, AUSTOR, even before Nathaniel had joined the lab, then he tired of midnight shifts and requested something less demanding. The pickings were slim, but Jerry wasn't ambitious, entertaining no thoughts of a PhD. He floated around a long time, ended up overseeing one of Toshi's ideas and assisting Nathaniel part time. Machuzak had first found it strange that Wilson was older than he, but they both got over it. One thing was certain: if the MTF went, Jerry went with it.

"The MTF is safe for the moment," Nathaniel assured him. "You have my word, but I'll talk to Toshi."

Wilson thanked him and disappeared into the next room. Today's ignition meeting was due to begin in ten minutes. Nathaniel would collar Toshi there. He drove to the main building, tore off the top sheet of the deadline calendar and took two steps at a time up to the ASSET conference room.

* * * *

Toshi was not present. The others were, though it made no difference. Four days had passed since Moravec's ultimatum, but no one could see how to ignite Prometheus short of putting a torch to it. Everyone had the same thought: to hell with long pulses, just get the power up, way up, if only for seconds. Push the magnets to the limits. Ignite, disrupt, claim victory. Seeing the state of affairs, Nathaniel asked if anyone knew what had happened to Matsushima, and he was unable to ascertain from Thaddeus Hasschler whether Toshi had even been informed.

"He's too busy levitating," cracked Kettering, pressing his palms together and making a mock bow in all directions. "What's he doing at CRFC anyway?"

Nathaniel was not amused. "Tom," he said, "let me put it hypothetically. If I had an ignition deadline to beat and you asked me to put my money on the entire lab or Toshi by himself, I wouldn't hesitate…"

Thad instantly rose. "I find that insulting, Nat. I demand an apology." Had Hasschler been wearing a glove, he would have hurled it to the ground. Aye, Hasschler's difficult temper was already leaking out at the knowledge that his would be the responsibility for coaxing the impossible fire out of that great, sullen machine. Who is this man? The question came unbidden, but Nathaniel asked evenly whether he had any ideas. Caught empty-handed, Thad sat down again and said gruffly, "In any case, there is nothing to be done until Prometheus is ready." He shot a smoldering glance toward Abbuhl.

"My apologies, Thad," Fred replied with his signature calm, "I only got three shifts on the boards a couple hours ago"—he glanced at his watch—"and we won't be up to strength 'til tomorrow. You're going to have to give us a few weeks, maybe a month."

"Then let's cancel these damned meetings until then!" Hasschler erupted.

Diana Cochran quipped that one of the concrete platforms supporting the helium factory had cracked and needed repair. Nathaniel leveled his gaze at Diana. They'd always irritated each other. As their eyes met, the same spike of suspicion caught in his throat. No, here is nothing more than the usual conflict of personalities. I regard her as knee-jerk gung-ho and she finds my skepticism of the Mission treacherous.

At that moment Hasschler swiveled to Machuzak with a pointed finger. "It is your responsibility to get Moravec to relent. This is our only hope."

"Take him to a surge room and electrocute him," Kettering cut in.

"Moravec's in Copenhagen," Nathaniel replied, peering at the tritium head with incredulity. "I'm meeting him in Dallas day after tomorrow." That silenced the insurgents, but as they adjourned Machuzak took Tom aside, about to interrogate him on the remark. Catching himself, he cursed audibly and backed off.

"What's your problem, Machuzak?" the ex-marine asked sternly.

"Sorry, nothing," Nathaniel answered, turning away awkwardly, putting a vague mental question mark by Kettering's name and certain only that it was essential to enlist Matsushima at once.

* * * *

Toshi Matsushima had also been exiled to Alpha Site by Krieg-Zuber and Nathaniel was forced to drive over again. To his surprise, he found the Japanese physicist in place, trim and agile at fifty, sitting on a tatami mat drinking tea.

"Why weren't you at the meeting?" he demanded.

"I wasn't informed," replied Toshi without apparent interest. As Nathaniel had suspected. "In any case, why should I join such a group of bots?"

"If you don't," said Machuzak, "we are certain to fail."

"What is that to me?"

"'You have the right to your labor, not to the fruits of your labor.'"

The exhortation obliged Toshi to smile. "Hoisted on my own petard," he said, knowing he had recommended the Bhagavad Gita with its famous advice to Nathaniel. "So how are you holding up, Prince Arjuna, on the eve of battle?"

Nathaniel chuckled morosely. "I am just trying to do my duty, *dharma*, isn't it?"

"Correct," Toshi responded, offering Nathaniel some tea. "But remember, the message of the Gita is that one does his duty whether one likes it or not. And now you will tell me that this applies to the both of us."

"Yes." Nathaniel declined the tea but sat down without invitation and bored unrelentingly into Matsushima.

Toshi understood. "The others are of course paralyzed, without ideas. You expect me to work the required miracles to spare the impossible Mission immolation. Will I be canonized, Nathaniel?"

"'You have the right to your labor, not to the fruits of your labor.'"

Toshi agreed only to consider it. Nathaniel well knew that Matsushima's exile to Site Alpha was spiritual as well as physical, that he would resist impressment; he tactically changed course to Jerry Wilson's request: What had Krieg-Zuber been up to?

"It is very much like the situation when one company buys another with its own money, isn't it?" Machuzak didn't quite follow. "You well know that the funds for my experiment come directly from the pocket of our exalted benefactor Richard Garrett. So if Krieg-Zuber was planning to scrub it, he would be canceling an experiment he did not fund. This is typical of The Terminator's ego."

When Matsushima spoke of "his" experiment, he meant one of his ideas, which others like Wilson were carrying out. Toshi could probably tie his own shoelaces, but tightening a bolt would have been beyond his range. That Garrett had been personally financing Toshi's experiment was public knowledge; it was too far out for anyone else to take seriously. "So, if I continue to pay Jerry at the MTF, you can ante up your half?"

Toshi smiled like the Buddha. "Is Krieg-Zuber able to hear our laughter?"

Despite his surname, Toshifumi Matsushima was half Korean and much of what he said had the flavor of a Zen koan, something that demanded completion yet could not be completed. This was typical of Matsushima, if anything could be called typical. An encounter with him left you inspired or perplexed, sometimes annoyed, rarely unaltered.

Toshifume Matsushima was in every respect the most singular character Nathaniel had known. He came from the six hundred thousand or so *Zainichi* families, ethnic Koreans, remaining in Japan, and Nathaniel often wondered whether his internal exile had shaped his destiny. He thinks qualitatively differently than you or I. "It is like a goat going up a hill and coming down a camel," he will describe a nuclear transmutation. Toshi's quicksilver mind allowed him the luxury to work on what amused him and he'd made contributions to several branches of physics. His great speed was equally his downfall. Toshi bores easily and has never carried through anything to the bitter end. He once confessed he could win his freedom only by receiving the Nobel Prize. Nathaniel laughed, reminding him that no one gets Nobel Prizes for plasma physics, and pitied him.

As Nathaniel glanced at his watch, the older man said, "Don't forget your deep-breathing exercises, Arjuna. Breath is the first thing that goes." Nathaniel nodded good-bye as Matsushima offered to show him his latest geometry problem, which he felt worthy to hang on the tree, but Machuzak had already disappeared, wondering, as always, who Toshi was.

FIFTEEN

Leaving Slava behind, T. J. had walked forthrightly into Balard's outer office to see the ITER director giving instructions to his secretary. She extended her hand and said, "Professor Balard, I'm T. J. D'Abro with CFRC, and I want to apologize for Dr. Archangelsky's behavior earlier. You can imagine things are a little tense over there." A true Frenchman, Balard counted it a good day when an attractive woman glanced at him, and to resist the enigmatic smile being cast in his direction was altogether beyond his capabilities. Allowing him no chance to recover, T. J. asked whether they might speak and he unhesitatingly offered a gracious bow, ushering her into his inner sanctum.

With a glance at the classical artifacts adorning the office, T. J. continued to improvise. "Hopefully things at CFRC will calm down once we determine the cause of the accident," she said, taking the seat offered, "and then you'll see that this is all a gentleman's misunderstanding. As a matter of fact—"

By this time Balard was smiling. "Gentleman's misunderstanding?" he interrupted with his heavy accent. "Mademoiselle, permit me, ITER is one of ze largest scientific projects ever undertaken, and doubtlessly ze most important for ze future of mankind. You see—" he gestured to a wall chart behind him that showed the dozens of countries and agencies involved. "What you cannot detect from zis chart is how small a role the United States is playing, approaching zero. Your country could have been the leader, but no, thirty years ago America turned its back on ze future. Your fundamentalist politicians, who live in a medieval world, have much on their shoulders, rejecting science for superstition, habitually pulling out of signed international protocols. What's more, when Rasmussen had the chance to correct these mistakes, what does he do? He swindles billionaires to invest in his ridiculous consortium, for no other reason than to serve his own vanity, which I assure you is unsurpassed. From ze beginning he has attempted to sabotage ITER. He steals from me scientists, engineers, he has diverted dollars to CFRC that were rightfully ours... If you think I will allow t...that *voleur* to beat ITER to ignition by one second—No. I will stop him, so help me God..."

As the director clenched his fist, T. J. saw that she was witnessing an outburst that verged on approaching the earlier one in the corridor. Balard simply could not disguise his hatred of Rasmussen. "How will y'all stop him, sir?" D'Abro asked simply, silencing her phone.

"W…what, what do you mean?" Balard abruptly halted. "I will stop him with every means. I will play his game. I will entice his best scientists with higher salaries, better cuisine, lovelier scenery. I will be sure that every cent of American fusion dollars comes to ITER instead of CFRC. I will push my people to the limits of their endurance and we will show Rasmussen what it means to challenge Pierre Jules César Balard." As before, the immense man thumped his chest angrily. "Leonard has asked for a race and now he has one. Give him regards from his former student, mademoiselle."

"Y–you were his student?" T. J. stammered in full amazement.

"His first doctoral student, *oui*, half a lifetime ago."

Boy, was this personal, T. J. began to suspect. "I'll be sure to tell him," she swallowed. "I'm curious, Dr. Balard, a lot of people here seem to have connections to the States."

"Of course, physicists are some of the world's best jet-setters, unfortunately not always of their own choosing. When funding for one lab is cut, the lab farms out its physicists to another site, sometimes for three, five years. Lives are changed, disrupted, divorces… Often one's home lab becomes a mere pied-à-terre… For many years the brain drain has been running in reverse, since so little goes on in America… But of course you know all this…"

"Of course. Do you still keep in touch with anyone there?" T. J. asked as nonchalantly as she might, peering at one of the Roman vases that adorned the desk.

Balard leveled his big shining head at her. "Why do you ask?" he said, less with suspicion than with perplexity.

"You said you were Leonard's student, that's all. Are any of your own students in Austin?"

"Perhaps, but for the past years I have had virtually no contact with anyone at CFRC, except for those who want to come here… Why have you come here, mademoiselle?"

She'd feared the question. "Just vacation, sir." T. J. told him, winging it. "I've been pretty stressed out recently. I'd never been to Provence and Dr. Archangelsky thought I might like to visit ITER."

"Better, mademoiselle, I should show you Avignon," Balard said. "Tomorrow, if my schedule permits."

"That might be very pleasant," answered T. J., if we haven't been deported.

"In any case, why don't you be my guest for dinner zis evening, Mademoiselle... D'Abro, is it? and we can have a more leisurely conversation—"

At that moment Balard's phone rang and he excused himself to the next room, saying the call would take a few minutes.

T. J. didn't know what she was looking for, but she lost no time, walking around his uncluttered desk. A blotter occupied the desk's center. She pushed aside a few papers. The blotter was a mess of notes, doodles, memos. It took a few seconds for the tangle to resolve. Emerging from the rest, the words *Rasmussen Rasmussen Rasmussen Rasmussen,* penned no fewer than four times. A cartoonish portrait next to the names with a sword stuck through its head. "I would slice him without a knife, good." That was all.

T. J. started when she heard Balard sign off in the next room and quickly returned to the chair. The director general entered. "Please excuse the interruption," he said. "That was ze Chinese director. India and China joined the program very late and have been a constant headache with their demands. Where were we? Dinner? Shall we say in two hours? My secretary will arrange rooms for you and Dr. Archangelsky at ze castle tonight."

* * * *

After dinner, T. J. said to Slava, "There ain't room in Fusion Town for Rasmussen and Balard both. Julius Cesar is gunnin for him, no question. Apart from detailing the ways he'd destroy Rasmussen, you know what he said over dinner?"

Of course Slava had no idea; he'd spent the past hours on the castle tower attempting to contact the people in the video they'd identified so far.

The Frenchman had leaned over to T. J. with wineglass in hand and tightened his lips. "Mademoiselle, you will forgive if my remarks earlier seemed, umm...heavy-handed. I am of course upset by zis week's events. Were I to do in Rasmussen, the method I would choose would be much simpler, requiring neither money nor theft. I require merely ideas."

"What do you mean?" T. J. asked, wrinkling her nose, checking for text messages.

"Mademoiselle, everyone hates Rasmussen. All that is required to make certain ASSET fails completely is for one of his team to feed him an idea." Balard examined his wineglass. "It should be a bad idea, but one that appears...good. There are many of those in science, you know. In fusion, a cleverly bad idea, disguised as a good one, would be enough to detour your program for years—forever."

When Slava heard this, it chilled him to the core. The scientific mills grind finely but ever so slowly. Balard was correct: in present circumstances little would be required to turn the impossible task before them into a catastrophe.

Archangelsky got to his feet atop the castle and stared at the light-flecked river below. T. J. was saying, "Slava, you gotta believe Balard's planted a mole among you folks. I don't know who, but Monsieur Director General sure wasn't leveling with me about not havin contacts at CFRC."

Slava suddenly wanted very much to get back to Texas.

SIXTEEN

Early Friday morning, en route to the lab, Nathaniel received a message from T. J. with a smiley; they'd reached their destination. Glad for that, he tore off the top sheet of the calendar as he arrived for the daily ignition meeting. Matsushima failed to appear and the meeting went precisely as far as yesterday's. As the division heads logged off their Facebook pages, he announced he was shutting down access to social networking sites. He knew he'd just deprived them of mother's milk.

The sensation that remained as they adjourned was one of futility absolute. While they stood paralyzed, the deadline had notched forward twenty-four hours. The single bright spot was that Abbuhl believed his team had identified all the Chinese bolts and that they could be removed. Kettering would contact Savannah River within the hour to make arrangements for new tritium shipments.

At Site Alpha, Nathaniel searched for Toshi, futilely. He returned to the MTF next door, thinking to send him a note, saw the on-screen warning again, halted. Instead, he tried to learn something about Moravec, whom he'd meet tomorrow. Machuzak uncovered much about Globe-Tex, but its CEO left few electronic footprints, an extraordinary feat in the post-Google world. With little to show for his efforts, Machuzak found himself staring into the empty beaker of his cold-fusion apparatus, wishing, as always, that the thing would work.

* * * *

It was only at seven that evening, a day postponed, that Nathaniel turned onto Red Bud Trail in West Lake Hills, where natural twilight alone shrouded the streets. Probably another power outage. Electricity had been vanishing at state borders from the nascent smart grid, but in fact he'd probably never discover what exactly had happened. Since the local papers had folded, no one really knew what went on in this town… Ah, by the time Machuzak pulled into the Rasmussens' driveway, the lights were back.

Theresa Rasmussen welcomed him at the door with a wineglass in her hand. Entering, Nathaniel kissed her on the cheek and complimented her on the elegant evening dress, which fairly slinked around her tall, almost bony figure. Theresa would have sooner fled town than be caught in a pair of blue jeans, Austin's official uniform. Like Leonard she couldn't escape an air of formality, *breeding,* Nathaniel had to call it, but she never allowed the likes of mongrel CFRC scientists to feel uncomfortable in her presence.

"What is it, Mac?" Theresa asked. "You look troubled."

Machuzak chuckled grimly, accepted the proffered wine with gratitude and saluted Leonard, who already sat at the dinner table. Leonard slowly raised a hand in return. "I think I've faced more trouble in the past week than in the rest of my life all together." After this day and its manifold problems he felt yet unfocused.

"Well, relax for a few minutes."

Together they strolled through the house. Here a Japanese wall unit full of mementoes: honorary degrees from a dozen universities in the United States, Japan, China, Korea, France; a citation from the president of Korea, a bullwhip from graduating students, government medals. Here the rare books: French novels, Enlightenment philosophy, a first edition of the *Arabian Nights* with illustrations by Dulac. Leonard's presence overwhelmed and, as at his office four long days ago, Nathaniel felt he was treading on hallowed ground.

"I'm surprised Leonard collects fairy tales," he said, leafing through the *Arabian Nights,* but the illustrations, soft and suffused with kindness, failed to stir him. "He always assured me that reality is far more interesting than any literature."

"That's why he's a scientist. Those are mine," Theresa replied, though her answer hardly surprised him any less and he asked what she found in them. "Truth," she said. "It's not just in tokamaks, you know."

They walked into the rec room. There, one of those walking machines for the hyper-energetic, complete with drink holders, fiber-optic connection. Behind it an African mask, bold, modern in its lines, frightening. Opposite, a clay sculpture, a nude, half finished. "Is that yours?" Nathaniel asked with curiosity.

She nodded. Nathaniel hadn't known Theresa was a sculptress, but she protested that she wasn't very good. He said she was wrong. "With Leonard's health I... I haven't been able to work much recently. Sometimes I get upset and smash everything, Just..." With that she bit her lip and turned away. Slashes disfigured the piece's legs, arms.

Nathaniel found no reply. Leonard was dying; that was the long and short of it. For the first time Nathaniel noticed gray on Theresa's ordinarily brown hair, and it seemed to him that she'd cut it short, the thing women do in a crisis.

She led him by the arm back into the living room. The wooden beams arching across the space, separating skylights, gave the fabulous house a rustic and Oriental feel. They stopped before the big windows overlooking Austin. Behind the house, the setting sun threw a soft purple veil over the city. Downtown, the mirrored buildings cast back the light, although little trim was left on after dark these days; farther north the university's tower glowed a faint orange.

"Did UT win a game today?" Theresa asked with the tone of someone who has been sidelined from world events.

Nathaniel shrugged no less than she. The window glass, separating them from the town, represented exactly how he felt. Austin, The University, belonged to another planet.

"Well," said Theresa with sudden cheer, "you've had three minutes. What is it?"

Nathaniel focused on the music that had been playing all the while. "*Dies Irae* from Zelenka's D minor requiem, I believe."

Theresa smiled. "You're very hard to fool." She dropped into silence for a moment, then, "Do you think you can do it, Mac?"

"No. It's impossible," he answered flatly, "but we'll go down trying."

"Don't say that to Leonard." She led him toward the dining room. "And Leonard's told me what happened," she said, disappearing into the kitchen.

* * * *

Machuzak sat down across from Leonard, confused. "You've told her about the sabotage?" he whispered.

Leonard nodded with difficulty. "She is my wife, you know."

Nathaniel found himself concerned and relieved. Too many people were learning about the true state of affairs, but he was thankful that he wouldn't have to lie to Theresa.

When she reappeared with salads for the two of them and soup for Leonard, Theresa paused to light candles and asked how Nathaniel was holding up. "The worst thing is that since this thing happened, I have to force myself to look people in the eye. I walk down hallways, crossing them off some mental checklist of personalities, motives, opportunities, catching words in my throat, glancing over my shoulder, wondering if in the next hour, minute, the machine is going to be hit again—or blown to bits. It's the strangest sensation I've ever known—distrusting one's friends. I... I know so little about them. I guess I'll have to live with it." Throughout Theresa and Leonard remained silent, expressions downcast. "Otherwise, I've enlisted a, umm, private detective and we've started an investigation. We have almost no clues, but she and Slava got to ITER today."

Leonard started, such as he was able. "ITER, why?" he said slowly.

Nathaniel disclosed that they'd received communications from somebody there who apparently knows something. "That's all I can tell you." He omitted the information that the someone was a virtual dragon who'd morphed into an armadillo.

"Jules Balard will do everything to prevent us from attaining ignition," Leonard continued with genuine alarm. "I've known him thirty years. He's the worst son of a bitch on the face of the planet."

"I can't believe he would go so far as to sabotage Prometheus!" Nathaniel exclaimed. "That's preposterous!"

With difficulty Leonard wiped away a line of soup dribbling down his chin. He reminded Nathaniel that Prometheus had been sabotaged once. The only question was, Who would do it twice? "I wouldn't put it past him," he spat. "The man steals everything he can get his hands on. He has stolen so many ideas of mine that he blocked me from winning the Nobel Prize."

The candlelight could not disguise the anger contorting Rasmussen's face. Nathaniel had never seen the older man display such vehemence. "Tell me," he changed the subject but put it directly, "did you authorize Krieg-Zuber to install a cell-phone wiping and jamming system? To block, monitor Internet traffic?"

Leonard's expression now dissolved into one of pain. "Cy felt the lab was being run too loosely, that the Mission was being compromised. Four years ago he decided that something needed to be done. I had other responsibilities and did not pay much attention, Mac. You understand, don't you...?"

"Len," Nathaniel replied, staring at him in disbelief, "while you weren't paying attention, The Terminator transformed the lab from a scientific establishment into a—You know why I am at Alpha Site—" Without thinking he slammed his fist on the table, nearly overturning his glass. "He's already threatened to take over again as soon as he's able..."

Nathaniel recounted their conversation from two days ago, but Rasmussen simple refused to believe it. "You must be exaggerating," he said.

"Mark my words."

"Maybe you could appoint him your deputy," Theresa suggested.

Nathaniel merely stared, as if she'd made a bad joke. Leonard thought the doctors had sidelined Krieg-Zuber for several months, but agreed to speak to him. Then as Theresa served salmon, he pressed Nathaniel for his ignition strategy. Nathaniel described the fruitless meetings, his determination to include Matsushima, the opposition to that on all sides, including Matsushima's. "The worst thing is the lack of ideas."

To Nathaniel's disappointment, Leonard offered no proposals that he hadn't already heard, adding only, "It might help to pray." At his own remark, a dark twinkle appeared in Rasmussen's eyes and he said, "Austin is the buckle of the Bible Belt more than ever before. We'll hire an televangelist to uncover biblical passages prophesying fusion and set up an eight-hundred number to raise funds." It was a relief to see the unexpected flash of good humor, despite…and Nathaniel smiled for the first time this evening.

"Could we start a Mideast war to drive up oil prices?" Machuzak asked, not entirely facetiously.

"I tried it once," Leonard answered with perfect gravity. "Unfortunately, there is always a war in the Mideast. I also promised the Saudis for a sum not to develop fusion—naturally I intended to funnel the money into ASSET—but they refused the bribe. Neither has Congress accepted my repeated observation that we could develop fusion for what they spend each month defending oil fields."

Leonard's voice bore no trace of its famous April Fool's Day impishness and it gave Nathaniel pause; he seemed to be telling the truth. Failing as always to imagine the exalted circles the director traveled in, Nathaniel changed the subject to Moravec. Here too Leonard was of little help. As it turned out, they'd met only virtually. "There is something strange about him," Leonard conceded, but added that GlobeTex's chief was no fool and a hero to environmentalists. Before Nathaniel could press him for weaknesses, Leonard asked to be excused. Theresa helped him to the bedroom and returned shortly, suggesting that she and Nathaniel adjourn to the living room.

* * * *

They stood again by the front windows with Austin in the distance. Nathaniel said he was sorry, Leonard's illness must be very difficult for her.

Theresa nodded, took a drink. "It's given me time to prepare. 'You plan a tower that will pierce the clouds? Lay first the foundation of humility.' That was Augustine, wasn't it?"

She'd done it. Theresa's internal dialogue had taken her across continents and momentarily short-circuited Machuzak's ability to follow.

"Oh, I was just thinking of the tower," she said, sitting, "that's all."

Nathaniel frowned, at himself. He perceived that at this moment Theresa Rasmussen herself was not excepted from his past days' revolving unease that he was surrounded by strangers. For all their years of acquaintanceship what did he know of Theresa? At a party, here, when Krieg-Zuber was pontificating that Einstein was the most important person of the last century, she casually asked him, What about the researchers who had vanquished tuberculosis? The inventors of birth control? Stalin? And what after all was one century? The Byzantine Empire had lasted fourteen. The Terminator was soon noticed to be missing from the party.

Theresa was no professional historian. Coming from a well-to-do family, Nathaniel doubted she was a professional anything. She'd been groomed to be the gracious wife of an important man, but ornamentation didn't suit her. Sprung from college, she hoisted a pack onto her shoulder and set off. Europe, Africa, Asia; Machuzak wasn't sure why or where. To touch Earth. Her *wanderjahr* lasted until the years left her rootless, and she returned. Once married, she headed committees and arts organizations. No less than Leonard, Theresa disdained idleness, and when she was not leading worthy charges, she delved into all sorts of strange byways. Her tastes ran in every respect to the obscure. She rejected the Great Men theory of history and was convinced that most of what is important in the world has gone unrecognized and unrecorded.

Nathaniel knew that much. He once asked why her aversion to jeans and she replied, "It smacks of indiscipline." In an age when 120 characters counted as epic, he'd rarely seen her without a book, often printed.

Theresa patted the spot on the couch by her side. "Sit," she said.

He obeyed. "I think I must disappoint Leonard," he said.

"Why no," her eyebrows lifted. "He's always said you had some of the best physical intuition of anyone he'd ever met. You just saw how an experiment would turn out. That's why he made you a division head. I'm sorry you haven't gotten farther at the lab. I think it's because you're too honest. You're the most honest person I know, Mac. It's a bit quaint in this age, wouldn't you agree?"

Machuzak stood again. "I'd rather be quaint and forgotten than take after some others and be shrouded in glory. Theresa, you can be sure that during this past week I've found it difficult to be as honest as I'd like. Slava's right. Google changed the definition of honesty. It's optional now. In science too. These days, I don't always remember why I got into this business, but you can be sure that by the time all this is over, I will have found out."

"Bravo, Nathaniel, bravo!" Theresa exclaimed, clapping, but Machuzak felt embarrassed, as if he had revealed too much.

"Maybe it's time for me to leave," he said.

She stood, took his arms, searched his eyes. He and Theresa were both in that plateau of years where it is impossible to guess another person's age, and he had always assumed, merely, that she was slightly older than he. Theresa ran her hands down his arms and lay her head against his chest, crying softly. Flustered, he allowed her to remain for several moments with his arms around her, then gently released himself. She kissed him lightly on the lips, lingered a beat too long, and he disappeared into the night.

SEVENTEEN

Well before dawn on Saturday, a ringing next to his ears shattered Machuzak's dreams. Bedbug. "Doc, we're going to be a little late. I'll call ya later," she said and abruptly hung up. He'd intended to rendez-vous with T. J. and Slava on his return from Dallas, where he was to meet Moravec. Puzzled, unable to return to sleep, he roused himself, headed to the lab, watched Hasschler and Kettering nearly come to blows at the ignition meeting, cursed, received the first resignations on his desk, cursed again and departed for the airport.

Garrett had put his private jet at his disposal and two hours after he'd left CFRC, Nathaniel entered the domain of Moravec, GlobeTex's CEO. After the call five days ago he did not know what to expect—male, female or otherwise. Stepping into the huge corner office Machuzak was equally unable to decide whether it had been modeled after a Hollywood set or vice versa. The plush carpet, the heavy purplish drapes. The rose-wood conference table. The 3-D displays, remote conferencing studio, scale models of solar plants, a wallful of awards and citations from environmental organizations.

The opening pleasantries. A tall suited figure, in no way resembling the one he'd seen once before, stepped out from behind the desk and extended her hand; today Machuzak was willing to guess at the gender, but he remained unsure whether facing him was a living human being or a bot. "I know what you're thinking," she said in a voice no more devoid of intonation than a Californian's. "Who am I? It's difficult to keep a low profile in this day and age, so I hide in broad daylight. I rarely make public appearances, employ doubles—no two of whom look alike—project various virtual images to confuse the enemy, if you will. Call it electronic chaff. I find it keeps the intruders at bay, not knowing exactly who they're dealing with."

Multiple personas, Machuzak thought, not unlike any Web citizen. Perhaps Moravec has forgotten who she is. "I should think it would spur curiosity, not decrease it," he said.

Moravec smiled faintly but didn't answer. "I know you are here to talk about the ignition deadline. Let's get down to it, shall we? Scotch?"

Nathaniel thanked his host for meeting him, and on a Saturday, accepted the proffered chair but declined the scotch. Moravec sat down stiffly opposite him, across a small lounge table. The being facing Nathaniel was taller than he, elegantly if sexlessly dressed, with silvering hair and a pale complexion that spoke of rare hours beneath the sun. He couldn't read her expression, which seemed of one accustomed to intimidate crossed with a discomfort at live conversation. It was not altogether unkind, but Machuzak chose his words carefully nevertheless.

"Many people at the lab have long felt that your membership in our consortium was a ploy, that GlobeTex intended to shut us down at the right moment. That does appear to be what you are doing—"

"—to eliminate the competition from fusion, just as GM destroyed public transportation, the Lear engine and early electric cars. Yes, I've heard that theory myself." To Nathaniel's surprise, Moravec revealed a slight bemusement. "In fact, apparently I staged last week's accident to give GlobeTex an excuse to pull out."

You took the words out of my mouth.

"Mac, you'll agree—I understand everyone calls you Mac; is that okay?" she said that with a typical female intonation, confusing Nathaniel further. "You'll agree that there would be little point in such a move given that our contract expires in six months...minus a few days."

Again anticipated. Machuzak leveled his gaze. "You know that deadline can't be met."

Moravec reacted only by standing and turning away. "I'm sorry. There's no choice in the matter. We've been putting far more money into your lab than the Republic or federal government. For a time Leonard Rasmussen convinced me that success was inevitable. He was, it appears, exaggerating. You may have heard that a controlling interest in our company has been bought by the Germans, who are much more enthusiastic about solar than fusion, especially with ITER causing so much controversy. GlobeTex's current plans are to establish the world's largest wind farm and solar facility in the panhandle, and push harder on cellulosic ethanol along the Brazilian model. I'm sure you'll agree that America's detour to corn-based ethanol was a total failure."

A diversionary tactic, Machuzak thought, but he did agree. Ethanol was, in a word, stupid. It wasn't energy efficient and its development only caused people to starve elsewhere. "I didn't come to talk about ethanol," he said. "I came to ask you for more time."

"How much?"

"A commercial fusion plant is still decades away. To demonstrate feasibility, ignition, a few years...four, five..."

Moravec chuckled while pausing before the award wall. "Mac, you're talking like your predecessors have for seventy years. We took a big risk investing in CFRC. People who support me are opposed to fusion—these days they're leaning toward ordinary fission now that Japan is forgotten—and GlobeTex is not prepared to wait any longer."

"Two years—give us two years." Nathaniel suddenly felt as if he were bargaining with the devil in a three-button jacket.

The CEO turned from the wall, raised her glass toward the physicist. "Tell me, Mac, what are the odds of success in two years?"

"Ten percent," Nathaniel replied, flinching internally, as he well knew the meaninglessness of placing odds on a single event.

"Not a risk any businessman would accept. Leonard would have answered one hundred percent."

"He would have lied. I am not Leonard."

"To your disadvantage, Mac."

That cut. Machuzak knew that he had no experience in these matters and must be coming across as a neophyte. "A year," he said.

Moravec laughed, this time Nathaniel might have said sardonically, and absently spun the blades of a miniature wind turbine standing on the desk. "If the odds are ten percent in two years, surely they are less in one."

"Tell me," said Nathaniel, now rising, "imagine we do the impossible and achieve ignition in six months." He stepped toward the reclusive CEO. "Then…?"

For the first time since the audience began, Moravec paused. "A fair question. We are obliged to extend your contract, I suppose."

"You suppose. For how long?"

At this, the executive's silence was slightly, perceptibly longer. Machuzak realized that she, it, hadn't considered the contingency.

"That would depend."

"On…?"

"On how promising the results look, I imagine." Moravec glanced away, the discomfort Nathaniel had noticed upon entering flashing briefly.

"You wouldn't accept ignition as promising?"

"I didn't say that. But as I understand it, the definition of ignition is not so clear-cut. Is ignition for one second ignition?"

One second is an eternity in physics. "You're shifting the goalposts."

Moravec set down her glass, no smile now. "Mac, do not class me with those reactionary politicians who have ruined Texas by fighting restrictions on carbon, fuel standards or research into alternate energy."

For an instant the CEO's voice was infused with a sad anger. "I too am of the future. But I no longer see fusion as part of that future."

She said the last in an earnest, nearly importunate tone. Nathaniel nevertheless perceived that Moravec's answer was a shameless evasion. She, it, had no intention of rescinding the deadline. "You've never visited the lab, have you?"

"Only by remote."

At that instant, her cell phone rang. The ringtone was a jaunty one, unusual, and a few seconds passed before Nathaniel placed it as an electronic version of the *Nisi Dominus* from Monteverdi's *Vespers*. Moravec cut her caller short, saying she was occupied, and returned to her guest.

"Why don't you visit, see what you are destroying?" Nathaniel said before Moravec could resume speaking.

"I don't relish the thought of being blown to bits," she replied.

Nathaniel tilted his head. "What makes you think that would happen?" he asked curiously.

"No reason," Moravec shrugged, "undue suspicion. I suppose I owe you that much, but I'll be traveling for the next six weeks. Make an appointment with my secretary."

They stood. As Nathaniel prepared to leave, he noticed on Moravec's shelf Sun Tzu's *Art of War*, beloved of movie executives. "Doesn't Sun Tzu write that it is better to take a state intact than ruin it?" remarked the scientist.

"If possible," reacted Moravec with surprise.

"He also writes that moral superiority is the first weapon in waging war." Nathaniel shook Moravec's hand and said he'd make the appointment.

EIGHTEEN

Early Saturday morning, as they left Cadarache Castle, Slava had found a message waiting in the foyer. He opened the envelope and handed its contents to T. J., who read, "Your presence in Cadarache is not required." Lost in thought, Archangelsky lagged behind while she walked in the brisk air down the steps through the garden and toward the parking area. Suddenly, she froze, and in that instant the two were buffeted by a deafening roar as their car went up in flames. Even now her instincts told her to take cover; she pulled the physicist after her three steps and together they dove behind a five-hundred-year-old stone wall. When their ears had stopped ringing, the two got to their feet, dusted themselves off. T. J. pulled a leaf from Archangelsky's beard but did not pause to ask for an explanation. As the castle staff came running, she gripped him by the arm, marched him to the other end of the lot and shoved him into an idle taxi.

* * * *

Only late that evening did Machuzak link up with Slava and T. J. at the Salt Lick in Driftwood. Even as Nathaniel entered the rough-hewn lodge, choking on the smoke that poured from the barbeque pit, D'Abro and Archangelsky signaled him from a bench in a far corner. Despite the dimness of the place, he perceived that the expressions worn by the pair went beyond jet lag.

They ordered brisket and ribs, which arrived on paper plates, beer in cups. Only a couple of Republic of Texas Defense Force militiamen immersed in computer games a few tables away and emitting alien shrieks disturbed the unusual quiet.

With an expression that appeared no less grim to Slava and T. J. than theirs to him, Nathaniel shook his head, ran his fingers over the wooden table scarred with knife wounds and began. "Nobody has any ideas. Toshi has vanished. People have begun to quit." This morning: one tech, two engineers, a physicist. He reported his negative results detecting nitrogen and SF6 in the surge room, to which T. J. smiled faintly, and he then relayed his meeting with Moravec. "He, she is a new species, *homo virtualis*. I'm not even sure I met *the* Moravec, but I'm convinced whoever or whatever I met can't rescind the deadline even if she, it wants to. Someone is forcing her to do this. I invited her to the lab, but…"

The deadline remained, immovable. The wheels of their great task were slowly beginning to turn. At this very moment, cooling-water checks, leak checks of the neutral beams would be proceeding. In the next day or two, techs would seal up the torus, further leak checks… The bakeout could take weeks. The cooldown would overlap but a month might yet pass before the desperate games could begin. Even Moravec could not fast-forward Nature. "Did you find the dragon?" Nathaniel asked, suddenly impatient.

Archangelsky and T. J. glanced at each other. "We got video of some people at chess tournament and have identified them," replied Slava somberly. Dima, true to his word, had found the names in the administrative offices and Slava received them over the Atlantic. "This is not main thing—"

"Did you find—"

"Doc," said T. J., "those ITER people don't like us." To Nathaniel's cocked head, Slava reluctantly described the corridor scene between him and Balard. When he finished, D'Abro added, "What you called a race with ITER before is gonna look like a pissant go-kart in a bowl of Cheerios compared to what's shapin up now. Believe me."

Machuzak glared ferociously at the Russian. "Yaroslav Borisovich, I send you to ITER on a reconnaissance mission and you start a war! I can't believe…!"

"Sorry," said Slava.

"Are you sure Balard would…?" Machuzak managed once he'd calmed.

T. J. described her encounter with the director, the note on his desk, the dinner conversation. "Doc, my theory is he's planted a mole here at CFRC who's determined that ASSET will fail—permanently."

Nathaniel disdained nonscientists' use of the word *theory* for any idle proposition. Archangelsky scorned it no less but said, "She's right, boss."

To prove her case, D'Abro shoved a phone toward Machuzak. "The whole conversation is there, and the voice stress analysis. Wanna hear it?"

Nathaniel was still absorbing the fact of the phone lying before him when Slava revealed what had happened that morning at Cadarache Castle. As the Russian finished, Nathaniel stared at him as if nothing had penetrated. Nothing had, so impossible was it to believe what he'd just heard. "You with us, *brat*?" said Slava, waving his hand before the other's eyes.

After an infinite space, Machuzak blinked. "I'm glad *you* are, *brat*...
Who knew you were there?"

"By this morning? Every plasma physicist in the world, probably."

"Balard sure wouldn't have forgotten," put in T. J. "It was just a
warning. We weren't anywhere near the car and if they'd intended to kill
us, they would have."

It seemed preordained when at that moment Nathaniel's phone
signaled. Holding his breath, he logged on to the Real World and, sure
enough, found the dragon perched on a crag above the same volcano.
"There will be another," the dragon roared with flared nostrils, and took
wing.

Its wake left the three of them staring. After eons T. J. breathed.
"Believe me now, Doc? We've *got* to locate those folks in the video.

"I'm working on it," Slava said.

Even as they were en route to Europe, T. J. had contacted the Real
World administrators to get the dragon's user information, but they naturally demanded a warrant. "That'll be tricky with me on leave. The other
choice is to hack in." She abruptly lit up. "Can you boy scientists do it?"

Machuzak glanced at T. J., to the phone on the table, back to her. At
length he said, "Maybe with enough—. I don't like the idea—"

"When it's this urgent—?" T. J. was staring at him with the ravenous
eyes of a teenage download pirate.

"Damnit, Bedbug, it's illegal!" Nathaniel shouted loudly enough so
that the militiamen glanced up from their computer games. "I shouldn't
be telling you this." All of them stared at the Real World volcano bub-
bling on the screen, as if to decide who was going to capitulate first.
"No," Machuzak finally shook his head, "I've had it up to here with
people telling me to do the wrong thing all week. What's happened to
this world?"

"To freedom of information," Slava raised his glass.

"Look," Nathaniel went on, "if we hack into the Real World we'll
only end up with a whole daisy chain of proxy server addresses that'll
lead nowhere. What we need is the Real World's cooperation to snag Mr.
Dragon next time he logs on. If we can trace him in real time, we might
at least get a geographical fix."

"We should have thought of this before flying to Europe," muttered
Archangelsky.

"We've *got* to smoke out the mole," T. J. insisted. "I tell you, when
Balard told me he had no contacts here anymore, I believed him about as
much as I'd believe that Pam Anderson's tits were real."

"Because of a cheap piece of software?" Nathaniel mumbled to himself, pushing her phone away in disgust. It did remind him, though...

"Krieg-Zuber has evidently been monitoring email traffic for some time." He told them about the back-room splitter. "You might check if there's been any communication with Balard."

Now T. J. cocked her head. "Much obliged, Doc. Are you sure it's legal?"

"I'm not, The Terminator apparently was." An awkward silence descended but then Nathaniel's eyes suddenly twinkled. "You know, why wait for the dragon's next appearance? Why not lure him online?"

"How?" T. J. asked, puzzled.

He wasn't sure. "Announce a meeting: 'radical ideas for ignition.' God knows we need some. Maybe he'll show up, in one avatar or another. If we're lucky, the Real World can trace him while we're on."

"This is not-bad idea," said Slava, "disinformation."

T. J. agreed. "Good to know you're thinkin, Doc; it's worth a try."

Nathaniel nodded and fell to contemplation. Slava called a halt then, saying he needed some sleep. The lines on his face were evident and D'Abro wasn't looking any better. With a wave Archangelsky abandoned the other two in the parking lot, and since T. J. had left her car at home, Nathaniel offered her a lift.

* * * *

She lived in Hyde Park north of the university, which after all these years retained its reputation as a hippie enclave. Machuzak pulled into the gravel driveway in need of weeding and suggested that she also hit the sack. T. J. nodded wearily, getting out of the car, but after a few steps halted and with a backward glance asked if he wanted to come in for a drink. He agreed. She unlocked the door to the smallish house, frowzy and single storied, switched on a light and apologized for the disarray. Ironing board in the dining room, clothes scattered hither and yon, books piled studentlike in corners, on unvarnished pinewood shelves. T. J. dropped her sweater onto the sofa and disappeared into the kitchen, leaving Nathaniel to glance over her collection. The young woman had not lied about being a physics groupie. Prominent in the stacks, *Entropy: The Key to America's Decline; Cash In on Climate Change; 1001 Theories of Everything; Reenchanting Everyday Life Through Quantum Mechanics.* He smiled, pondering the chasm between such treatises and the nitty-gritty of science, noticed the genuine biology, physics and chemistry texts interspersed among them.

T. J. returned then, holding out a glass of bourbon, saying she was too keyed up now to sleep.

"I can imagine," Nathaniel answered, as she cleared a place on the sofa for them to sit. "First week on the job, you pass a radiation course, almost kill yourself in a tokamak, nearly become a murder victim… Not bad."

"Yeah," she smiled faintly. "You know, Doc, when I resigned I was feelin real burnt out, too much from all sides—work, cyberspace, chores… I'd been thinkin of spending some time in one of those Buddhist retreats up in the hills. The online ones didn't help. My plan doesn't seem to be workin out, does it?" She smiled dimly again. "And we still don't have any idea of what's goin on."

"It's been less than a week, T. J. Scientific problems often take years…"

"Investigations go cold in a day." She plunked down on the sofa and motioned for him to sit. "You know what was goin through my mind at ITER, Doc?" she said, facing him unabashedly. Nathaniel shook his head. "That I missed you."

Reddening, Machuzak swallowed and managed to say, "I missed you too." He realized he meant it.

"What do you want to do?"

Nathaniel was taken aback, here, not earlier than midnight, watching D'Abro lean closer with her elbow resting on the back of the couch. Her hair flopped over her face, almost into her glass; she flicked it back, chuckling in a way that was as embarrassed as he felt. "What do I want to do?" he said. "We have a job, T. J."

"Upstanding Nathaniel doesn't believe in mixing business with pleasure?"

Machuzak answered that intense situations bring every kind of… emotion…illusion. "We're very different, you and me."

"About as different as they come." She made a nod that might have been taken for pensive and silenced her earpiece. "Opposites attract but don't stick, huh?"

"Do they? Anyway, it's dangerous, getting involved with coworkers, in science especially. Look at a woman the wrong way and—there's hell to pay."

Again D'Abro chuckled, rolled back against the sofa with her eyes toward the ceiling. "Doc, I'm not a scientist, in case you're still confused on that point. I know. No office romances, too unpleasant when they go sour. No next-door neighbors, same reason. Forget subordinates, superiors, students, you name it. In fact, the only place when romance is legal is when it's…virtual." T. J. sat up, clasping her glass with two hands and took a drink. "You know," she said abruptly, "according to your radiation manual, the greatest health risk to a male is staying single. Ten years off your life."

"Are you suggesting I take up smoking?" Nathaniel asked dryly.

"You'd gain seven years."

Nathaniel couldn't help but laugh, not perceiving where these two people were heading. Neither were the sculpted curves of T. J.'s figure lost on him as she lay against the couch with her eyes half closed and her blouse loosely buttoned. He was tempted to reach out his hand, and she might have welcomed it, but he hesitated. "Surely," he said, finally, "someone as attractive as you must have…commitments."

He sees that T. J. finds the words funny. "Umm, occasional commitments," she replies. "You already know I have trouble stickin around."

"Then why, I mean why me?"

"I told you I'm a physics groupie."

"Anyone at the lab can explain what a plasma is."

Again she rolls her head toward him. "Maybe, but not everyone has the Bhagavad Gita lyin on his desk."

Without thinking, Machuzak stretches his hand across the small space and runs his finger down her cheek. She does not oppose him, indeed attempts to nuzzle his hand. "The Gita won't help with tokamaks, but I keep hoping it will help with life. It reminds me to do my duty, that's all." Somehow he has not expressed himself well, he feels, an especially common state with women. "T. J.," he says, reluctantly withdrawing his hand against all desire, "we have a long row to hoe and… I'm not sure you entirely trust me."

She looks up at him in her fatigue. The moment may be slipping. "You keep a lot to yourself, Doc, you really do. Or else you're so damn naïve that you have nothing whatever to hide. I'm not sure which is scarier. It's the wrong century for someone like that." Her blue eyes are locked on to his, as wide as he'd seen them, limpid and imploring. "What haven't you told me?"

He shakes his head, puzzled.

"I hope you're right, partner."

She loops her arms around his neck and nestles her head against his shoulder. A moment later she is asleep. Machuzak sits there until late becomes early, gently disentangles himself and goes home.

NINETEEN

Machuzak again arrived early at the MTF, a foam mattress and sleeping bag in tow. After yesterday's warning from the dragon he found himself edgy, convinced against his better judgment that another attack on Prometheus was inevitable, imminent. The insane events at Cadarache left no doubt of the prognosis and what he'd feared most was taking place: he could not empty his mind of suspicion.

A mole? Who could Balard have turned? Who at CFRF reviled the program so fiercely to throw the race to ITER? Machuzak began scanning a mental list of CFRC scientists who'd worked on ITER or visited Cadarache itself. He lost count. Hasschler, Krieg-Zuber, Slava… No, not even Archangelsky was jaundiced, crafty enough. Nathaniel clasped his head between his hands.

The hiss of a valve caused him to jerk upright. He breathed, thought to check ITER's daily report and instantly regretted it: Balard had moments ago announced that he would bypass deuterium-deuterium experiments altogether and go straight to the high-powered deuterium-tritium mix within a week. Machuzak struck the desk hard with his fist. "Damn you, Archangelsky!" he shouted. The empty lab echoed with his vain curse but as T. J. had predicted, the race between ITER and ASSET was no longer one between pissant go-karts in a bowl of Cheerios.

He cast about for a way to turn the situation to their advantage and ordered the nearest webcam on. Moments later he'd recorded an announcement that CFRC scientists, under the leadership of Toshifume Matsushima, had conceived a radical new magnetic field configuration that would allow ASSET to achieve ignition in record time. Experiments would begin within weeks. It was a complete lie, but Machuzak added an upbeat soundtrack and after sucking in his breath readied his finger to release it to the world.

Was he out of his fucking mind? They yet had no warrant to tap the Real World. What if the ruse succeeded and the dragon logged on today? They'd have gained nothing, absolutely nothing. Nathaniel lowered his finger.

* * * *

As he sat in the gloom-shrouded lab, chin resting on knuckles, the MTF's third worker walked in. Nathaniel looked up, smiled faintly at Mercedes Ramirez. He hadn't seen her in a full week. Seven days past the event, she appeared in a state of shock, eyes large, red, a sleepwalker's. Perhaps it was the hour. Perhaps it was her.

"Hello, Mercedes," he said.

She didn't reply, exactly, instead pulled off her earbuds and shook out her hair, staring at him for a moment with a pinched, sullen expression. Without a word she walked into her lab, which adjoined his own. He followed and asked how she was doing.

"The whole thing freaked me out," Mercedes at last answered. She stood facing him in a brown vest and set her portfolio on the bench. The space wasn't much different from Machuzak's own next door. "I'm sorry, I just didn't want to come in."

A few years younger than Nathaniel, Mercedes was more of their generation. Permanently plugged in and insensible to her surroundings, she could give T. J. a run for her money as poster child for the smartphone stare, the gaze into cyberspace that was the indelible brand of the age. Nathaniel often wondered why Mercedes had become a physicist. Like many of their contemporaries, she wielded video-game reflexes but was less than adroit with true experiments, having been schooled since birth to view a nuts-and-bolts laboratory as an artificial thing. A refusal to confront a world in which systems fucked up and could not be reset at the blink of an eye had become the most intractable dilemma facing modern science. For all his mathematical shortcomings, Machuzak at least respected the mathematical process. Mercedes regarded calculus, even algebra, as software. Like most CFRC hands, when presented with the simplest problem her first move was invariably to the computer. It never entered her mind that a mathematical problem might have an exact solution and that humans were capable of finding it, occasionally. The very concept of an exact answer had disappeared from the face of the Earth, as extinct as the dodo and the polar bear.

They'd briefly danced around an affair and Nathaniel couldn't deny that she was an attractive woman. But despite her Latin name, Nathaniel found Mercedes to be brittle, uptight, taken to offense and imagined slights. She also suffered from that androgynous, sexless quality that seemed to be the hallmark of the few women who entered physics to this day. Machuzak readily conceded that she may well have felt the same about the men, but as he regarded her, he wished D'Abro were standing before him.

Had Mercedes taken up with Krieg-Zuber last year? Those were the whispers, but if anything was going on, they'd kept it under the radar and Nathaniel didn't consider it his business. Had she'd ever worked at ITER? Yes—he scanned her face her uncomfortably—he thought she had. "I've invited Moravec to visit next month," he said. "We'll show her—"

"—Her?"

"Them, maybe. We'll show her the MTF, the accelerator. It may be our last chance to convince her to rescind this hopeless deadline. Will you do the honors?"

At that moment a tool clattered loudly to the floor in the next room. "What was that!?" Mercedes Ramirez exclaimed, going stiff from head to toe.

Machuzak also flinched, against his will. "Something fell, that's all… Are you okay?"

"I'm fine," she said, sniffling.

"Good, I'll talk to you later. I'm late for today's meeting."

Nathaniel made a quick exit, leaving Ramirez standing sullenly in the MTF, wondering very much who she was.

* * * *

As the meeting, the paralysis he'd described to T. J. and Slava last night continued. The realization that one false step could send them down a blind, fatal alley had completely incapacitated the division heads. Hasschler was arguing that they couldn't dare anything exotic. But if they refused to essay the radical, they'd fail. And Toshi? After leaving Mercedes Ramirez, Nathaniel scoured the MTF for him in vain. Archangelsky hadn't showed either, and with jet lag from Europe he shouldn't be sleeping late.

"Pierre Balard announced today that ITER will go to DT within the week," Machuzak told them in the midst of it.

Instantly, the division heads sucked in their collective breaths as if they'd been punched in the stomach. They stared, but no brilliant suggestions came to their lips. In the vacuum, Fred Abbuhl distributed a list of immediate repairs: turbine on cryoplant pump #4 ; five high-voltage capacitors for pulse-cleaning; two klystrons for rf heating… Nothing major. Nor the stuff with which to serenade your true love. When all was said and done, Nathaniel understood, that was our problem—lack of romance. We are too much engineers.

* * * *

As he left the conference room a call came through. Krieg-Zuber, now at home from the hospital, on the line. "Fuck DD, old boy," he commanded. "Go straight to DT." Machuzak clicked off and blocked the number.

In the next moment he collided with D'Abro, who'd been looking for him. "Doc," she said, with no trace of awkwardness from the previous night, indeed with some unspoken, melancholy intimacy, "I've been thinkin, maybe you do need someone on active duty. This is getting beyond my pay—"

Without a word, Machuzak silenced her, grabbed her arm and rounded up Slava. Outside in the fountain's spray, T. J. revealed herself to be as on edge as Nathaniel himself. "Doc, another attack is a sure thing and I'm not in the position… Geez, I'm already calling in a couple favors to get a Real World subpoena and DNA tests." She shook her head at a loss, then stared at Machuzak sadly. "Look, why don't you put me on the accident investigation, if it's not too late."

"It's not too late," Machuzak said sympathetically, laying his hand on her shoulder.

She smiled faintly. "Then I can at least interview everyone who was in the power area. But I won't even be able to take DNA elimination samples unless we break cover."

"She's right, boss," Slava interrupted. "This covert ops business has strung us by the ham. Maybe best to get unstrung."

Machuzak was surprised to hear this from Archangelsky the subversive, but evidently they'd all been thinking the same thing.

"Until we're not," D'Abro sighed before he could answer, "I'm gonna raid all those emails your former superiors have hoarded and flag Cadarache traffic. I'm also gonna bury myself in your personnel files and do a lotta cross-checking with what passes for your surveillance records. Believe me, I won't surface before sundown, CSI reruns notwithstanding."

They had no better plan. Slava remarked that he'd contacted most of the Europeans in the photo, and that they all seemed to be in the clear. "No reply yet from Asians and I doubt asking whether they are posing as dragon in Real World will help. Best bet is to snag Dragonmaster next time he logs on. We need their help, with or without warrant."

Nathaniel then revealed the video he'd made and come to within seconds of launching two hours ago. "I almost torpedoed the show."

"Don't beat yourself up, Doc, you'll be a rock star soon enough. The minute we get the Real World's cooperation, you're online."

"A microsecond after I'm online, everyone at CFRC will know I'm lying and about ten milliseconds after that so will ITER. We have no ideas, none, to achieve ignition in record time."

Archangelsky stroked his beard, shrugged. "We merely adjust truth to lie. Governments do this all the time."

"True," nodded Machuzak with something that might pass for a smile. "Standard operating procedure." He then got up and walked back toward the main building, preparing to wait, for exactly what he didn't know.

TWENTY

T. J. was pissed off and scared. Pissed off because she was pain-fully aware that her training, life, had not prepared her for what she'd stumbled into. Why'd she let Mac talk her into such a mess? What was this "we're all amateurs" bullshit? Pissed off enough, for sure, to request the sheriff's department's cooperation in an official-like investigation, reminding them that CFRC was fronting the bill. Outsourcing sounded good to Austin; with the sheriff's permission she filed for the Real World subpoena herself, fast-tracking it online. And now she fidgeted, waited. Damn, she had so looked forward to that Buddhist retreat.

Scared because she couldn't comprehend her surroundings. For sev-eral days she'd been poring over surveillance files. Mac'd been right. There was no coverage, none, in the bowels of Prometheus. Whatever world this laboratory belonged to, she'd never seen its like at IMAX. Nor could she understand a tenth of the jargon she found in Krieg-Zu-ber's email cache. Stubbornly she persisted, staring at her monitor until bleary eyed, cross-checking against personnel files images of anyone the cameras had caught at the pentagon entrances within twenty-four hours of the event, cross-checking her fingerprint matches against the same, checking all personnel files for scientists who'd worked at Cadarache, which were many. None had an obvious connection to Balard.

Damnit. T. J. abruptly got to her feet, walked out of the security of-fice into the darkened lobby. Not a word she'd read during the past hour had penetrated. She walked over to the opalescent firebird, whose wings glistened even at midnight, and pressed her forehead to the display glass. For a moment she wondered again at the mad artisan who had spent months fashioning the thing. No multitasker.

Thoughts obstinately refusing to organize themselves, she checked her messages. Nothing new in the past ten seconds. T. J. glanced at the shadowy exhibits surrounding her and glumly conceded that, maybe, truly, she wasn't cut out for science, at least at a place where the experi-ments took not seconds, not years, but lifetimes.

She returned to the office and, with a bad taste in her mouth but a curiosity she couldn't deny, went through Mac's file. He hadn't spent time in Cadarache, but Slava had and neither much liked Krieg-Zuber.

They'd already admitted bein in the power area before the accident. Krieg-Zuber's database coughed up a dozen pairs of prints that matched those she'd found in the surge room; a few were too smeared to identify. How old they were she couldn't know, but every name attached to the matches appeared on the access records. The only prints on the damned busbar were Mac's, Slava's and Lipman's. Professional amateurs, sheesh. Oh, that strange reticence of his... She'd rarely ever met anyone so diffidently smart; she'd even asked him about it. "The Greeks tell us true valor has no need to call attention to itself," he'd replied, smiling. She couldn't understand. Not to advertise was practically un-American.

To hell with this. Now an official member of Lipman's accident investigation, she sent the tech a list of people she wanted to interview tomorrow, but not until she spoke to Krieg-Zuber. She turned off the lights and slept on the floor.

* * * *

Only after Krieg-Zuber confirmed with Henderson that D'Abro was a new hire at CFRC did he agree to take her call. She spoke to him from the big field, amid the buffalos, figuring that put her out of range of cupped ears.

"How are you feeling, sir?" she asked the clean-shaven, imposing blond man of about Mac's age who stared at her from a living room chair.

"Not badly, mademoiselle, thank you. The burns are healing, my left arm is still partially paralyzed and may take some months to return to normal, but have no fear, I intent to resume the directorship as soon as possible. Only the plebian doctors have prevented me from returning already."

"As you know, we're conducting an accident investigation," T. J. said, observing even over the phone that the deputy director rarely blinked. "I need to know why you ran into the surge room against all safety regulations."

"Mademoiselle," Krieg-Zuber replied with visible, unblinking annoyance, "that has already been explained to Lipman. In my younger years I fixed tokamaks every day. By the time I arrived on the scene, technicians had already racked out the circuit breakers and the system should have been entirely discharged. Obviously it wasn't. I may be a foolish statistic now, but this far from the first electrical accident at a laboratory. You shall determine the cause."

"This is our intent, sir," T. J. answered with complete honesty as a buffalo nuzzled her. "Apparently you told Dr. Machuzak that you felt dizzy in the surge room?"

At that Krieg-Zuber cast at her a wide-eyed startled glance. "I don't remember much if anything about what happened, but yes, I told him that. Why did he ask?"

"Just a theory. He thought you might have fainted in the excitement."

The convalescent snorted disdainfully. "Hardly likely, and irrelevant. Young lady, people like Machuzak have deluded themselves into thinking that their minuscule problems, observing the dent an ion makes in a piece of titanium, grants them mastery of the universe. These humdrum physicists, engineers—they are interchangeable, their ideas, their personalities. They can be bought and sold in bulk for discount rates. You certainly don't realize it, but this war with ITER is the best thing that could have happened. Machuzak has no vision. A strange quirk of fate has catapulted him to the directorship, but be assured, he will not maintain that high position long."

"May I ask, sir, what is your vision for the laboratory, the ignition campaign?"

"ITER is a historic boondoggle. It was never subjected to true scientific scrutiny; it was an entirely political decision and is billions of euros over budget. No one believes that it can achieve ignition—"

"Then why, sir," interrupted T. J., petting the buffalo, "are you in a race?"

"We did not ask for this, but now we must win." Krieg-Zuber clenched his fist. "The world must know that fusion can be a reality and for a smaller cost than ITER—"

"ASSET is a ten-billion-dollar machine, sir, and it's a tokamak."

"Not all tokamaks are identical, mademoiselle, and as CFRC is overwhelmingly privately funded, no one can accuse it of siphoning money from other research."

"Could you tell me, sir," it suddenly occurred to T. J. to ask, "what ideas you have contributed to ASSET to make it different from ITER?"

"Ideas? Miss D'Abro, that has been explained to you one minute ago," he said with his unnerving stare. "Ideas in science are a dime a dozen. If one person doesn't have an idea, another will. No one cares who has the ideas. The man who understands people, mademoiselle, he is the man who changes history. I have led this project. There can be no greater contribution."

Krieg-Zuber's scoff or sneer or condescension would have been impossible to surpass. "I see..." said T. J. pensively. "May I ask one other question? Have you worked at Cadarache?"

"I visited for a few months four or five years ago. What, young lady, can that *possibly* have to do with the accident?"

"Nothin really, but y'all seem like a big, incestuous family, you physicists. You're friends with your rivals and rivals with your friends and have no allegiances except to the place you've parked your overnight bag. Well, thank you, Dr. Krieg-Zoober. I'll send you a copy of the report."

T. J. signed off, uncertain of Krieg-Zuber's vision for Prometheus, certain that every one of these high-minded folks wanted fusion on their own terms and no one was about to retreat. She walked back across the field toward the pentagon. It was time to interview the techs.

* * * *

They all had plausible stories. Red Ehlers had been down there just twenty-four hours before the dedication, doing some last minute high-potting. What that meant, T. J. hadn't the faintest, but in the gloomy dungeon he demonstrated, as did the other techs. She began to understand why judges hated expert witnesses.

Their resentment at recent events leaked through everything they said. "The Terminator saw two guys having a mock knife-fight with screwdrivers"—Frosty Patton spat on the floor—"and fired them on the spot. If they were still around, they'd have thrown the big ass into the surge room themselves."

By evening, T. J. had a numbing headache and no more reason to believe one tech wanted to sabotage the machine more than the next—or had refrained. It seemed unlikely to her that the techs were involved. How would a tech have known she and Slava were in Cadarache? Well, Slava had said it: by the second day probably every plasma physicist in the world knew their location with GPS precision. That wasn't the point. How many knew *why* they were there? A tech? No way. Had Balard guessed?

T. J. returned to the security office and stayed late again. The DNA tests came in that evening. Progress. There'd been a few samples on the busbar. She'd retrieved one of Slava's hairs from her sweater after the Cadarache incident and one of Mac's from her couch. With a knot in her stomach, she'd sent both in for testing. The results left no room for interpretation.

She'd also found a few hairs in the surge-room vicinity and those tests had come back too, but unless she broke cover she couldn't get elimination samples. Fuck… She wandered again out into the lobby and peered into the firebird's display case. "Why don't you help, bird?" The unblinking jeweled eyes merely stared at her.

Abruptly T. J. glanced over her shoulder, but the only other occupants of the lobby were shadows and her own echo. She felt very stuck and she needed a drink. T. J. closed the security office door and this time went home.

* * * *

By morning the Real World under subpoena had turned over their logged IP addresses for Dragonmaster. Meeting Nathaniel and Slava early in the MTF, T. J. gave them the bad news. The addresses led to a server near Cadarache. The two physicists glanced at each other. "You were right, Mac," she bowed. "It's a proxy that disguises the original address."

"I'd have been surprised had it been otherwise," remarked Slava.

Machuzak pondered their situation. "I suppose that means we need another subpoena," he eventually replied.

"Doc, you don't get it. I can't subpoena a French service provider. I'd need cooperation from the French law enforcement agencies, and to get that…"

She stared at him significantly, but Nathaniel had no intention of resurrecting his adolescent hacking skills; the idea daunted and disgusted him equally.

Archangelsky felt the same. "Looks like it's time to launch your infomercial, Boss," he said.

They huddled around the computer and Nathaniel posted his video, with enhanced graphics, on CFRC's website and then on the big video sites. Forty-eight seconds later the first burst of rage and disbelief came back from ITER. Machuzak nodded. Good. By the time this morning's ignition meeting was over, the announcement should have gone viral.

* * * *

The division heads were watching the video as Nathaniel entered the conference room and met him with fierce outcries from all sides. "What the hell have you done, Machuzak?" Diana Cochran shouted. "It's a bald-faced lie."

Absolutely. He feigned a smile and lied again: "It's only to keep ITER off balance."

At which Thad Hasschler exploded. "Off balance! You have made what was impossible inconceivable! Not only Balard, but the whole world will be breathing down our necks and know us for frauds!"

"If you don't want the world to know us for frauds," Nathaniel now answered icily, "I suggest you come up with some ideas. You're *way* behind schedule." With that he canceled further ignition meetings and left.

TWENTY-ONE

An hour later, blogs being posted on the four corners of the Earth but no sign of Dragonmaster, Machuzak headed to the pentagon, hoping that if the damned physicists couldn't keep a level head, his chief engineer could.

Nathaniel found Abbuhl in the test cell, where now two balloons of Edvard Munch's *Scream* face guarded the entrance. Technicians had sealed up the torus a few days ago and had been pumping hard on it since. Leak checks were proceeding. Machuzak stood at Fred's side watching the techs climb in and out of the cryostat as they sprayed helium gas over every surface of the inner vessel. Meters below, diagnosticians checked whether the helium showed up in the vacuum-pump exhaust.

"Looks good," Andy Lipman reported. "Seals are tight."

Machuzak audibly expelled a quantum of tension. They'd run into no major catastrophes, like the plastic pails or latex gloves that techs had sometimes inadvertently left in machines after the hand washing, household items which easily contained enough gas to destroy the vacuum they were attempting to achieve. More than once the discovery of such objects had cost them months while the tokamak was brought up to room pressure and reopened. The thought sobered: a rubber glove in the wrong place today would be the perfect sabotage. Our nemesis should have thought of it. But he hadn't: after days of pumping the gauges would have already hit a latex iceberg.

"When can you begin the bake?" Machuzak asked.

"Mac," said Abbuhl, "you know as well as I do that it takes a week to get down to operating pressure." Meaning no pressure at all, one hundred billionth of an atmosphere.

Once there, Abbuhl would begin the vessel bake, heating the torus to nearly 400 degrees Celsius to drive out recalcitrant impurities and water. That would take…

"Mac, sir, even Balard can't rush this. The bakeout before the dedication took two weeks."

"Push it," said Machuzak and winced even as he uttered the words.

Abbuhl glanced sideward at him. "*Herr Doktor* Professor, let ITER fuck itself."

Nathaniel barely heard him; he was already considering helium. While the torus baked, the big cryostat surrounding it would be pumped out too. After ITER's, it was the world's largest vacuum vessel. More leak checks. The magnets themselves would then be flooded with liquid helium, slowly bringing them down to operating temperatures, 4.2 degrees absolute. Should they get there, the hottest place in the solar system would reside next to one of the coldest, only a vacuum jacket separating them. Machuzak was grateful that vacuums are the best insulator.

Three weeks for the cooldown. At the same time Abbuhl's team would be checking out the heating systems. "How long to condition the neutral beams and the rf drives?" Nathaniel asked.

"Mac, it takes a month—you know that as well as I do."

"Push it," said Machuzak and left the test cell without waiting for the chief's protest.

* * * *

He found Diana Cochran conferring with two of her engineers in the cryoplant, which occupied pentagon No. 3. The trio stood below the nitrogen factory with its boxlike plant towering above and its maze of multicolored pipe-works and holding tanks that resembled supersized hot dogs. To the best of Machuzak's knowledge, it was the second-largest liquid nitrogen factory in the world and the helium factory near it was larger. They both churned 24/7, 365 days a year.

Nathaniel approached and perceived that Cochran's expression was not welcoming. "What's wrong?" he asked. The others could hardly hear him over the high-pitched whine of the compressors.

First she scowled. "We've been getting nonstop response videos about your commercial, Machuzak. You really raised the stakes with that one. We needed this like a hornet up our ass."

"What else?" Nathaniel said; he always felt itchy around Cochran.

"One of the nitrogen refrigerators failed," she answered above the noise. "We're going to have to replace the motor."

"What about helium? Abbuhl's ready to start cooling." That was a stretch.

"The tap is on."

"Make sure it stays on. I want that machine superconducting in two weeks." A larger stretch.

Cochran turned away from him and muttered something, which the noise rendered indistinct. He thought he heard, "If I were you, Machuzak, I'd pray."

It suddenly felt like he'd been doing that his whole life.

* * * *

The afternoon had half run its course when Machuzak's wrist, handset and office phone went off simultaneously. "This is it," he whispered to Slava, who'd just stopped by. Too late he realized that it was not the Real World pinging him but an obscure, unfamiliar website. Even as they ran outside to the fountain they got a rough fix on its URL: Cadarache.

Within a moment Machuzak found himself walking along a desolate plain at twilight. To one side, on a beach under a black-red sun, he spied a group of small creatures, which for some reason he took to be the Eloi, huddled around a campfire while they filled the air with a final song. As he traveled along the plain, to either side stood ruins of past civilizations. Here the stark pillars of the Roman forum, there the colossal wreckage of the Bibi-Khanym mosque in Samarkand and the remains of Ulugbeg's observatory. Farther on, the Parthenon, a pile of rubble that was once the great Buddha at Bamiyan, a half-excavated Pompeii with its ash-encrusted mummies, casts of citizens in the final moments of their lives as they futilely struggled to escape the inescapable. Nearby, the Qin Emperor's tomb, with its row upon row of terra-cotta warriors, here headless, armless, lifeless.

As he passed the mummies, one rose and approached. "You have ignored my warnings," it said in a thick Scottish brogue.

Not in the mood for games, Nathaniel grabbed the mummy by the throat. "Are you the saboteur or are you trying to help?" he demanded, his pent-up anger and frustration surging forth.

"If you persist, Prometheus will be destroyed," the mummy said flatly with blank eyes that revealed nothing.

An instant passed before the words sank in. When they did, Machuzak reeled. Dragonmaster's two previous messages might have been ambiguous. Not this one. "Who is going to destroy it, damnit?"

"Not to act is to act," the mummy replied.

"Tell us what you know!" Nathaniel shouted but the avatar had already dissolved in his hands.

Under the fountain Archangelsky sighed. "At least there were no flying samurai."

For his part, Nathaniel remained silent long. "Looks like Dragonmaster knew we'd staked out the Real World," he finally said.

Slava glanced around, pausing at a wild turkey that had wandered onto the drive. "Not clear. Maybe he was just smart enough not to show up on same website too many times. He must realize we are after him."

"Not to act is to act," Nathaniel muttered, stomach knotted again as in the past days. "I destroy the machine by continuing on course…?"

"You could abandon the effort," Slava proposed heavily. "We have no chance anyway."

"Damnit!" Machuzak exploded again. "How can we do that now?"

Slava stared hard at him with a beard glistening from the spray. "Nat Edward'ich, avoid becoming Krieg-Zuber. You give the word, project ends. Lab ends. ITER wins. Machine survives, no one is hurt."

"I give the word, Krieg-Zuber steps in."

The two men stood facing each other until the Russian bit his lip. "Well, Dragonmaster has outfoxed us. He won't appear in Real World again. We need way through that proxy server, or around it." As Machuzak cursed aloud, Archangelsky offered the latest on the Cadarache video: "I contacted Asians. No surprise Japanese fellow is at what's left of Naka Fusion Institute, the Korean was at KBSI—" that was the Korean Basic Science Institute, site of Korea's fusion program. "The Chinese are at Hefei, of course."

"They all check out?"

Slava nodded. "That leaves only one person unaccounted for."

"Who's that?"

"Whoever shot video."

Nathaniel peered at the Russian. He had half a mind to throw Archangelsky on a plane, but said only, "Find him," and, "You're also going to start showing up to ignition meetings."

"They've been canceled," the Russian replied.

* * * *

The complexes at CFRC were already sparkling with the glow of evening when T. J. appeared at the MTF. She wasn't happy to learn about the meeting at the End of the World, not one bit. What they needed was help from the FBI Cyber Division, which wasn't gonna happen. "You say this server was Cadarache again?"

"Doesn't mean a damn thing," Machuzak growled, still seething, "and you know it." He cut off further discussion by showing her some of the messages that had been pouring in throughout the day: nearly two hundred from France alone. She didn't need to be a physicist to see that the ITER team had gone ballistic over Mac's infomercial and was already planning tests for later in the week, just to stick it to CFRC. His attempt to bait the Dragonmaster, Nathaniel acknowledged, had unquestionably failed in every purpose except to put them in a more precarious position than they'd already been in. Hasschler was very right about that…

"It was a good idea," T. J. offered, "even if it hasn't worked."

"Slava's ready to throw in the towel—"

"Don't."

The ever-present clacking of the vacuum pumps receded under the plea in her voice, but Machuzak's only reaction was to strike the desk hard with his fist. At that moment a call from Abbuhl came in. His team had located a cracked flange on one of the neutral-beam boxes. "I'll be right there." He took D'Abro by the hand and fifteen silent minutes later they stood in the test cell with Abbuhl. Luckily, it was no emergency. The chief told them that they'd need to replace the flange and pump the box down again, but there was no further damage and the vacuum in the cryostat was holding. Then he vanished to take care of other business.

D'Abro glanced up at the massive steel monoliths covered with cable, and perhaps wanting to change the tone of their previous conversation whispered, "It's way past time you explained to me what these damned things are. Maybe if I knew, it might help with this here investigation. As far as I've made out, neutral beams have something to do with heating that plasma to twenty times the temperature of the sun, but your household Radar Range doesn't come close, does it?"

"Well," Machuzak began slowly, if nothing else also wanting to change the previous conversation, "after holding the plasma, heating it is our biggest headache. A tokamak being the world's largest contraption, we use several methods." Apart from merely squeezing the plasma with the magnets, which wasn't popular because of the water balloon problem he'd explained last week, there was the toaster method, there was in fact the Radar Range method and there was the billiard-ball method.

"The toaster method is pretty simple minded. A plasma is like toaster wire; zap it with a few million amps and it heats up. But it's sort of a reverse toaster wire—the hotter it gets, the less it wants to heat up further, until it stops, period. The toaster method gets you only to twenty or thirty million degrees."

"Only," T. J. grunted, wondering what the incomprehensible amount of plumbing above her was for, wondering whether nanobots could change her hair color.

"Yeah. You can do better with the Radar Range method. We call it rf—radio frequency heating." Machuzak pointed to the racks of microwave guides running into the test cell above their heads and disappearing into Prometheus. "Essentially we nuke the fuel with microwaves and on a good day it heats it up beyond what the toaster method can achieve. But to get the temperature way up we use the neutral beams—"

T. J. stopped crunching the peanuts in her mouth and said, "Go on—the suspense is killing me."

Machuzak nodded. "These huge boxes are actually particle accelerators, which accelerate deuterium and tritium to high energy and inject them directly into the plasma. The nuclei collide with the particles already inside the torus and—"

"A break shot," T. J. interrupted, now with him. "Cue ball slows down, other balls speed up. Doesn't sound so complicated, Doc. You might have told me before."

Nathaniel laughed soberly. "Bedbug, the devil is much in the details. The electric field in the beam boxes can only accelerate charged particles like deuterium and tritium nuclei. Fine. But the Earth's magnetic field deflects cosmic rays. How do you get charged nuclei past the tokamak's own magnetic field into the machine?"

The cocky expression on D'Abro's face dissolved. "Let's just say we do a fast two-step—we change the neutral tritium and deuterium atoms into charged ions by adding electrons, accelerate them, then strip away the extra electrons to neutralize them again. Then the deuterium and tritium can pass through the tokamak's magnetic field and clobber the particles inside. Sort of a bait-and-switch operation. The neutral beams not only supply the fuel, but bring it up to operating regimes, four hundred million degrees."

"Humph," T. J. snorted pensively, then abruptly asked whether there was reason to sabotage the neutral beams as opposed to anything else.

Not that Machuzak could think of. "It's one of the biggest systems and dozens of people work on it. As you see." Techs were already swarming around the cracked flange.

"Well," she said, "I think I'm gonna visit with Krieg-Zoober." Nathaniel cocked his head at her. "He's back on-site today. By the way, Doc, I've been meanin to say, about that night at my place…"

"I know, don't worry about it."

"I'm not worrying," she smiled bravely, and they parted company.

TWENTY-TWO

Moments later, T. J. rapped on the third-floor door of Cyrus Krieg-Zuber's office, glancing at the posters of the Arc de Triomphe, Napoleon's tomb, the pyramids and Westminster Abbey hanging in the interstices of the teak cabinets that lined his spacious office walls. This was the first time she'd actually seen him in the flesh. She'd read his personnel file with the others and knew that Rasmussen had originally recruited Krieg-Zuber about ten years ago from Advanced Cryotech, which had manufactured ASSET's magnets, and where he'd received some highfalutin CIA security training. He'd spent time at various ITER sites but as deputy director at CFRC had become Rasmussen's right-hand man and four years ago decided to tighten up security. That's when things, as Mac told it, began to go seriously amiss.

The man who sat at his monitor today wore a blue silk shirt and necktie and grumbled even as he stood up, his left arm hanging somewhat stiffly at his side. "He has shut out the director, he believes..." he spat, annoyed at having to adjust his tie with a bad hand.

"Dr. Krieg-Zoober," T. J. said, already unsettled by the man's wide, unblinking ice-blue eyes, "I'm surprised you're in. What brings you here?"

"Zubér. Mademoiselle D'Abro, isn't it? What do idiot doctors know? No one can prevent the director from performing his duties. To what do I owe the pleasure of this visit?" T. J. was equally unsettled by his demeanor, bow-string taught. Before she could answer, he interrupted himself. "You have obviously seen the video that was launched this morning, if you did not assist in producing it. What could have possessed Machuzak to make such untrue and hazardous statements?" He trained an incendiary stare on her and she involuntarily backed up a step.

"I believe Dr. Machuzak wanted to light a fire under the division heads," she swallowed, suddenly doubting that this man and the one she'd spoken to by phone were entirely the same. "Get their asses in gear."

But the two were the same, externally. The deputy director paused, running a finger along the scar on his face. "Mademoiselle, if one wanted to 'light a fire' under the division heads—quaintly put—far more effective tactics may be brought to bear. Threaten them with replacement, announce that we have offers of help from the best Japanese, Korean and Chinese teams. Shame is a most compelling weapon against cowards who shirk from laying down their lives for their cause."

T. J. regarded with curiosity a small sculpture of San Sebastian hung on the wall, complete with dripping wounds and piercing arrows. "Dr. Krieg-Zubér," she said sweetly, turning her glance slowly from the statue, "why not just line them up against a wall and shoot them?"

A thin smile spread across Zuber's lips and he blinked once, slowly. "A sufficient threat should suffice..." He walked to his desk, put his nose to a flower, then raised his head so that he appeared be staring up at her almost through his eyelids. "You have come about the accident investigation."

"Exactly, sir."

At that Krieg-Zuber gazed at her in amazement for an instant, then nearly spat out a laugh impossible for him to contain. "You cannot expect anyone to take such a charade seriously!" he snarled. "With the ignition campaign under way, crucial evidence has already been erased. You will find nothing—if you ever intended to."

T. J. now shut the door behind her, leaned against it. "I came to find out what you remember."

"Mademoiselle," Krieg-Zuber answered with dripping fatigue, "stop playing games. You have been told what I remember. If you are truly attempting to get to the bottom of this, then you have been examining access records and our pitiful supply of surveillance files. You surely cannot be so naïve to believe this was an accident, can you?"

"What makes you think that?" T. J. said, suddenly feeling more nervous than she hoped she appeared.

"There are no accidents in this world, Miss D'Abro, but there are myriad enemies who would like to see this program end, apart from Moravec. Look at my arm!" he exploded without warning. "What they have done to me!"

"Sir, someone in your condition should take it easy," T. J. said, nearly jumping backward as Zuber stooped to examine his own desk for bugs. "Can you be more specific?" she ventured, hoping that she continued to prop up her innocence. "I mean, about who would like to see the program end?"

"No," Krieg-Zuber answered, abruptly breaking off his search and sitting down at his desk, where he began to play absently with the toy trains there. "But there is more here than meets the eye."

T. J. frowned at the cliché, at the same time dying to know what this man knew. "Well, sir, if there is, I hope to discover it, but the surveillance records haven't been as helpful as I'd hoped."

"How surprising." He no longer attempted to disguise the sneer in his voice. "The people who designed the CFRC security system were amateurs, but there are other records."

"I am aware that you monitor email, Dr. Krieg-Zuber—"

"Routine!" The wave was angry as he got to his feet again. "CFRC has completely lagged behind the times. You have, young lady, undoubtedly noticed that the damned fingerprint-reader system has not yet even gone online."

In one sense it had. "I also know that you were monitoring all Internet traffic to this laboratory." T. J. thought that Krieg-Zuber paused and cocked his head at her, but then decided no. She was finding him difficult to read, since his penetrating stare met her eyes and did not.

"Accepted practice and legal," he said, with slightly less anger. "Surely you do not need to be reminded that CFRC is a private lab." T. J. couldn't argue. The practice *was* accepted and legal, and it hadn't disturbed her nearly as much as it had Mac. "Stupidly," Zuber went on, "Machuzak has pulled the plug; this you obviously know."

"Are you offering something, sir?" she asked.

For a moment Krieg-Zuber glanced at his arm sorrowfully, whimpered, said, "The director's archives are yours, mademoiselle."

At that he fairly bowed toward her, but in a way that his blank eyes made T. J. uncertain that she was present. "Tell me, Dr. Krieg-Zuber," she said, swallowing, "a random question: have you ever met Pierre Balard?"

Zuber stroked his chin thrice, nodded. "Certainly."

"Is it true that he was Dr. Rasmussen's first doctoral student?" T. J.'s question was genuine and Krieg-Zuber's smile knowing.

"Quite true," he replied. "Balard despised Rasmussen for stealing his ideas, which were significant. They haven't spoken to each other for twenty years."

"As I suspected," T. J. answered. "I'll let you know if I require your assistance, Dr. Krieg-Zuber." With that she opened the door, noticed the damp she left on the knob, and stepped into the hall, feeling no less stuck than she had for the past days, and a notch more ill at ease.

TWENTY-THREE

Machuzak, Fred Abbuhl and Diana Cochran stood in the ASSET control room, watching the downward tremble of the temperature gauges. The cryostat had been pumped down to a billionth of an atmosphere, a vacuum that would serve to insulate the magnets, and liquid helium was flowing from the helium factory into Prometheus' great coils. The cooldown had begun. Fred had been right: they could hardly hope for better than a degree an hour and that would mean—weeks. Someone had hung a big deadline calendar under the captain's deck, with more than two weeks crossed out. They'd heard nothing from Dragonmaster since the encounter in the ruins and Nathaniel could only wonder which of the remaining dates was marked.

"Is extra tritium coming in from Savannah River?" he asked.

"Kettering ordered it over a week ago," Abbuhl replied. "We should have a shipment in a couple days."

Cochran was not happy. "There's another helium shortage in Amarillo," she told them and Machuzak understood. The Federal Helium Reserve in the panhandle produced a third of the world's helium supply, but over the past decade industrial demand had risen ten times faster than predicted and they'd intermittently been running dry. The spiking prices meant that helium cost fifty times what it had a few decades back. "If we have to bring Prometheus up again…"

"I know, pray." Nathaniel bit his lip, trusted that Diana was merely engaged in her habitual grousing. Prometheus and the helium factory form a closed loop and there should be no losses. Under normal circumstances. He took his leave.

* * * *

T. J. intercepted Machuzak at lunchtime on his way to the cafeteria, a pseudo Spanish-style mezzanine of pink marble that opened to the back courtyard. The same constrained agitation gripped him now as the other evening, and unfortunately, she was not about to make his life easier. She pointed her handset at him, he glanced at it, frowned in her direction, walked over to a microphone that stood before a big mural of cowboys riding into the sunset. Bill Balustradi had taped his smiling face over one of the cacti.

"Today ITER has begun DT experiments," Machuzak announced. Exactly as threatened, Balard had skipped the low-yield DD, going directly to deuterium-tritium. These were just low-power test pulses but it meant that ITER had suddenly jumped ahead of CFRC by a month. At Nathaniel's words, a veil descended over the cafeteria and silenced it. Good, we deserve this. Together he and T. J. descended with sandwiches from the mezzanine to a picnic table below.

D'Abro gazed across the grassy place, which yielded to asphalt and the pentagon in one direction, to vast fields and Site Alpha in the other, and turned to Nathaniel. She had intended to report her meeting with Krieg-Zuber. Instead, observing his dark expression, she said, "What is it, Doc?" even as she knew the answer. Suddenly she wanted to take his hand.

"Damnit, T. J.," he erupted, "what good is having a machine when you have no idea of what to do with it?"

Before she could respond, her attention was distracted by a slim figure who entered the courtyard, walked up to the big oak and looped a small wooden tablet over one of the branches, where it began to rattle hollowly in the breeze with all the others. For a brief moment he stood with his head bowed, then walked toward the cafeteria.

"Who's that?" T. J. asked.

"That"—Nathaniel clenched his teeth as he rose—"is Toshi." He strode over to the older physicist, grabbed his arm and dragged him back to the table. "Where the hell have you been?" he demanded angrily. "I've been looking high and low for you—office, home… You dropped off the face of the Earth. Who do you think you are, a killer bee?"

The older physicist only shrugged and sat down cross-legged on the grass before the fishpond, where he opened a container of rice. Finally he said, "I have been doing geometry problems."

"Geometry problems! Damnit, Matsushima, in case you haven't heard, I canceled the ignition meetings because no one has come up with a single decent idea—"

"This is not surprising," Toshi replied, gazing straight ahead. "What do you expect from a group of people who exist only as appendages to computer terminals? They have never learned how to think, only to calculate. They have never learned that where heaven and Earth meet, this is where you have attained proficiency in the art of swordsmanship. This is where knowledge lost is knowledge gained, where to win is no more than to lose." Briefly he halted. "And why, Nathaniel, do you think these bots will accept my ideas any more than they have in the past?"

Listening, T. J. was instantly captivated by Matsushima, but at last a shadow of perspicacity fell. "Dr. Matsushima, sir, doesn't this lab mean anything to you?" The question surprised her as much as the others and Matsushima's silence was uncomfortably, disturbingly long. "Doesn't the future mean anything to you?" she continued with an even more importunate tone when he didn't answer.

"There are many futures, Miss D'Abro," the physicist finally replied, "but the gods have not given us the vision to choose the one we want."

"If we don't choose, who then?" she said, verging on despair. "Didn't all those gurus used to say, 'Not to decide is to decide'? Haven't we not decided on this planet too long? Dr. Matsushima, if you people don't decide, who? I'd really like to know." She squinted at him fiercely until she embarrassed herself. "Excuse me, Professor. I'm out of line." She turned away, blushing as the physicist stared with a puzzled expression.

Not to act is to act, Nathaniel couldn't help thinking, but seeing the state of these two, he attempted to rescue both. "Toshi, I know how you feel about Krieg-Zuber and being out in Alpha Site—"

"Do you, Nathaniel? What do you, a mere foot soldier, know? These rumors that I believe in levitation and ESP? Being reduced to foraging for funds when I should have been creating. Here I am, banished to Alpha, where I am invisible and shorn of respect. I might have changed the entire fusion program had anyone listened to me."

"I am sorry about what Krieg-Zuber has done to you—"

"Krieg-Zuber!" Toshi snorted.

T. J. was following the exchange with widening discomfort, uneasily deciding to check Matsushima's file. She saw equally Mac's displeasure at being stripped of rank and expected him to anger again, but he did not. Instead he answered, "'They are forever free who renounce all selfish desires and break away from the cage of *I, me* and *mine* to be united with the Lord. This is the supreme state.' Toshi, if you could only listen to yourself."

The older man stared at Mac momentarily with an annoyed expression, which then saddened. "Do not be clever, Nathaniel."

"I am not being clever, Toshi," he said, shaking his head with a sadness that exceeded Matsushima's own. "I am asking you to put aside your feelings and turn your talents to the task that called us when we were young and idealistic, when we willingly, bravely became scientists to understand the intricacies of Nature and with our understanding turn her to the benefit of the future. Maybe Nature will not bend, outwit us as she always does, but let us make our struggle with her, with our understanding, not with the past or with personalities we dislike. Let us act without regard to rewards or consequences, and we will succeed even in failure."

"Again you try to outwit me, Nathaniel. When the Master governs, the people barely know he exists. I see you are becoming a master. My compliments."

"Please, Dr. Matsushima," T. J. entreated, again surprising herself.

Once more, Toshi agreed only to consider the request, but his reply was amiable enough that T. J. allowed herself to rise. The two physicists watched her walk over to the oak, where Toshi hung worthy geometry problems, and she began turning the tablets over one by one, pressing the flat of her hands against them, even sniffing them, as if by these actions she could absorb the mathematics she so claimed to dread.

"Sacred geometry," she said almost to herself as she returned to the pair, staring in befuddled wonder at Matsushima.

Toshi overheard. "Ah," he said, "who knows what is sacred in the world of Samsung and Toyota? But many are the gods to be propitiated and hopefully a few digest mathematics."

"Professor," T. J. asked, at this moment with more genuine curiosity than professional acumen, "I've heard a lot about you, but I don't think I know what you do here."

Matsushima, calmer now, leaned back on the grass and smiled. "Miss D'Abro—that is your name I believe—it is quite clear none of us know what we are doing here. As for me, I am robbing the rich." T. J. asked for his meaning. "Since my present ideas are considered—how do we say it in polite company?—not to lie along the Eight-Fold Path, I am forced to beg alms on the street."

Nathaniel put in that Garrett paid Toshi out of his own pocket.

"What sort of ideas are you talking about, professor?" T. J. pressed, her conversation with Balard suddenly loud in her ears.

But Toshi only snorted. "Miss D'Abro, it is not the ideas; it is the implementation of the ideas. Ideas are cheap. Machines are expensive. When the US government trashed all approaches to fusion beyond the tokamak, it was rolling billion-dollar dice, not to mention our future. Of course, partisans claimed the other devices never would have worked, but some of them were simpler than tokamaks, being mere cylinders rather than doughnuts, and with a few modifications they might have outperformed America's favorite. Geometry, Miss D'Abro, is destiny and it is far easier to remove the waste products of fusion from the ends of a tube than from a doughnut, and to service the machine. You wrinkle your nose. Indeed, these are practical concerns—hardly poetic, but they are important for a real, not imaginary reactor. A tokamak, in my view, is an imaginary reactor."

"Why is that, Dr. Matsushima?" In Toshi's remarks, T. J. heard an echo of Archangelsky's on the airplane. After three weeks at CFRC she had begun to perceive the deeper faults in this hermetic community, and now she wondered whether she had too jokingly called it a pit of vipers.

"Oh, everyone knows how tokamaks are prone to failure. I imagine a field the size of several football stadiums filled with giant tokamaks, such that when one nosedives and requires servicing, another is brought online. Each of these machines should be five times the size of ITER, volumewise—"

"Five times the size of ITER!" T. J. choked. Her first sight of that unbelievable construct, and her reaction to it, returned in full force.

"Oh yes. This is when Nature bestows her favor on tokamaks. But to attempt fusion with something so insignificant as ITER or ASSET is a waste of time. Of course, none of these ideas helps us in our current predicament, but there are more subtle possibilities that might allow us to cheat a deadline. They involve technical matters that I am sure do not interest you. Now, if you'll excuse me, Miss D'Abro. It has been a pleasure."

* * * *

Toshi got to his feet and moved off, leaving the other two alone. "What a character!" T. J. blurted out, then abruptly, soberly peered at Machuzak and whispered, "Doc, is he angry enough to have done it?"

Nathaniel replied with a strange disgust etched across his face. "I trust him more than anyone, except Slava perhaps. He's a difficult, vain man who sees everything with crystal clarity—except himself. I suppose in that he is human." For another moment Machuzak continued to gaze intently at T. J., then he nodded with comprehension and switched off.

D'Abro saw that Machuzak had just become one step more of a stranger. "You really don't think I trust you, Doc, do you?" she said after one heartbeat, then another. "Even now?" The anguish in her voice was audible.

"It's your duty not to trust me," he replied. "I don't hold it against you."

The genuine equanimity of his response coerced from her an incredulous shake of the head. "Sometimes you don't make it easy, partner," she began, but he'd already changed course.

"Maybe Abbuhl is right—you can't hurry the process."

"Huh?" T. J. asked, not following.

"They say it's important to be stuck," Machuzak replied, as if somewhere else. "You know, Siddhartha wandered for six years before he sat himself under a fig tree, where for forty-nine days he was assailed by every force and temptation. When he finally arose, he was the Buddha. It is necessary to be stuck."

"I'll order a fig tree planted in the courtyard," T. J. said quietly.

Machuzak's only response was to stand and clench his fist. "It cannot be as difficult to achieve ignition as enlightenment."

"I hope you're right about that, Doc," she said with continued wonder, "because we are truly, truly stuck."

That state lasted another minute.

TWENTY-FOUR

Machuzak's wrist and handset when off simultaneously, as well as the laboratory's emergency warning system. An instant later, Abbuhl was on the air, paging him.

"Mac, sir, you'd better get down to the neutral-beam area. Fast."

Machuzak clicked off, not entirely understanding what had hit him; he grabbed T. J. by the arm and ran.

"It's happened, hasn't it?" she managed.

"I don't know, but when Fred Abbuhl sounds like that, it isn't good."

They sprinted at full speed out of the courtyard, across the asphalt and to the pentagon. With a yank, they picked up Slava, who stood rubbernecking in the crowd already gathering by the test cell entrance, and shoved their way inside.

"Where's Abbuhl?" Machuzak shouted.

He got no coherent response. "Downstairs," someone finally answered and the three clambered downward, still pushing their way past equipment and onlookers, all of an unearthly pallor under the sodium lights. Siren wails growing louder each second gave Machuzak an intense sense of déjà vu. With half the lab in tow they reached the neutral-beam supply area and the surge room, what was left of it. Abbuhl stood in front of the door, which had been blown outward, as if a bomb had gone off in a ship's hull. The inside was a tangled mess and a confusion of smells. Two technicians sat on the concrete floor nearby, bleeding; one lay stretched out, badly mangled and unmoving.

Lipman.

Machuzak knelt beside the tech's body and put his hand on the bloody chest. "No!" he roared in futile defiance. "No!" Abbuhl and D'Abro pulled him to his feet.

"Sir..."

Machuzak shook them loose, breathing hard, and walked over to Faberman, one of the survivors, who lay against one of the huge girders supporting Prometheus above. "Are you, okay, George?" he asked, kneeling again. Faberman admitted that he'd felt better. "What happened, can you tell me?"

The tech nodded. "The schedule's tight, you know…" Yeah, Machuzak knew. Come on, George, don't faint on me now. "The sulfur hexafluoride in the switches was low, so we refilled them this morning. Just now we were checking the ignitrons. Suddenly there was this explosion…"

Nathaniel stood up. Sulfur hexafluoride? Explosion. What? Sulfur hexafluoride is an inert gas. This wasn't even the same surge room where Cyrus the Great had touched lightning. Instantly, everything became clear. It was one of those moments you live for as a scientist, when you see a problem clean through, when the pieces of the puzzle suddenly fall into place. Machuzak cursed. Why hadn't he seen it before? "Where's the SF_6 bottle?"

Faberman pointed to a nearby alcove. The bottle was one of many, the usual gray, labeled sulfur hexafluoride. "Does anybody have a balloon?" Nathaniel asked. "A plastic bag? Something?" His eyes surveyed the crowd. After a few moments, someone produced a condom. Machuzak filled it, tied it off, put a match to it. With a loud pop, it exploded, a miniature Hindenburg. Every face in the crowd was etched with the same astonishment.

"Sulfur hexafluoride, my ass."

"But Mac, sir," said Fred, as the astonishment transformed into perplexity. "Flammable gas bottles have left-hand threads."

"Yeah."

Nathaniel told Abbuhl to deal with the emergency people but refer any questions to him. Grabbing Slava and T. J., he led them away from the pentagon, but not before he and T. J. loaded the bottle on its dolly into the freight elevator. And not before she turned to Abbuhl and said, with ringing authority, "Nobody, I repeat, nobody, enters this area. Nobody touches those cylinders. If anybody tries," she looks Fred straight in the eyes, "shoot him."

When they were barricaded in the MTF, Nathaniel glanced from one to the other, lasers beaming from his own pupils… Did they understand?

"Looks like your gas theory was correct, brother," Slava said, putting a cigarette to his mouth. "After all."

"Yeah, wrong gas."

"Huh?" said T. J., struggling to keep up.

"Deuterium," Nathaniel explained. "Chemically it's just hydrogen. Explosive. The lab's full of it." He waved his arm over his own space. "For the taking. No one keeps track of it."

"Whoa," T. J. insisted, silencing her phone. "This wasn't a second strike?"

Nathaniel shook his head. "Almost certainly not."

"Then what the hell happened?"

"What happened, three weeks ago, is that during the demonstration, someone had a deuterium bottle venting gas into the surge room. By cutting the busbar in half, the saboteur created a spark gap. He was hoping that at a high enough voltage he'd get a spark and blow the neutral-beam supply to bits. This was no sophomoric prank to stop a demo. He was trying to spike the machine."

"Clever idea," said Slava. "You must admit."

Always the scientist's appreciation for the technically sweet. Machuzak did not find himself filled with admiration.

Why didn't it work? the detective wanted to know.

"As I recall, we got a fault light before the highest tap, just before going to half a million volts. I don't know, maybe he was counting on a spark at the highest voltage. The gap itself knocked out the protection circuitry, so it must have caused a component to fry in time. The saboteur defeated himself."

"No quite," Slava remarked, contemplating his unlit cigarette.

Machuzak nodded. "Krieg-Zuber—you, me—we did get dizzy, not from nitrogen or sulfur hexafluoride, but from hydrogen."

"Why'd it blow today?"

"You heard Faberman. The techs refilled the high-voltage switches with this insulating gas, sulfur hexafluoride—what they thought was sulfur hexafluoride. Then they started testing the ignitrons, those giant crowbars that short the circuit in an emergency. Ignitrons have real spark gaps in them and when they fire, they truly fire. The saboteur got his spark all right, just a few weeks late." The switches, as usual, were leaky.

D'Abro was shaking her head sadly as the lab phone began to ring. "There's no way I could have pieced all this together."

Machuzak sympathized; the admission must be hard for the young woman. "T. J., no one expected you to. Anyway, it took an explosion to bring me to my senses."

T. J. now returned the favor. "You expected to get all that?"

"If I'd thought of deuterium, Lipman would be alive."

"Doc," T. J. stretched out her hand, "nobody can live with standards like that."

"Nat Edward'ich," Slava put in, "she is correct. Your intuition was amazing. I salute you. But there was no way to have seen everything."

Nathaniel breathed deeply and silenced all the ringing phones. "Okay. Maybe we at least have a decent clue—a deuterium bottle."

"They'll be some prints for sure, if not dozens, and I thought you said deuterium is all over the lab."

"You heard Fred. Flammable gas bottles get left-hand threads. Someone filled an SF_6 bottle with deuterium—"

"—or merely relabeled a deuterium bottle as SF_6. That's what I would do."

T. J. glanced sharply at the Russian.

"Christ, what then? Try to trace a discarded deuterium label? It's been thrown away weeks ago."

"Doc," said T. J., putting her hand on Nathaniel's shoulder. "We got big problems. One of which is that this explosion's blown our cover sky high. Another of which is that you now got a murder on your hands."

After a pause during which the truth sank in, Machuzak nodded grimly. Lipman's death was the worst and they couldn't avoid a public investigation. By now everyone at CFRC realized that no accident was responsible. Everyone in the world realized it. "Well, we've been complaining that covert ops has shackled us. We bite the bullet. Tomorrow morning I hold a press conference."

Archangelsky scowled. Yes, he'd also questioned their strategy, but now he had second thoughts about his second thoughts. "Nat, don't be hasty. Maybe there is yet—"

"Yaroslav Borisovich, fifty or a hundred people down there saw sulfur hexafluoride explode in a condom."

"Beware of what you wish for—"

"*Brat*, put a steamship in it."

D'Abro was half out the door with the dolly. "I'll be back. I'm impounding this bottle."

Slava recognized defeat and threw his cigarette in the trash. "Well, if that is so, let's turn out the lights and throw the grenade."

They switched off the lights.

TWENTY-FIVE

The auditorium was overflowing. People crowded the aisles and spilled out into the lobby, where the oversized closed-circuit displays had been switched on. Latecomers hung over the stage apron and pressed against the big doors, which as they had been since the deadline ax fell, remained closed.

Machuzak scanned the room filled with familiar, unknown faces. Security guards, technicians, engineers, scientists. Leonard and Theresa sat in the first row, Leonard frozen at the aisle in his wheelchair, Theresa holding up a few tentative fingers. Nathaniel hadn't seen her since their strange dinner a few weeks earlier and he'd scheduled this press conference without seeking Leonard's approval. Slava's wife, Nastya, had shown up and threw a friendly, forlorn glance Machuzak's way before sitting down with her occasional husband. Mercedes, Lise. Garrett himself, having flown in from Fort Worth, marched down the aisle as he waved his hat to the cameras. The flash of phones was continuous, the clashing ringtones. It had been like this all morning, every channel, every station, every website, every minute.

When at last the time came, Machuzak waved the crowd silent and squinted against the lights. "For any of you who don't know, my name is Nathaniel Machuzak, acting director of CFRC. This is lieutenant T. J. D'Abro of the Austin Sheriff's Department." T. J. had reluctantly requested and received dispensation to continue the investigation, and they decided to call her by her rank. No longer in a security guard uniform, she nodded to the audience. "As you know, about three weeks ago Cyrus Krieg-Zuber, the lab's deputy director, was seriously injured in what appeared to be an accident. Early the next morning one of our technicians, Andy Lipman, uncovered evidence that someone had tried to sabotage Prometheus, CFRC's large tokamak. Since then, Lieutenant D'Abro and I have been conducting an investigation in an attempt to find out exactly what happened and who was behind it. In order not to cause further alarm, or to tip off the saboteur, we decided on secrecy." Machuzak let pass that Leonard Rasmussen had insisted on it. "Unfortunately, before we were able to apprehend the culprit, yesterday's explosion took place. You all know about it. There is no point in trying to pretend it didn't happen. Apart from killing a valued technician and injuring two others, the blast has shown conclusively that sabotage was involved."

A murmur rippled from one end of the hall to the other.

When the noise abated, Nathaniel described his theory about how the explosion took place. It was a vast relief to get it off his chest, to empty himself of all the accumulating poisons. No, self-censorship remains at work. He withholds mention of dragons and mummies, not only because of what the press will do with it, but because uncovering Dragonmaster's identity, as implausible as it sounds, may be their best hope now. Nathaniel also attempts to peer into the near future and fails miserably. If the deadline seemed unattainable before, at this moment it appears unimaginable.

"Do you have any suspects?" asks a reporter across the link from Shanghai.

"We have evidence," Machuzak answers vaguely. "Certainly the detailed knowledge of the power system indicates that a member of this lab was involved, perhaps someone in this room." The wave of awakening that runs through the crowd is audible. "Unfortunately, after yesterday's events the saboteur will be even more difficult to apprehend." He elides mention of ITER moles.

"What about terrorists, Dr. Machuzak? Isn't CFRC high on the terrorist hit list? Won't all of south Austin become uninhabitable if CFRC is hit?"

It is a worried local jumping to her feet, shouting, agitation as genuine as it is extreme. For a moment Machuzak stares at her, perplexed, remaining amazed at how often he has heard the preposterous claim. He tries his standard answer: "My guess is that terrorists would sooner target the nearest Taco Bell and do us all some good." The joke garners a few laughs. "Look, CFRC is a civilian lab. There's nothing here a terrorist would want. Terrorists train their sights on human targets, train stations, office buildings, not machines."

"What about the tritium?" a talking head from Mumbai objects sharply. "Can it not be used in bombs?"

Here we are again, always. Nathaniel suppresses a sigh. "The amount of tritium you need to make a bomb is classified. I don't know it exactly myself, but you'd have to steal a good fraction of CFRC's inventory to produce a tactical weapon. In any case, the tritium supply is secure. Yesterday's blast caused no radiation leakage." There, he'd said it.

"But do you think a terrorist attack is possible, Dr. Machuzak? Possibly a Middle Eastern country that wants to prevent the development of fusion?"

Great minds do think alike. "I'd say this: The Middle East has been going nuclear for some time. And why should Middle Eastern terrorists destroy the fusion program, when our own government has destroyed it for them?" The political quip is obvious, but it at least garners black chuckles from some quarters of the auditorium. "In any case," Nathaniel adds, "why CFRC and not ITER?" He should perhaps not be giving anyone any ideas.

At that T. J. stands and interrupts. "Sir, we are exploring all leads. I do not think we should be more specific. And I'd like y'all to remember that this is not the result of any carelessness of neglect on the part of CFRC. What's more, yesterday's explosion was planned to have gone off weeks ago. Since then there haven't been any others, so we have no reason to think this is part of a prolonged campaign." Machuzak and T. J. exchange forced smiles at the lie. "Please do not panic."

Nathaniel is glad she has said it, not him, although the admonition will certainly have the opposite effect. Only at this moment does he sense realize the fear they are discharging over the entire laboratory.

* * * *

For the better part of an hour the pair were besieged. Machuzak answered the questions over and again, drew diagrams of the surge room. He explained neutral beams and spelled *tokamak*. "Do you investigate cold fusion?" "No, we do not." "Why not?"

When it was over the two looked at each other, breathed.

"Well, the good news is that more people know what fusion means today," said Slava, approaching the stage.

Nathaniel pushed his way toward Rasmussen but was intercepted by Richard Garrett, whose imposing form was also making its way down the aisle. "Son, I admire your guts. That couldn't have been easy." Easier than he thought. Telling the truth generally is. "Leonard, did you know about this?"

Rasmussen looked truly terrible. "I knew there was trouble," he said from his wheelchair.

Nathaniel still hadn't told Leonard everything. "Are you going to pull out?" he asked Garrett point-blank.

"Nope, I'm behind you until this is over, if you still think you can do it, show that son of a bitch Moravec that he, she, whatever isn't the only energy honcho in the Republic of Texas."

"The damage wasn't too extensive. We can carry out the repairs in parallel with the cooldown. If nothing else happens we shouldn't be set back."

"Go to it," said The Chairman.

"Take a hike, old boy," said an unmistakable voice behind Nathaniel just as he extended his hand to Garrett.

Machuzak swiveled to see Cyrus Krieg-Zuber, who'd entered the auditorium and now, mobbed by reporters, was announcing that today he felt fit enough to take back the reins. For an instant, Cyrus the Great's presence confounded Nathaniel, then: "Sorry, old boy, I'm director."

Both turned toward Garrett, who nodded sternly. "Sorry, Dr. Krieg-Zuber, that's the way it is. When they found you in that surge room, you were as dead as a can of corned beef, and when they carried you out, you were in about the same shape as a centipede with sciatica, so enjoy your rest. If you don't, I'll bar you from the lab."

Stunned, Krieg-Zuber raised a finger at Machuzak, but for the first time that Nathaniel could remember, he found no words. Then he stormed out of the auditorium.

Slava whistled. "'I perceive you now, beginning of high and turbulent days.'"

"You've said that before," answered Machuzak.

The Russian shrugged. "Look on the bright side. Now the saboteur is trapped with the rest of us. No one will dare resign after this. Even take vacation."

Da, from this moment on they were all prisoners.

TWENTY-SIX

Evening had fallen by the time Machuzak reached his home on the lower slopes of West Lake Hills. The house had become foreign to him, a mere crash pad, hardly even a life preserver in a sea without shore. His kitchen resembled an earthquake zone, counter and table strewn with empty cereal boxes, a refrigerator that had been cleared of everything but archaeological odors. He glanced at the Kandinsky clock on the living room wall. Usually it was with a momentary disbelief before he crashed onto his bed, awoke, threw on the nearest clothes, hopped into the jeep.

Tonight he was home earlier. After the press conference he had escaped the lab alone, not wanting to talk to anyone. He'd gazed into his cloudy crystal ball and could not be cheered by what he perceived. Would ITER relent as its rival collapsed? Hah. Nathaniel glumly searched for something to eat, tossed out a shriveled apple. This entire series of unintended consequences was of their own making. His water was off too; was this a scheduled outage?

He flipped on the television, eight channels simultaneously. The local stations ran nonstop with the press conference; it played very high on the national news and even got twenty-three seconds on the BBC. As he watched, several of the newscasts cut to the Austin office of Senator Roy Whitman, where the white-haired politician addressed the cameras.

He'd received a leaked copy of the preliminary accident report, which T. J. and Lipman had just finished before the explosion, and named it "pure whitewash." That it was, Nathaniel sighed. Yesterday's disaster was due to a cover-up by the acting director and unless the laboratory didn't expedite a proper inquiry, he'd call for a congressional investigation.

Nathaniel felt his mouth go dry. "Big Bad Roy," as he styled himself, was a leader in the fight for Texas autonomy. To this day he opposed all energy and environmental legislation, figuring the Republic would soon enough make its own rules. But he was the powerful head of the Senate Appropriations Committee's Energy and Water Subcommittee, which oversees fusion, and almost from the day Leonard had founded CFRC, he'd proclaimed the lab's work fraudulent. Otherwise, Machuzak knew little about Whitman, except that he could cause a lot of trouble; he just had.

Nathaniel ran his tongue over his lips. Who could have leaked the report and how? Machuzak was on his feet when his handset went off. "A couple weeks late, Cassandra, but not bad." Archangelsky. "Have you seen Whitman?"

Da, Machuzak confirmed and signed off. Aye, on that first night he'd vaguely predicted to Slava that a week wouldn't pass before the politicians jumped in. He sat for moments, resolving that until Whitman stopped barking and began biting, the proper tactic was to ignore him.

The doorbell rang then, he shouted, "Come in!" and Theresa Rasmussen entered to find him before the wall screen. The senator was still on the air, claiming that "taxpayers must be protected from footing the bill for a pie-in-the-sky project that has no chance of providing any benefit to our citizens." Like the space station Whitman voted for way back then, Nathaniel thought.

"Oh, he is an evil man!" Theresa exclaimed, catching sight of the image before her. "He's just a plain, lying idiot. When you meet these people at banquets, you tell yourself that their platitudes and homilies are merely for public consumption. Then you meet them in private and discover that they talk on the inside the same way as they do on the outside. That is Whitman, outside through and through."

Nathaniel was momentarily taken aback at Theresa's vehemence, and surprised to discover that she had encountered him at any number of official functions. On reflection, he realized he'd been naïve.

"How I dislike that man," she went on, almost to herself. "He enjoys power. It positively oozes from him. I'd like to make him pay."

Nathaniel knew then that he might have found a powerful ally in Theresa Rasmussen, but he had no idea why she had appeared at his door.

"I'm sorry, Mac," she said, only now remembering to greet him, "I was on my way home from shopping and saw your car. I didn't say anything today after the conference. I think I was overwhelmed. What you must be going through... How about some wine? I have a bottle in the car." Nathaniel nodded absently and Theresa went to fetch it.

Holding out the bottle for an opener, she asked, "Is this our final defeat, Nathaniel, the end of Prometheus?" She spoke as if ASSET belonged to her. But then, Theresa had always been part of the lab.

"I haven't raised the flag," he said, putting a determined face on it, "but what happened yesterday...and now Cyrus..."

"Don't worry about the big oaf," Theresa said. "We'll take care of him."

"Theresa, the oaf has trashed my career once already. How's Leonard taking things?"

Theresa stared down into her wineglass almost as if it weren't there. Abruptly coming to, she cupped it in both hands and took a deep gulp. "Not well, Nathaniel. How would you take seeing your life's work being destroyed before your eyes? He is a strong man, but...he can't... This will make the end..." Suddenly, Theresa lifted her eyes to Nathaniel and threw herself into his arms, kissing him passionately on the lips and face.

At first he responded reflexively, then with intent. They moved almost clumsily into the living room, practically tripping over the coffee table and falling onto the couch. Theresa would not be delayed and soon her fingers had unfastened his shirt and were running greedily over his bare chest. Neither would she wait for him to undress her; she bared herself for him, tossing her shirt and bra to the floor. His hand was to her breast and his lips to her stiffening nipple. They managed to get off the rest of their clothes, she laughing, and he felt the gooseflesh of her buttocks above him, and before there was time to consider she'd slipped him inside her and groaned.

They went at it with abandon, but when they were done and she lay atop him, the guilt arrived quickly. "Theresa, what have we done?" Nathaniel asked.

"Shh," she replied, putting a finger over his lips. "Consider it a gift to me. I needed it... It's been a long time. Leonard would thank you. You don't need to become my lover...umm, maybe occasionally." She smiled, almost wickedly.

Stroking her flank, Nathaniel remained surprised at what had just taken place. He'd always viewed Theresa as a patrician educated back East in a series of those unaffordable girls' schools and colleges. He could only imagine with difficulty that those women had sex at all.

"Come now," she said slyly, arching her neck, "what do you think we think of all day, locked up in those unaffordable girls' schools?" She lay her head on his chest, and he saw her contemplating a lone African mask on his wall. "Tell me," he said, once again he realizing how little he knew about Theresa Rasmussen, "why did a young upper-class chick go to Africa?"

"Penance, I think," she answered, looking inward. "I felt so removed from the world, from reality almost... I needed to help, do something... I didn't get very far rebelling, did I?" She chuckled throatily, with self-deprecation. "I remember the songs of the black neighborhoods around Cape Town. There was such poverty and violence, but also a sense of motion, of something worth struggling for. That's what I miss here. I see no sense of the greater good, just slow fragmentation. Whatever happened to the idea of a covenant, Nathaniel?"

He couldn't answer. He'd read about it once. The Republic of Texas was for sure no place to find a covenant, but now for the first time Nathaniel saw Theresa as one of them. Of CFRC, certainly, but he meant as one of the small group of globetrotters, cosmopolites who paste no flags on suitcase or car bumper. That group whose nation consists only of the best they find anywhere, the best of culture, the best minds, the deepest souls. Machuzak was unashamed to pledge his loyalty to the fraternity of the dispossessed. He'd have none other. No scientist would. Theresa as well.

When the urge to separate overcame intimacy, Mrs. Rasmussen got up and dressed. She again told Nathaniel not to worry, that she'd never force herself upon him, that this was a gift. For him too, he replied. It was largely, mostly, for Leonard that he'd undertaken this impossible task. At this moment a stronger determination gripped him. He hoped it was not guilt, but he surely owed it to Leonard now. Theresa kissed him lightly on the lips and stepped into the evening.

TWENTY-SEVEN

The first protestors showed up at dawn. Three or four locals, a family it seemed, were lounging on lawn chairs outside the main gate, but they carried no placards and voiced no demands. As Machuzak passed, he couldn't determine whether their intent was to keep people out or radiation in. "May I help you?" he called out.

"Nope," was the response. "Just keeping an eye on things."

"Good—I need all the help I can get," Nathaniel answered, but by afternoon they were gone.

Joking had stopped at the guard booth. The security staff, after years faced with a job, opened trunks and inspected undercarriages, and did not exempt the acting director. D'Abro herself was up early, briefing guards on suspicious behavior, and Machuzak watched them grill an industry rep until tempers flared.

As he tore the day's page from the deadline calendar, Nathaniel saw that someone had drawn a dagger thrust into Bill Balustradi's forehead. He checked in briefly at his office; the single door open at this hour closed quietly as he passed. Five abrupt resignations flaunted Slava's optimistic prediction. At the pentagon, techs averted their eyes and, though first shift was well manned, he felt as if he were walking the streets of a west Texas ghost town. For a few minutes he watched the crew work silently on the surge room repairs and scrub the floor of bloodstains. Back in the control room he found Abbuhl and glanced at the magnet temperature gauges. They stood at 200 Kelvins now, hardly colder than a winter's day. Nathaniel asked Fred about the vessel bake.

It had begun. That meant they'd pumped the toroid itself down to less than a billionth of an atmosphere. "There's a lot of junk comin off the walls, Mac, sir," Abbuhl told him without expression. "You're going to have to give us a week or two." He went on to report that they were also conditioning the neutral beams and rf power supplies, checking insulation problems...the normal start-up activities, but the engineer's empty voice betrayed none of his signature laid-back humor or engagement.

"Fred," Machuzak said, "don't fold on me. If I can't count on you, we may as well throw in the towel now, let ITER do it."

"Would that be so bad, Mac, sir? At least Balard doesn't have a saboteur runnin loose." Abbuhl paused, finally offering a rueful smile. "Well, this is Alamo country, isn't it? At least because of that misguided demo, *Herr Doktor* Professor, all the systems are in pretty good shape."

This afternoon he'd begin testing the motor-generators, the 700-ton flywheels that powered their experiments. Those dumb pieces of steel, built for a hydroelectric plant, had performed flawlessly for a decade and Fred saw no reason that they couldn't perform for a decade more, if the lab existed.

"Fred, I'm firing up the ignition meetings again, or we'll have a machine and nothing more."

His chief stared at him with an expression that would have passed for ironic had it not been so filled with trepidation.

"In an hour." He slapped Fred on the back and made his way upstairs through echoic corridors.

* * * *

With the division heads gathered before him in the ASSET conference room, Machuzak announced that the bakeout and cooldown were proceeding with only minor glitches and that barring unforeseen difficulties experiments could begin in two weeks. Not a person at the table reacted to the good news and as Nathaniel surveyed the blank, downturned expressions before him, he perceived that Abbuhl's mood had been upbeat. He reported that today ITER had announced a ten-second low-power burn—a mere warm-up—but his chiefs hardly stirred.

"What is the point?" Hasschler asked finally, rhetorically. "We cannot beat them in…our circumstances."

"I know how you are all feeling," Nathaniel replied. "One of our colleagues has been killed, a saboteur lurks among us, the lab will shut down, ITER will win. But remember, we have five months and a week to create a star on Earth. Imagine! Look your colleagues in the eyes, get the gloom out of your systems… Let us try to create a star."

Still, the uncomfortable, shifting silence continued until Nathaniel moved toward the door, at which Hasschler spoke up gruffly. "Crespi has made an interesting proposal…" It was a start, but from the way Hasschler wiped his bald crown as he attempted to explain Crespi's idea, Nathaniel knew that it was also no more than a disguised shot in the dark.

"Anything else?" he asked.

"We have, of course, the usual parameters, but—"

"—the usual parameters will not get us ignition, will they?" said Toshifume Matsushima, entering the room with Yaroslav Archangelsky behind him. "Thank you for your wisdom, Mac, the other day," Toshi said, bowing at the waist toward Nathaniel. "You have cleared my eyes."

Machuzak did not know whether his courtyard speech or the explosion had turned Toshi around, but he breathed a quantum more easily, seeing that Matsushima had finally decided to put his mind to work.

All eyes were on the Japanese Korean. "Gentlemen, ladies," he said, "from what I have heard, these meetings have taken on the aspect of Abraham Lincoln's cabinet—strife and stagnation. As is clear to everyone at this unfortunate laboratory, our kairos is rapidly diminishing, and if we wish to take our place among the immortals, we shall have to create fusion, not fission."

Pretty words were too much for Kettering, today, now. "For God's sake!" he shouted, "I'm sick and tired of hearing about fucking kairos. What's kairos got to do with this ignition campaign?"

Matsushima smiled. "This is indeed your problem, Tom. To an anteater everything is an ant; to a soldier, everything is a campaign. What we require is a new mode of thought."

Hasschler was falling back into his previous humor, if indeed he had left it. Again he wiped his head with his bare hand. "Talk is cheap. We are entering new territory. What concrete ideas do you have to contribute, Toshifume?"

"If we were entering old territory," Toshi responded, "we would be there, not here."

"This isn't science, this is bullshit," snarled Diana through clenched teeth, pointing at Toshi and Machuzak.

An instant later everyone in the room was roaring. Nathaniel yanked the CO_2 extinguisher from the wall, aimed the nozzle toward the ceiling and pulled the trigger. "Halt!" he shouted superfluously, for the carbon dioxide cloud filling the room had already sent everyone scrambling into the corridor. He followed. "Toshi, I want you to talk over Crespi's idea with Thaddeus, unless you have any of your own."

As they coughed and cursed in the hallway, Richard Garrett appeared and told Nathaniel he was taking up residence at the lab "for the greater good." Machuzak stared at him quizzically before he continued on, past a lonely water cooler.

* * * *

With their cover blown, T. J. lost no time in getting down to taking elimination DNA samples from anyone who could have been in the power area immediately before the accident. She spent two mornings swabbing the techs she'd interviewed, but the only DNA certain to match the samples she'd already collected was Lipman's. He'd probably been the last one in the area the night before the incident, and he wouldn't talk, ever. No, there were two other certainties: Laurel and Hardy.

The atmosphere hovering over the cafeteria would have better suited Death Valley, and T. J. soon began to retreat to the new office they'd given her, where like everyone else she sealed herself tight. When the knock came it startled her. She put down her sandwich, got to her feet, hesitantly opened the door and saw Cyrus Krieg-Zuber.

"Mademoiselle D'Abro," he said, wedging in, closing the door behind him. "You are in need of my services." She didn't reply; he didn't wait but rather inspected the bare office, a spare room devoid of ornament, only eventually bringing his eyes around. "With the crisis mounting, it would serve everyone's interests to have the investigation concluded as soon as possible, would it not?"

Krieg-Zuber's intense gaze seemed to be focused behind her in a way that, as at their first meeting, left her unnerved. "That goes without saying, Dr. Krieg-Zuber," she answered at last.

"How far have you gotten?" the sinewy man asked.

T. J. didn't see the harm in revealing public knowledge and told him about her interviews with the techs and the elimination samples. "I don't think they're involved," she said, then ventured a little further. "My theory is that whoever carried out our little act of sabotage is working for Balard."

"Your instincts are good. Follow them."

His reply, made with a smile as he lifted with curiosity the single ornament from her monitor, a red garter with a holstered six-shooter from Billy Bob's, surprised her and she decided to probe further. "I've been checking traffic between here and Cadarache and can't pinpoint anyone communicating directly with Balard." To be sure, in the past days she'd ransacked four years of captured messages and installed an alert to trigger on Balard's name; now she was being beeped dozens of times a day.

"Mademoiselle," Krieg-Zuber said, rubbing his scar, "only an idiot would communicate with him through the laboratory server. Why have you wasted your time? The lesson of Osama bin Laden is one of low-tech." Mac or Slava had said much the same, T. J. recalled. "As I have told you, there are other archives. Here." He dropped a memory ring on her desk and before she could thank him the strange man was gone.

T. J. plugged the ring into her computer, found dozens of video files. Opening them at random, it quickly became apparent that they'd been recorded by Krieg-Zuber himself. Why he'd given them to her, she couldn't fathom, but she now started from the beginning, having no idea what they contained, or omitted. Soon she stumbled across Krieg-Zuber and Machuzak arguing in the deputy director's office.

"Mac, we're canceling your experiment," Cyrus Krieg-Zuber said.

"You're joking," Nathaniel answered. "It's the best work I've ever done."

"And it has nothing to do with building a reactor."

Krieg-Zuber then said in his most affected accent, "You're too good to let go, *docteur*, so we're giving you a couple of options…" The deputy director, standing stolidly before Nathaniel with crossed arms, assured him that casualties were high, that virtually everything was canceled except ASSET. They now had a mission. One was to show the world that ITER was not the only game in town.

"You'll crush the light out of this lab with your Mission," T. J. watched Nathaniel tell him in not-quite-lifelike 3-D.

"Don't take it so hard," Krieg-Zuber responded, "old boy. What did the general say about Vietnam? 'Our mission is to drop ten bombs in the same hole.'"

At that Nathaniel stormed out of the office.

T. J. called in Machuzak and replayed the scene. She was only momentarily taken aback when he did no more than sigh, "I'm hardly surprised that the fucker bugged his own office," and nod. "Yeah, I remember this. It was a year after ANFRL became CRFC. It was still possible to do research here, and I was continuing my project from Princeton."

"What was it?"

"Well," Machuzak talked readily enough, "I'd abandoned my boyhood dreams to create a unified field theory, but I hadn't given up my determination to learn something about plasmas, and I'd been making progress with a novel idea about plasma heating. The thing was, I'd finally reached the moment when intuition kicked in and I was able to outmaneuver the damned gas. I didn't need equations or computers. I *saw*. That's the moment you live for as a scientist. Enlightenment, Toshi'd call it."

"It must have been hard," T. J. said with genuine sympathy.

"Very."

"What did you do?"

"Ended up working on ASSET with everyone else, until a few years ago when The Terminator assigned me to the MTF."

D'Abro looked up at him. "Why d'ya figure Krieg-Zuber gave me these here archives?"

"Why do you think?" With that he glanced at his wrist, saw a message from Kettering—"tritium shipment from Savannah River scheduled to arrive within hour"—and excused himself.

TWENTY-EIGHT

Kettering was waiting for him at tritium operation's loading dock, pentagon four. The delivery truck was already backing in, but Machuzak's eyes were riveted elsewhere: on two guards, armored and carrying automatic weapons, standing before the vault entrance.

"Compliments of the Republic of Texas," Kettering said. "Thirty seconds after your press conference, the governor went fucking nuts about tritium being stolen."

"Who authorized this?" Machuzak exclaimed angrily.

"Your inspector lady, who else? If you ask me it's a good idea, with all the rumors flyin around. Show the public we mean business."

Rumors were right. The local media speculation about tritium's value to terrorists has been ceaseless, and at this moment real and robotic reporters are running in his direction to watch the fateful delivery. Machuzak momentarily stares in disbelief, then decides to enlist his unwanted militia. "Keep them back," he orders. "They are *not* authorized."

Kettering has already shifted his attention to the federals accompanying the shipment. He counts the aluminum UC-609s, signs the bill of lading. As the guards keep the scrum of journalists at bay, Machuzak helps with the offloading and glances at the surveillance cameras. This is the one place at CFRC where security is exactly what imagination demands. Peering from every direction are radiation monitors and at the other end of the cameras' optic nerve sits a guard posted twenty-four hours a day.

Ignoring the shouts from the press about infiltrators and safety, Kettering steps before a camera at the vault entrance, requests authorization to enter, signs in. After getting an okay from the duty officer, he presses his thumb against the fingerprint reader—this one has always functioned. The heavy door, plastered with a dozen variants of Secure Area, swings open with a slight whoosh and they step into the negative-pressure zone, designed to contain tritium like an Ebola virus at the Centers for Disease Control.

The reporters think they are invited and Machuzak must order the guardsmen to keep them at bay while the delivery crew transfers the UC-609s onto the freight elevator. Each of these oil drums lined with space-age padding contains an LP-18, a smaller bottle containing eighteen liters of tritium at negative pressure. Two flights down a second airlock, more surveillance cameras, further warnings.

Machuzak halts at this second door, deciding there is no need for him to proceed further. He is satisfied that sufficient tritium has arrived to carry forward the beginnings of an ignition campaign and goes above to tell the journalists to get the hell out of here.

* * * *

That evening, T. J. walked into Machuzak's office, where he was speaking with Archangelsky, without a word plugged the flash ring into his computer and stepped back. Before anything happened, Machuzak ordered the computer to pause and turned to D'Abro. "Did you request those guardsmen?"

"I didn't request anything, Doc. The governor phoned this morning, as freaked as a whore in church, and I agreed to his request. The blogosphere has gone ballistic with tritium. Everybody's waitin for somethin to happen. Think about it." She commanded "play" and the video recommenced. This time it was a furious Machuzak confronting a Cyrus Krieg-Zuber, who stood surrounded by trophies and stroking his chin. Nathaniel nodded soberly, watched.

"You've been pocket-vetoing papers!" shouted Machuzak. "You intercept them, they disappear, then what—they come out with your name on them? How dare you!"

"Don't exaggerate, *docteur*. Nothing's come out with anybody's name on it, but we can't have CFRC scientists wasting time with research irrelevant to the Mission."

"You're to decide that?"

"Yes."

"If this isn't illegal, it should be. This is blatant thievery. You've never had an idea in your life and you're stealing them."

Krieg-Zuber's face momentarily flushed, then the retort: "Worthless hack! Don't flatter yourself that your ideas are worth stealing, old boy. This conversation has ended."

Back in the office Machuzak nodded again. He well remembered the scene from four years ago. That skirmish he'd won. He reported Zuber's scheme to Rasmussen and Leonard had immediately ordered it scrubbed. Watching the show, Slava's reaction was similar to Mac's the previous day. "*Eb tvoiu mat'*," he muttered. "Richard Nixon had nothing on us."

"Yeah," said T. J., "I'm beginning to understand why you and Cyrus the Great weren't exactly bed buddies, but if you're surprised that administrators keep an eye on their subordinates, you've been living in an alternate universe." She opened another file.

The time line had jumped to about three weeks before the recent commissioning. Machuzak and the deputy director were in the midst of a heated argument. "What is all this about?" Nathaniel watched himself shout. Krieg-Zuber feigned ignorance. "Why the secrecy?" Machuzak pressed. "Why are we checking out the turbine? We won't be ready to use it for three or four years—if ever."

The deputy brusquely reminded Machuzak to "do as he was told." They needed to put on a show. If necessary they'd explain to the public how a turbine worked. Even now, The Terminator's patronizing tone struck Nathaniel as calculated to enrage; he'd raised the art of condescension to a new level entirely.

"Do as I'm told?" Machuzak fell for the bait. "This is a scientific laboratory—sorry—" he raised his hand—"this was a scientific laboratory."

"Perhaps you'd be happier at ITER," Krieg-Zuber responded.

Nathaniel didn't respond. Instead he said with steel, "I want to know what the hell's going on. It's fucking nuts. The guys are already exhausted."

Watching the replay, Machuzak was amazed that he hadn't seen through the whole bloody deception then and there and that Krieg-Zuber had managed to keep his true intentions under wraps. As he now saw his earlier self storm out of the office, T. J. said, "Doc, I asked you to tell me what you weren't tellin me. I'm askin you again, for your own sake."

Archangelsky, appearing as if he were about to vomit, wasn't paying attention, but having had a moment Machuzak answered more calmly, "T. J., you just saw me have an argument with The Terminator. I've never hidden how I felt about what he was doing to CFRC."

"You defected to ITER?"

As on the earlier occasion Machuzak didn't respond, but at this moment the image of Duke Lorenzo at his doomed ball was bright. "Why don't you ask Krieg-Zuber what you're not seeing?"

"I intend to. Look Doc, I know there's nothin conclusive here, but somehow you missed telling me that you and Cy were at each other's throats. Now, I've been goin through these here videos. Lots of hours. It'll take a while, but given that the *only* forensics we got puts you and Slava down in that surge room, I'd start bein more careful, Doc. I gotta make you understand, this is capital sabotage now—whoever spiked your machine is lookin at a murder charge, period."

"What about the deuterium bottle?"

"It's safe," T. J. replied, "at the police lab. But the prints on that bottle are yours and a couple of technicians, one of whom is dead."

"T. J.!" Machuzak erupted. "You and a hundred other people saw me with my hands all over that bottle, filling a condom with deuterium."

"What do else do you fill your condoms with?" she cracked, but her voice didn't reveal mirth enough to put either of them at ease.

"Bedbug, do you suspect me of being Balard's mole and the dragon at the same time?"

They were staring hard. "Doc, I don't see any reason to believe that those two people are the same and I don't pretend to know yet how this all this is gonna fit together. I'm just actin like a good little scientist—followin the evidence. You don't hold it against me, as I recall."

Both of them paused, painfully aware that their relationship was fast mutating beyond their control. "No, I don't," Nathaniel said finally. And neither would he be careful, because he had nothing to fear, from her or anyone.

Slava's handset pinged then, alerting him to a new broadcast by Big Bad Roy Whitman. They switched the monitor to a webcast of St. Cecilia's talk show. What could he be on about? Nothing whatsoever had happened since his volley two days ago.

That was precisely what irked the senator. St. Cecilia pointed out that, despite recent events, the Prometheus experiment seemed to be proceeding on schedule.

Whitman, dressed in a fringed buckskin jacket, scoffed at the thought. "There's no chance that their endeavor can succeed," he countered. "Those fusion people have been promising to deliver the goods for seventy years now, and despite two hundred billion dollars of investment, they ain't one day closer now than they were then."

The figure Whitman had just quoted was ten times more than the federal government had ever put into fusion. Nathaniel wasn't so much staggered by the politicians' innumeracy but that they got away with it; he looked down to see himself clenching a fist.

"What they say they're trying to do is frankly impossible and what they're in fact doin is duping the public. They know they can't reach this so-called ignition in five months. And since I last spoke, they've made no progress on their investigation either. Cecilia, let me tell you, I *will* institute a congressional inquiry. We can't let these people get away with their crimes and I don't mind telling you, as far as I'm concerned CFRC should be shut down."

"How much progress does the *svoloch'* want in two days?" Archangelsky hissed at the monitor.

Nathaniel was perched on the windowsill with his hand on chin, watching Whitman intently. "He's afraid we're going to succeed."

"Doesn't sound it to me," Archangelsky objected.

T. J. didn't hear it either. "Why's he so out to get you, Doc?"

Climbing down from his perch, Nathaniel shook his head. "I don't know. Whitman goes back before my time, but even a couple years ago he was saying things so harebrained I could only guess he was a complete idiot or completely evil. 'If the Earth is getting warmer, why is Minneapolis getting colder?'" Without another word Machuzak called St. Cecilia's studio. Hearing his name, the screener put him through immediately.

"Everything you've said in the last five minutes, senator," Machuzak said on the air, "is complete bullshit," and he proceeded to tell the listening audience why.

Nonplussed for only an instant, the senator became suddenly affable and replied that he would be glad to discuss the matter with Dr. Machuzak in private.

Any time, any place.

And so it was scheduled then and there: Colt versus tokamak, high noon, tomorrow, the Federal Building.

When he'd hung up, Nathaniel breathed deeply. Watching him, D'Abro was taken aback; she hadn't seen before such a look on his face. Fortitude, purpose, she wasn't sure what to call it, but he seemed to have grown several inches. "I don't know what he's up to, or why, but when Big Science and politics tangle, science always loses, and as I have the misfortune to be acting director, it's my duty to get him off our backs. After tomorrow he will be." A pause and then: "How am I going to do that?"

Without a blink D'Abro answered, "I'd tell him to visit Durham Cathedral." She walked up to Nathaniel's bulletin board, unpinned the photo and handed it to him.

He looked at it, at her, while she gazed at him with far more sympathy than she had in the past half hour, and at the same time cast at him the most challenging expression she'd yet sent his way, an expression he took to proclaim, "We may be on different sides now and you may think I'm crazier than a locoed bedbug, but our orbits intersect in more ways than you, Dr. Machuzak, have imagined." He replied with a soft nod, which satisfied her, for they both knew it was a moment she would find difficult to surpass.

TWENTY-NINE

The Cathedral of the Church of Christ and Blessed Mary the Virgin is probably the masterpiece of Anglo-Norman architecture and dominates the old English town of Durham. From its position on the hill, the river and entire countryside are visible. Durham Cathedral was begun in 1093 and not wholly completed for four hundred years. Work on the more elaborate York Ministry began when Durham had already assumed recognizable form and took two centuries to complete. The foundation for Notre Dame du Paris was laid in 1163 and the nave and towers were completed a mere ninety years later, but the chapels and other embellishments took a further century to consummate. Notre Dame at Chartres was begun in 1145, almost entirely destroyed by fire fifty years later, and rebuilt almost from top to bottom in less than three decades, which maybe says something about progress.

Looking back on these works the most incomprehensible thing is the mentality of the people who produced them. I do not wonder at the great shafts of light ascending to heaven. I stand there, illumined, and ask what sort of person would devote his entire life to constructing an edifice he would never see completed.

* * * *

The question runs through the life of fusioneers; it has run through my mind more than once in the weeks since the accursed accident, and surely now as I crawl up I-35 to meet Senator Roy Whitman. During fugitive moments, it has pleased me to compare fusioneers with cathedral builders. I have liked to believe we are doing something beyond ourselves, something noble, something for the greater glory, but in the harsh light of the before-noon, I see that the comparison is not wholly flattering. The reality is that when the fusion programs began in the 1950s, the pioneers had no inkling how difficult the task would be. The trailblazers may have been working for the greater glory, but they were no fools. No one planned to sacrifice his career for an unattainable goal.

The long truth dawned slowly. Mayhap it was exactly this self-delusion that led to the persistent, overly optimistic predictions from the fusion community, from as far back as the 1940s when the Brits prematurely patented a fusion device. Rosy claims that have haunted fusioneers through tokamaks, stellarators and the rest, and that politicians throw into our faces even now. It was not for nothing that Lyman Spitzer named the original classified US fusion program Project Matterhorn, a steep climb.

Since those legendary times fusion has become the most international of endeavors, but we have not been able to cleanse ourselves of our sins. Nor have we been able to convince the public that NASA holds no monopoly on great adventures, that performing somersaults in a space station is not science and that science is not glory.

Only politicians and project leaders have failed to learn the distinction, that science is the wrong arena for glory hounds. With 150 names trailing the title of each paper coming out of CFRC, Krieg-Zuber once remarked that that worked out to two-thirds of a percent glory per author. Glory drippings, he called them in his standard fashion. But even those glory drippings are collective. In that we are like the cathedral builders. Anonymous.

Aye, off to Hollywood or Washington, ye glory seekers. Not for you the realm of science. Nature is the ultimate equal-opportunity employer, offering her fruit to anyone with enough insight to pluck them from her branches. "If you don't do something," Slava has always maintained, "somebody else will and in the same words." Slava is right. Why do we keep at it? The money's not great, the glory nonexistent. The curiosity is good.

For all my misgivings, I have not lost my belief that there is something noble in the endeavor to harness the energy source of stars. Whether we are in fusion for glory or money or mere curiosity, it remains a good deed. Ours is not a galaxian visit to realms far from human concerns.

The Earth is a finite place and the presumption that what is best for humans is best, that we know best, is dangerous beyond words. If we are to accept stewardship, let it be with reluctance and the greatest humility. That would be an achievement in this tattered federation of the perpetual present, where history began moments ago, where the future has been infinitely distant and humility is never considered a virtue. Would that we could learn at least this from the cathedral builders.

* * * *

Having carried out the miracle of parking, Nathaniel sat for a few minutes on a hard stone bench amid potted trees on the Federal Building plaza, intending to still himself, but the sterile plaza, where two solitary souls sat immersed in their screens, served only to oppress him and he went round to the far side, stared at the Great Seal of the United States and opened the door. Passing through the detector, he received a visitor's badge and decided he'd hardly left CFRC. "God has favored our undertaking," he said to the guard as he was patted down and took the elevator up. The guard stared after him suspiciously.

Whitman's office, like Moravec's, was much as he might have expected, lined with intimations of power and wealth: walnut, mahogany, the heaviness of law, brass fixtures and sports trophies, a shaft of sunlight cast onto the massive desk. Nathaniel's adversary was of the same proportions: nearly as tall as himself but no lanky scientist. Before him stood a man certain of his weight, with a broad, fleshy face, complexion still ruddy though he was fifteen years his senior, or twenty. Despite the three-piece suit, Nathaniel wouldn't fancy meeting him in a boxing ring. They shook hands consciously, coldly, staring.

"The famous Dr. Machuzak—please sit, why don't you."

Nathaniel ignored the regretful remark, which he'd heard more than once in the past days, and accepted the chair proffered, a chair designed to make visitors want to leave.

The senator also took up his position behind the desk, picked up, tapped an unlit cigar on an ashtray. "Dr. Machuzak, I don't appreciate being called a liar on the air, although I gotta admit I admire your directness. You're obviously not a politician."

"That's tautological." He didn't think Whitman got it and didn't pause either. He was resolved that this man would cease to be a distraction. "Senator, I'm not here to apologize. We have a genuine crisis down at CFRC and the last thing we need is your unjustified attacks. I came to tell you to lay off. Stop interfering. Period."

Whitman snorted, surprised at the belligerence of the scientist facing him, but tough arenas were nothing new to him. "Dr. Machuzak," he said, turning on the same honed affability he had displayed yesterday on the air, "take my advice—don't run for office. Why should I lay off? Everything I said on St. Cecilia's show was true—"

Machuzak merely burst out laughing. "You began by claiming that the amount of money fusion research receives is ten times larger than in reality. You've obviously confused fusion with the space station. ASSET and ITER, the largest fusion projects ever attempted, have cost more like ten billion apiece, and the US government ain't payin. I remind you, Senator, that CFRC has been run by a private consortium for a decade now."

"Dr. Machuzak, I *am* the chairman of the Senate's Energy and Water Subcommittee and have an obligatory interest in what goes on in your lab. You know as well as I do that CFRC is a public-private consortium and continues to receive eighty million a year from the government—"

"More like ten, Senator, but who's counting?" Theresa had been right: Whitman was a plain, lying idiot. "And when you say there's been no progress in fusion, get real. The first tokamaks produced a thousandth of a watt of power, not even in the same league as a Christmas tree lightbulb. Now we routinely produce fifty megawatts, fifty billion times more. Most people would call that progress. Sixty years ago we held a plasma for twenty milliseconds; now we can hold it an hour at a time."

"Not at that demo you didn't," Whitman inserted the knife cleanly.

… and only at low densities, Machuzak conceded. Forced to reconnoiter, he feared he had not understood exactly what he'd intended to accomplish at this showdown, or adequately prepared his mind. "Prometheus was not ready, is not ready, I admit it. But soon we'll achieve ignition. Will you then claim there's been no progress?" Internally he winced. I pray that we reach ignition. We will achieve ignition. If we survive.

His opponent plainly detected his weakness and didn't need to consider his words long. "Dr. Machuzak," Whitman said, leaning back regally in his chair, "you people have been saying 'soon' since Adam and Eve. Funny how 'soon' always turns out to be the next generation."

As money gets shorter, horizons get longer, Nathaniel thought, even as he reluctantly conceded the truth in the ancient charge. "You know," he said, "Durham Cathedral in England took four hundred years to build. What if it had been halted at the towers?"

Now Whitman merely laughed, crossing his arms high on his chest; an amateur faced him. "Machuzak, a cathedral is only a cathedral once it's finished. The fact remains that there is no evidence your scheme is going to work, and even if it does, that it will be economical. I've seen the studies—you're talking about a twenty-, thirty-billion-dollar plant. Who's gonna fork over that kinda money on a long shot? That Moravec character has apparently seen the light by imposing the deadline."

Again Nathaniel had to yield to truth in Whitman's remarks. Even if they could make the damn thing work, they didn't yet know how to make it cheap. This duel wasn't going well. "You know Moravec?" was the only thing he could think of to say.

The offhand question brought a derisive shake of the head and an unguarded answer. "Of course not. Bandits like him have caused a lot of problems for the fossil fuel industry, lobbying for unattainable emission standards—it's all to line their own pockets, of course, sons of bitches."

"Unattainable by Texas," Nathaniel said caustically. "Texas is by far the leading CO_2 emitter because of people like you." It must have been Whitman whom Moravec, with hardly less vehemence, had referred to as a reactionary politician. He preferred the strange GlobeTex CEO.

"Ya know," the senator continued, confident now of mopping the floor with this lightweight intellectual who held the pointy-headed delusion that his opinion counted, "you liberals are all extremists." He got to his feet, began pacing. "Those studies you always cite have more holes in them than Swiss cheese. Hockey sticks..." Now the senator waved his cigar in big aerial loops around his head. "You know, the EPA is unconstitutional—they have no right to regulate anything, yet alone CO2, which isn't a pollutant. What's wrong with global warming anyway? I've visited Greenland. The folks there rejoice at it, believe me they do. You remember that ice storm we had a few years ago—freezing rain, airports shut down for days, me having to scrape the ice off my windshield in the damned cold. I welcome global warming, Machuzak, I do welcome it. By God, Texas *will* be a republic again, and we'll have beaten the feds..."

Machuzak listened to Whitman rant in amazement. There was a grain of truth in what he said. Much of what the public thought it knew about climate science was simply wrong, but for all that, the danger this politician fails to understand is not that science can predict the future, but that it can't.

Nathaniel knew that Whitman was backed by Big Oil, that if Texas seceded, it would become far easier to build new plants. As he watched his antagonist pace, he could only guess that independence was somehow behind the senator's hostility to their endeavor, but Machuzak in his haste hadn't checked. Damn, if only he'd readied himself for this confrontation...

"No, Machuzak, you haven't convinced me of a thing. The money the government spends on your lab is money down a rathole and I'm gonna do my best to see it put to better use. In fact..." Whitman regarded his cigar, placed it once more in the ashtray "... if Texas is going to invest in fusion, I personally feel that laser fusion is more sensible than your tomahawks."

Nathaniel cocked his head. "You're talking about NIF?"

The senator nodded somberly.

"That's a defense program."

"In part. But they achieved ignition years ago and will mop you up in the race for a commercial plant."

For a moment Nathaniel stared at Whitman in true puzzlement. The National Ignition Facility at Lawrence Livermore *had* gone online years ago. NIF blasted rice-grain-sized pellets of frozen deuterium and tritium with 200 multi-trillion-watt lasers, imploding the capsules, triggering fusion. The original idea behind NIF was to create miniature hydrogen bombs so that the government didn't need to test real ones. Some exciting science concerning matter at ultrahigh densities had come out of the facility, but after the initial hoopla many of its results became strangely classified. Personally, Machuzak considered NIF one of science's great boondoggles, but the true swindle was calling it a prototype for a commercial reactor. NIF did produce more energy in one of its pulses than it consumed—what they hyped as ignition—but they'd never managed more than one or two shots a day, each a billionth of a second long. To call this a prototype for commercial fusion was weapons-grade horseshit.

"Senator," Nathaniel answered, gimlet eyed, "laser fusion is for Star Wars enthusiasts. Better you should shut them down."

Whitman remained unimpressed. "Dr. Machuzak, I remind you that France and other countries have opened similar facilities, so your opinions are far from universally shared. However, as aspects of such programs are still classified, I am not at liberty to discuss it with you."

Naturally. The senator moved toward the door, letting his visitor know in no uncertain terms that the interview was terminated. Nathaniel rose, understanding that he had accomplished absolutely nothing except to increase Whitman's enmity for the lab—and the fault was entirely his own.

Abruptly Machuzak said in a tone that was closer to a command than an invitation: "I'd like you to visit CFRC in two weeks." He should have begun here.

"The cook's tour?"

"The real tour. I intend that experiments should be under way."

"Already? Well, I don't relish the thought of being blown to bits." Strange, Nathaniel thought, I've heard that phrase before. "But all right." As he ushered the physicist out of his office, with his arm across his shoulder, Whitman said, "You have more guts than I expected, Machuzak. I like that, boy." Without waiting for a response, the politician went on unperturbed. "One more thing: you people should look into this cold-fusion business again. I'm sure you academy types are missing something. That I would support. It'd sure save a lot of taxpayer money."

Well, Fermilab did get funds by claiming they could build quark bombs, and UT's old Relativity Center was started with navy grants for antigravity research. "Do you know, Senator," Nathaniel said, "you can get substantially more energy out of fusion if you use helium-three as a fuel instead of tritium, and it's nonradioactive."

"Then for God's sake why don't you people try it?"

"It's only available on the moon."

Machuzak walked out then, stopping at the secretary's desk, vowing to himself that someday he'd take this senator down.

THIRTY

Shaking from his performance, once back at the lab Machuzak headed directly to the pentagon, where he found Abbuhl in the test cell. The magnet temperature stood at 120 absolute, on schedule, but the bakeout had stalled: The damned electric heater that forced hot, high-pressure helium gas through coils wrapping the doughnut to bake it and drive out impurities, had blown a filament. Fred assured him it would be repaired immediately. The coils themselves, thank God, hadn't sprung a leak. That would have sunk them without trace.

"Fred, we've got to get a first plasma in two weeks—"

"Mac, we're on schedule but—"

"Fred—"

Fred saluted and Machuzak left, punching both balloons of Munch's *Scream*.

* * * *

Even as Machuzak exited the tokamak bay, Archangelsky was summoning him to the lake. He found the Russian sitting beneath the fountain while he got an approximate geographic fix for an IP. "Cadarache!" Slava hissed. "Fucker." Machuzak looked on, puzzled, as his colleague entered the site that had alerted him, Fusion World.

"Fusion World?" Machuzak wrinkled his nose.

Indeed, the place was a theme park, all glittering and brightly lit against an evening sky, with a giant tokamak taking the place of Cinderella's castle. Passing through the gate, Archangelsky was greeted by an antique DeLorean, which glided up to him and raised its gull-wing doors. He entered as bidden, not failing to notice the "Mr. Fusion" reactor protruding from the trunk. As the door closed over him and he was swept into the sky, a silken female voice began to explain the basics of fusion.

"Many visitors want to know," she said, "the principles of the Mr. Fusion reactor on the DeLorean. This is a cold-fusion reactor, not a conventional hot fusion reactor, which is the subject of research at laboratories worldwide."

Forcing himself not to retch, Slava asked severely who she was, but like all customer-service representatives his disembodied guide was preprogrammed. The chirpy voice merely kept on while the car zoomed through the mountain-sized device, pointing out key features of a reactor. A short time later the car deposited Archangelsky back at the gate. At his feet lay the same chess queen with the shot-glass crown they'd seen before and next to it a little dragon—no, a fish. Then the whole place abruptly dissolved into a fireworks display.

"These messages are breadcrumbs," Machuzak said as Archangelsky vainly attempted to log on again. "One of your friends from that damned tournament is trying to tell us something. Have you remembered who shot the video?"

Slava shook his head. There was a limit to memory. "Good site," he finally said. "Designer knew what he was talking about. We should copy it. Guide pointed out the power supply; it's been hit. Maybe a hint."

"Could be coincidence. What else?"

"Cold fusion. She talked about cold fusion."

"What fucking good did that ever do anybody?" Machuzak said, stymied. He told Archangelsky to meet him at the MTF in two hours and departed.

* * * *

At sunset, just before he was about to depart for Site Alpha, T. J. rapped on Slava's door and found him at his terminal. He told her about Fusion World.

"Cadarache again?" she sighed. "Jesus. The Austin Cyber Crime Unit has finally gone beyond porn, and I might be able to twist some arms over there. I already contacted the FBI. As I expected…nada. To enlist the French…" She sighed again, feeling as stuck as ever, but Slava had already turned his attention back to the screen, slowly stroking his beard at what he saw there.

"What's that?" T. J. asked, peering over his shoulder at a simulation of brightly colored vortexes and spiraling paisleys that resembled tadpoles swimming in a whirlwind.

"This is what I do for a living when I'm not chasing cyber dragons or having my car blown up." The simulation was, in fact, what to Archangelsky a plasma looked like, a fluid chasing the magnetic field lines inside a tokamak. "In case I haven't told you, I design magnetic fields. We are going to need creative designs soon, I think."

"You can change those huge magnets in Prometheus?"

"Not magnets themselves, but we can play with the fields. Maybe I should say computer plays with fields. Our models have gone beyond human intuition. This disturbs me; it leaves soul hungry and is always dangerous."

T. J. knew if she pursued the provocation he would leave her behind. "Why don't you wear your wedding ring, Slava?" she asked, plunking herself down on the edge of his desk.

"How many women do you know who would put up with this?" he pointed ruefully to the monitor. "Nastya and I need space, that's all... How many couples live in same area code these days? If 24/7 work week didn't put end to age of love-conquers-all, gasoline price did. What do you want, T. J.? Your expression tells me this is not social call." He peered at her with those beady eyes that never failed to startle her.

"Mac wants to see us at the MTF," she said, glancing at her wrist.

"No," Slava shook his head. "What do you want?"

For a moment her gaze rested on an icon of the Mother of God, which Slava had hung on his office wall. As she regarded it, the tender expression of the Virgin enveloping the Child and all who gazed on it seemed so alien to what she knew of this physicist that she found herself speechless.

"Well, Slava," she began, "all the techs downstairs are cleared. Their inspection sheets back them up, meanin they can show me where they were repairing this gizmo or replacing that one. Ya know, DNA doesn't lie, and sooner or later you gotta start listenin. The only DNA I've got is you, Mac and Lipman, and I've never rightly understood what you PhDs were doin down in engineering country—"

"Klop—"

"Who's *Klop*?"

"Russian for bedbug. *Klop*, we've told you what there is to tell. We were staffed short, pulling triple shifts. Lipman asked for our help. Nat Edward'ich and my badges are good for all areas; check the files. That's all. You've seen how things are around here."

"After the fact, yeah." Without a further word she inserted her ring into the nearest port of Archangelsky's computer. Suddenly Slava, facing the camera, was arguing with Krieg-Zuber, present only in voice.

"He shot this with phone?" asked Archangelsky, scarcely raising an eyebrow.

Slava's utter resignation slightly surprised T. J. She nodded, brushed back her hair, glanced at her playlist.

Krieg-Zuber is telling Slava to stop wasting his time with some idea of Matsushima's connected to that thing called a mirror device.

"Contract says I work twenty percent on anything I want. Keeps brain alive. Working nonstop on tokamak keeps brain dead."

"Your contract is going to change, old chum. We can't waste resources anymore on dead-ends."

Slava starts, angers, peers at the camera with that anarchist expression already familiar to D'Abro. "You know mirror machines are more stable than tokamaks, have higher betas. If Toshi's idea is correct, no need for doughnuts. *Pfft*. This is dead end? For tokamaks, yes."

"Dr. Archangelsky, you have a choice: one hundred percent of your efforts to the Mission, or one hundred percent of your time to searching for a new job."

"I'll speak to Rasmussen about this."

After a flicker, the video jumps to the director's office and this time Archangelsky did register surprise. "He bugged Leonard's office too?"

The detective nodded slowly; Slava searched for any sign of profound disgust on her face, but all he could make out was a shallow resignation. In the video two men are now visible, captured by a ceiling camera.

"Krieg-Zuber has threatened to eliminate me unless I give up work on other projects," Slava heard himself say.

"I'm sorry, Slava," Leonard Rasmussen apologizes contritely. The director appeared to be in good health, as he should be according to the time stamp of a year ago. "Cyrus is correct. I have held this lab together by force of will alone and we can no longer afford the luxury of exploring secondary avenues. Toshi's idea is a long shot anyway, hardly worth your effort. We need you for the Big Push, Slava." Leonard clenched his fist. "ASSET will achieve ignition before ITER or I'll die trying."

"And what will you do with Toshi?" Archangelsky watched himself anger. "You can stop such a man from thinking his own thoughts? Hah. He would sooner leave lab than sell out own ideas."

"Then he will leave the lab! Of what use is he to me? I will not allow Matsushima to threaten our great endeavor, do you hear?"

Both men recoil in surprise at the outburst and for a moment stare silently at one another. T. J. could not but recollect Matsushima's own outburst the other day.

"Perhaps you should consider working elsewhere," Rasmussen says at last. The sun streaming through the windows of the octagon sparkles off Leonard's desk and the daruma doll on the shelf.

"*Pravda*." Slava storms out of the office and the show ends.

Yaroslav Borisovich turned to D'Abro. "So, like Nat said, you have seen argument. What does this prove other than we work in Gulag?"

"Not much," T. J. allowed. "But like I keep sayin to Nat: be careful, Slava."

Archangelsky, in full Rasputin mode, threw at D'Abro a visage she wasn't likely to forget and growled through his teeth, but otherwise made no protest.

"Let's get over to the MTF," she said.

* * * *

Machuzak was waiting, but before he uttered a word, Slava waved him silent and nodded to D'Abro, who'd brought a palm-sized bug detector from her car. "What's going on?" Nathaniel wanted to know. "The investigation is public now."

"Too public," Archangelsky spat as they climbed over everything, sweeping the lab for listening devices and cameras. "Edward'ich, things were worse than we thought, fucking Stalinists." He said not a word more until he and Machuzak had rigged up a noisy spark generator from parts on the lab bench.

When Machuzak heard Slava's report he found himself far angrier at D'Abro than at Krieg-Zuber. "Who are you after, T. J.?" His gaze was adamantine.

"I'm after the man trying to destroy your program," she answered sullenly, sadly, but she didn't capitulate and rolled another video.

Once more it was Machuzak speaking to Krieg-Zuber, this time about three years ago. "We're taking you off ASSET," Krieg-Zuber said to Machuzak. "You have a choice: leave or become division head at the MTF."

"You're exiling me with Toshi, banishing troublesome rivals?"

"You're perpetually griping that we've neglected materials research for decades. Take it or leave it."

Machuzak took it and worked hard at it, but it wasn't good enough. Without pause, T. J. played another scene stamped only six months ago. Once again the scene is The Terminator's office. "I've decided to close down the MTF. Time for you to pack."

Nathaniel saw himself before Krieg-Zuber shaking, and an expression of absolute disgust written across his face.

"On second thought," Cyrus went on, abruptly nonchalant, "I shall merely incorporate the MFT into another division. We might require your services for the upcoming ASSET dedication. Consider yourself put on notice."

Machuzak hardly had time to react before the scene jumped again, this time only days after the dispute over the secrecy of the dedication that D'Abro had already shown him.

"Old boy," the affect at once returned, "I'm shutting down the MTF in three weeks. You're history, Machuzak." Even recorded, the snap of his fingers jarred.

The Nathaniel in this playback, though, managed to possess himself. "You're bluffing," he said coldly. "You been making noises for a year. What good is your reactor if you don't know what to build it of? You know as well as I do it's the last hurdle to creating a commercial machine."

"*Docteur*, materials research is as sexy as my ass and I've put up with your virulent insubordination long enough. I shall speak to Rasmussen the moment we've commissioned ASSET."

"Speak to him. He'll tell you you're all ass."

The monitor went blank.

T. J., facing Machuzak, asked bluntly why Zuber hadn't closed down the MTF.

The answer was as evident as Machuzak's expression: "He died, alas not permanently." They stared at each other without flinching until Nathaniel said, "D'Abro, you've become hypnotized by video hearsay. Who knows how these videos were edited?"

"Krieg-Zuber swears they're not and he's opened his entire archives without subpoena. Doc, I've been warnin you to watch out. I'm givin you *real* good advice: watch out." Although she didn't add "please," the petition in her voice was unmistakable.

"Some partnership," Machuzak muttered after a moment during which both of them retreated. At last she asked why he wanted to see them here.

He scratched his head as if he'd forgotten, glanced nervously over his shoulder in a way that saddened her. When he turned back, the anger had disappeared from his face, the entreaty from hers, but he could not put aside the strange bond that had formed between them. "I saw Whitman today and got him to agree to visit the lab with Moravec. I want Prometheus ready."

T. J. was certain Machuzak had derailed. "That's it? You didn't knock Whitman out of the picture?"

"No, I blew it. The only thing left is to convince him that we're not the charlatans he claims—and that's not going to be easy. He's dumb but not as dumb as I thought." There was one other thing. "I want to learn why the senator has it in for CFRC."

"What's that have to do with me?" T. J. retorted, mystified, frustrated, even as the little flame on the physicist's test cylinder distracted her. "I've got an investigation to run."

"You do, and I've got a lab to save."

THIRTY-ONE

But how? A month after he'd taken the job, Machuzak had no idea how to disperse the intangible haze, neither autumn mist nor smog, that now shrouded the final descent into the valley. Outside the main gate the family was gone, but a larger group of locals had taken its place, brandishing posters for Nuclear Free America, Save the Environment, Solar People. Nathaniel couldn't be certain whether this was protest or advertising. Along the drive, over the big sign proclaiming the number of accident-free man-hours, someone had spray-painted the number of sabotage-free hours. Not many. Nathaniel called maintenance.

Below Bill Balustradi's photo inside the lobby, a small tangle of action heroes charged about blindly, colliding with one another. Machuzak puckered his lips, tore off the top calendar page and descended to the control room where he found Abbuhl. Without hesitation he pressed again whether they'd be ready for first plasma by the time Moravec and Whitman arrived.

"Mac," Fred turned around. The engineer's lined face and drooping eyelids immediately told Machuzak that he'd been at it round the clock, in violation of the two-shift rule. "Don't try what Krieg-Zuber tried," he said wearily.

"I said first plasma, not ignition."

Abbuhl only stared blankly at Machuzak's testy response, as if nothing was computing. "Mac, have you seen today's ITER release? Balard just completed a thirty-second low-power burn—and we haven't even started. They're thumbin their noses at us, sir."

About to reprimand the chief for his safety infraction, Nathaniel's attention was suddenly caught by a temperature display. The magnets had fallen below 77 degrees absolute, nitrogen's boiling point. The giant niobium-tin coils were getting seriously chilly. Civil war might well break out in the 60 degrees that remained before they became superconducting, and everyone could die of exhaustion in the further 14 degrees before they reached operating temperatures, but Machuzak did not reprimand Abbuhl. Instead he stared with a faint feeling of amazement.

After two weeks of pumping, the torus itself stood below a ten-billionth of an atmosphere. The task ahead of Fred was to get rid of ninety percent of what remained. Machuzak heard in his mind the puttering of the troglodyte roughing pumps, larger versions of the mechanical jobs in his lab or a high school chem class. They'd begun the process, then—

The test-cell hotline cut off his thoughts. "Fred, we've got a problem." Faberman, back on the job. "One of the fan blades has broken," he said, referring to the turbomoleculars.

"It was about time this happened," replied Abbuhl with a resignation as heavy as it was undisguised. The tech couldn't be sure what exactly had occurred. Operating in what beginners consider high-vacuum, turbomolecular pumps remove air molecule by molecule, spinning at fifty thousand rpms. Even a small leak sometimes proves too much for the delicate fans and a blade shatters. This late in the pumpdown...?

"Call France," said Abbuhl. "Get one overnighted and take this one to the airport." As Faberman signed off, the chief turned again to Machuzak. "We'll have it fixed by tomorrow evening, *Herr Doktor* Director," he exhaled, and it seemed his entire chest collapsed.

Nathaniel laid his hand on the engineer's shoulder. "Fred," he replied, "organize a basketball game for this afternoon, then take the rest of the day off."

* * * *

It was time to find Mercedes. Machuzak headed to the MTF but didn't see her anywhere. With trepidation he checked his mail: three more resignations. At this moment he could not force himself to check the ITER website. On YouTube, dozens of videos proclaiming a government conspiracy to cover up cold fusion. At last sensing another presence, Nathaniel walked through the adjoining lab into the cavernous, decaying accelerator room and circled around the linear accelerator there.

"How are you, Mercedes?" he said, finding Ramirez at a workstation.

She practically jumped at the sight of him and knocked over the styrofoam cup of coffee on the desk. "Damn!" she exclaimed, removing her earbuds as Machuzak moved to help her mop up.

"Sorry, Nathaniel, you surprised me. I haven't seen you for weeks."

"Yeah, I've been scarce. You look better than last time. Are you getting any work done?"

Mercedes nodded wanly and brushed back her hair but suddenly protested with a shrill edge, "What's the point? I'd be wasting less time looking for another job..." Not for the first time Machuzak was struck by how dark her skin was, nearly as brown as one of Gauguin's natives. In truth, he might well have been regarding a work of art, for any friendship between them had receded into the still past and the person before him now was in every sense a stranger. "I've been a little on edge," she grudgingly backtracked, "I guess like everybody else around here. It's scary, not knowing what's going to happen…"

"One thing that's going to happen is that in less than two weeks Whitman and Moravec are coming to visit—"

"What for?" she cut him off as shrilly as before. "They plan to get killed?"

"No, the motherfuckers want to show their audiences that they're reasonable men. Will this be in running order?" He pointed with his thumb to the accelerator. "Can you show them something?"

Mercedes nodded. "Nothing much can go wrong with this thing. I could irradiate them, I suppose."

"Don't tempt me," said Nathaniel and turned to leave. For a moment he regarded the machine, a big white cylinder nearly forty meters long. He could hardly look at it without flinching. The accelerator was the main reason the MTF cost millions a year to run and was the locus of all of Krieg-Zuber's threats. Threats or no, it produced neutrons, the deadliest particle, and for that reason it was important.

The Terminator well knew that what to make a reactor out of so that it wouldn't literally collapse after twenty years of neutron bombardment was probably the most serious hurdle between the now and commercial fusion. As the scene D'Abro had sprung on him yesterday made too clear, Zuber also knew that solving it wouldn't make anyone's name; that is why he viewed the MTF with such contempt. Nathaniel's problem was another. On the hierarchy of romance, the materials' challenge occupies the lowest rung; for that reason he'd balked at becoming its division head. As for Mercedes…well, she probably wouldn't find much else.

"Come to the barbeque this afternoon," he said to her, then phoned Lise to organize one. "In fact," he told the secretary, "schedule one every week."

* * * *

This pall's enough to choke on, thought T. J. along the main drive. She didn't like the look of those protestors, no way. Even the armadillos scampering across the road seemed sullen, sluggish, and yes, someone had painted radiation hazard symbols on their armor. She wasn't amused.

In the lobby she cast her eye at the shrine of action heroes, which she took to be the gods lab personnel expected to save CFRC. About to tear off the day's sheet from the calendar, she saw that Mac had beaten her. She wondered how long it would be his privilege and felt sick. God, what was springing up between them? He'd said it: they had a job to do. Science goes where it goes; investigations go where they go. Why couldn't he just level with her? Again she glanced at the figures at her feet. Dang, even for her this was a little weird.

She was surprised to find Cyrus Krieg-Zuber waiting at this early hour outside her office. Wishing him good morning, she unlocked the door and stepped in. He followed without invitation, glancing around the naked space, at the red garter adorning her monitor, the single flower vase now adding a solitary cheer. "I should give you a poster, mademoiselle," he said in his low voice. "Cheer the place up…"

"What can I do for you, Dr. Krieg-Zuber?" she replied without answering.

The deputy closed the door behind him. "I understand you have found my archives helpful. You are making progress?"

T. J. glanced at the tough, angular figure before her. "Some," she said after a pause long enough to reveal her uncertainty. "Patience is the name of this game, Dr. Krieg-Zuber." Lord, give me more. "I've seen a lot of videos of Machuzak and Archangelsky duking it out with you, behavin as if they're ready to defect to the enemy, but nothing that points conclusively to ITER, despite my instincts."

"As I told you," Krieg-Zuber offered, "only a fool would use the CFRC server for such communications."

T. J.'s claustrophobia was increasing, but Krieg-Zuber appeared entertained, with himself or her as he rearranged one of the flowers in the vase. "What would you do?" she asked finally.

"Mademoiselle, please," he replied with an expression dividing contempt and amusement, "if *I* were Balard's mole, I'd attempt some nonstandard method of communication…and in that case I'd be an even bigger fool. Detective D'Abro, you know as well as I do that communications taking place on company property, on company time are subject to scrutiny…" Here Zuber began to pensively stroke the scar on his cheek. "A few weeks before the dedication I became aware of some shortwave transmissions—absurdly low frequency by today's standards, but effective for long-distance communication and difficult to pinpoint. The signals seemed to be coming and going from the lab at irregular intervals."

"How were you aware of them?" T. J. peered at him skeptically.

"Miss D'Abro, until recently I *was* in charge of information security—"

"I've been meanin to ask," interrupted T. J., "doesn't the deputy director have more important things to worry about, like running the lab?"

Krieg-Zuber abruptly broke off stroking his scar and exploded. "Nothing is more important than security, mademoiselle, nothing!" In an instant he'd calmed down and now fixed on her a stare of benevolent surprise. "And I would be shamefully slipshod in my duties if I failed to monitor all frequencies. Any fool can do it with a store-bought scanner. I captured several transmissions, although the messages were of course encrypted. I have not yet attempted to break the code, but, but if the parties haven't been serious enough to use one-time pads, the messages can be cracked. I am certain ITER is involved."

"Just how are you certain, sir?" T. J. replied, conscious that Krieg-Zuber's story had riveted her.

"Each transmission is prefixed by 'The Way Forward' or 'The Way Backward' in an artificial voice. Obviously the parties are being careless, assuming no one would be interested enough to listen in."

She and the docs had done their best to keep everyone at CFRC ignorant of their search for Dragonmaster, but with Krieg-Zuber's fastidiousness in such matters, T. J. could no longer be certain he was in the dark. With the prospect of a second strike, the FBI's lack of interest and Machuzak's preoccupation with ignition… T. J. clenched her teeth. She'd see an end to this.

Rising, D'Abro faced the deputy straight on. "Dr. Krieg-Zuber, I'm not uninformed of your background," she said with a glance at a pile of folders on her desk. "You came to ANFRL from Advanced Cryotech and have had super-deluxe CIA corporate training. You think we're all amateurs next to you. You may also believe I was born yesterday or couldn't hit a bull's ass with a banjo, but, sir, I'm well aware of your antipathy toward Dr. Machuzak and have no doubt you'd like to see this investigation go in a certain direction—"

"No, no," he held up his hands in protest, "you misunderstand completely, young lady. I'm merely interested in getting to the truth of the matter. How can I be blamed if that fool decides to jeopardize the entire Mission with amateurish undercover tactics?"

"That was my call."

"My sincerest apologies, Detective," he bowed. "But understand, you and I are on the same team."

"Dr. Krieg-Zuber," T. J. said, peering at him, "since you are presently inactive, I'd ask you to decode those messages. Let me know when you have something."

"It would be my pleasure, mademoiselle."

THIRTY-TWO

Surveying the gang of squabblers and potential mutineers gathered around the conference table, it remained beyond hope that they could pull off the miracle required of them, but to Machuzak's astonishment everyone was present, including Toshi and Slava. More remarkably, no one was arguing. "In a week we have visitors coming," he said. "This you know. If we haven't lost the chance already, it will certainly be our last opportunity to convince Moravec and Whitman that CFRC scientists have some idea of what they're doing. Can we show them that Prometheus can hold a fire?"

All eyes turned toward Abbuhl. "I'd say that's a possibility, Sir Director." Fred didn't look much better for the sleep Machuzak had ordered him to get a few days ago. "The vessel bake is nearly complete, so far so good. We're running tests on the neutral beams and rf systems and getting ready for coil energization tests. The cooldown is nearly finished. With luck, in a couple days we'll be at operating temperatures...with luck..."

Nathaniel thanked him, then gave them the bad news: "I'm sure you've seen today's report from ITER. Their numbers are going up and it looks like they'll attempt breakeven within a week or two." Breakeven, at which you get as much energy out of the plasma as you put in. "What do you thi—?"

"Let's go for it," Kettering now jumped in. "Kick their butts."

Hasschler appeared undecided; it depended on the mood of the neutral beams.

"Mac," said Fred, "don't try it on opening day. It's too risky."

"You're right. Somethin nice and easy. Maybe a mega-amp at five Teslas—"

"DT," said Kettering. "Fuck DD."

Nathaniel did not respond. "The rest of you guys"—he bore down on Hasschler and Matsushima "—had better be generating ideas, because you're on stage next."

"We have been generating ideas, Nathaniel," replied Toshi, "but as the wise man said, to die for an idea is to place a high value on conjecture."

* * * *

An hour later, Slava's wrist was again summoning him to Fusion World. This time he crossed himself, alerted D'Abro and waited without making another move until she and Nat were dashing into his office from opposite directions. The trace dead-ended at the same region in southern France.

When Slava entered the site, the plaza before the Cinderella tokamak was jumping with 3-D animations of the inventions of Nikola Tesla. Lightning bolts smash into the ground from his famous Long Island tower. Tesla coils send Frankenstein sparks climbing into the air; the face of the inventor hovers on giant helium balloons over everything, while the whole show is accompanied by an ear-shattering rock beat: "*Into this world came a man out of time…*"

"At least Dragonmaster has a sense of humor," Machuzak remarked to Slava alone, utterly perplexed. No longer trusting that the detective held the slightest trust in them, this morning he refused to acknowledge her presence.

"Nice track," D'Abro observed.

"He is nutcase," Slava said to Nathaniel.

Attempting to make sense of what they were seeing, Nathaniel ticked off some of Tesla's achievements: "He was into wireless energy transmission, early radio pioneer. Teslite legions credit him with atomic energy, nuclear fusion, cold fusion, not to mention the twentieth century."

"Like you said," Archangelsky nodded, "Dragonmaster has sense of humor."

As if to confirm Nat's words, the DeLorean pulled up then, no guide, and as Slava hopped in a voice reminded the passenger that the car's cold fusion power source was made possible by the visionary work of Nikola Tesla. "Definitely has a thing about cold fusion."

Today the car didn't provide a fly-through of the giant tokamak but instead passed over a rocky, barren cove overlooking the sea. There was little to catch the eye except a few radio antennas and a small concrete obelisk.

"Where the hell is that?" asked T. J.

"Poldhu, Cornwall," Slava answered, face growing ashen. "Site of Marconi's first transatlantic radio transmission."

"And how do you know?" she swiveled on him; her disbelief showed.

"Was radio amateur as kid. Without shortwave, was hard to learn anything in Russia. I still keep transceiver." He pointed to a cabinet.

Archangelsky waited for D'Abro's reply, but to his surprise her only response was a tightly clenched jaw as the tour ended with a fireworks display that created the shot-glass crowned queen and a fish.

"He's your friend, Slava," said Mac. "Find him."

"Damnit!" Archangelsky slammed his fist on the desk. "How many times have I told you, I contacted everyone in video. *Klop*, if you're so fucking sure Dragonmaster is coming through ITER server, talk to their system admin."

"I have. It's not their machine. Just nearby. I've put in a request to the French police." T. J. hoped that she'd concealed her outright lie. It *was* an ITER server, but Dragonmaster had slipped up by coming through it. The ITER administrator had immediately cooperated and the trace led to—Austin.

After a long, uncomfortable moment passed, Slava muttered, "Better an anthropologist to trace this guy than a hacker. Useless pud-puller."

Nathaniel glanced at the blank screen, at the wall clock. "Slava, I'm moving ahead." Without a word to D'Abro he left the room.

* * * *

Just before five he was receiving a report on the motor-generator tests when D'Abro, Richard Garrett in tow, cornered him and dragged him to Slava's office. Her bearing was even more distant than it had been in the morning, and several degrees angrier than when she'd sprung the last video on him. Once again she plugged her ring directly into Slava's computer without uttering a word.

The image quality was not nearly so good as in the previous surprises. The picture jittered with noise; sound poor, perspective odd—as if it had been shot from the top of Slava's desk. According to the time stamp, the scene took place only weeks ago, during the run-up to the demo. Archangelsky was checking his office, lifting up the icon on his wall. Eventually he sat down opposite Machuzak. Exactly how angry he was, was difficult to determine, but no one would bet that he was sober.

"Nat Edward'ich," Archangelsky heard himself say as he filled two shot glasses with vodka, "Balard has offered me job at ITER. I will accept."

"You will?" Machuzak makes his reply with evident surprise, peering over the tumbler he holds in his hand. "How can you, Slava?"

"What can I do here? Program is a mess. The Terminator blocks everything besides ASSET, reduces me to programmer, then engineer. Balard is bastard, for sure, but one bastard is better than two or three. He suggests maybe I can stay in Austin but work for him."

"H–he'd pay you for ITER code development?"

Archangelsky nods. "He would annex CFRC. *Anschluss*." Slava slams his fist on the desk and for a moment the image goes missing.

"Balard always claims idea was his when he was grad student and Leonard appropriated it. Let's organize coup, overthrow regime."

"Hmm, h—how would we do that?" asks Machuzak, now showing the effects of the substance in hand.

"This requires planning, but you know, lab needs a spanner thrown into the works."

After a pause, during which he wryly consults the alcohol, Nathaniel answers, "I agree." He sets down the glass and the scene goes black for a second and final time.

"How was this shot?" Machuzak demanded angrily, once he'd recovered from his stupefaction.

"Do you deny that it took place?" T. J. insisted, dismissing the question.

"How was it shot?" Machuzak repeated.

Slava was beside himself. "I thought I knew all tricks… I was even sweeping office for bugs—" Suddenly, he faced D'Abro with a finger practically at her nose. "This was smart dust, wasn't it? Synthesized image?"

With reluctance T. J. nodded.

Slava ran his fingers across his desktop, ornamental ashtray, as if wiping them clean of disgust. Fangs fully bared, his visage belonged to a wolf.

"What do you expect?" T. J. said defensively with anger and sadness warring for her face. "Two seditious employees, you think your superiors aren't watching? Admit it, this don't look none too good."

Machuzak snarled. "Only The Terminator could have come up with this…"

Garrett, who'd remained silent 'til that moment, raised his hands. "Now y'all calm down. I saw two disgruntled scientists blowin off steam during a rough patch, that's all. Anybody can see they're joking…can't you?" Machuzak didn't like the question mark at the end of The Chairman's sentence, or the squint of his brow. "I suggest a twenty-four-hour cooling-off period. Agreed?"

D'Abro was gone.

The Chairman put his arms around the two scientists' shoulders. "Boys, the situation here is obviously worse than I thought. I can't believe you two were up to anything other than sharpenin your horns, but if you were, I'm askin you to confess—now."

"I'm wanted in the test cell," Machuzak said, also making for the door. "By the way, Richard, don't forget, Moravec and Whitman are showing up in a week."

* * * *

By the time the days ran their course, Fred Abbuhl appeared, if possible, more exhausted than Machuzak had ever seen him, barely able to stand. Indeed, excusing himself, he took a seat at one of the computer stations, next to a pot of coffee. Nathaniel withheld reprimand because, despite everything, his astonishment today surpassed even that of a week ago. The cryopumps had completed the evacuation faultlessly as air molecules dutifully wandered onto their liquid-helium cooled panels to stick there like frost to a windowpane: the pressure inside Prometheus stood at a hundred-billionth of an atmosphere.

As if to ridicule Cochran's warnings, the liquid helium factory had also kept up its end of the bargain and the magnets rested at operating temperature, 4.2 degrees above absolute zero. Fred's team was putting the coils through their paces, but remarkably all systems seemed go: this morning, the magnets were superconducting at 15 Teslas, which made them—except for bench-top jobs the Dutch used to levitate frogs—along with ITER's the most powerful on Earth. Moments ago, the techs had begun the machine-area scrub. They'd clean every nook and cranny of metal or debris, and not for nothing: they had no intention of allowing an ultrahigh magnetic field turn a forgotten wrench into a rocket-propelled grenade.

What had they overlooked? Machuzak clearly saw he was asking for trouble, that a visit was the perfect opportunity… But if they'd overlooked nothing, if they'd been meant to overlook nothing, Moravec and Whitman could watch a first plasma. "Fred," Nathaniel said as he had on the other occasion, "get some sleep. That's an order. We're just beginning."

THIRTY-THREE

A strange welcoming committee gathered outside the main building to meet two black limos and one orange and white with horns, which were converging by the lake. More than the visit had forced Machuzak to run his tongue over his lips as he passed through the outer gate. Overnight, the number of protestors had quadrupled to one hundred and a dozen National Guardsmen stood poised, weapons ready, to keep the troublemakers at bay. Worse, media vans parked at the fence told him that word of the visit had leaked. Worse yet, as Nathaniel drove between the opposing forces, he sensed that the antagonists were itching for a fight; he waved cheerfully.

Now he stood in a Western vest with Archangelsky to his right, whose blue sports jacket, lanyard and beard put him in full punk-tsarist mode. To his left, Toshi immaculately suited in a high-collar Maoist jacket and Theresa, who insisted on joining them, promising a surprise, effervescent in a shimmering gray-green skirt and blouse. Leonard lolled in his wheelchair beside the curb.

The decision to exclude T. J. sat hard. He couldn't blame her for doing her job; he could blame her for not seeing where a scientist's duty lay. And as long as she hadn't arrested him the call was his. While the fountain's spray caressed them, Machuzak discerned the expectant quiet in the old westerns before the gunfight, the deeper shadows, the glint off the windows, the crunch of gravel under the boots. The hairs on his arm stood too, though he thought that had more to do with the distant clouds heralding the onset of Austin's wet season. He was wary of gunfights after his showdown with Whitman. Today he had no hope of eliminating the senator, son of snake pus. Today he'd devote to reconnaissance and hope that the experience of a functioning laboratory would cause Big Bad Roy and Moravec to relent.

As the chauffeurs discharged their passengers, Whitman emerged in his buckskin carrying no less than an Alamo-vintage musket. But the cornball stunt paled next to the two bodyguards armed with pistols and Uzis who climbed out ahead of him and closed ranks. The confrontation had begun.

"Sorry, Senator," Nathaniel said, "I won't have weapons on the premises."

Leaning on his musket, Whitman measured the physicist facing him. "Dr. Machuzak, I'm risking my life coming here and have no intention of being taken down by a terrorist or those folks at the gate. Either my men come or I leave."

Despite the banality of the senator's words and his own better judgment, Nathaniel saw little choice. Moravec's trick was craftier but no less TV-ready: one of the CEO's pleasant faces appeared on the screen of a remote and expendable bot, which now unholstered a pistol from beneath its jacket and handed it to the chauffeur.

Atmosphere corroded, Theresa and Slava forced on smiles and handed out the traditional personalized hard hats, which Moravec politely declined. Leonard wished the guests a pleasant tour and departed, while Garrett attempted damage repair by trading Aggie jokes with Whitman. When The Chairman asked the visitors whether they'd ever met, both said no, and shook hands so mechanically that Nathaniel all but laughed.

* * * *

The sky growled as long black trails became visible against the horizon. Nathaniel ushered everyone onto a van, which hummed over to Site Alpha. While the senator's heavies scanned the drive for loose saboteurs and protestors, the wandering eye of Moravec's avatar showed that, even remotely, the CEO could not fully armor herself against the laboratory's scale. That had been a small part of the plan.

The bodyguards swept into the Materials Test Facility as if expecting to be met by automatic-weapons fire. Mercedes, who'd been waiting but never for this, caught her breath, shot her hands into the air and cast a frozen, terrified glance at Machuzak. Only once he reassured her that all was well, did she manage to stagger the few steps to her test stand.

"T–the Materials Test Facility," she told them, plainly quaking as Theresa and Nathaniel distributed coffee, "is dedicated to one of the most basic challenges in building a commercial reactor: what, uh, do you build it of?" Pulling herself together with difficulty, she reminded everyone of the ultrahigh magnetic fields Prometheus required, fields that attempted to twist iron into corkscrews, and so you needed to construct the machine out of nonmagnetic materials. "The old tokamaks were built from stainless steel, nonmagnetic but soft and heavy, whereas Prometheus is constructed of superalloys and titanium, stronger and lighter." Ramirez's disquiet at this moment understandably went beyond her usual high-strung behavior, but even so, as she droned on with a bloodless face, she reminded Nathaniel of one of those department-store mannequins from a 1950s display kitchen and he wondered whether she was aiding the cause.

"The problem with stainless, and to a lesser extent titanium, is that they, uh, absorb neutrons." At the n-word, Mercedes flinched visibly, then reluctantly confessed that after twenty years of bombarding itself with neutrons, a fusion reactor would become so radioactive you'd have to bury it.

"Like that place in Russia… Chernobyl," the senator snorted, his first comment. It didn't help. "If a reactor's so dangerous, why build it at all?"

Mercedes swallowed and Slava jumped in. "Dirigible is dangerous too, if you build it out of wrong stuff."

"Yes," continued Mercedes, recovering as Whitman shot an unfriendly bolt at the Russian. "This is why we're developing activationless materials." She ushered everyone into the accelerator bay, which is large enough to convince visitors that the scientists are up to something. The accelerator, she explained, lit to ghoulish green under the fluorescents, slammed deuterium nuclei into a target of frozen tritium.

"Like NIF," Whitman said, a quantum more brightly.

"Uh, something like that."

"Tell me," the senator suddenly asked, smiling brightly, "can you find God with this machine?"

Ramirez involuntarily freezes again, totally flummoxed, utterly immobile.

"No," Nathaniel answers the senator with humor and derision, "for that you need a much bigger machine."

"I knew we should have built the Supercollider," Whitman says.

Slava leans over. "You idiot," he whispers into Machuzak's ear. "You should have asked for funding."

Mercedes, spooked into her full zombie persona, now continued as if the interruption never occurred, explaining that on the one hand neutrons are necessary because they carry off most of the energy of fusion reactions, but on the other they are dangerous, because by slamming into the machine, they cause it to become radioactive and weaken the superstructure. "At the MTF," she said, handing a Geiger counter to Moravec, "we investigate low-activation materials: vanadium, silicon carbide, chromium-titanium alloys…" The counter rattled obscenely as the avatar passed it over a steel sample lying on the benchtop, then dropped to a rare click on the vanadium. Whitman stole a glance at his watch.

Leading the group back to the adjacent lab, where Jerry Wilson on his back like a car mechanic fiddled beneath a great steel clam several meters across, Mercedes droned on. "The public is understandably afraid of radiation, but of greater concern to us here is that after several decades of neutron bombardment, the reactor's superstructure will collapse under its own weight."

At once the scene loops in Machuzak's mind: Krieg-Zuber threatening to shut down the MTF; he, Machuzak, arguing that unless this problem is solved, the proceeding decades of effort will have been in vain.

"Nature is a challenging mistress," Mercedes said and went on to explain that materials which don't weaken under neutron bombardment aren't the best for holding a vacuum or resisting the heat of the plasma. "A commercial reactor will be subjecting its inner walls to an amount of heat approaching that radiated by our sun over every square meter." Rapping on the big chamber, she explained that in this experiment they bombarded various materials with sunlike plasmas to see how they stood up.

The only reaction was from the bodyguards, who nervously scratched their weapons and convinced Nathaniel that he was witnessing a lifeless laboratory. Finally, Whitman interrupted, asking whether all this had any practical applications.

Without a blush Theresa ticked off the list: microcircuitry etching; waste disposal; the coating of materials, like chrome on car fenders, long a billion-dollar industry. Advanced welding systems. Rocket engines.

Once Machuzak got over his surprise, he realized that Theresa, if anyone, would have been well rehearsed in such matters.

"Chrome on car fenders," remarked Whitman. "That I can understand."

Moravec was less impressed. "Those spin-offs can be accomplished directly, without building enormously complicated reactors."

As they departed the water-stained MTF, Mercedes threw at Machuzak a glance of pure hatred. Absorbing it, he leaned over to Theresa and said, "This isn't going well." She shrugged off his concern, reminding him that the morning was young, but outside, just as they rounded the building, a slew of journalists ambushed them.

"Two can play this game, boy," said Whitman as he waved on the reporters.

"Senator," one of them asks, eyeing his goons, "aren't you worried about your safety here today?"

"Of course I'm concerned," he smiled broadly, patting his musket. "As you see I've brought protection. Nevertheless, it's my duty to see that taxpayer money is spent properly, and so despite the substantial risk I have come today to CFRC to assess the situation. But Texas—" he brandishes Ol' Betsy above his head—"is prepared!"

The bastard knows who he's playing for, Machuzak fumes with unconcealed admiration, and it ain't us. Simultaneously, Archangelsky makes a move for an imaginary pistol, then shrugs empty-handed at the reporters.

"How do you assess the situation?" the journalist follows up, ignoring the Russian clown.

"I see no advantage to fusion," Whitman replies. "By the time it is a reality, we can have built a hundred nuclear reactors and exploited every drop of shale and offshore oil."

"Exactly," interrupts Moravec, for nearly the first time saying anything at all, "every drop."

The reporters turn to Moravec's avatar as the morphing assemblage rocks toward the van. "You don't agree with the senator, sir?"

"No," he emphatically replies from afar. "The senator should ask how many lives have been lost to respiratory disease due to his perpetual war against federal regulations. Personally, however, I am not convinced that fusion is possible, yet alone economical. I wish it were—"

"Then why have you imposed the deadline on CFRC?" A bot from the *Statesman* site shoves her ring mic into the other bot's face.

"My company's direction is solar and wind. As for fusion, you might agree that a century is a long time line for an investment." The exec sounds so reasonable, so irreproachable, that no one watching this show will doubt her good intentions. Even to Machuzak she, it is convincing. "The size of the investment for fusion is certainly colossal." Moravec seems genuinely embarrassed, even remotely, by the attention. "The ITER project with all its overruns is costing twenty billion euros."

"Yes," Whitman jumps in, intending that the CEO should not grab the spotlight, "and for all that money it won't even produce any energy."

Machuzak won't let that nonsense go by. "ITER is a scientific experiment, not a commercial reactor. It's not meant to produce net energy."

Theresa had remained virtually silent since the start of this, but the creases around her eyes showed that she was following the exchange intently. Seeing an opening, she suddenly invaded Whitman's space and faced the crowd. "You must not believe the senator's feigned disinterest, people. His brother Thomas ran the Office of Energy Research at the DOE several decades ago and together they have been trying to kill fusion ever since."

Machuzak himself started, hard. The Office of Energy Research at the Department of Energy—now the Office of Science—oversaw energy research at the major US laboratories. He hadn't known Whitman had a brother who'd been director there, let alone one who opposed fusion.

Several decades ago Nathaniel was in college. What do college kids know? What is Theresa going for?

"Mrs. Rasmussen," the senator said, unable to conceal an umbrage that penetrated his buckskin, "it's true that my brother was at the DOE. What of it? As director of the Office of Energy Research he had many assessments to make."

"Of course he did," Theresa returned with a stiletto smile, "and wasn't one of those assessments to divert fifty million dollars away from the magnetic fusion program?"

Leaning on his musket Whitman scratched his chin in an attempt to look as much like Fess Parker as possible. "I have a dim recollection of him making proper use of discretionary funds, but perhaps you should ask him, Mrs. Rasmussen, not me." He beamed broadly.

Suddenly they seemed to be poised on the verge of open hostilities, but with Whitman's final remark the brakes were switched back on. Theresa herself climbed into the van and they drove back toward the pentagon and tritium ops, media caravan in tow.

THIRTY-FOUR

Kettering greeted the entourage at pentagon unit four. By now a light sprinkling descended from the gloomy sky, but neither the drizzle nor Whitman's bodyguards nor the too-tempting opportunity for a saboteur prevented the journalists from pressing the senator on Theresa's allegations.

Big Bad Roy's demeanor, rifle tenderly cradled, remained placid. "Folks, if a government appropriation doesn't get spent in one place, well, it just goes back into the pot and surfaces somewhere else."

"Like in harbor dredging," Theresa finished. "That's what my husband originally thought happened and he protested to Congress. But isn't it true, Senator, that your brother in fact diverted the money to the Star Wars program?"

"Why, that's preposterous, Theresa!" Whitman retorted with the stage anger of politicians, "and I didn't come here to discuss my brother's ancient history."

"Why did you come?" Theresa asked, but the senator refused to respond.

The exchange riveted Nathaniel. The magnetic fusion program was on the civilian side of the DOE, Star Wars on the military side. If Theresa was right, the other Whitman's action had been blatantly illegal. At this moment Nathaniel truly wished Theresa had prepared him for her surprise. He also understood that visiting the sins of one brother on the other was a dangerous tactic.

"Wasn't your brother forced to resign his position as a result of this misappropriation of funds?" Theresa went on without flinching.

Nathaniel did another double take but had no time to consider, for Whitman answered. "Theresa, after five long years he just wanted to spend more time with his family—nothing more mysterious than that."

Despite the senator's smooth defense, Theresa had apparently accomplished what she'd intended. Reporters huddled around her, asking for information. Despite the long history etched on her face, she pleaded ignorance and suggested only, "Why don't you find out why Whitman's brother resigned as director of the Office of Energy Research, and see if it was a result of family values."

Nathaniel grabbed her arm and took her aside. "Theresa," he whispered, "I hope you know what you're doing."

"So do I," she answered with a smile less confident than her speeches, "so do I."

Moravec, with Toshi by him, could not hide her amusement. "'In battle, confrontation is done directly, victory is gained by surprise,'" she chuckled.

"'Therefore those skilled in the unorthodox are as infinite as heaven and earth,'" completed Toshi.

The bot rotated to the physicist with curiosity. "I see you are a dangerous man, Dr. Matsushima," it said. "Dr. Machuzak also recognized Sun Tzu. Is the *Art of War* a favorite of physicists?"

"Nathaniel has learned a few things from me," answered Toshi.

As he stood at the door to tritium ops, Machuzak's only objective at this minute was to get the show back on track. "Today we plan to produce a first plasma—our first shot since the dedication, to convince you that we've recovered. The experiment will require tritium and I thought we'd show you how it's prepared."

"Is there any danger of radioactivity?" Whitman asked, suddenly as cautious as a scared eight-year-old.

"None." Nathaniel crossed himself.

"Why not then?" the senator said with an uneasy glance around. Moravec displayed no worries.

Nathaniel motioned for Kettering to lead them down, but the National Guardsmen at the vault entrance diverted everyone's attention and one of the reporters called out, asking the reason for their presence.

"Just security," replied Nathaniel as he followed Kettering.

The reporters and Whitman's bodyguards all pressed forward, but Machuzak held up his hands. "Sorry, no tourists allowed in the tritium vault."

One of the media people called out, wanting to know what he was hiding. "Has tritium been stolen?"

"Nothing has been stolen. You have not been cleared ahead of time for entry into the vault. End of story. You can wait here. That goes for you too." Nathaniel faced Whitman's guards.

When the muscle didn't retreat, Kettering stepped up to them and said, "Micro model, nice piece. Three hundred fifty meters per second muzzle velocity. You want to release enough tritium to kill everybody on this site? Stand down." At his nod, the militiamen interposed themselves between the VIPs and the others, all arguments ceased. The guests turned toward the entrance to the River Styx. Whitman handed over his musket to his men.

"The tritium we have down there wouldn't kill anybody," Machuzak whispered to the tritium chief.

"They don't know that," Kettering returned.

Clearing his fingerprint, the chief leads the group past the security cameras, through the door and into the negative pressure area, then follows the steps downward into the realm of Hades. No one chuckles or dies of a heart attack at the No Pacemakers advisory, and the radiation warnings silence everyone completely. But as they enter the vault, the atmosphere instantly changes. The area is brightly lit and the tritium handlers, some of whom resemble bikers and a few of whom do sport leather, gather round to greet the visitors. The shock and awe of the guests is extreme. They expected men in white lab coats or something.

While Bill Balustradi's merry visage says, "Hi gang!" from every closed-circuit monitor, a couple of the guys request autographs from the senator and Quintanilla drapes his Harley jacket over Moravec's avatar. Once more in his element, Whitman whisks out his cigar, but Markowitz, who bears an uncanny resemblance to Groucho, snatches the stogie from his fingers, holds it up to one of the radiation monitors and pockets it. "No chewing in radiologically controlled areas," he scolds. In fact, the radiation level in the vault is less than the Austin background.

Truly, the tritium handlers are a little different than everyone else at the lab. They cheerfully recount their stories about the weekly urinalyses and joke about the times they've experienced a "direct uptake," officialese for being doused by tritiated water—what the hell? "Nothing is more fun than a real 'line break,'" they tell their visitors, a genuine cleanup operation requiring moon suits and all.

Fusioneers do have a different take on radioactivity than the public, thinks Nathaniel, grateful for the reporters' absence. The problem isn't that tritium is radioactive; the problem is that tritium's a bitch. It's light, flammable, it combines with everything—water above all. That's when you've got to watch it.

"The body doesn't distinguish H_2O and T_2O," Kettering is telling the guests. "But hey, if you swallow tritium, the best treatment is beer."

"Beer?" Moravec remotely exclaims in spite of himself.

"Affirmative. You know the effects of beer."

With the guys posing with Whitman's cigar in front of their Miss Fusion calendar, Kettering turns to a glove box and connects one of the LP-18 bottles to a mass spectrometer for assaying. Pure tritium, close.

Despite all the clowning, Machuzak inadvertently gulps, suddenly realizing that he doesn't know a single one of the handlers. What better place, time...? What has he done?

"When we need to pump tritium into Prometheus," Kettering continues, "we heat these beds of depleted uranium, onto which the tritium has been adsorbed, releasing the gas." He points out the uranium beds inside the glass-walled box, but they're hidden within an extraordinary maze of plumbing that, like everything else at CFRC, must seem the creation of Rube Goldberg gone mad. In fact, the whole tritium ops section is an import from the old weapons labs.

"Ready when you are Mac," Kettering says, "and thanks for staying the course—sir." He snaps to attention and salutes, Machuzak merely acknowledges with a dumb nod and follows him down the corridor. "It's pretty routine," the chief goes on, leading everyone to the recycling plant, which reclaims the tritium after it leaves the tokamak contaminated with all the garbage from the machine walls. Along the loop molecular sieves remove the tritiated water. "It's basically kitty litter," he says, though surely no one believes him. "We store it in steel barrels." Beer kegs, actually.

When all is said and done the recycling plant, towering over them by several stories, glittering with lights and gauges, is a distillery. Put the mess in one end, each component of the contaminated gas comes off at its own boiling point, tritium itself at about 25 degrees absolute. Repeat the process until you're left with the pure thing.

"Generally," Kettering remarks, staring Moravec's bot in the screen with his invariable pugnacity, "the recycling works so well that we rarely need to import tritium from Savannah River. But we have a fucking deadline to beat."

Moravec takes the hit without response. Everyone is eager to climb from this somber subterranean realm, but Slava, who's been examining the recycling plant, turns to Kettering and asks, "Can you make vodka with this?"

"Let's turn the machine on," says Machuzak and they ascend.

THIRTY-FIVE

Outside heavy droplets were by now splattering irregularly on the asphalt and concrete, while thunder snarled in the distance. The reporters lay in wait and the first question to split the air was, redundantly, "Has any tritium been stolen?"

A ring shoved in her bot's face, Moravec had little choice but to reply. "This is hardly for me to say. The security down there is impressive, but the entire operation seems unduly complicated. Nature perhaps does not believe in fusion on Earth."

Slava, two steps away, overhears. "A century ago," he answers, "computer would have seemed unimaginable. If there is one percent chance of supplying world with energy for millions of years, is not endeavor worth undertaking?"

Moravec isn't buying. "The age of fusion has passed, I am afraid. With solar and wind power here to stay, it's increasingly difficult to see why fusion is necessary."

"Y'all know," muses Slava, scratching his head, "where I come from the sun don't shine half the year. That's a might lotta batteries, and solar's never gotten as cheap as advertised."

During the general laughter Whitman sees his opportunity, asserting that Texas would do better on its own and that the private sector handles these things better than any government.

"Like the way the private sector handled health care and finances." Theresa is visibly angered by the senator's insistence on an imaginary past and she throws in a few government failures "like the Manhattan Project and the Internet" for good measure. "But you may be right, Senator: if Texas manages to become an autonomous Wild West, it will flourish until the big neighbor surrounding it declares war."

Watching the show unfold before a global audience, Nathaniel can't but admire Theresa's refusal to kowtow before the politician, but he senses that her antipathy goes well beyond theatre. She did say she despised him. By some miracle, though, this movable kitchen debate hasn't exploded and Whitman's reply is simply to cradle his rifle and put his arm around Theresa's shoulder.

"Theresa," he says with a practiced chuckle, "you really should consider running for office." With the others, Nathaniel looks on with amazement, certain only that they are neither winning friends nor destroying enemies.

* * * *

At that moment T. J. appeared, jogging up to Nathaniel, as if she'd dressed specially for the occasion. "Doc," she said, smiling radiantly in a black dress suit, "you wouldn't want me to miss this, would you?"

Nathaniel raised his finger, swallowed his tongue and waved the entourage toward the test cell. He only pointed out pentagon five, housing the radio-frequency supplies, nothing more than a hundred-megawatt radio station that provides Prometheus its microwave heating through the large microwave conduits running overhead.

As he prepared to lead the crowd into the central hub, the door unexpectedly swung open. Instantly Whitman's bodyguard's pistols are out; the senator himself hoists his musket. With hands raised high above his head one of the techs, Joe Johnson, is glancing in every direction, terrified. Joe's a big black guy—a very big black guy—and his dreadlocks stream loose and unfettered through the slits he's cut into his hard-hat liner. This morning he's made matters worse by wearing an African dashiki.

Normally Nathaniel would have cracked up, but today he quickly interposes himself between tech and goons, pushing down their firearms with his forefingers. "*Where* the hell do you think you are?" his voice lies between a growl and a shout. Turning to the tech he says with full exasperation, "Joe Johnson, meet Senator Roy Whitman."

Whitman, flummoxed, must apologize live. "I guess I can't count on your vote next time around," he concedes weakly, lowering Ol' Betsy.

Joe merely walks off shaking his head.

* * * *

Experiments about to begin, the test cell is off limits and Fred Abbuhl escorts everyone to the visitors' gallery. Nathaniel offers a silent thanks to Prometheus. At the sight of the device, all arguments subside as the inevitable quiet descends, the familiar sign that the guests are failing to cope with sensory overload. Before them stands a machine much different from the one he pulled D'Abro from on her first night on the job.

The bay is clean, the donut and magnets invisible, enclosed in the great vacuum flask. They are able to make out microwave guides feeding ASSET from pentagon five, diagnostic lasers and spectrometers sprouting from every crevice, conduits from the cryoplant, a few of the neutral beam accelerators, each several stories tall and covered with so much cabling that they conjure up the monster from *20,000 Leagues Under the Sea.*

When one of those beam boxes was delivered on a tremendous lowboy, Fred recounts, the driver got his route mixed up, collided with a bridge spanning an interstate and—took out the bridge. The beam box remained intact. The neutral beams had been delivered from Japan; all the specialists here had retired or been RIFed and no one knew how to build them.

"This is the usual course of technology," interjects Toshi with a shrug, one of his few comments. "Who knows nowadays how to cut a quill pen?"

Nathaniel doesn't quite catch the point, but Whitman goes for it. "Is that bad, Professor?"

"Your predecessors at Independence Hall, Senator, understood the value of pausing for thought."

The exchange goes unnoticed, for everyone else is staring at the huge deadline calendar, big as a movie screen, that Fred's crew has hung on the test cell's east wall. Six weeks are X-ed out and a mushroom cloud rises above day zero, but Moravec merely purses her lips on-screen, and Nathaniel can't read any more into it.

* * * *

Fred accompanied the group past techs stationed at strategic locations and through the dank three-hundred-meter tunnel to the control room. "I've wanted to say, Mac," he offered, "thanks for getting us this far. You've done a good job."

Before Nathaniel could do more than smile, a tech overtook the group at the entrance to the control room and asked, "Is this Moravec?"

More or less, Nathaniel nodded.

"Put it to work. We've got a deadline."

There was no trace of humor in the command, none, and it didn't escape the media. "Dr. Machuzak, wouldn't it be wise to advise your employees not to insult your visitors?"

Angered, Machuzak snarls, "This is a scientific laboratory, where people traditionally think for themselves, not the bloody marines." He swivels on Whitman with a raised finger. "Leave your thugs outside." This time the senator retreats, handing over his weapon to his men and posting them at the control room doors.

Inside, a KXAN reporter wants to know whether, having seen Prometheus, Moravec has changed its mind.

"To the contrary," the CEO responds. "In fact, it seems inconceivable to me that such a monstrous…*contraption* could actually work."

"There's still oil," quips Whitman, "and we still can't live without it."

The remarks sets Moravec off and right there, brightly lit amid the decades of terminals and displays, the two launch into a heated argument, fossil versus bio, North Pole oil versus Dakota wind, animated stogie against swiveling screen, flailing buckskin contra suited plastic.

The two loathe each other, Nathaniel observes once more as accusations of "doomsayer" and "dinosaur" fill the air, but when he interposes himself again between the combatants, it is Moravec, not Whitman, to whom he turns with a determined expression. "We're now going to show you that our *contraption* can work… Thad, take the helm."

Hasschler is onstage. He nods to Larissa Davidson, the chief operating engineer and, as on that other day, the countdown abruptly begins.

"Sixty seconds to current ramp-up," she announces.

As the digital clock on the wall begins ticking down, Machuzak explains, "Ladies, gentlemen, except for the start-up tests we've been conducting, this is the first time we've run the machine since the dedication. You're now going to witness our first plasma, a genuine shot, no tricks."

"Is there any danger?" Whitman suddenly asks again.

"Not if you keep your hands to yourself," Machuzak replies and the senator immediately goes stiff, arms clamped to his side.

"Preparing for DT injection and current ramp-up."

Machuzak attempts to direct their attention to the big screen, but it is now T. J. who interrupts. "Doc, y'all really gotta get with it." Abruptly she links her handset to the COE's system and at once the hammering pulsations of a synthesized music track are accompanying the countdown and have set the audience in motion. "See?" she says, jiving. "Now it's real."

The clock hits zero.

"Beginning current ramp-up."

They hear the crack. As on the earlier occasion, the speakers pipe in the tremendous metallic wrenching from the test cell. T. J. involuntarily flinches, stops snapping her fingers and grips his arm; he does not remove her hand. Everyone—Slava, Theresa, Toshi—is transfixed by the glow on the monitor, the bright red glow, which this morning persists.

After about ten seconds, when Larissa announces, "Three hundred thousand volts, one mega-amp," Thad says, "Let's leave it there," and the burn ends.

"What just happened?" Moravec asks, bewildered.

The diagnostic teams are already turning to the shot analysis, but Machuzak knows the answer. "Nothing happened. We just created a low-density plasma in the machine and held it for ten seconds, without problems."

"This isn't fusion though, is it?" the CEO replies skeptically.

"No, this was just a test, but it was a successful test of our *contraption*."

At that instant Abbuhl steps up to Nathaniel. "Mac, this just came in from ITER. Ten minutes ago they achieved breakeven." He hands Machuzak the printout.

"What exactly is breakeven?" Moravec wants to know.

"The point where the plasma gives you as much energy out as you're using to heat it. Jules César Balard isn't wasting time."

"Let's go for it," Kettering shouts from beyond a row of consoles. "Now."

Machuzak firmly shakes his head. "No. Let's have lunch."

THIRTY-SIX

As they gained the cafeteria, Machuzak walked up to the traveling light display that had been installed above the cowboys in the big mural to broadcast safety messages: *Every finger plays an important part. Protect yours... Bill Balustradi says have a great day...* He stooped, pulled the plug to the applause of those gathered for lunch and made his announcement:

"Today we achieved a first plasma in Prometheus. The machine functioned perfectly." Another round of applause and some cheering greeted him until he gave them the news from ITER.

"Let's catch them!" came the instant shouts from several quarters of the mezzanine amid hissing and booing.

"We have a different race," he said, raising his hands for quiet. "Let us concentrate on that, and the rest will follow."

Moravec's avatar, whose head turned owl-like as it surveyed the faces in the cafeteria, swiveled to Toshi. "Your director seems amazingly calm, considering. Everybody here will be dying to beat ITER."

"As ITER will be dying to beat us," Toshi replied. "Let us hope that neither side takes those words literally."

"It may increase your chances of beating the deadline."

Moravec's remark lay somewhere between a statement and a question, but Matsushima shook his head. "Nathaniel is correct. Too much fervor and the saboteur could easily defeat us, not by homemade bombs but by slipshod ideas. Here is how it could go: We are making progress toward your deadline when a team member puts forth an outrageous proposal allowing us to leapfrog ahead of ITER. By then everyone is so panicked that we foolishly attempt it and bring about complete catastrophe. We lose the race, miss your deadline and you shut us down."

"What do you think it would take to ensure that such a scenario plays out?"

Toshi only shrugged noncommittally. "A guarantee to support more promising roads to fusion might be looked on favorably by some."

"Hmm," replied Moravec, "that would be a substantial risk for an investor."

"Less risky than a tokamak. On the other hand, given that there is not one chance in a thousand that we can beat the deadline imposed by Jinghiz Khan the Merciless, it is perhaps an unnecessary prec—"

The conversation went no further. Two nearby lightning flashes, followed in quick succession by a pair of deafening thunderclaps so percussive that stomachs shook and glasses toppled, caused Matsushima to duck. Nearby, as the lights blinked, Machuzak stiffened, nearly dove for cover under the nearest table, while others did. But the thunder didn't abate and the roaring continued, an uninterrupted bellow that only slowly revealed itself to be something else, the roar of an earthquake or an avalanche. There are no mountains at CFRC and no earthquakes in Texas.

Machuzak ran to the edge of the mezzanine, from where he could see the pentagon. A huge mushroom cloud was climbing high into the dark sky. "My God," he whispered, first walking, then running down the stairs into the courtyard.

The journalists were at once after him, D'Abro and Whitman's guards as well. "Is it an atomic bomb, Dr. Machuzak?" one of the reporters shouted.

"If it were an atomic bomb," he replied with a sudden, purposeful calm, "you wouldn't be asking the question—and I wouldn't be answering it." For a moment he paused, gazing up at the cloud that must have now risen to five hundred meters. No, this was some gas venting. It hit him then—helium, from pentagon three. God, that was bad enough.

Nathaniel sprinted across the asphalt past the test cell and on to the helium factory. Cochran stood inside amidst the giant storage dewars, gesticulating wildly and shouting to her techs above the ear-shattering whine of the compressors. Machuzak couldn't hear a word and took her aside.

"What's happened?" he shouted into her ear.

"It was the lightning strikes," she said. "We lost primary and emergency power. The gauges were going nuts. We were about to regenerate the cryopanels in the beam boxes with a little helium, but somehow liters got in there."

"*Liters!*" Machuzak shouted in disbelief.

"It boiled off and completely overwhelmed the pumps—"

"Diana if those pressure disks rupture—"

"I know, I know. Emergency power is back on. It looks like the sensors caught it in time and vented the main dewar. Boy, did they." She glanced upward.

Machuzak motioned her after him and they rushed up the access ladder to the roof. The cloud above their heads was already dissipating, but the exhaust vent had been built to point downward and the roof was—frozen solid.

"Jesus," the two breathed simultaneously. "We'll have to replace the whole roof."

T. J. had followed them by seconds, annoyed at having to make the climb in her dress suit, but now saw what they saw. "Do you know what caused this?"

"Helium, very cold helium."

"I mean the failure."

The lightning strikes, Diana told her.

"Are you certain?"

Cochran and Machuzak turned toward each other. No, they were not.

When they'd climbed down again and gotten away from the noise, D'Abro asked for an explanation. "We often inject a little helium into the neutral beams," Machuzak answered. "As it boils, it cleans the hydrogen frost off the cryopanels. Somehow liters got in there and when helium boils it expands seven hundred times. I guess with the power failure the pumps weren't functioning and the pressure completely overwhelmed them. If the emergency pressure disks on the beam boxes blow, the atmosphere rushes in and the whole system needs to be repaired, purged and pumped down again. Luckily the power came on and the sensors vented the main dewar, relieving the pressure."

"So is this a freak accident or…?" D'Abro asked, shaking her head.

Machuzak had hardly been thinking that far, and without answering turned to Cochran for her opinion. She also remained silent for a long time, at last shaking her head. "I've never seen anything like this. We hadn't actually injected the helium when the lightning hit."

"Could even a lightning strike cause several liters of helium to get into the beams?"

"I don't see how. But then somebody would have had to override the programmable logic control."

Machuzak breathed heavily, faced D'Abro. "You see how easy it is to torpedo one of these systems. If it's deliberate our man has gotten more sophisticated—we can't even tell whether it is sabotage."

Fred was struggling to keep the press at bay nearby, but there was nothing for it. Machuzak told the journalists simply that they weren't certain yet what caused the event. Immediately they asked again about atomic bombs and whether radiation was leaked. "No, just helium gas," Nathaniel assured them. Helium was vital to cool the magnets and without it Prometheus couldn't function.

Machuzak and D'Abro walked silently back to the main lobby where the dignitaries were waiting. Whitman, in a manner that attempted to mask his evident fear, huffed, "Well, Dr. Machuzak, I told you I was risking my life coming this morning. Are we quite safe?"

"There is no danger," Machuzak replied sullenly, wishing the politician would dissolve.

"Well, then, I think we've had sufficient excitement for one day."

Machuzak only watched as Whitman motioned for his men to follow him. A few steps on, the senator's phone rang. He answered, said he was busy and disappeared out the laboratory door and into his limo. Nathaniel stood rooted to the spot. It was the same ringtone that he'd heard in Moravec's office, the *Nisi Dominus* from the Monteverdi *Vespers*.

"I need to see you and Slava," D'Abro said soberly. "Meet me in the conference room in thirty minutes."

* * * *

It didn't happen like that. From his handset Slava was monitoring five or six of the news broadcasts originating at the lab and watched to his horror as over the course of three minutes news of the helium venting went viral. But helium has become confused with tritium and the protestors at the gate, having survived the thunderstorm, are convinced that tritium has been leaked into the atmosphere. At that moment—a call from the guard booth. "Dr. Machuzak, you'd better get out to the main gate."

He arrives, Theresa at his heels, to find a near riot, half the protestors running for their lives, the other half attempting to storm the lab. As he sensed earlier, the National Guard is in no mood for games and rifles are aimed.

Nathaniel wades in, interposing himself between the militia and the civilians. "Don't antagonize them!" he shouts, pushing aside one of the rifles, even as he holds back a struggling student. "Shout 'More pay to the Guard!'"

The kid, who Nathaniel recognizes as the same one from the day of the dedication, stares at him as if he's out of his mind.

"You've just had a nuclear accident at this place," the kid texts, even now refusing to talk. "You can see the cloud!"

"Must be a mighty small one," he says, nearly repeating himself. "We're all still here." Indeed, and at this instant he recollects his vow to explain tritium to the kid. "Look, why don't you come in and see what's going on. I'm not afraid, see?" He moves toward the gate.

As on dedication day, there is uncertainty, hesitation, then a few brave souls step forward. The guardsmen resist until Machuzak orders them to stand down, at which the crowd begins to stream through and he leads them across the field to the MTF, into his lab.

There they are, sitting on the floor, the benches, the lab tables, standing, overflowing into the adjoining rooms. He doesn't know their names. There are tie-dyed and "Save the Whales" shirts, mostly adorning college-age bodies, but others are older, gray hair tied in ponytails, lanyards with lapis and silver brooches, faces creased by the southwestern wind and sun. The press is persistently underfoot until Machuzak orders them to leave. They don't, but they too stand down.

"So," he says, "I'm Nathaniel Machuzak, acting director of the lab. Why don't you tell me what's on your mind."

The ensuing silence persists long enough that he begins to think this wasn't such a good idea, but finally one of the older women spits with her voice focused into a nasty spear, "No nukes in Austin."

"Fair enough," he answers, feeling impaled by her hostility. "Does that mean you think this is a nuclear plant?"

She seems uncertain. "Well, we don't want any radiation around." Gaining with that a dose of bravery she adds, "And we don't want no bombs either."

Nathaniel explains patiently that they don't build bombs here. He says it with the matter-of-factness that comes with the knowledge that theirs is a perpetual action to be waged.

"The place ain't classified?" someone interjects loudly.

"Nope, never has been."

"Damn!" the fellow exclaims, snapping his fingers in disappointment.

Nathaniel tells them a little about fusion and plasmas, to which he gets the usual "blood plasma" response. They are welcome to have a look at Prometheus. It becomes clear that they aren't so much hostile as afraid. Rightly so.

They talk about the tritium safeguards and how the other fuel, deuterium, other than that it can explode, poses no threat. "You see this big cylinder," Nathaniel introduces them to his test stand, "and you see this little flame here?" He locates a flint and strikes a fire. "People sometimes worry that we're releasing deuterium into the atmosphere, so I burn off the excess to make heavy water." It occurs to him that he has a sample on hand and he grabs the small flask from the cabinet next to his desk. "It's perfectly harmless," he says, unstoppering it, and he empties the flask in a single drought. Heavy water tastes pretty terrible, worse than distilled water, and he makes a wry face.

A few laugh, but one of the students isn't satisfied. "Fusion is centralized power. You're just increasing industry's hold over everybody. You should be advocating solar, decentralization, not centralization." He gets a round of applause. Nathaniel nods. A law of nature: every time you mention fusion, somebody else mentions solar.

"Actually, I'm in favor of insulation... Um, look, some of us who work at CFRC believe in fusion; after all that's why we work here. But I doubt you'd find anybody at the lab who's against solar. Look at all the panels on the roofs. We are scientists. We believe our experiments and calculations more than this month's political flavor. Solar is good, but it's not so cheap and to provide the entire country with electricity, you'd have to cover four or five Rhode Islands with panels. Well, Rhode Island's smaller than the King Ranch." A few more laughs. "Anyway, why don't you take one of those electric vans over to the main site and somebody will show you around. Then if you have any questions you are welcome to come back and argue. I apologize for the guardsmen. They got a little excited."

Long before he finished, Richard Garrett, Slava and T. J. had arrived, wedging themselves in with the rest. When the crowd had departed, Garrett said, "You handled that about as well as can be imagined, son." He grasped Nathaniel's hand warmly. "Congratulations."

Nathaniel only managed a long sigh. Theresa glanced at him with undisguised pride, but as T. J. looked at him, her eyes came close to filling with tears. "Doc, we have an appointment at the ASSET conference room." She motioned to Slava and Garrett as well. "Let's go."

THIRTY-SEVEN

During the drive over to the administration building in D'Abro's car no one spoke. Machuzak was still attempting to make sense of everything that had taken place this morning. At the ASSET conference room, he and Slava ran their eyes over Chen the armadillo, the safety posters and the rest, but nothing penetrated except that Cyrus Krieg-Zuber and Mercedes Ramirez faced them from the conference table. Zuber could not disguise the satisfaction written on his face.

D'Abro motioned for Machuzak, Archangelsky and Garrett to sit, while she took her place at table's head. "Docs, we've got a big problem," she begins without prologue, lingering on Archangelsky. "Slava, you told me you keep a shortwave transceiver in your office."

"That is true," Archangelsky replied cautiously, distantly, already vaguely feeling ambushed. The entire day had been one of attempted ambushes.

At his response, Garrett exhaled unhappily and fingered the rim of his Stetson, which he held in his hand.

"Dr. Krieg-Zuber has intercepted a series of shortwave transmissions to and from the lab using an obsolete code called, hmm…"

"The Baudot code," Krieg-Zuber finished with a twitch as Archangelsky now hurled a sharp, furious glance at him. "The original five-unit telegraph code. It hasn't been used in a century, and so it took some time to recognize and decrypt. The only additional encryption, carelessly, was that it was in Russian."

"Slava," T. J. asked, "have you had shortwave communication with ITER?"

"I have."

"Why shortwave, Slava?"

Archangelsky drilled into Krieg-Zuber with a fiery eye. "Why not? When it becomes clear this bastard monitors every keystroke, every breath taken at laboratory, what recourse do we have?"

"If one has nothing to hide," Zuber fairly hissed as he stroked his chin, "of what need is there to protect oneself?"

"What need!" Slava erupts, addressing D'Abro but pointing his finger at The Terminator like an Old Testament prophet. "To this maniac, every conversation is plot, every accident sabotage. You think we are robots? How can one exist in place like this?"

D'Abro does not directly react, instead slides a sheaf of printouts across the table to the Russian. The others watch the blood drain from his face.

Garrett takes the papers from his hands and reads aloud: "Slava, Balard has authorized me to tell you that with your original work on plasma transport you could be of great benefit to ITER. He says it may be even more advantageous if you remained off-site. What do you think? Dima, for Balard.'"

"Do you have his reply to this?" Garrett asks of T. J., leafing through the printouts, but she shakes her head. "Do you, Dr. Archangelsky?"

Slava, doubly dazed now, manages a denial. "Most ITER work done at off-site labs; permanent staff at Cadarache actually small. But rivalry between ITER and ASSET is so great that to work here for them might be spying. I don't like dictators. My friend Dima has shortwave and sent me that. I told him no way. If Krieg-Zuber is intercepting transmissions, why doesn't he have reply?"

"What's this mean?" Garrett furrows his brow. "'Situation here is untenable. Deputy director needs to go or I do. I would slice him and his program without a knife.'"

T. J. again sees the words scribbled on Balard's desk while Slava swivels to Machuzak in disgust. "*Brat*, I tell you it's time to get out of this business." He stands and puts it directly to Krieg-Zuber. "Who the hell do you think you are, goddamned KGB?" And with a turn of his head to The Chairman, "I don't have words for this except that this laboratory has been turned into political prison. This man makes me want to vomit. I resign."

Garrett, startled and alarmed, jerks his head. "Hold on a minute, Dr. Archangelsky," he urges, patting the air with his hands. "Just calm down and tell us what that message meant."

"Meant exactly what it says. Either Krieg-Zuber resigns or I quit. Now I quit."

Krieg-Zuber, having sat through the entire exchange unperturbed, now says fiercely, "Dr. Archangelsky, whether you resign is of no concern to me, but if you were planning to slice me or the program without a knife, you'll answer serious charges."

"What the hell are you talking about?" Slava shouts, incredulous. "'Slice without a knife' is Russian expression, '*bez nozhá zarézal.*' Just means to fuck somebody over. You fucking idiot." He spits out the words at Cy, forcing his face so close to his that Zuber nearly falls backward.

"Why did I find those words in Balard's office, Slava," D'Abro interrupts with more calm, "on his desk?"

"Maybe he thought they were cute. Dima must have told him." This is all too much on top of the before-noon and Archangelsky, in no way placated, is waving his arms in front of the ASSET letters. "Why don't you ask Balard?"

"I may do that," D'Abro responds without pity.

Recovered, Krieg-Zuber nods to Mercedes, who proceeds to tell them in a manner little different from the tour she gave hours ago how two nights before the dedication she was working late in the MTF and overheard a conversation among Machuzak, Archangelsky and Lipman. Curious, she came unnoticed to the door of Machuzak's lab and, alarmed by what she heard, recorded it with her phone. As she drops each word, she fixes her eyes to the table, not so much as glancing at Machuzak. D'Abro plays back the scene.

"The guys have had it," said Lipman, standing near the workbench. "The Terminator won't say a word about what's going on, but everybody's ready to blow the place sky high."

"Sounds like a good idea to me," Machuzak chuckled from his desk.

"Shouldn't be difficult." This from Lipman again. "We got enough hazmats on-site to do the job.

Slava, pacing back and forth between the other two: "All we need is a spark. End of our problems and beginning of bright future for mankind."

Nathaniel visibly disagreed. "No, beginning of reign of terror. Zuber would—"

"—Maybe we can get rid of him too."

The playback ends while Machuzak and Archangelsky stare speechless at Mercedes, but she holds her fingers interlocked and gaze riveted to the table.

"Isn't this scenario precisely what transpired, old boy?" Krieg-Zuber asks with dripping satisfaction.

"Are you crazy?" Nathaniel fully shouts. This has gone beyond belief. Luckily, Archangelsky's grilling has given him a few minutes to collect his wits. "What evidence," he growls, "do you have that we were even down there?" Too late he perceives his slip.

"You know we have the evidence, Doc," T. J. says quietly. "We've had it from the beginning."

Machuzak jaw goes slack and he can find no instant response. The lights are very harsh.

"We also know from the access records," Krieg-Zuber adds, "that Lipman was certainly the last person in the power area the night before the incident, after midnight. We also know that you rarely work so late, weren't assigned third shift, yet you showed up just before twelve. Very strange. Especially as your name is missing from the access sheets."

"Anybody's missing who isn't there."

"But you were there. The GPS log from your vehicle," Krieg-Zuber answers with absolute control, "was captured at 11:47 p.m."

Machuzak is on his feet. "You cocksucking motherfucker!" he slams his fist on the table, knocking over coffee cups and startling everyone.

Despite himself, Zuber is taken aback by the figure leaning into his face and he clenches the table with his good hand. "It's clear what happened. Lipman strangely doesn't report a busbar having been sawed in half the very night before the event—"

"He didn't *inspect* it the night before and it was camouflaged to make certain it wouldn't be detected!"

"You tailgated on Lipman's badge and set the trap then—"

"I resent that you son of a bitch!" Machuzak shouts at the top of his lungs, tilting into Zuber's face.

Archangelsky spits simultaneously, "*Yebyona mat'!* This fucker is totally nonlinear, chaotic."

"Shout all you wish," says Cyrus, crossing his arms, one with difficulty, across his chest. "The fact remains that you were there."

"Yes," Nathaniel hisses, "and Lipman plants a deuterium bottle next to the surge room that three weeks later kills him."

"Accidents happen, conveniently. We also know you didn't stay long enough, old boy, to help out with anything. According to your GPS log you departed at… 12:37."

"You—!" Machuzak pushes aside the chairs and grabs Zuber by the knot of his tie. For a moment it seems he will strangle the deputy director, until D'Abro and Garrett forcefully wrestle him away.

"I'll have you on assault, Machuzak," Krieg-Zuber sputters, loosening his tie with one hand in an attempt to breathe.

But Machuzak isn't done and again moves toward him. "And you'll try to pin what happened today on us too, huh?" he snarls as The Chairman inserts his own bulk between the two.

"We shall discover that the two are linked."

Garrett is now himself angering while he holds the two at arm's length. "Do you have anything else?" he demands of Zuber.

"Your days are over," Cyrus says to Machuzak, raising his good arm.

"If you have nothing more, will the three of you excuse us?"

The deputy director, whose left arm still appears paralyzed, and Mercedes, who yet refuses to meet Machuzak's eyes, leave the room.

* * * *

A moment, two, passed in silence; Garrett motioned for everyone to sit. "How bad is this, Lieutenant D'Abro?"

She slowly ran her tongue over her lips. "Some of that evidence would probably be inadmissible in court, and there might still be exculpatory evidence buried in Cy's files, but in terms of figurin out what happened here, it looks pretty convincing."

"Convincing?" Machuzak cannot believe his ears. "This is all some nutso conspiracy manufactured by The Terminator, which you've bought into."

"Nutso? Conspiracy? We got your prints all over the place, we got your DNA, we know you were down there in the right time frame and we've got videos and radio transmissions—for Christ's sake—showing that you've been acting like a bunch of anarchists. Exactly."

"We never did a thing," Machuzak protested.

T. J. slammed the flat of her hand on the table. She'll have none of it. "Damnit, Mac, you didn't tell me any of this. Why?"

What is there that he can say? "We knew how it would look. I hoped we would have gotten to the bottom of it by now."

"Looks to me like we have."

Her blue eyes are drilling him, but Machuzak resolutely shakes his head. "We were just trying to do our jobs."

The Chairman put an end to the duel. "Mac, whatever happens from this point on, you've become too much of a liability to remain acting director. We're a week or two short of two months, but I'm askin you to step down."

"Fine," Machuzak stood again. "Who do you have to replace me?"

The Chairman fingered the rim of his Stetson. "I don't see that there's much choice but to put Dr. Krieg-Zuber back in charge. He maintains he's fit."

Machuzak nearly threw up. "Richard," he glanced at the clock as he moved to the door, "remember the moment when you destroyed the lab."

Slava also stared at Garrett in revulsion. "I say again: I resign."

"Not so fast, Docs," T. J. moved to block the exit.

Nathaniel asked whether she was arresting them.

"Not yet, but don't leave town. I keep tellin ya—this is murder. Slava, I'm gonna need to see your laptop."

"Get a warrant," he replied and walked out. Garrett also slowly picked up his hat and T. J. and Nathaniel were left alone.

"I know you won't believe me, but I'm sorry about this, Mac, I truly am." Her searching eyes told him she was telling the truth. "But you should have leveled with me from the start."

He returned her gaze sadly, wearily. "I just told you why we didn't say anything, and I'll tell you two other things now. One: I don't like having my life x-rayed by people who have it in their heads that if they've got the gadgets, they've got the obligation. Two: we've got a conspiracy on our hands, just not the one you thought."

T. J. blinked and asked what he could possibly mean.

He told her about the ringtone on Whitman's phone. "It was the *Nisi Dominus* from the Monteverdi *Vespers*—the same ringtone I heard at Moravec's office."

D'Abro wrinkled her nose, not in an amused way. "Are you sure?"

"Yes, I'm sure. I may be too quiet for my own good, and wrong about a lot of things, but my musical memory is as reliable as DNA. Those two characters claimed they never met and they obviously despise each other. But they're connected."

"You want me to put this *Nisi Dom*—whatever—a *ringtone* against everything we've got against you?" she flailed her arms angrily.

"That's exactly what I want you to do," he said and with a glance at the armadillo exited the conference room.

THIRTY-EIGHT

When Machuzak got up and headed south with the dawn, he could find no reason for doing so except force of habit, and that hardly convinced him. He was dismayed but hardly surprised by a crowd of protestors and the National Guardsmen facing off again at the gate. "Let them in," he said without expecting, or getting, a response, surprised nevertheless that the guards allowed him to pass. His badge operated the gate and the door to the MTF, but the pentagon units refused him entry. Death by deactivation.

He put up with frisking at the guard booth, not needing to ask where the order originated. The main lobby door was unlocked, but he tried his badge anyway and it functioned; someone, though, had already torn yesterday's date from the calendar. He bounded upstairs to see other guardsmen posted outside Krieg-Zuber's office. Past the atrium and the sweet scent of flowers, he knocked at the octagon, but it was too much to expect that Leonard Rasmussen would be at his desk this early, if at all.

Nathaniel descended slowly to his own office, where a ringing telephone met him. His only words were "No comment" and when the ringing became ceaseless he unplugged the phone. After sitting motionless for the better part of an hour, he walked to Archangelsky's office to find the Russian contemplating the books he was removing from the shelves.

"Don't do it, Slava," Machuzak said.

Slava continued to pack his books into a cardboard box, glancing at each one for a moment, perhaps recollecting what he had learned from it, or the course he had used it in as a young man, before he sealed it away. "Nat Edward'ich," he said without turning, "it's no use. You should be packing too."

"We've got an ignition deadline, remember?"

"Edward'ich," Borisovich went on, refusing to look at him, "we are soon to be arrested. The ignition deadline is theirs, not ours."

"We have a saboteur to catch."

"I hope he blows the place sky high."

"For me, stay."

Archangelsky's unruly locks swayed as he shook his head. "People like us did science for joy of it, for those rare moments of truth. You know what I mean. There is no joy here anymore—and no truth."

"What will you do?"

From behind, Machuzak could see only the shrug of his shoulders. "Maybe I go to work for Balard. They want mole, now they've got one." Slava moved toward the wall and gently took down the icon of the Mother of God and lay it atop the box. Only then did he face Nathaniel and offer his hand. "Good luck, Nat, you know where to find me." Slava's beard made it difficult to say, but Nathaniel thought he saw a tear rolling down his friend's cheek. Archangelsky switched off the light and walked out.

* * * *

Machuzak secluded himself in the MTF. The morning was not gone before an announcement came around that Krieg-Zuber had resumed his duties as acting director, that Mercedes Ramirez had been appointed deputy director. Nathaniel smiled faintly. No further explanation for her behavior required. The websites were full of yesterday's gallimaufry at CFRC and it hit hard to see his own headshot inserted above the shoulder of local newscasters. Thirty minutes later Krieg-Zuber's first memorandum appeared: according to the best intelligence the saboteurs had been apprehended and the ignition campaign could now move forward with calm and assurance. Another five minutes and a second edict: the weekly barbeques instituted by the previous acting director were heretofore canceled, all work-related computers were to be physically disconnected from the Internet and access to social networking sites was, as of now, permanently disabled.

A few media were following up on Theresa's suggestion to investigate Whitman, but interest peaked by afternoon and, as Big Bad Roy himself made clear on his site, the apparent second act of sabotage served only to ratchet up his determination to terminate the lab. Moravec also issued a press release saying that yesterday's events had convinced him that canceling CFRC's contract had been right. The saboteur had accomplished his mission, Nathaniel conceded. We are finally, absolutely alone.

While Nathaniel contemplated the state of affairs, someone knocked on the door. His call "Come in!" went unanswered. Eventually he swiveled around to see D'Abro leaning with her elbow on the doorframe, biting her nail. She appeared nervous, or trying to find the proper balance between civility and distance. For her thoughts, Machuzak would have given far more than a penny.

He spoke first. "Are you taking me in?"

To her, he seemed grave rather than angry, at least not as angry as he should have been. "If I had my druthers, Doc, I would, but the folks downtown will decide when there's enough evidence. In the meantime, let me give you a piece of advice." D'Abro, with her signature distraction, had begun to wander around the lab, inspecting the plumbing, microwave conduits, most of all the deuterium bottles lined up against the wall. "You might not believe me, but most crimes ain't solved by fingerprints or by DNA. People get guilty consciences, twenty, thirty years after the crime, they start talkin, braggin, confessin… If they would just keep to their silly stories, as idiotic as they are, there's nothin the law can do to touch them. That's my advice."

"Have you heard me confessing? Detective, whatever you are this week," he motioned for her to sit, "you've been violating the first commandment of science: 'Thou shalt not love thine own theories too much.' You've caught me and Slava grousing about Krieg-Zuber—"

"That's putting a new spin on euphemism," she interrupted, leaning against the workbench but continuing to stand.

"—and you've ignored everything else. You know how Slava hates Balard. Why would he become his mole?"

D'Abro momentarily glanced around the space with which she had become so familiar over the past months. "Maybe Slava's a good actor, maybe he hates Balard less than he hated Krieg-Zuber. It's hard to know people, Doc, even friends." She leveled her eyes.

He met them. "Yeah, Detective, and so maybe you've neglected the possibility that Slava and I had nothing to do with the sabotage and that we've just pissed Balard off so much that he intends to run us into the ground."

"Whaddya got to prove it?"

"A ringtone."

D'Abro merely scoffed. "How many people could have that ringtone?"

Machuzak returned an equally dismissive scoff. "My guess would be three. The *Nisi Dominus* from the Monteverdi *Vespers* can't exactly be topping the charts."

"I don't have time—"

"In science you explore all leads, Detective."

"No you don't," she shook her head decisively, picking up a piece of metal stock that could have served for a busbar. "You follow your nose, you said so yourself. You learn what's promising and what isn't. Same where I come from."

"All right, then," Machuzak asked abruptly, "what was in that deuterium bottle you impounded?"

Surprised by the question, D'Abro squinted and replied, "Deuterium, just like you said it would be."

The scientist frowned. "Your lab rats downtown must have run it through a mass spectrometer. What else is in it?"

Not much of anything, as far as she knew. They'd only given her a verbal report.

"Get the cracking charts, will you, and let's see what was in that bottle."

T. J. still showed herself to be puzzled.

"The devil is in the details," Machuzak said and for a moment the two ceased speaking. "What did you want here, Detective?" he said finally. "Today?"

"A wrench and a regulator would do," she answered.

Now it was the physicist's turn to be puzzled. He pointed to an oversized crescent wrench lying on a tool cart amid the clutter and a spare regulator on the bench.

"Where do you keep the empties?" the detective said, picking them up.

It took a moment before Nathaniel realized what she was after and he pointed to a collection of half a dozen deuterium bottles strapped together like a bundle of hay against the wall. Above them a hand-scrawled sign read "Empties."

D'Abro walked over, fit the regulator stem to each bottle in turn, trying to tighten it. After a few minutes she reaches one that won't go. She fiddles with it a few times to be sure, stops and looked at Machuzak. "Right-hand thread."

"So?"

It was hardly a reaction. "Do you remember how after the explosion Abbuhl said he couldn't understand how deuterium got into a sulfur hexafluoride bottle because flammable gases get left-hand threads? It sort of passed me by, with everything else… Just this morning it popped back into my head."

"Yeah." Machuzak did remember. "Slava said it would be easier to swap the label. The bottles look the same."

"They sure do." D'Abro pointed the wrench at the bottle. "I'm willin to bet that this here is a sulfur hexafluoride bottle."

At once Machuzak exploded. "Why on Earth would I bring it to my own lab?"

"Inventory. I did a little checking." T. J. was flipping the wrench in her hand. "Things are loose around here but not that loose. Procurement likes to keep track of who has how many bottles and where. Take one outta the lab, gotta bring one back. Make sure it's empty, send it out to be refilled. End of evidence."

Machuzak made an expression far deeper than a scowl. "Nobody pays any attention to that sort of thing. That would be the dumbest—"

"The way you guys have been behavin hasn't been the smartest... Anyway"—she stopped flipping the wrench and laid it back on the cart— "I'm gonna impound this bottle. Sulfur hexafluoride is a very heavy gas. Maybe there's a pinch left."

"Why don't you just breathe it," he suggested. "If you end up sounding like King Kong, it's sulfur hexafluoride."

She declined the invitation, handed Machuzak a pair of gloves and asked his help in loading the bottle onto a dolly. Grudgingly he obliged and they took it out to her car. "As I said, Doc, don't leave town. If this sulfur hexafluoride checks out, I am gonna call the DA's office about seeing you charged with criminal mischief, that's willful destruction of property, and if I can get it, capital sabotage—which, as I've said, includes murder." She stepped into the car and looked up at him with a half-angry, half-resigned expression. "And what was that, *Nisi Dom* by Monte... Monte—"

"*Nisi Dominus* by Monteverdi, Claudio Greenmountain," Machuzak answered and slammed the door shut.

THIRTY-NINE

Machuzak stood for a long time in the parking lot after the detective drove off. Inside the MTF he remained immobilized, incapable of thought, and checked mail. During his five-minute absence Krieg-Zuber had issued a new memorandum: the staff will immediately prepare for crisis-response simulations, including terrorist attacks, cyber warfare and budgetary exigencies. As late as he is mad, Nathaniel blinked at the descending cloak of unreality, but the staff posted no protest videos.

He tuned in distractedly to the control-cast, now accompanied by a music track. Despite his removal, experiments were proceeding and Hasschler's team had coaxed a twenty-second low-power burn out of Prometheus. Machuzak felt nothing at all, not even the ache of exclusion, only a distant recognition that Thad was carrying on. In the coming days Hasschler would shoot for breakeven, to show ITER that they had a contest on their hands. Good, Machuzak supposed. Abruptly he decided to go home.

This time he ignored the increased numbers of protestors at the gate and continued north. A few minutes later he felt the first onslaughts of panic, the rush of adrenaline and shallow heaving that short-circuits everything else. But as the dread threatened to overwhelm him, a call came through from Archangelsky who wanted to meet at Town Lake. The familiar voice brought him round and he breathed. Thatch your mind.

* * * *

By the time he found Slava sitting with a tablet on a bench at river's edge, Machuzak was beginning to feel that he might still be alive. The Russian didn't notice his state and only pointed to the screen of his computer where another invitation to Fusion World beckoned. Archangelsky had already traced the address to the Cadarache region. "I still don't think location is important. He has been trying to confuse us."

"And doing a good job," Nathaniel replied, yet agitated by the other crisis.

The next few minutes passed quickly. Once again, Slava was invited to a tour of the Cinderella tokamak; the DeLorean's electronic guide pointed out some of the main features of the machine, which were high-lighted by starbursts in the form of smiley faces.

"Wait," said Slava. "Look here. The power area and helium factory are highlighted—they've already been hit." He couldn't remember what had been lit up on the previous tours.

The news confirmed that what happened yesterday was no light-ning strike but a perfectly disguised sabotage. Nathaniel got to his feet, focused now but scratching his head. "His first messages were vague warnings. Now, he's showing us what's already happened. His crystal ball is cloudy."

"The helium balloons last time were warnings? Hmm, perhaps you are right—he lacks perfect information."

In short order the tour ended—no more smileys—and the site faded, as before the familiar dragon and a fish resting at Slava's feet. This time there was also suspended in air a little glass bottle with some electrodes protruding from it.

"Shit," was Nathaniel's only reaction. He walked to the water and hurled a stone into it. After a moment, Slava put the computer aside and joined Machuzak. Kneeling, he put his hand into the river.

"Nat Edward'ich, why should we worry about this? I have resigned; you are no longer director. D'Abro intends to arrest us both. What's in this for us?"

Picking up another stone, Machuzak hefted and skipped it. "How about self-preservation, *brat*?" Now he turned fully to the Russian. "Less than two hours ago, D'Abro threatened to charge me—and that means you—with murder. You want to stay out of prison, let's find out what's going on. That's our profession, isn't it?"

"We're already in prison." Borisovich's reply was sullen.

For a moment Machuzak gazed distractedly across the river to Aus-tin's downtown, which felt tawdrier with each passing year, and then he shrugged, panic now fully evaporated. "Anyway, what else will you do with your free time?"

"Good point," Slava chuckled and stood. "Wait a minute," he sud-denly exclaimed. "I still have the video, don't I?" He walked over to the bench and picked up his computer. "Where did I put that thing...? I should have thought of this before—D'Abro should have thought of it right away."

Confused, Machuzak merely watched as Archangelsky downloaded some freeware. "What are you doing?" he asked.

The Russian didn't reply, only crossed his fingers and stared in-tently at the screen while he ran the app. Seconds passed, then: "Yes!" Slava breathed and clenched his fist in a small victory. "*Vot.*" Machuzak followed the outstretched finger to a number in the upper right corner of the video shot in Cadarache.

"Digital watermark. We're lucky video wasn't too old or too altered. We still don't know who shot this but we now know exactly what camera did. Canon. All we have to do is trace it."

We must turn this information over to D'Abro, Machuzak told him, but Slava shook his head. "The women intends to charge us with murder, *brat*. Let her figure it out. She has copy and I still have friends in Moscow." Then and there he created an account on a tiny public network and sent an encrypted email to Moscow, asking his friend to learn where this camera had been sold.

* * * *

The half-moon was already bright when Nathaniel appeared unannounced at the Rasmussens' door. Theresa called out sharply, telling whoever it was to let himself in. Nathaniel did, quietly, searching for her. As he passed the rec room he caught sight of her in a clay-streaked smock, angrily pummeling a standing nude into formlessness. Only after he'd stood watching for an eternity did she become aware of his presence and her electric start revealed pain and relief.

"Mac," Theresa said, sniffling. She wiped a tear from her eye with the back of her hand, walked over to him and kissed him on the cheek. "It's good to see you." She sounded as unhappy as she did truthful. "Let me wash up." Vanishing into a bathroom, Theresa emerged clean and smiling a few moments later and picked up a wineglass that stood by what remained of her sculpture.

Nathaniel was undeceived by the mask of cheer. "What's wrong?" he said and put his own concerns aside.

Theresa attempted to wave him off, saying she was just so up and down with Leonard's health. "Some days I almost think he might recover, some days it's worse... I don't know what to do..." She laughed aloud at some distant, surfacing memory. After the instant it took for a quizzical expression to pass across her face, Theresa collapsed without warning on Nathaniel's shoulder and said, "Oh, Mac, sometimes I want to put a bullet in my brain."

Neither of them had spoken of their encounter of several weeks' past since it had taken place, but it now seemed beside the point. Seeing her state, Nathaniel understood he had come to no purpose. Within a moment, though, Theresa had pulled herself together, led him by the hand into the kitchen and held out a glass. "Forgive me, Mac, you should be crying on my shoulder. I heard what happened yesterday with Cy."

"D'Abro said she might charge me with murder," Nathaniel said simply. "And Slava."

The words forced a gasp of horror from Theresa. Her hands went to her face and she only slowly perceived that Nathaniel was far calmer than she was.

"Don't worry. I don't think she wants to, I doubt she has the evidence…"

As she peered at him, Theresa's curiosity was overt. "How can you take it so well? I'd be hysterical." She managed a faint smile and took a gulp.

"I had my five minutes of panic this afternoon; now it's time to deal with the problem." His own fate was not paramount. "Krieg-Zuber will kill the lab," he said. "I need to speak to Leonard."

Theresa led him into the study, where Leonard was watching television. He looked noticeably better today than yesterday. "Leonard," Nathaniel said, "if you want this ignition campaign to have any chance of success, force Garrett to correct his fatal mistake. He must remove Krieg-Zuber from power, immediately."

"Nathaniel, I can't," Leonard replied, with an acute irritation that penetrated the pain of his expression. "I… I've abdicated the throne, you know that. Garrett is in charge. Period."

Machuzak insisted, knelt by the wheelchair. "Tell him you'll lead the ignition campaign and he'll relent."

"I'm sorry, Nathaniel," Leonard replied, both angry and near tears, "sorrier than you know."

Machuzak had no understanding of this, but Leonard's tone was final, and he saw that nothing more would be gotten out of the great man on that front.

"Dear, what can you tell us about Thomas Whitman's resignation from the DOE?" Theresa asked abruptly.

The change of subject caught both men off guard and Rasmussen didn't immediately react, but after an instant true wrath spread across his features. "Those two bastards… You know, when the lab was still AN-FRL, a review team came to visit. Thomas Whitman stacked it with fat laser-fusion cats to ensure that our funds would be cut and siphoned in their direction. I screamed bloody murder to DOE and the collusion was so obvious that the DOE chief ordered an investigation. A new review panel was appointed and I saved the lab."

"Is that why Thomas resigned?" Nathaniel asked, surprised at the history.

"That was something else," Leonard replied sharply, "after Thomas diverted fifty million dollars away from magnetic fusion. I lobbied like hell to get it back, but Senator Roy, the devil incarnate, blocked my efforts and Congress supposedly reallocated the funds. What we might have done…"

Leonard had confirmed Theresa's accusation of yesterday, but Nathaniel wanted to know how Thomas Whitman could divert so much money.

"Discretionary funds," Leonard answered. "He could do anything he wanted."

"Even divert money to the military side of DOE?" Nathaniel pressed.

"They said it went to harbor dredging," snapped Leonard. "It's part of the same budget pool. Thomas soon stepped down and I never found out exactly what happened."

It seemed that Theresa had dangerously overshot in her allegation, but then she interrupted. "Darling, what do you know about a company called Exosystems?" Nathaniel snapped his head toward her and Leonard revealed only puzzlement. "An out-of-work reporter from the old *Statesman* phoned me today and said that the Whitmans once owned the company, but that they sold it well before Thomas became director of Energy Research."

Leonard pleaded ignorance. "It could be. What happened was always shrouded by closed congressional testimony. I don't know anything about it."

Theresa and Nathaniel glanced at each other and, seeing Leonard was tired, bid him good evening.

* * * *

In the kitchen, Nathaniel expressed surprise at the existence of Exosystems and found it odd that Leonard knew nothing about them.

"He doesn't know everything," Theresa shrugged, "and he doesn't tell me everything he knows. And if it all happened under wraps…" She offered Nathaniel another glass, which he declined with a wave of his hand. "There's virtually nothing about it online, either. The company hasn't existed for decades."

"If it's not on Google, it never happened… Theresa," Nathaniel said, clasping her by the shoulders, "Slava and I are in big trouble, but the lab is in worse trouble. I need you to investigate this Exosystems. That's your assignment."

"Willingly accepted, sir," she smiled. "I'll work with the freelancer. We'll do our best."

Theresa led him to the front door with her arm around his waist. There, she kissed him on the lips, the kiss of a lover, but graciously permitted him to depart.

FORTY

With his usual slowness, Nathaniel suspected his presence at CFRC was not required when he saw that several Greenpeace members and Scientologists had swelled the ranks at the gate only to be outnumbered by a new contingent of National Guardsmen. When the sentry at the booth gaped at him as if he were a dead man walking, his suspicions hardened, though he managed a friendly gesture for the fellow to raise his jaw. By the time he perceived that CFRC had overnight been turned into an armed camp, where the rooftop of the main building bulged with sandbags and bristled with rifle barrels, his fears had crystallized. Bill Balustradi alone offered a smile, despite the dagger stuck through his head. Anyone he encountered, all strangers now, gawked uncomfortably for an instant, turned away, gawked again. More than one colleague growled for him to leave. When even Lise recoiled at the sight of him, he felt compelled to remind her that he hadn't been charged and she burst into tears.

Obstinacy rising, he attempted to visit the control room, where two guardsmen barred his entry. "I have every right to be here," he protested, but they refused to allow him to pass until Abbuhl intervened. He instantly regretted his decision. Larissa, the COE on duty, baldly picked up the phone to call security. Cochran ignored him, or pretended to, and Abbuhl could do no more than plead desperately with his hands. Martyrdom was not cause enough to prolong the visit. "You should automate this," he said, flipping a small deadline calendar on the COE's console and walked out.

* * * *

Very well, the MTF would serve as leper colony. Strangely, it struck him, he hadn't woken up last night in a cold sweat. As yesterday's panic fell away, he felt increasingly unburdened, enveloped by the same aura of tranquility he heard in Schubert's last works, though he hoped the outcome would not be equally fatal. Nevertheless, his duty now was to see his way through this bog. The moment of grace and opportunity was at hand.

Machuzak did not know exactly what he intended. He checked Monteverdi ringtones online, not finding what he sought. He spent some time sitting, thinking, before he switched on the control-cast. Instantly he recognized that in the two days since first plasma, the control room's aspect had drastically changed. Virtually every division head was on hand; the neutral-beam and rf control areas full of people, bags of chips and soda cans stacked up for the long haul. Technicians darted in and out, phones rang ceaselessly. For the first time in nearly two months, the number of scientists vied with the rest. Spectroscopists and other diagnosticians sat at some of the centuries of terminals filling the room. Today the displays indicated that a genuine scientific experiment might be under way. To call what was taking place an experiment didn't put exactly the right spin on it, Nathaniel, everyone, understood. To a trendy music track they were entering the final battle for their lives.

Bald Hasschler stood on the captain's deck, arms akimbo, giving orders in his crusty style, while Krieg-Zuber, dealing with his bad arm, made notations on an electronic pad and ordered one of the techs to lose the potato chips.

Over the next few hours Machuzak intermittently tuned in while he prowled about his own space. DT shots proceeded all morning, ten or twenty seconds long, each result informing the team when they had taken a step toward ignition and when they had stepped backward. The machine was behaving and within a few days they ought to achieve breakeven, a fabled benchmark forty years ago, but one that should be child's play for Prometheus. The question remains: what happens in the territory beyond?

Suddenly, commotion envelopes the room, fault lights begin blinking everywhere and Machuzak stands, riveted. A few minutes streak by when Faberman dashes in, announcing that Fluorinert is spilling onto the floor of pentagon five, the microwave heating facility. No one needs to tell Nathaniel what thought is coursing through the mind of every person in the room. He yet has no idea of how the "accident" of two days ago could have been engineered. He knows only that another act of sabotage is now superfluous.

Even as Faberman makes his announcement, Zuber's face is reddening. The tech attempts to assure him that it is no more than a routine leak of coolant for the megawatt radio tubes employed in the rf heating system. Cleaning it up is nothing a refrigerator repairman couldn't handle. Faberman's words reassure everyone within earshot, except Zuber, who has gone so far ultraviolet that he rips off his tie. Machuzak recollects some years ago the epidemic of Chinese students poisoning themselves with the stuff to prevent their deportation.

A moment later the division heads' phones went off with a message, "This is not a drill. Report to the director immediately." Perplexed, the chiefs, most already present, gather round Krieg-Zuber. "What plans do you have for investigating this accident?" he barks to Fournier, head of rf heating, and he doesn't wait out Fournier's stuttering reply. "You will begin investigating at once, per our new procedures, which we will rehearse in exactly one minute upstairs. This accident reeks of intent." Fournier manages to point out that the saboteurs have been apprehended, at which Krieg-Zuber starts, answering, "We can never rule out copy-cat incidents." Suddenly: "Are those webcams on? The entire world is witness to your incompetence! Our opponents are able to capitalize on every mistake, every accident, every piece of data posted!"

"Scientific data is posted, by long and honorable tradition," Matsushima reminds him.

"This is not a scientific experiment, Dr. Matsushima, this is the final crusade for the salvation of the human race! Those webcams will be turned off!"

A few seconds later the scene goes dark.

* * * *

The following morning the webcams were again broadcasting, although as he watched from home, Machuzak wondered whether Krieg-Zuber knew it. Overnight the betting had begun. On one of the control room's big whiteboards, crew members had scrawled possible outcomes with the odds being offered. Beating the deadline ran at 750 to 1 against, beating only ITER 10 to 1. Machuzak could not understand it would be possible to win against ITER without beating Moravec. The only favorable odds being offered were 1 to 1 on Moravec's assassination.

Toward noon, Abbuhl entered the control room and suggested cleaning the cryopumps. Krieg-Zuber again turned crimson and swiveled around a full 360 degrees before he objected. "Damnit, Monsieur Abbuhl, the machine is behaving, and I expect breakeven tomorrow."

"Yes, sir," Abbuhl replied, "but those pumps are getting pretty dirty. I recommend we regenerate them."

Krieg-Zuber remained intransigent and by day's end the cryopumps failed and had to be cleaned anyway. Breakeven was not achieved the next day.

* * * *

Machuzak's pulse hardly rose a notch when toward the end of the week D'Abro appeared at the MTF with a warrant for his arrest.

"That was a sulfur hexafluoride bottle," she said, entering his lab, "and your prints are on it—nobody else's. I'm sorry, Doc." Her tone left no room for interpretation.

"Don't be," he answered, dead calm, "but I'm not budging."

D'Abro regarded him with a newfound professional incomprehension. "Resisting arrest is a criminal offense, Dr. Machuzak," she replied levelly. "I can charge you with that too."

"Before you do," he nodded pensively, "did you bring the cracking charts for the deuterium bottle, like I asked?" He regarded the lieutenant, who with shimmering hair and designer suit had lost none of her flamboyance. A few weeks ago he would have given himself over to fantasy at the sight of her, and for one night at least, she'd curled her arms tenderly around his neck. Today he would have settled for a kind word lofted across the abyss between them.

D'Abro did hesitate. "I don't know, Nat, your analytical mind should appreciate my dilemma. If you're the man I'm after, you'll do everything to lead me astray. On the other hand, if you didn't do it, I could use your help, because this report doesn't say anything to me or anyone else downtown. Like you predicted, there was more than deuterium in that bottle."

"Trust me," was Machuzak's only reply as he stretched out his hand.

With perceptible indecision she finally turned over the printouts. They weren't cracking charts, exactly, but at least a summary of lab results.

"As I thought," he said—one glance was enough. "Silicon carbide."

"Huh?" she asked, taking a step forward to look over his shoulder.

"Your report lists silicon and carbon impurities in the deuterium bottle," he tapped the paper with his fingertips. "They come from silicon carbide, one of the materials we test at the MTF–"

"—which means it came from this lab," D'Abro said with a pained, saddened glance around the room. "You're hangin yourself, Doc."

"Maybe." He got up from the desk and motioned her over to the familiar test stand. She accommodated his request, keeping a distance. "The MTF consists of three adjoining labs, plus the big accelerator room. We all do experiments on the same substances, share equipment and deuterium bottles. You remember the little flame I rigged up to placate the environmentalists?" D'Abro nodded as Machuzak pointed to it on the exhaust side of the test cell. "It means that virtually all the deuterium I use is burned to heavy water."

The detective motioned for him to demonstrate and he was not unprepared. The pumps were already chugging and he needed only to connect a deuterium tank to the input nozzle, light the flame and turn on the equipment. After some minutes the two observed drops of heavy water slithering down the glass distillation tube into the hose, which ran, covered by a metal strip, along the floor and through a hole in the wall. He took her to the window, where she could see the water dripping onto a patch of withered grass outside. This was how it worked.

"That's what I do with my deuterium," he told D'Abro. "So how did traces of silicon and carbon get into that bottle?"

The detective shakes her head, not seeing the answer, but there is no way she can.

"Let's try an experiment," he smiles. D'Abro follows cautiously as he walks next door to Mercedes' laboratory. There's no danger of finding Ramirez here; she cleared out last week with her rise to power and hadn't set foot in the place since. Her experimental setup is much like his own, except that Mercedes usually recycled deuterium. With a glance around her lab, Nathaniel wheels over a fresh deuterium tank, connects it to the input and an empty to the output. He finds a silicon carbide target on Mercedes' workbench, nothing more than a flat, slick black square the size of his hand, and mounts it on the clamps inside her test cell. Now he flicks on the pumps. The familiar clacking, pitch ever rising as the air is evacuated. When the pressure is low enough, he starts the diffusion pumps.

During the near hour that goes by while they wait, D'Abro's only remark is, "I will get to the bottom of this, Mac."

"So will I." Machuzak meets her gaze head-on and the conversation ends.

At last, he lets in a stream of deuterium and switches on the high voltage, which strips the gas of its electrons and slams the deuterium nuclei into the target.

Allowing the experiment to run for ten minutes or so, he fills the empty bottle from the test cylinder, disconnects it and wheels it over to the mass spectrometer in his lab. Before long he has a cracking chart. Deuterium with trace abundances of silicon and carbon.

D'Abro objects that the abundances are significantly lower than the crime lab report, but Machuzak only shrugs. "The concentration will depend on how long we run the experiment and the number of times the deuterium is recycled. First try and we're within a factor of ten. Exact matches are rare in science, DNA notwithstanding. You see the principle. Mercedes recycles deuterium; I don't."

D'Abro stared at the physicist sullenly, fiercely. Her reluctance to accept his argument was written all over her face, but he did not particularly care. "Why do you think Ramirez could be involved in this?" she asked skeptically.

"I don't know," Machuzak conceded. "According to rumor she's been having an affair with Krieg-Zuber—" At that D'Abro raised her eyebrows. "Oh, I see you haven't heard that one. Mercedes doesn't like me very much and she does like power. At least she'd like a better job. She's no way a terrific physicist but she is good with computers."

"Was she down in the power area?"

"Everybody lent a hand during the run-up to the dedication. She didn't usually work there, but then again, neither did I."

D'Abro rose. Flicking the arrest warrant sharply against her hand she said, "You've bought yourself a little time, Doc, that's all. I'm gonna double check the access records, but I don't recollect any prints matching hers, so don't get excited."

As she turned to go, Machuzak asked her, "Did you trace that ringtone?"

T. J. only scoffed and vanished.

FORTY-ONE

It was nothing more than a vague hunch—she still didn't understand the intricacies of the enormously complex systems that had surrounded her for two months now—but T. J. decided to ask. She sought out Diana Cochran at her outpost office in the helium factory, pentagon three. "As I understand it," T. J. said, having announced herself, "y'all are convinced last week's accident was sabotage."

Cochran leaned back from her monitor. "Yeah, someone injected liters of helium into the beam boxes and when it evaporated—!" She produced an explosion with her hands. "Liters! Usually it's—" she made the other gesture, the universal "an itty-bitty bit." "We're lucky the sensors caught it before it ruptured the pressure plates."

For a moment D'Abro regarded the cryo chief, who with her bobbed blond hair and athletic build struck her as the kind of woman she once encountered at swim meets. "How do you control the amount of helium you put into those neutral beams?" she asked.

"The operator uses a programmable logic control circuit. Used to be manual switches."

T. J. asked if she could watch it done, and Cochran obliged, donning a head mirror and demonstrating the point-and-click system that guided the helium flow. "Who's got access?"

"Only a few of us," Cochran replied, "me and two operators."

"Could someone have hacked the system?"

The engineer tilted her head. Krieg-Zuber, losing not a second, had ordered them to investigate that possibility, but with experiments under way, they hadn't gotten to it yet. "The system's pretty secure, but if someone stole a username and password, they could do anything." Without saying more, Cochran brought up the log file for the past days and ran her finger down the list of IP addresses. "These guys are our operators…wait." She hesitated halfway down the screen. "This looks wrong… And it was exactly at the time of the accident, to the minute." At once Cochran determined that the address was local, as it must have been for the saboteur to know precisely the moment to strike. "Machuzak and Archangelsky…" she whispered to the detective.

D'Abro peered at Cochran with curiosity, puckered her lips, reflected. At length: "Would have been a good trick, given that a hundred people saw them in the cafeteria arguin with Senator Whitman when lightnin struck."

Cochran disagreed sharply. "Once you were in the system you'd program it and push the damn button on your phone at the right moment like a roadside bomb." She demonstrated with her thumb.

"You don't like those two much, do you?" T. J. said. It was not a question.

A pugnacious expression crept across the cryo-chief's face. "Those two? CFRC isn't some do-what-you-feel-like university department. It's a dedicated lab. That pair hates anybody who tries to get the job done. At least with Krieg-Zuber at the helm we stand a chance. Nah, Archangelsky and Machuzak, they act like some prep school snots, thinkin they're better than the rest of us. I wouldn't put it past them to have sabotaged Prometheus, just so ITER could win; they're socialists, you know…"

"Remember, ma'am, hot words lead to cold slabs," T. J. saluted and left, having gotten the picture.

* * * *

It was time to call on Mercedes. D'Abro found the physicist in her new third-floor office with a splendid view of the administration building's central atrium. "Nice digs," she said, appraising the ample space. "Mind if I sit down?"

Mercedes cocked her head, revealing a small surprise at the lieutenant's appearance. She followed this with a "Please do" of equal disinterest and, almost as an afterthought, rose slightly to shake D'Abro's hand. They hadn't yet been officially introduced. "How may I help, Detective?"

T. J. got down to it and asked how she suddenly became assistant director of CFRC. A quizzical expression passed across Mercedes' face and she pinched her nose, as if it hadn't occurred to her that anyone might question her good fortune. She replied simply that Krieg-Zuber had made the offer.

"Do you have any prior administrative experience? I don't see any in your file." T. J. paged through the tablet in her hand, then leaned over to examine a pretty Talavera vase on Ramirez's desk. The physicist had already begun to decorate the office with Mexican earthenware and folk items, which appeared incongruous at CFRC.

"No, I guess I haven't," Ramirez admitted, "but with the crisis the options were limited." She smiled faintly.

"The thing is, it happened within hours after Krieg-Zuber was appointed acting director, which means, I'd think—wouldn't you—that you folks discussed it ahead of time, no?"

Ramirez's annoyance showed plainly in her expression and in her voice. "Yes, well I suppose we did. What of it?"

D'Abro shrugged. "Just seems a little odd, that's all, like you planned it. Tell me," she went on without pause, "why'd you record that conversation between Machuzak, Archangelsky and Lipman?"

"I explained that the other day," Ramirez answered with a ragged edge. She really had become annoyed, quickly too. "I was working late, overheard them and decided it was important, so I recorded it."

"Do you always record important conversations?"

"There's no law against it!" The woman had abruptly passed beyond annoyance and her voice was ugly. "And they *were* talking about sabotage—if not worse."

T. J. got to her feet, began to examine a gray-and-blue weaving that hung on the wall. She was starting to understand why Mac didn't like Mercedes very much. "You never joked about doin in your boss?"

"They were plotting," Ramirez dug in. "You heard them."

"Tell me, the access records show you were down in the power area three, four days before the dedication. That's a long ways from the MTF. What were you doin there, on foreign territory, Dr. Ramirez?"

The physicist's exasperation at the question reminded D'Abro of Machuzak's own. "I was helping out," she said, "like everybody else… with some inspections. I… I helped replace some old capacitors. Surely, Detective, you can't think…" She suddenly frowned with the utmost contempt and forced herself not to laugh.

"Is it true you've been having an affair with Krieg-Zuber?" D'Abro asked abruptly.

Mercedes Ramirez froze in her place. Then: "How dare you bring my personal life into this!" She fully exploded.

Again T. J. merely shrugged. "Well, you've accused a couple guys of sabotage, maybe worse. That's pretty personal, wouldn't you say?"

At once Ramirez was on her feet. "Detective, I haven't accused anyone of anything—"

"Neither have I," D'Abro answered, smiling sweetly.

"I offered a tape—"

"In exchange for what, Dr. Ramirez? This office?" D'Abro glanced toward the ceiling and spread her hands. "You'd sell your soul for an office?"

"I resent that, Detective." There couldn't be any doubt; a very unpleasant expression contorted the new assistant director's face.

"Excuse me, ma'am, I guess it is brighter than the MTF."

Ramirez now leaned over her desk, almost into D'Abro's nose. "Lieutenant, you've gone way too far," she snarled. "Machuzak got himself into his fix. For five years I was stuck in that dungeon and he never batted an eye—"

"Ah—"

At that moment Krieg-Zuber himself appeared at the door asking about all the commotion. In the time Ramirez hurled a ferocious glance at D'Abro, then at Krieg-Zuber, T. J. said, "We were discussing why you appointed Dr. Ramirez as acting assistant director, or would that be deputy acting director?"

"As you know," he replied sternly, "the lab faces a crisis. Dr. Ramirez expressed interest in the job. She is very talented with computers." He nodded in Mercedes' direction.

"You were about to close down the MTF and offered her a parachute, is that it?"

"Fortuitously, young lady."

"Win-win, I guess. But with a thousand people at this lab—minus a few recently—you picked somebody with no background in running such a joint. What was the deal? A tape? Why's it important that she knows computers?"

"Your question has been answered," Krieg-Zuber replied. "There is nothing more to say about it."

Ramirez glanced at Zuber in a way that T. J. couldn't read and then, having regained a quantum of composure, interrupted with a steel voice, "Lieutenant, unless you have some concrete evidence to connect me with these crimes, I'll ask you to stop fishing and leave."

T. J. yielded. To be sure, she had no forensics of any kind on Ramirez, and the woman apparently had never worked at ITER or had had any contact with Balard. "I've traced the deuterium bottle to the MTF," she did reveal, "and that includes your lab." D'Abro opened the door. "Oh, one other thing, given that you're so handy with computers, I'd like to have a look at yours."

"There's nothing in them of any possible relevance," Mercedes stammered. "I...it's private."

"Funny how that works, isn't it?" T. J. really couldn't understand this private-life stuff. Promising to get a warrant, she left Mercedes petrified and staring and ran after Krieg-Zuber, who had already disappeared.

* * * *

T. J. glimpsed the deputy vanishing into the elevator and only caught sight of him again on the ground floor as he crossed the central atrium.

He was walking fast, so fast that she needed to sprint to intercept him in that sun-dappled space, infused with the perfume of flowers. The man who reminded her of an arrow was in no good mood, and not only because of the scene moments ago. As she overtook him, he was cursing aloud that the fools under him hadn't attained breakeven. "They're dragging their feet intentionally, mutineers." ASSET was weeks behind ITER. "The pygmies have no sense of history," Krieg-Zuber smoldered, putting his finger under his collar.

"The director is listening, mademoiselle, for a moment," he paused in midstride and swiveled around when he sensed T. J.'s presence. "How do you expect him to concentrate on life and death with you dogging his heels?"

T. J. abruptly sat down on a rock beside one of the pools into which water cascaded over a miniature fall, for a moment swishing her hand in the water and disturbing the fish, for a further moment shielding her eyes against the sun as she glanced up at the executive offices peering down on them. "I'm still tryin to understand why you made Dr. Ramirez assistant director. Yeah, imagine she'd jump at the chance to get out of that MTF cave, especially in that you were about to shut it down. But you were within an inch of axing Machuzak, why not her?"

"That was explained upstairs," Krieg-Zuber snapped, but he did stop in his tracks.

T. J. liked this spot, the only place in the immense, claustrophobic lab of steel and electricity where she felt outdoors. She stood, took into her hand a cluster of bird-beaked flowers of a brilliant sea green, brought them to her nose, inhaled. "What is this called? A jade vine? I'm not very good with flowers, you know. Why'd you accept her application? The recording?"

"Are you saying, Lieutenant, that she, or I, manufactured evidence?" Krieg-Zuber peered at her with his unblinking, disdainful blue eyes. Then he merely scoffed.

"No, the crime lab tells me the recording's pristine. That was the deal, wasn't it? The eavesdrop for the position. Sure got Machuzak out of the way—Bam!"—D'Abro struck her hands together—"and got you the directorship, cleeen as a whistle."

Krieg-Zuber, peering, stroked his scar, then to T. J.'s great surprise pulled a banana from a nearby tree and offered it to her. Too shocked to do otherwise, she accepted the fruit and began peeling it. "The directorship was Krieg-Zuber's, by contract and by right, Mademoiselle D'Abro, and he will not apologize for fighting for it. Do you know, young lady, his boyhood dream was to become a champion yachtsman and sail the world without a care. He was an accomplished sailor and won a number of races. 'I could have danced all night...'" Without warning Krieg-Zuber took T. J.'s arms and led her in the first steps of a waltz, then abruptly sat himself at the atrium's grand piano and attempted to play the famous tune. With the banana in her hand, D'Abro was speechless.

But when his bad arm betrayed him, he slammed down the keyboard cover and cried, an abyssal injury, "The sacrifices I have made for the Mission! I would sell my soul to achieve fusion, Ms. D'Abro... No one wants it but they shall have it!" He pounded with his fist and stood.

Flummoxed, T. J. chewed slowly on the banana, swallowed. "A man in your condition should take it easy, sir," she said at last, "but I'm still confused. Ramirez made the recording before the event. Seems a mite convenient, and that deuterium bottle could have come from her lab." Krieg-Zuber leveled those eyes. "Oh, you didn't know. We traced it to the MTF."

"Machuzak. It fits with everything."

"Hmm, probably, but I've also heard that the two of you were having an affair. True?"

She put a cute question mark on it, as if she were intending to post it on Facebook, and Krieg-Zuber did a double take, scoffed. "You are not serious!"

T. J. admitted the information might be inaccurate. "But I've also learned that Mercedes met Balard in the Real World last year and asked him for a job." The Real World's cooperation was finally proving interesting in that respect, but T. J. hadn't yet found anything to suggest that Balard had offered her a position in return for services to be rendered. That's why she wanted Ramirez's computer.

Hearing this, Krieg-Zuber shot at her a look which attempted to hide the wound of betrayal; whether the injury was personal or professional proved impossible to say. "And this adds up to what, young lady?" he at last said, already moving in the direction of the control room.

"Not much," T. J. admitted. "Not much."

* * * *

Late. Very late. Returning home exhausted, T. J. showered, peered at herself in the mirror, didn't much like the lined face staring back at her, modeled a scarf around her neck, which didn't improve matters, plunked herself on the living room couch butt naked except for the scarf. For a while she felt herself all over, but it gave her little pleasure, and soon she found herself mindlessly surfing the big screen.

She glanced over at the books stacked on the floor and remembered reading somewhere that when scientists are confronted with facts that don't fit their theories, their first reaction is to ignore them, and this goes on for a long time, until somebody rubs their noses in it. Sounds like law enforcement. Part of her felt terrible about what she was doing to Machuzak but he sure hadn't made it easy for himself, dumbass scientist; it's almost like he wanted it this way. Maybe she did. Sigh. Some office romance this is turning out to be. T. J. cast around on the Web for some self-help along those lines and, finding none, downloaded what she thought was the Greenmountain tune Mac had been insisting on. Pretty cute, she thought before falling asleep on the couch.

FORTY-TWO

The deadline calendar stood at 125 days and the control room was buzzing. Abbuhl's team had regenerated the cryopanels without incident; Prometheus once again was a functioning machine.

Watching from his lookout, Machuzak saw from the number of runs posted on the big screen that they'd been working all night. Hasschler slumped over a small table on the captain's deck surrounded by styrofoam coffee cups; he'd been at it three shifts running.

The violation of regulations wasn't what had turned Krieg-Zuber's face scarlet. He strode purposefully into the control room and announced from the deck, "Whoever turned those webcams back on is undermining the Mission and has forced me to implement drastic measures. Iris scanners will be installed at the control room entrance, and the unauthorized shall not escape detection."

"Excuse me, sir," Abbuhl interrupted in his most laid-back drawl, one greatly amplified by his weariness. "I turned the webcams on. It's important for us to be in constant communication with our colleagues around the lab. More important, I'd say, is that Austin folks and Big Bad Roy should know what's goin on here. We're sproutin National Guardsmen, more protestors are showin up every day. You want a riot—turn this place into a weapons lab and by God you'll have a riot. Now, if you're insistin on punishment, take my resignation. To hell with this race."

Bravo, Fred, Machuzak applauded. In his slow Southern way, Abbuhl has floored Krieg-Zuber. The Terminator couldn't doubt that if Abbuhl went, the show was over. He crossed his arms as of old, but with difficulty, blinked in disbelief, but could find nothing to say other than, "The blameless must protect themselves, this you fail to comprehend" as he abandoned the control room.

Ari Socarides of Hasschler's team was urging Thad to get some sleep, but the chief had other ideas. He gulped down a cold cup of coffee and announced that it's time to go for breakeven. In the old days, magnets gobbled up so much power that the machines never produced as much energy as they consumed, but superconducting magnets had made the task easier and the accounting more scrupulous.

Despite the risk, Machuzak found himself delighted at the spontaneity of it. Creativity is usually the last thing to make the tight schedule on a big machine. But as t-minus sixty seconds approaches, Fournier breaks away from a frantic huddling for a conference on the deck with Hasschler. At length Hasschler turns to Matsushima, standing beside him. Machuzak zooms in on Toshi, who shrugs listlessly at Fournier's suggestion. Whatever they've decided seems a go, and Thad gives the nod. The parameters are programmed in at the various consoles, Larissa says, "Okay, everybody ready to rock and roll?" and suddenly, without further ado, the countdown begins.

"Sixty...fifty-nine...fifty-eight..."

Not fifteen seconds later one of the diagnosticians interrupts the electronic voice and loud clicking of the digital clock. "Local bet! Local bet!" he shouts and a few bucks exchange hands in a far corner of the room.

"Ten...nine...eight..." At almost the same instant, the door opens and D'Abro wedges herself into the room to stand among the rest. She is smiling at her contribution, the music, but the sight of her suddenly amplifies Machuzak's pain of absence. There is nothing for it and he can only watch with the others.

"Four...three...two...one...zero..."

The current begins its ramp-up. The neutral-beams are injecting their high-energy deuterium and tritium nuclei into the tokamak, providing the fuel while heating the plasma. The radio-frequency drives add their muscle. Within as many seconds, five mega-amps of current are circulating in Prometheus and the magnets are happily producing four-Tesla fields. The tokamak's interior is all bright and red, which lasts for about five seconds more, then it goes dark.

By the time the shot ran its course, real-time data was flashing on the diagnostic monitors and Hasschler had his result: 45 megawatts of fusion power. But the rf and nb heating systems required 50. At least nothing crapped out. After a quick consultation with the diagnosticians, Hasschler called another huddle and fifteen minutes later decided to try again with higher magnet current.

They start over.

To eyes worldwide looking in, the scene remains unchanged: the countdown, the electronic voice, the onset of the pulse followed by that high-pitched screeching piped in from the test cell. The music.

This time when the results are in: 53 megawatts.

Immediately cheers go up throughout the room and five scientists simultaneously grapple with one of the champagne bottles set aside for ignition. Krieg-Zuber, rushing in at the last second, blinks in shock or disbelief and turns red, but refrains from action or comment. Machuzak himself makes a fist. "Yes," he breathes. They'd achieved breakeven. The benchmark was meaningless in terms of a commercial reactor. At the close of the twentieth century, the Joint European Torus in England had grazed breakeven and AUSTOR regularly surpassed it a few years later, but Machuzak could not deny the satisfaction that this week two reactors had for ten full seconds produced more energy by fusion than was required to run them.

Before the champagne had stopped foaming, Krieg-Zuber dictated a press release to Mercedes announcing the achievement under his direction. Moments later an email addressed to "our friends at CFRC" came back from Balard, congratulating the team on "having achieved what we at ITER accomplished a week ago."

* * * *

"You have failed to heed me," Krieg-Zuber said to Hasschler on the captain's deck. "Balard is lurking, and the foolish shall repent."

Even as he cocked his head at the strange words, Hasschler recognized the truth in them and tuned into ITER's own webcast. The numbers on their big screen are clearly visible as they ready a high-field shot to soothing background music. Thad won't stand for it and calls for an even higher power shot to jump ahead. This time, five seconds into the run, the fault lights begin blinking. All action grinds to a halt, every handset comes alive.

Hasschler, completely losing his aristocratic cool, pounds the rail on the deck and shouts, "Fuck!" Others make similar gestures at their stations.

So, pulses have begun to race, thinks Machuzak. Krieg-Zuber is stomping about as he tries to determine what went wrong. Tebrill, an operating engineer, waves his hand in frustration. "No, I don't know what the hell happened!" at which The Terminator blinks and grasps his collar. A few minutes later, one of the techs announces that there has been a big short circuit in Prometheus and some cables have vaporized. It will take several hours to fix. The chips and salsa are opened, the boots go up, the grim jokes begin.

Not for long. Soon one of the scientists complains that his terminal has locked up, that his network connections are totally frozen. Before long, nothing whatsoever is functioning and every scientist in the room is throwing up his hands, cursing. At once everything comes back online. Shortly afterward Mercedes Ramirez appears, announcing that all systems are in order. Zuber takes the horn: new cyber-attack protection software had just been tested; vigilance must be seamless and perpetual. Machuzak knows it is going to be a long day.

FORTY-THREE

In the bunker two unshaven beam operators engaged in a chess match as the machine was being readied for the next shot, and the rest of the team milled around while it waited for experiments to resume. A tritium guy picks up a guitar and begins twanging "Big Science Blues."

"Break for basketball!" Krieg-Zuber announces unexpectedly. So impossible is it to believe what they've just heard that not a single person budges. "That's an order! Go! From now on, basketball, volleyball, every day at two o'clock sharp!"

Eventually, a few of the technicians headed apprehensively for the door, but when The Terminator made no effort to stop them, the room cleared out quickly. For a week, precisely at two o'clock, Ramirez or Krieg-Zuber appeared and the control room shut down for an hour. The webcams also went down but before the first afternoon's blackout, a snippet of audio leaked through from an off-stage conversation.

"How can I trust you!?" Machuzak heard Krieg-Zuber shout to Mercedes. "Communicating with Balard! You have committed high treason!"

Thinking that this didn't sound like a lovers' quarrel, Nathaniel listened to Mercedes retort, "You have no one else to trust, Cyrus."

That was all before she exclaimed, "The cams are on!" and the empty control room went dark.

Nevertheless, for the next days progress was made with a series of shots above breakeven. At the end of the week, Zuber entered the control room just as everyone was exiting for the afternoon game. "Where are you going?" he demanded. It was time for the break, they told him. "Who authorized you to leave?"

"You did," said Abbuhl, "in case you've forgotten."

Hearing the exchange, the beam operators who preferred chess to basketball broke off their match. "No!" Krieg-Zuber told them, "continue. Play nonstop while Balard closes in on immortality. Have you seen today's ITER release? A Q of two, do you hear! A Q of two! They approach a burning plasma! And you sit here playing chess! Forgive me. Organize a competition to take your feeble minds off our great task. Do it now, a competition!"

The two operators stared at each other, jaws wide, and at Krieg-Zuber, whose neck muscles had assumed the outlines of steel cable. The fellows attempted to return to their stations while Hasschler judiciously called for a new shot, but The Terminator prevented them. "Have you heard me?" he shouted. "Forget the ignition campaign. Play basketball! Play chess!" Then and there he launched into a macabre jig and with a wild swipe of his good arm knocked the board and all its pieces to the floor.

Silence shrouded the entire control room, each person glancing uneasily at the next. Even a very nervous Mercedes warned that he should calm down, for his own health. "Nothing can get in the way!" he shouted at the top of his lungs, staring. Then, suddenly, swiveling full circle as if to address himself, a double, he said, "Excuse me, that was uncalled for. My apologies." He picked up a chip from the bag on the console, dipped it in the jar of salsa that had survived and bit into it with a loud crunch. He straightened his jacket and exited.

* * * *

Hours later Fred Abbuhl discovered Machuzak wandering through the MTF. "Mac, you've got to do something," he said, describing what had taken place. "We'll never make it through another month, yet alone to ignition, with that guy in charge."

"What would you have me do, Fred?" Machuzak responded, raising his eyes from the folder in his hand. "He got you to breakeven, didn't he?" Machuzak handed Abbuhl a hard copy of the ITER press release, which had triggered today's scene: a Q of two. Fusionese's most common term, Q, was going to be heard a lot more often in the coming weeks. Q represented the ratio of the energy a plasma produces to the energy needed to heat it. Breakeven—a Q of one. Ignition—Q approaches infinity. Between one and infinity lies reality: a commercial reactor might settle for thirty. ITER and ASSET were hoping for ten. Five was the magic number. At Q equals five, the theorists foretold, a plasma should begin to heat itself; it should burn. No one had ever achieved a burning plasma before. At Q equals five France or Texas would declare victory.

Abbuhl tossed away the press release. "The question is, what's going to burn first, the plasma or us?"

"Fred, in less than a week I will be arrested."

"*Herr Doktor* Director," the chief engineer remained adamant, "unless The Terminator has a heart attack we've got to organize a counter-coup. That nutcase didn't hesitate to topple you with any means at his disposal. Fight back, Mac, sir. Even if you are guilty as charged," Abbuhl smiled faintly, "I'd still prefer you at the helm."

"Let me think about it," answered Machuzak.

* * * *

The following afternoon he met Theresa at the Laguna Gloria museum with its feel of a Mediterranean villa and canopy of trees, porticos, bells, suspended chimes and moss. "Theresa," he said at once, "you've got to become director of the lab."

Caught by surprise, she threw a bewildered look at him. "I thought you wanted to hear about Whitman."

"Later." He grasped her arm as they began walking through the dried leaves of the largely barren sculpture garden. Only at this moment did Machuzak realize that autumn, such as autumn is in Texas, had crept up unnoticed. He smelled the good air, breathed. "We've got to overthrow Krieg-Zuber if this campaign is going to have any chance of success." He related what had occurred yesterday.

"I… I'm not a physicist," she objected.

Neither were some others, despite their PhDs. "You know the lab, the people respect you. Let them pursue their desperate business and you deal with the press. In three months it will be over. Leonard will advise you. I'll help…if I can."

Theresa's demeanor told him that she was not persuaded and she revealed that she'd been getting up three or four times a night, reading until four in the morning. When that failed to put her to sleep she'd try a pill, two…

This wasn't good, and with the alcohol…

"Do you think I'm capable?"

"Yes." He clasped her by the shoulders and looked her in the eyes. "That which doesn't kill you… What have you discovered?"

"Tamasin Ara—he's the out-of-work reporter—he knows his way around obscure archives and the Congressional Record. The Whitmans did own a company called Exosystems, but they sold it so Thomas could become director of Energy Research and avoid a conflict of interest."

"I thought he said they'd sold it much earlier."

"That's what the Whitmans told everybody, but it seems to have been a result of the confirmation hearings. Now it is forgotten."

"Leonard never heard of it."

Theresa shrugged, kicking the leaves. She'd already said it: Leonard didn't know everything.

What did the company do, Machuzak asked, and who did the Whitmans sell it to?

"We're working." Theresa had climbed onto a solitary sculpture, a concrete-and-iron piece reminiscent of a sundial, one that pivoted with a squeak and was overgrown with weeds. "Mac," she said from the perch, "I'd like to plan a memorial for Leonard."

"He's still alive," Nathaniel answered, puzzled by the turn of conversation. "You said he might pull through… There's still hope." Nathaniel vaguely realized he was spouting the usual platitudes but saw no need to press home the matter.

"I want it to be some sort of living memorial…" Theresa went on as if not having heard. "'Forward!' should be the slogan. Not 'Backward!'…" She jumped down, wrapped her arms around herself and shivered, though it wasn't cold. "We can't turn our backs to the future. Did the Huns know their millennium would be lost? Somehow we must succeed, you must succeed, Nathaniel. It *is* our kairos. Do it for Leonard."

Theresa appeared to have forgotten that he was no longer director. "It is largely for Leonard that I undertook the task," Machuzak acknowledged, perhaps to himself for the first time. "Theresa, snatch up the baton. Speak to Garrett. Convince him. Success would be the greatest tribute to Leonard."

They sat down by river's edge and a few moments later were kissing each other passionately. They shucked off their clothes and made love in the secluded spot, amidst swaying reeds. It was convulsive, desperate lovemaking, she avoiding his lips, he kissing her sides, with every kiss she squirming—delight, fear, he could hardly say. As his tongue went between her thighs she flinched and produced a guttural noise; her command, he thought, to enter. The animal sounds continued, but there was a frantic anger in them both, an anger enveloped by the other nervousness of being discovered. It was soon over. They did not afford themselves the luxury of lying in the reeds long, tangled, sweated and uneasy, and they quickly pulled themselves together. They watched the boats, the water skiers, the ducks. As always in the recent past, it seemed to belong to a walled-off world and because they could not touch it, they sat only for a few moments and departed.

FORTY-FOUR

Twenty-four hours later Richard Garrett received Theresa Rasmussen and Cyrus Krieg-Zuber in the office he'd commandeered and without ceremony said, "Dr. Krieg-Zuber, I'm relieving you as acting director. I don't like the way things have been going around here."

Krieg-Zuber's first reaction was to bore unblinkingly into Garrett with his laser orbs, then dismiss the news as a perverse joke. When Garrett assured him it was not, Zuber slammed the flat of his hand on the table around which they were seated and shot up. "I demand a hearing before the board."

The only response was a gimlet eye from Garrett, which said, "You're looking at it." To eliminate misunderstanding The Chairman became explicit: "It was my mistake to have appointed you and as of this moment I am correcting that mistake."

"I remind you, old boy," Krieg-Zuber protested, sweeping his finger before Garrett's nose, "that under my leadership this morning we achieved a glorious Q of two. We are closing in on ITER. Think—!"

"A Q of two, whatever that means, will be your epitaph, Dr. Krieg-Zuber. I hope for your sake it doesn't refer to an intelligence quotient."

Turning to the door, then swiveling full around again, Krieg-Zuber was breathing hard as he looked down at the seated man. "You are making a grave error, a fatal error, and if you persist this laboratory shall reap the whirlwind."

"Are you threatening me?" The Chairman returned a gaze reinforced by offense. "He who sleeps best is on his guard. I know your motto, Mr. Terminator, but I'm tired of your apocalypses and they're going to cease, now."

"You'll regret it, money bags."

"Mr. Krieg-Zuber, I'm half a second from barrin you from the premises. Now, if you don't want that to happen, shut up, leave the room and take a well-deserved rest."

Once Krieg-Zuber, after a moment of stasis had blinked in disbelief and departed, Garrett allowed himself to deflate and turned to Theresa, advising her to get rid of him altogether.

She demurred, saying that Leonard had spoken highly of Krieg-Zuber's administrative talents and that she'd find something for him, but when she proposed that Nathaniel Machuzak be made assistant director, The Chairman put his foot down at once.

"That is not a good move, Theresa."

"I need a scientific advisor," she said. "Otherwise I can't do this job."

"Theresa, one thing I've learned around here," Garrett answered, "is that ridin herd on scientists is like tryin to catch a greased pig. You'll have plenty of advisors, not a single advisee. You want to lean on Machuzak in private, well that's between you and him, but your job is to inspire this lab for the next hundred and ten days and to be its face to the outside world."

"I intend to start broadcasting tonight, Mr. Chairman. Wish me luck."

He shook her hand.

* * * *

Because his badge no longer functioned, Slava parked outside the main gate, within sight of the pin oak where several dozen protestors gathered in the daily ritual, ducked behind a tree and hopped the fence. He walked the kilometer to Site Alpha without interference and found Nat and Toshi at the MTF. Machuzak did not conceal his surprise at seeing him, but Archangelsky refused to say a word until they were outside.

"Moscow friends traced camera," he said simply.

Machuzak waited.

"It was bought in Seoul, six years ago."

Little else needed to be said, but Machuzak said it: "KBSI," the Korean Basic Science Institute, home of Korea's fusion program. Toshi asked for an explanation and they recounted from beginning to end their fruitless hunt for Dragonmaster. Matsushima asked if he could see the mysterious dragon and fish emblems and Archangelsky obliged, bringing up a Fusion World Web page, which he'd captured.

Toshi shrugged. "This is obvious: the Dragon Carp from Korean mythology. You must know it: The carp freed by the fisherman has struggled upstream for a thousand years, jumps over the royal gates and becomes a dragon, so Koreans consider him a symbol of bravery and perseverance, not to mention wealth… Of course craving for wealth ruins the foolish… Your Dragonmaster is obviously Korean and trying to help. Why didn't you ask me sooner?"

Machuzak and Archangelsky glanced at each other and sighed.

* * * *

At high noon T. J. D'Abro appeared at the MTF with more than one warrant in hand. "Where's Archangelsky, Doc?" she said severely. "Looks like he's cleared out from his house. I've seized the computer there. I want his laptop. You must know where he is."

Machuzak broke off from the work he was doing on the test chamber. "No, I don't. Why do you want his laptop?"

"That server in Cadarache was at ITER," she frowned, revealing what she'd known for some weeks. Machuzak granted her a raised eyebrow. "Their system administrator has been cooperating with me and we've traced an address to Archangelsky's computer." She omitted the assistance she'd received from the Austin Cyber Crimes Unit, which had briefly put aside child molesters. "Slava's Dragonmaster. Which means you're in on it, Mac."

Nathaniel shook his head, nothing more.

"Damnit!" D'Abro pounded her fist in anger on the workbench next to her. "I warned you guys not to skip town. Where is he, Doc?"

Machuzak shook his head again. "What about Mercedes?"

T. J. glanced down at the clutter, the shining bits of metal. "She surrendered her laptop and has wiped a lot of files, but we've subpoenaed her backups and recovered a lot. Six months ago she asked Balard for a job; he declined. She's a climber for sure, but that's not illegal and so far I have nothin else on her. Which means you're under arrest." She looked up at him, bit her lip, said, "Sorry, I didn't want this to happen."

Machuzak's only response was "Cuff me."

The detective obliged.

FORTY-FIVE

Once he landed at Incheon airport, unwashed and weary beyond travel, Slava lost no time getting into Seoul. As always, the Koreans were ten years ahead of the West. On the metro each and every passenger was glued to a video game, leaving the wagons dead quiet; not a book was in sight and a special car was set aside for conversation. From Central Station Slava headed south on the KTX. Here too, the Koreans held on to their lead: at speeds above 300 kilometers per hour, talking had become forbidden except when mocking slower countries. In less than an hour Slava arrived at Daejeon and hopped into a cab. Despite the dreary concrete apartment blocks, the city retained its futuristic appearance, in part because of the old World's Fair grounds, which had been transformed into a science park, and in part because Daejeon encompassed Daedeok science town, Archangelsky's destination.

Daedeok was a more modern version of those *akademgorodoks* of Slava's homeland, research enclaves hosting dozens of government facilities and private firms, and could easily have passed for a Western corporate park except that the architecture was two steps more adventurous and at its center stood the Korean Basic Science Institute. Archangelsky stepped out of the cab and regarded KBSI's unusual façade, with what he had been told was a stylized ship's prow protruding from the front wall. To him it resembled a giant diamond, somehow out of *Things to Come*. Inside stood the Korean tokamak, a successor to KSTAR, whose American design had been sold to the Koreans when the DOE canceled the project.

Only at this moment did Slava fully confront his predicament: he didn't know anyone here well enough to claim an invitation, and KBSI was a government facility, not famous for showing its hospitality to unannounced visitors. The jerks didn't even give public tours. While he stood at the entrance, the doors opened and several employees emerged. Slava grabbed the handle, saying that he was to meet Professor Kim. They nodded absently and he entered. In the small, immaculate lobby a polished grandfather clock vainly attempted to slow time and Slava glanced quickly at the directory, hoping someone's name would jump out at him. None did. Not wanting to be caught in the open, he signaled the elevator and ascended to the third floor accompanied by pleasant chimes and soothing voices.

He began to prowl up and down the corridors, peering into each office, examining the nameplates on the doors. No one paid much attention to him, naturally assuming that he belonged here, but neither was he finding the person he sought. Eventually he risked a secretary, asking whether she knew of a grad student or post-doc who had spent time at ITER about five years ago. She bowed her head in the pleasant Korean manner; several post-docs on the second floor had been there.

Archangelsky descended, still having no face in his mind, but as he strode down the corridor, a young Korean walking in the opposite direction caught sight of him and inadvertently started. Slava shouted, "*Stoi!*" as the fellow bolted for the stairwell. Archangelsky was after him, down to the first floor, out the lobby doors and main gate to the road. He pursued his quarry past one institute after another until his lungs burned; such activities sure weren't the average physicist's daily workout—Oblomov, forget it. Abruptly the Korean skidded into the back lot of a lonely shedlike building with a weedy lawn and made for the door. He yanked the handle, intending to dash inside, but a card was needed to unlock it. Caught in the open, he fished for his wallet and in that instant Slava reached him, pinning him against the door.

"Sangjun Park," he panted, the name finally coming back to him. At long last he was in possession of the most important thing—a name. "I think you have wanted me to find you, Dragonmaster."

Park shook his head wildly. Slava vaguely remembered the young man from Cadarache with a reputation for being socially inept and equally unbalanced. Slava had no doubt the first was true, describing as it did at least half of all physicists. "Yes, you have." The little Russian had his hand around Park's throat. "I have never been more in the mood to strangle someone," he said, inflating himself like a toad to twice his size, "and if you don't tell me what you know, I will haul you off to police and tell them you're terrorist."

"Let's go inside," Park said in his differently accented English.

Archangelsky retained his grip on his hostage and motioned for him to swipe his card. They entered the building, which was empty of other human beings. A glance at the equipment told Slava that it was the magnet fabrication facility for the Korean tokamaks. He motioned for Park to sit at the base of the big vacuum chamber and picked up a large wrench nearby. Koreans might be the gentlest people on the face of the Earth. Russians weren't. "Talk."

The Korean remained silent.

"You know who's trying to sabotage our program," Slava said as he videoed Park, "and you're going to tell me."

"What can you do to me?" Park answered haughtily. "You aren't police."

Abruptly Slava slammed the wrench on a bench and the sound echoed throughout the huge space. He'd often imagined interrogations, usually from a different perspective.

Sangjun Park jumped to his feet and this time Slava did whack him on the shoulder. "Trust me," he said, motioning with the wrench for Park to sit again, "three months of threats, explosions, deaths have put me in mood to use this. Tempt me and I bash your brains out." An acetylene torch was standing nearby. Archangelsky picked up a striker and stroked the regulator fondly.

The Korean's alarm as he looked up at the Russian was genuine. That beard and bloodshot eyes could only have belonged to Christ on the cross or one of the Ten Kings of Yama. "I—I am not working for Balard, if that's what you think," he sputtered and wiped aside his jet-black hair. "I don't believe anybody is working for Balard. Y–your machine is in danger. I have been warning you."

He expected gratitude? "Your warnings have been as useful as bullets made of shit. Why didn't you just tell us what was going to happen like good stool pigeon, instead of belching dragons and Fusion World tours? Why have you hidden from us?"

As Slava moved to light the torch, Park flinched and averted his eyes. "You think I want to be involved with this! I don't know exactly what will happen. Clues were obvious. I thought you'd stop bothering me. Stop bothering me!"

"You have strange sense of who is bothering whom," Slava replied. "Helium balloons were warning helium factory would be targeted?"

"Yes."

"And Marconi's shortwave station was warning that my communications with ITER were being monitored?" Park nodded. "How did you know about shortwave? Are you working for Krieg-Zuber?"

Sangjun Park jerked his head up, wildly startled. "No... I... I don't know him."

It appeared to Archangelsky that the disturbed young man was telling the truth. "Then how?"

"I know the people involved. They talk, they can't help themselves. I hear things. ASSET remains in danger, don't you understand? Great danger."

"What friends? Where are they? You are the accomplice, letting this happen, endangering whole program, machine, lives." With those words

Archangelsky did light the torch, contemplated it, turned to Sangjun Park. "Names."

Suddenly Park jumped to his feet and lurched toward the door. Slava lost a few seconds quenching the torch and was after him, tripping over a large coil-winding form that lay on the floor. By the time he gained the door, the Korean was already out of the building. Slava pushed his way past the closing door only to have it slammed into his face. He clutched his nose and reeled, slumping down, half in and half out of the facility. As he slowly got to his feet, he saw Park a long way off. This time he would not catch up.

FORTY-SIX

Three hours after D'Abro cuffed him, Machuzak found himself in an upstairs cell at the Travis County Central Booking Facility, charged, exactly as she'd threatened, with criminal mischief and capital sabotage. His main impression of the booking procedure was that it was far more elaborate than he would ever have suspected from television, and during the three days of his incarceration his strongest sense was one of detachment, as if the humiliation were being inflicted on another person altogether. His only response to a brown-and-tan uniformed officer's warning that his fingerprints would "now be in every database from Austin to the FBI" was "My guess is you're late." Nor did he react when they threw him, clad in jailhouse grays, into an "open bay" for a suicide watch.

Suicide had not been on his mind. Once the cell door clanged shut, Nathaniel experienced a certain relief. He tested the bunk, thinking he'd slept on worse, and lay down. At last he is able to set his mind free in an attempt to understand what he does not yet understand, what he is missing in all this. He does not yet perceive the key, but gradually his mind relaxes and he feels he is approaching the verge. The solution will shortly be at hand.

When against his protests Theresa posted bail, which the judge set at an absurdly low $13,500, Machuzak's only remark was "The Wild West." A few hours later, to his continued protests, Theresa signed the check, reminding him that she required a scientific advisor. On the municipal court steps Machuzak told her lawyer that the single service he required of him was to make sure the grand-jury hearing took place at least 105 days from now.

To the well-tailored fellow's question, Why? Machuzak answered, "Because by then all this will be over and the charges dropped."

* * * *

Nathaniel had no intention of impaling himself anew on the spears of his colleagues. The morning after his release he bypassed even the guard booth by driving through the utility company's right-of-way access directly across the range to the MTF. Media babble held that the saboteur had been arrested and the police were wrapping up the investigation. More than one supermarket aisle had revealed the expected space-alien connection, while rock-video ballads appeared online by the minute. Big Bad Roy alone remained mute, a lofty "I told you so" penetrating the silence. His single action, yesterday, was to formally request that the Energy and Water Subcommittee rescind all unspent CFRC funds for the current fiscal year and zero funds for the next. No opposing voice was raised except Theresa's in her new nightly webcast, but hers was in a far wilderness. Machuzak belatedly began to perceive the power of a US senator.

Arriving at the MTF, Nathaniel half expected Slava or T. J. to be waiting. Surprise overtook all three of them when they converged at the same moment. Archangelsky, fresh off the plane, recoiled. D'Abro snatched the shackles from her belt and moved to cuff him.

Slava held up his hand. "I found Dragonmaster."

"Yeah," said T. J., "I'm lookin at him. Those messages out of Cadarache were originating from your computers." She informed him of the trace she'd accomplished with the help of ITER's systems administrator and Austin's Cyber Crimes Unit.

Slava resolutely shook his head. "Then Dragonmaster hijacked my boxes with trojan horse. Believe me, he is Korean, not Russian. *Vot.*" He produced the video he'd shot in Daedeok. "This one confessed. His name is Sangjun Park. He was at Cadarache five years ago. He is now at KBSI, or was until day before yesterday. God knows where he is today. I doubt he hung around."

When Slava revealed the digital watermark T. J. displayed suitable mortification, but as the Russian ended his tale she exclaimed, "You let him get away!?" before attempting to retract the involuntary outburst.

"I would not put it that way," Slava answered with his own embarrassment, scratching the band-aid on his nose. "He is confused like his warnings. From him I understood more than one person is involved in attempts on Prometheus."

"He knows who they are?"

"Yes, and he knows that it isn't over."

While she lingered over the video D'Abro sighed deeply. "Fuck, how am I going to get the cooperation of the Korean police...?" She looked up, swept her finger before them. "This doesn't clear you guys of anything."

If she was going to arrest him, Slava said, he should call his wife. While D'Abro considered, the lab phone rang. Machuzak answered, listened for a moment, hung up. He turned to the others and said, "That was

Theresa. Looks like Mercedes Ramirez has shown up at ITER. She's fled the country."

T. J. whistled to herself. She'd learned more from the Real World administrators than she revealed to Krieg-Zuber. The Real World system naturally logged encounters, keystrokes, dialogue. Ramirez and Balard had been carrying on a virtual flirtation for six months. Although Balard had initially declined to offer a job, he eventually relented, indicating that something might be arranged. When Machuzak revealed the strange control-room conversation he'd overheard between Krieg-Zuber and Ramirez, figuring that The Terminator was also on to Mercedes, T. J. whistled again and stowed the cuffs. "No, I'm not takin you in, Slava," she said, "but you leave town again and your ass is grass." It was her first indication that perhaps she'd erred.

* * * *

Once the others were shadows, Machuzak drifted into Mercedes' lab and sat down at her desk. She'd departed in a hurry and hadn't bothered, or forgot, to clean it out. Little rummaging was required to uncover a list of passwords in her top drawer and he logged on to her machine. For hours he worked, restoring deleted files, reading old correspondence. He felt unclean at every moment, but each time the sensation of disgust boiled upward he forced himself to stare at her face in the conference room. He found no correspondence between her and Balard, although she would hardly have been so careless to use a lab machine for a discussion of treason, as Krieg-Zuber had put it. Undoubtedly that was what she had erased before handing over her box to D'Abro. Abruptly, Machuzak decided to search on "Sangjun Park." He went back five years, before The Terminator's security measures would have been installed.

Bingo.

Ramirez and Park knew each other. "An honor to meet you in the Real World the other day," their correspondence began.

The emails, between Austin and Cadarache, were few and concerned routine scientific matters: experiments, references, citations. Machuzak, unable to find more, attempted to think like the detective: Balard had, through the offer of a job, persuaded Ramirez to be his mole at CFRC, to sabotage the machine. She saw an opportunity to frame Machuzak and Archangelsky with the eavesdrop and traded her recording for the assistant directorship. That position would provide excellent cover, allow her to continue her treacherous activities without arousing suspicion. Except that over the months and years she had blabbed once too often to her pal Sangjun. Which explained how Park knew of Slava's shortwave.

The scenario was consistent, Machuzak felt, and physicists appreciate consistency. The acquaintanceship with Balard, Park and the eavesdrop were indisputable; the deuterium bottle likely originated right here, in her lab. He glanced around the room, phoned D'Abro.

When, toward evening, the detective appeared again at the MTF and he presented his theory, she puckered her lips and conceded that the case against Ramirez had rapidly become more compelling—especially with her attempted deletion of laptop files and flight from the country—but they were still missing any evidence that put her in the surge room near the time of the dedication.

"What about this?" Machuzak answered. He brought up an address he'd found buried deep and entered the username and password that was at the bottom of her list. He was into the helium factory's programmable logic controller. He also pointed out that she'd configured her browser to link through a proxy.

T. J. swallowed hard. "Let me have that list," she said to him and he turned it over. "Do you hate me, Doc?"

"Do you mean despite the fact that you've done everything to ruin my life and have nearly succeeded?" he returned.

"Hmm," she puckered her lips again and couldn't help but redden, "something like that."

"Not at all," he smiled faintly, looking up. She wasn't pleading, exactly, merely attempting to negotiate a peace. "You just forgot the maxim: Thou shalt not believe thine own theories too much," but I've said that before."

"I was right about the mole," she persisted, showing no intention to compromise too much.

"Evidently. Trace the ringtone, would you?"

"I owe you at least that," T. J. saluted and left the MTF.

FORTY-SEVEN

The Xs on the calendar have annihilated all but one hundred days. Theresa stands on the captain's deck and below her the control room is crowded with people. She has welcomed the press for this symbolic occasion, although the countdown toward Waterloo is anything but reassuring and the whole gathering has the strange flavor of a Day-of-the-Dead carnival. While the odds on the betting board fluctuate wildly, Hasschler and Matsushima huddle. The chief engineers are present, D'Abro too. Krieg-Zuber, whom Theresa has inexplicably allowed to be present, paces in greater agitation than the others. Today even Death has shown up, someone dressed in a skeleton costume, clasping a scythe. Very funny. The only persons missing are Nathaniel Machuzak and a Russian.

Watching from exile, Machuzak senses the tension pervading the room. A tech trips over the foot of one of the National Guardsmen who has stepped in to watch the circus and his hands shoot for the ceiling even as the guard reaches for his pistol. For a moment everyone stops breathing, but for all that Nathaniel cannot feel the raised arm hairs, the tensed muscles and sweat. That is what he misses; he also knows that for the moment his duty lies here.

Both ITER and ASSET have been operating well above breakeven for the past days, but ITER remains ahead and ASSET has been unable to close the gap. The time has arrived for creative thinking. Nathaniel doesn't know what the chiefs have in mind. The discussion will be highly technical, but surely Toshi wants to exploit the advantages of ASSET's shape over ITER's, which allows higher magnetic fields and the possibility of greater bootstrapping.

To be sure, Nathaniel overhears the fabled word from the deck. Tokamaks can generate only several million amps of current, depending on how fast you can crank up the ignition coil shoved right through the machine's doughnut hole, an ignition coil just like an antique car engine's. Several million amps is not enough. To attain fusion the plasma must generate its own current, just as the Baron von Munchausen pulled himself out of a lake by his own bootstraps. Despite Prometheus' smaller size, its shape is better suited for this feat than ITER's and that alone might be enough to let allow them to whip ITER's ass.

They're going for it. As usual, there is little for spectators to see and the control room gradually empties of nonessential personnel, but within an hour those who remain begin to see significant bootstrapping. The plasma is heating itself, higher, higher, until fully 98 percent of the current is self-generated for twenty seconds. The milestone has never before been achieved and Hasschler orders two bottles of champagne to be cracked. Krieg-Zuber's anger that the breakthrough did not take place on his watch is etched everywhere on his face and stiff demeanor; indeed he begins to shake.

But as if preordained, all manifestations of victory or disgrace are cut short when chatter bursts forth from the nb control center:

"Oh hell, we're getting a line of crowbars."

"The MG breakers have gone."

"I think we've lost Paraguay." One of the neutral-beam accelerators. For some reason the engineers have named them after South American countries.

Machuzak finds himself waiting for an explanation with the same intensity as everyone in the bunker. Some of the operators abruptly don iPods and begin dancing on the control room floor. Krieg-Zuber moves to stop it, only to be halted by Theresa. Machuzak can't understand why she allowed him to remain. The scientists break for volleyball while the engineers investigate.

A long hour passes before the problem is revealed. Some of the big transformers are filled with oil and the oil level is measured by a flotation device—well, a toilet-bowl float. "Uh," Abbuhl reports to Theresa, "seems the idiots who designed the things made the float out of metal; it unscrewed, floated against the transformer wall and shorted out the beast."

"Fuck this!" Orne, one of the operating engineers, suddenly exclaims when he hears the news, angrily shooting to his feet. "Sue the fucking company! A toilet bowl for Chrissake!" Everyone immediately sees the cosmic metaphor in a toilet-bowl float becoming the end of fusion, but Orne only runs to the betting board, ups the odds against beating the deadline and throws down a stash of bills. Why not? It will be the rest of the day before repairs are complete. While Orne waits vainly for someone to take up his bet, Death makes a sweep of the room with his scythe and vanishes.

* * * *

Shaking his head, Machuzak turns from the monitor. He stands, not angry that he remains in limbo, for limbo is exactly where he wants, needs to be. Again he moves next door to Mercedes' workstation, brings up the correspondence, ponders what is missing, what damns her. Why leave that address to the helium factory's programmable logic control here to be discovered, as buried as it was? Did she simply forget it in her exiting haste? True, there was no love lost between him and Ramirez, but his entire career, a scientist's career, is one of seeking out the holes, filling them, of being hard.

Once more he stands. At the door he finds himself hesitating like Buridan's ass, unable to decide whether to go left or right. He steps to the left, toward his own lab, goes right, drifting into the third room, the one with the big vacuum clam where they simulate the effects of interstellar plasma on satellites. He does not know what he is looking for; he's just following his sense of smell. For a while he wanders about the darkened place, filled with the aroma of oils, running his fingers over the rough deuterium bottles, the cages separating him from the high-voltage systems, the workbenches cluttered with tools and cannibalized electronics. No silicon carbide targets are lying about, none visible as he peers through the port of the vacuum chamber. He really has no idea. He passes Wilson's desk, scattered with papers and paraphernalia. Shoved to one corner is what appears to be Wilson's own cold-fusion apparatus, a glass bottle with electrodes. Nathaniel hadn't known that Jerry investigated cold fusion, at least he never talked about it. He suddenly recollects the Dragonmaster's obsession with that boondoggle and, abruptly, that strange bottle with electrodes that appeared after the last tour of Fusion World. It resembles almost exactly what Machuzak now sees before him. He glances up. Above Wilson's desk on a shelf stands a series of old loose-leaf binders, all plainly marked "cold fusion." How could so many volumes be devoted to that nonsense? Machuzak begins leafing. Wilson, like everyone else, had zero success in creating energy from water, heavy or otherwise. But the pages on cold fusion quickly end at a divider labeled "AUSTOR." Machuzak turns the page.

Wilson had been a diagnostician on AUSTOR years before it was decommissioned and he stumbled over to the MTF. His records consist of handwritten notes, pasted-in graphs, computer printouts. Nathaniel switches on a light so he can better make out Wilson's scrawl and sits down. It is late, Jerry has been recruited to do diagnostics in the control room and Machuzak knows he will not be interrupted. Wilson's first job had been to measure AUSTOR's plasma temperature and mostly what Nathaniel finds are data for numerous experiments, sometimes with exclamation marks next to a particularly bad run and occasionally embellished with Wilson's commentary: "Temperatures significantly low!" "This damn machine is not working as well as Rasmussen advertises to the DOE." Hardly compelling literature but the commentary provides a sort of narrative that guides Machuzak through the binders and he keeps at it, strangely fascinated. By the time the sun comes up the next morning, Nathaniel is convinced that either Wilson was a lousy diagnostician or that old AUSTOR was indeed a case of cold fusion.

·

FORTY-EIGHT

Noon has come and gone according to the clock when D'Abro enters the MTF and very nearly stumbles over Nathaniel asleep on the mattress he's brought from home. As he blinks up at her with waking incomprehension she remarks, less with sarcasm than with curiosity, "What is it, Doc, you post bail and prefer to stay behind bars? Well, bein that you're public enemy number one, I understand. I told the reporters outside to get lost. Hope I was right." Her speech hasn't fully penetrated, but she isn't far off, he thinks groggily: behind bars is where one often finds clarity. At this moment he senses none and she allows him to revive himself in the nearby men's room.

When he at last faces her, in a more or less human state, she bequeaths him the barest of smiles: "I have been workin on your ringtone," she says, "for some time. Hasn't been easy, but me and the Austin Cyber Crime Unit finally got it. Your prediction was dead-on. There are exactly three people in Texas with that Greenmountain tune: Moravec, Roy Whitman and Darrell Whitman."

"Darrell Whitman?"

T. J. nods. "Roy's nephew."

The pause is fleeting. "Thomas' son?"

Again a nod. "Lives south of San Antonio. The question is, So what?"

"So what," Nathaniel finds himself staring at the detective, "is that he's a direct link between Whitman and Moravec. The question is not, So what? The question is, Why?" He casts around for a cup on his desk, swallows a mouthful of cold coffee and then turns inward.

"What is it, Doc?" she asks.

He offers only a shake of his head. "Nothing, the name sounds familiar, that's all. I'm probably just confusing him with Roy."

"You didn't meet him at a Monteverdi concert?" T. J. quips, half out the door.

"Where are you going?"

"San Antonio." She raises her finger. "Don't leave town."

* * * *

With D'Abro gone, Machuzak tunes in to the control-cast. Since yesterday the Internet has been festooned with videos featuring giant machines disappearing down toilets, but in fact the engineers have quickly gotten ASSET back on its feet and the machine has been running at well above twice breakeven for the past six hours. Damnit, ITER has pushed closer to a Q of three.

Even across the Web the smugness in the Cadarache control room is sensible. They've been unable to resist posting their own records on big signs as well as cartoonish maps of Texas with a commode replacing the capital. Balard's smugness goes far beyond sensible; it is overt. "Our friends in the Republic of Texas should concede the race," he informs a journalist as he primps for the camera. "They have no chance. The game is over." He turns to the webcams and abruptly shouts, "Over, do you hear!"

Machuzak, watching Theresa in the control room watch the same broadcast, sees that she is seriously annoyed and Hasschler fuming. Balard observes their reaction on a big screen at ITER and grins, straightens his tie, salutes and nods to his COE. Thaddeus can read the numbers on their screen and knows well that his adversaries are readying a high-field pulse to put ASSET further in the dust.

The droplets of sweat dribble down Hasschler's dome, and Machuzak convinces himself he can hear the grinding of Thad's teeth. But without warning, ten seconds into ITER's pulse a tremendous *Bam!* ricochets clear across the Atlantic. Hasschler, Matsushima, standing at his shoulder, everyone—they all practically jump, then observe the confusion at ITER control, every ITERnik rushing to discover what went wrong. Even before Balard's team comes to its senses, all is clear.

"They've had a major disruption," Thad announces.

It has happened. In real time Machuzak watches the ITER director go completely nonlinear, tearing at his nonexistent hair. At an initial report from a diagnostician he clutches dramatically at his chest and nearly keels over. Is it a heart attack? Machuzak can't be certain; Balard's assistants are propping him up... When less than a minute later a second report comes in, Jules César turns green, begins to curse, rage, morphs into a psychic monster and storms out of the control room.

In his isolation Machuzak nods grimly, clenches his teeth and awaits the update. It is conceivable that ITER, all twenty billion euros of it, has just been ruined. Minutes ago the ornery plasma burst through its magnetic cage and slammed the tokamak walls with the energy of—? ITER's designers claim the huge machine can absorb small car-bomb-size disruptions. If they're lucky, this one was no larger than a stick of dynamite.

At this moment every plasma physicist in the world is holding his breath to hear a damage assessment. A half hour creeps by as the ITER team examines the interior of the machine with periscopes. Finally, Nathaniel senses the global exhalation. The machine is intact, although enough junk has been blown from the walls that the vacuum is seriously contaminated. The ITERniks will spend several days doing cleanup pulses and salving the walls with lithium, a balm for physical, as well as mental, wounds.

Machuzak himself breathes a sigh of relief. Winning this race is one thing, but nothing, nothing at all is to be gained for fusion or the world if ITER fails.

Yet this is no gentlemanly duel, one nobleman allowing his opponent to recover a dropped sword. Seeing his opportunity, Hasschler literally grasps a sabre he has brought, salutes Balard, who back in his own control room responds with a finger, and calls for a higher power shot, intending to leapfrog over ITER. The countdown commences. When Nathaniel hears the *Bam!* he nearly jumps from his seat again. Hasschler, unable to restrain himself, stamps on the deck, shouting, "Goddamnit!"

Prometheus has also suffered a disruption. Luckily as the reports come in, it seems not so major as ITER's; nevertheless the better part of a day has just gone up in smoke and the global audience can no longer doubt the difficulty of confining a plasma.

"We must get Archangelsky here," Matsushima says the moment he realizes what has happened. "Prometheus's advantage over ITER is that its shape allows it to hold a plasma at lower fields. This is what has just saved us, but Slava can best exploit its advantage and avoid such disturbances."

Theresa hesitates, uncertain of the best course. Krieg-Zuber, passing below the captain's deck, overhears Toshi's remark and replies as if he still wields power: "Gentlemen, I remind you that Archangelsky will shortly be arrested. He must not be allowed to step foot in this control room. Find someone else—experts at this lab abound."

"Most of them have been dismissed or have resigned," Toshi replies calmly. "Archangelsky knows the codes; after all, he wrote many of them. In any case, this is not your decision, Dr. Krieg-Zuber."

Noticeably rattled by the events of the last hour, Theresa, wondering how she will explain these events on her webcast, sternly calls for a halt, agrees to speak to Slava and exits.

* * * *

By the time she gets to her office the phones are ringing. Time and again she assures the journalists that there has been no permanent damage to the machine, no radiation leakage. But St. Cecilia catches her flatfooted by asking whether this could be another sabotage by Nathaniel Machuzak, who inexplicably is still employed by the lab. To her dismay, Theresa hears herself lamely protesting that his case has not been tried and that the sheriff's department has not closed the investigation. As she repeats her explanations, she feels the need to wash and has begun to understand Mac's self-imposed absence.

For the good of the lab he must come out of quarantine. His reluctance to appear at the main building is manifest over the phone, but he finally relents when she offers to walk him though the guard booth. It is evening when he arrives but the three guards cannot disguise their disappointment as they grudgingly allow the pair to pass unmolested. She leads Nathaniel up to the octagon, where they kiss each other lightly, holding each other at arm's length.

"Quite a day," he says to her, in unfeigned good humor but hesitant to speak in dangerous surroundings. He glances about the polygonal room, surveys the books, the famous daruma doll, moves to be certain the blinds are closed, passes his eyes over the books again.

With dismay she replays for him Whitman's webcast of an hour ago and her response from this very room. Whitman has kept mostly silent recently, but today he couldn't resist gloating over ASSET's disruption, claiming that it proved the impossibility of the machine's use as a commercial reactor. For her part, Theresa betrayed unconcealed defensiveness as she riposted that Prometheus was merely an experimental, not commercial, device.

"I can't see how you lasted two months," she says, switching off the spectacle. "Every misstep…"

"You're doing fine," he declares brightly, honestly.

To be sure, despite the cyclone into which she has been unceremoniously thrust, her spirits seem better than she acknowledges. Her morning exercises show in her muscle tone. He detects no quantum leaps in her conversation, no absentminded lapses, and she speaks no more about memorials to Leonard. She does think to ask, with concern shading her voice, "Can you see everything on the control-cast?"

"Enough, the best reality show on the Web. I can't feel it, though." He scratches his arm. "That's what I miss."

"Please come back." She takes cognizance of his cocked head, which betrays true perplexity and incomprehension. "I'm sorry about those horrible reporters… I phoned Slava. He won't even speak to me."

At that Nathaniel puts his finger to his lips and goes mum. Nodding, she leads him by the hand into the director's private bath, where she turns on the shower and undresses. He follows suit, although even as he smiles at the old countermeasure, he is uncertain whether it will be effective against modern bugging devices. He does risk raising his voice to a whisper.

"Theresa, half the lab suspects that Slava and I are guilty of murder, the other half is certain of it. I have work to do at the MTF, but I'll talk to him, promise."

"What work?" she asks as they soap down each other's flanks.

"Believe me, you'll know when I'm finished."

Theresa sighs, knowing not to pursue the matter. As they hold each other close, he abruptly, unexpectedly asks, "Why are you allowing Krieg-Zuber to remain in the control room? He's becoming more unhinged every day."

The director's reluctance to reply is visible everywhere on her face. Finally she offers, "He insists something terrible is going to happen, and he is the best trained in security measures. I keep him on a tight leash."

"What does he know?" Nathaniel presses, but getting no more out of Theresa than denials, he changes the subject again. "What do you remember about AUSTOR?"

This question also catches her off guard. "Not much," she replies, not able to perceive Nathaniel's direction. "Leonard pushed like hell to get the contract and was very proud of it. He put everything into it. I think he made some people angry along the way." She chuckles slightly under the cascade of water.

"How well did it work?"

Now she looks at him with open puzzlement and sweeps back her wet hair. "Why are you asking me, Nathaniel? You'd know better than I."

"I wasn't on the project from the beginning…" Another dead end is approaching, he sees, and takes a step back. "Who did Leonard make angry?"

"What a strange question!" Theresa exclaims, batting her droplet-studded eyelashes. "What's gotten into you?"

At this point Nathaniel feels blocked and remains silent.

"Mac," she offers, seeing his discomfort, "all I know is that you scientists never agree on anything and are constantly bickering over who has come up with some little idea first. I'm convinced you have no basis for your self-worth other than your ideas. They aren't so important to the rest of us."

"What is important?" he responds involuntarily, clasping her shoulders and forcing her to look up at him. It is difficult to digest such foreign thoughts.

She rests her head against his chest, reflects. "A largeness of spirit I would say. The ability to live. You know, I don't think we even have a word in English for someone with a genius for life."

"There's no job code for it on the tax form." Nathaniel has always liked Theresa for her perspective, at this moment, in this unlikely setting, more than ever. "Did Leonard have a genius for life?"

"Gusto, yes, genius…uh-uh. He was always too much like a steam-roller." She makes a planing motion with one hand atop the other and laughs, spitting out the water in her mouth. It feels awkward to speak of Leonard now, in the director's shower, in the past tense, but her laugh cheers Nathaniel. Nevertheless, no, he should also not press forward in this direction.

It is Theresa, though, who now changes the subject, revealing that her reporter has run into difficulties tracing Exosystems. "It's been harder to hunt down than we thought," she says, absently tracing a large *E* on the fogged shower window. "With the press clamoring, Whitman released the documents today. Did you see them?" No, he didn't. "They definitely sold the company before Thomas became director of DOE and it was liquidated shortly afterward. It just no longer seems to exist."

"Hmm," says Machuzak, wondering whether Theresa had seriously miscalculated in her accusations, and he turns off the shower.

FORTY-NINE

Machuzak decides to head home to fulfill his promise to Theresa to speak to Archangelsky. Midnight has nearly struck by the time he raises him and Matsushima together for a call, but despite the hour Slava's anger bursts forth from the screen before the discussion gets under way.

"Nobody in right mind would buy a commercial reactor prone to internal explosions!" he growls like a wolf, strangely echoing Whitman. "We should have built stellarator. Why are you pestering me, Nat Edward'ich?"

"You know why, Slava," Machuzak replies, watching Rasputin tear his hair.

"Were they using active feedback on the coils and beams?" Archangelsky grudgingly asks Matsushima. With a tenth of a millisecond notice, the software can adjust the fields to micromanage disruptions; what took place daily forty years ago have become rare events—below breakeven.

"Of course," Toshi replied, "but not with your neural-network model."

"Then I can do nothing," Slava answers, crossing his arms with finality. "Build stellarator."

* * * *

Machuzak sighs as the two launch into a technical discussion involving computer codes, which Matsushima loathes, but Toshi puts up with it for a time. Slava is not fully crazy. The enormous energy in those terrible disruptions comes precisely from the damn mega-amp currents that the tokamak uses to produce its own magnetic field. In stellarators, the tokamak's first cousins, external magnets produce the fields; there are no currents and no disruptions, simply. But the severe difficulty in fabricating the stellarator's baroque magnets, far more complex than a tokamak's, led long ago to the government's inevitable cancellation of the star generator program.

Toshi has had enough of software. Suddenly his expression brightens and, "Why not fabricate a nuclear catalyst? Like Chinese finger prisons, they would draw deuterium and tritium together to facilitate their union…"

"Toshi—"

Once Toshi has taken off there is no bridling him. He insists on importing a flask of supersymmetric particles from CERN. "They are heavy, exactly what we require—" He ignores Nathaniel's sarcastic response, "Why don't we just import the Large Hadron Collider?" and he soon vanishes in a puff of smoke.

After a silence, Nathaniel says simply, "Slava, they need you down there."

"I don't need them," is Borisovich's equally simple response. "And you aren't one to talk, Nat Edward'ich."

"Forget me, forget the others, forget everything but the work. This is your chance to do the work of your lifetime, your kairos, to light a candle to God."

At length, Slava agrees only to think it over. That, Machuzak accepts as progress. "Have you heard anything from Sangjun Park?" he asks, changing the subject.

Slava shakes his head. Park is certainly in hiding and they won't hear from him again.

"But he warned that the danger persists. When, what?"

Again Slava shakes his head. "Damnit, I don't know."

* * * *

In the morning when Machuzak comes upon the exceptionally large crowd at the gate, and the ugly, roiling atmosphere, he cannot doubt that yesterday's webcast duel was to blame. Not only did Whitman gain the upper hand, but Theresa's denials that any radiation was leaked surely convinced viewers of the exact opposite. Now they've gathered here, forgetting the risk to their health, to stridently voice their displeasure. Greenpeace members brandish *Fusion Is Madness* placards and *No Nuclear Accidents In Austin*. The Tritium Kid is back, convincing Nathaniel that he never got through to his protégé. Scientologists are distributing leaflets. He tells the National Guard to permanently open the fence, but the militiamen no longer recognize his authority. The only thing they recognize is that they are surrounded by barbarians at the gate.

Machuzak decides to risk the main drive and as he rounds the curve, four widely spaced signs march up one by one:

Dare To Care?

Share!

United Way

Burma-Shave

Bill Balustradi's annual joke. It is a relief to know that someone at CFRC has retained a sense of humor.

Every pulse/ Now is more/ Six seconds longer/ Than before/ By using Burma-Shave.

Why not? Nathaniel tears off again across the range. Even before arriving at the MTF, he puts in a call to Theresa alerting her to the situation, then one to Abbuhl, asking to meet as soon as possible.

* * * *

Theresa orders the Guard to admit the protestors, but though the militia grudgingly obeys, the protestors would rather block the gate and make noise. That afternoon, she is surprised by Krieg-Zuber at the octagon at the very moment Leonard emerges in his wheelchair from the director's bath. Zuber allows her no time to speak.

"Leonard, you are duty bound to reinstate me to my position as acting director, from which Richard Garrett has illegally removed me." Leonard, weakened as he is, seems not to understand and Cyrus repeats himself, lifting a finger toward a filing cabinet in the corner. "Leonard, reinstate me. Now."

"You are not to be reinstated," Theresa replies to both of them.

"My appointment as deputy is in writing," Krieg-Zuber says, pointing once more to the cabinet, "as is the agreement that I succeed him."

As he slides his hand into his breast pocket, Leonard nods feebly. "I…it is true, d-darling." His stuttering has become worse lately.

Theresa glares fiercely at The Terminator, planting herself between him and the cabinet. "I don't care, Cyrus, if whatever you signed is signed in blood. The deputy directorship has been dissolved and you cannot be reinstated to a nonexistent position. Hire a lawyer." She has no idea what this is about.

With jaw clenched Krieg-Zuber walks to the blinds, makes a chink and for a moment gazes down onto the atrium. The trembling of his entire frame is visible across the room. Suddenly he swivels about, raising his hand, bearing down with his hypnotic eyes. "Theresa, my friend, reasonable men cooperate and I am a reasonable man. Appoint me codirector. Reinstate the sensible countermeasures we have put in place—"

Theresa responds with a caustic laugh. "What an insane idea! Codirector! I have no intention of starting a civil war. Be grateful that I've allowed you to remain director of security—minus your foul eavesdropping. Now get the hell out of here before I lose my temper!"

After a moment of stasis, during which Krieg-Zuber seems about to shatter, he turns and slams the door behind him. Theresa faces her husband, who sunk into his chair attempts with little success to put his head in his hands. "I did sign…"

Theresa glances once at the filing cabinet, feels her eyes suddenly overflowing with tears and herself rushes out of the room.

* * * *

The disruption cleanup has occupied Abbuhl nonstop and by the time he gets over to the MTF darkness has again fallen. The lines of age on the chief's face are deeper than Machuzak has remembered them. Without asking, he knows that at this moment Abbuhl is dreaming of retirement.

Within this vale/ Of toil/ And sin/ Your head grows bald/ But not your chin/ Burma-Shave.

To the engineer's puzzlement, Machuzak, without saying a word, leads him outside onto the field, where the only sound to be heard is the occasional flap of a night bird's wings. "Fred, you've been around this lab longer than anyone. Tell me about AUSTOR. I came on board only a year or so before it was decommissioned." Nathaniel can see Abbuhl's perplexity deepen. Why has Machuzak got me here out in the grass in the midst of this crisis to talk about ancient history? Nathaniel elucidates, a little. "How well did that machine perform?"

Now Abbuhl draws back ever so slightly to a more guarded stance. "Mac, sir, you know that AUSTOR was not one of our shining successes."

"It worked okay when I was on it."

Fred nods and shakes his head in a totally ambiguous manner. "Ach, by the time you got on it, *Herr Doktor* Professor, the beast was doing well enough, but it never reached its design specifications, you know that. In the first few years…it wasn't even close."

"Are you sure?"

With every motion, the chief telegraphs his discomfort in talking about the subject and Nathaniel is far from certain how much to press him, but Abbuhl does reply. "Mac, sir, you're a scientist, a damn good one, if I may say so. You know that it's a miracle when two people get the same results for a measurement. It was like that. Some were low, some were a little higher, a couple were absurdly high. We eventually convinced ourselves that the high temperature measurements were more correct than the low ones, that's all."

It has grown too dark for Machuzak to weigh the words against the chief's expression, and he decides to leave it for the moment. He pats Abbuhl on the shoulder, says, "Thanks, Fred," and watches the elder engineer walk slowly off into the night.

FIFTY

By eleven o'clock rain is falling, a steady, heavy rain characteristic of this time of year, but Machuzak has no intention of heading home. Instead, he pulls up the collar of his jacket, grabs a flashlight and sets out on foot from the MTF to Site Beta. His badge no longer grants access to the pentagon or the main building and, anyway, guards will be posted, but he should be able to get into Beta, a largely abandoned complex of buildings that houses some old machines and smaller experiments. And he's betting that he knows CFRC better than the guards do, and maybe Krieg-Zuber.

On the approach to Beta Site Nathaniel glances west. Third shift is well under way, the pentagon is ablaze and the rain encircles all the floods with shimmering halos. His ears seem to be playing tricks, though, for he imagines he can hear the distant, giant cracks of the capacitors discharging, cleanup pulses after the disruption.

Beta is dark, not a single light from a shop or lab. He badges himself in, nodding, at the same time thanking the security gods that he hasn't been deactivated here, and he passes down a long corridor, through a cranky door and into the darkness of one of the old tokamak bays. Beta Site isn't built on the scale of Delta, the pentagon, but CFRC's standard yardstick—the football field—fully applies here. Even so, next to Prometheus the machines here were toys. Your fingers could almost reach the top of them if you stretched.

He lifts his flashlight, pausing for a moment to contemplate the remains of TEX-1, CFRC's first tokamak, built a half century ago. In those days science was waged on a human scale. A part failed and you asked the machinist at the shop to craft a new one. You knew everyone at the lab, which consisted of maybe fifty scientists, a hundred engineers, four or five secretaries and a director. A thousand-person city, half administrators, had yet to enter anyone's mind. Then again, TEX-1 held a plasma for a millisecond, attained a temperature of 50 million degrees. It didn't rank as a flicker.

Physicists rarely know nostalgia and tokamak robbers have stripped TEX-1 to the bones for newer experiments. Under the play of the flashlight its shadowy skeleton offers only a stepladder, the baseplate, the magnets surrounding what was once the toroid within; TEX-1 actually looked like a doughnut. As Machuzak ponders its ancient remains in this archaeological museum, he is certain that TEX-1's mummy holds a higher, metaphorical significance, but the air in Beta Site is so stale as to be almost unbreathable and he hurries on.

At the far end of the bay he descends, finds the entrance to the old tunnel connecting Beta to Gamma Site, the main building. They simply forgot to install fingerprint readers here. He badges himself in and walks through, ignoring the smell of dead rodents, surfacing in the basement. The lock on the door at this end has been broken for as long as he can remember. He yanks it open and takes the stairs, two at a time, to the octagon. They also neglected to confiscate his master key, but he sees that Theresa has anyway forgotten to lock the door this evening. He does not, however, forget to lock himself in.

The lights blink on. Automation be damned. He quickly hits the override, extinguishing them, and checks that the blinds are fully closed. Only the desk lamp. What am I looking for? Those journals he noticed yesterday, Leonard Rasmussen's famous diaries, from which he publically quoted, in which he kept a record of fin de siècle physics and who knows what else. Forty volumes at least stand on the shelves before him, leather bound, brown, embossed with gold trim, each dated with the proper year. It is the what-else that Machuzak bets is to be found in abundance within these sacred tomes and he decides to start twenty-five years ago, before the building of AUSTOR. He pulls down the first three books, sits at Leonard's desk, lowers the reading lamp and begins. A lab is an organism with infinite memory.

Before him, Leonard's formal, elegant script, written with a gold-tipped fountain pen, brings forth the history of his career. His successes, his disputes, his ideas. It is a myth, surely, that people keep diaries exclusively for themselves. As he reads Leonard's, Nathaniel becomes convinced that he wrote for posterity, one eye cast over his shoulder, looking out for the person he expected someday to be reading them. He never expected that person to be Nathaniel Machuzak.

The personality of Leonard Rasmussen's imagined reader is not difficult to pin down. It is someone who would accept his achievements and prize his ego. Which from the get-go appears so colossal that Machuzak simply cannot reconcile the emerging picture with the man he has known for ten years; he rejects the diaries as forgeries.

Yet, he is riveted. Balard, Leonard's first graduate student, appears everywhere, conflict present from the beginning. "J. C. B. objects to my name being on the alpha-channeling paper. How dare he? Yes, the concept was his, but he doesn't know what to do with it." Nathaniel pauses.

Rasmussen always billed that important idea as his own and he finds himself taking Leonard's side. Other disputed proposals march across the pages, year after year, each of which Machuzak had always credited to Rasmussen, but Leonard's pugnacity in every case is so fierce that his resistance to the picture taking shape begins to crack. He cannot pinpoint when the final break with Balard occurred, but it looks like J. C. B. wanted to be project director of AUSTOR. "I'd rather shoot him," writes L. R.

Nathaniel finds plenty about AUSTOR's construction. He must try hard to convince himself more than a single person was involved. Here is the bidding for the $700 million government contract, the promise to achieve first plasma by the contract date. "Hah!" Leonard gloats over the defeat of Oak Ridge and General Atomics. Then the infamous run-up and the first plasma at one fleeting minute before deadline: "Success. It is a great moment that shall be remembered. A week without sleep but we did it. I personally drove the crew to exhaustion. With justice this will teach the fools in Washington a lesson, but we will have to dismantle the machine."

Nathaniel, by now in a fugue state where he must accept the authenticity of the documents before him yet refusing to believe it, skips forward several volumes. The Whitmans have become prominent and he slows down. Here the visiting commission Toshi said was stacked with laser-fusion cats. Rasmussen squarely indicts Thomas, director of the Office of Energy Research. "How a man of such limited intellect can occupy such an office is beyond me. He should be sacked. He and Roy have singlehandedly made life hell for the fusion program. I am weary of the constant battles with this powerful fool. How much more pleasant to live in a society like Japan or Korea, which respect our efforts."

In truth, Rasmussen's entries on Japan, Korea and China are overflowing with praise, and he made considerable efforts to recruit Asian post-docs at ANFRL. Hmm. He has fond words for geishas and it also becomes clear that Rasmussen kept several mistresses. *A woman in every port* is the traditional phrase. Does Theresa know?

Something is not adding up. What about these Whitmans? Ah, Leonard's protest about the visiting committee to the director of the DOE. He succeeds in having the report trashed. "I have saved the lab," he breathes. Fast-forward again. Nathaniel takes another volume from the shelf and another. He halts: the infamous fifty million. "I protested to Senator Kennedy and others, and Thomas Whitman has finally been sacked. This man was a traitor to the fusion program and should have been eliminated long ago. We may never recover from the harm he's caused. Senator

Roy says the money went to harbor dredging; I am sure it went to the Whitmans' company Exosystems, which they claim to have sold."

At that Nathaniel starts hard. Leonard had blatantly lied. He'd known about Exosystems all along. According to the diaries, the fifty million was only the tip of the iceberg. Not only does Roy, in retaliation for the sacking of his brother, kill virtually all federal funding for magnetic fusion, but Rasmussen remains convinced that the brothers have siphoned off hundreds of millions of dollars from the expiring program into their own pockets.

But what did Exosystems do? What triggered all this? Nathaniel travels back in time to the volumes he skipped. AUSTOR is functioning, at last. Stop. "Wilson causing trouble. He insists on publishing his nonsensical low-temperature readings for AUSTOR and claims we have not fulfilled the conditions of the contract. Must act. Wilson is a mere spectroscopist, who has no interest in the program; he doesn't see the big picture."

Some entries later, without warning: "The young Whitman, this apprentice, Wilson's friend, is selling dirt on the lab to the visiting commission. I'll be damned if this will continue."

Nathaniel swallows hard. Darrell? Now he remembers why the name sounded familiar. Darrell Whitman once worked at the lab, before his own arrival. He was an intern, or something.

Machuzak reads forward again and it is not long before he finds an entry. "I fired him." He looks up. In the now, a night watchman is checking the door lock. Machuzak holds his breath, but whoever it is continues on his rounds. As the picture comes together, Nathaniel leans back. The dirt Darrell was selling to the Whitmans was Wilson's low temperature readings, which showed Rasmussen had bilked the government out of $700 million with false promises. Leonard fired Darrell, Thomas Whitman retaliated by lifting the fifty million. Rasmussen lobbied to get Thomas sacked. All politics is not merely local, it is personal. Machuzak understands that he is witnessing one side of a feud worthy of the Hatfields and the McCoys.

After that traces of Wilson vanish but for the cryptic remark, "Wilson taken care of." Machuzak rechecks the dates. How long has Jerry been jobbing around the lab? Since before I arrived.

The journals are scarcely exhausted. Indeed, he himself briefly emerges from the pages, when nearly ten years ago Leonard decides to cancel his old experiment. "Machuzak doesn't realize that his idea could threaten the nb heating push. I won't allow it and have already told Krieg-Zuber to deal with it. Cyrus is an idiot, but he has his uses."

Matsushima figures far more often and more vividly. "The man has so many ideas, most of them are crazy but enough of them are possibilities that he is becoming a menace. He must be *neutralized*. I told Zuber to get rid of him, but that fat nuisance Garrett intervened and the only thing I've been able to do is exile Matsushima to Alpha." He goes on to recount in obscene detail the steps he has taken to derail Toshi's career and make certain he can never work elsewhere. He does not flinch from spreading rumors about the physicist's belief in ESP and levitation.

Machuzak raises his head. So it was Rasmussen, not Krieg-Zuber, who canceled his own magnum opus, and it was Rasmussen, not Cyrus the Great, who did all to make Matsushima's life miserable. Leonard would kill anything or anyone that threatened his status as Father of Fusion. Strangely, Machuzak feels no anger at all the revelations. It was a decade ago; the past has detached and become impotent. At the same time he is forced to conclude that Rasmussen saved this hidden facet of his character for the Olympian battles, which took place above the clouds, and that it cost him little to appear kind to the foot soldiers. The other possibility, he concedes, is that Machuzak has been a fool.

At last he gets to his feet. There must be some record around of what happened to Darrell Whitman. Lise, Leonard's personal secretary, would probably have it, straight through that door. He walks into her office, adjoining the director's, and glances at the computer. It seems that he remembers her password; she'd given it to him once in one of her anti-computer fits when she needed assistance. He logs on. It takes only a moment to find a record for Darrell Whitman, who'd worked at the lab for just a year as an intern, then a technician and then was fired—within a week of Leonard's diary entry. Machuzak thinks to check Wilson's file. It seems that he too was fired, but suddenly reinstated a couple years later. Machuzak remains puzzled over this, but he will now bet that Leonard Rasmussen ruthlessly and without remorse destroyed Jerry Wilson's career.

The sun will soon be coming up. Machuzak knows he'd better get out of here before anyone appears. Theresa. Has she read the volumes surrounding her? He considers leaving a note. No, if she has read them, she knows; if she has not, she will soon enough. He replaces the diaries where he found them and, making sure no guards are to be seen, retraces his steps through Beta Site. His single thought on the drive home is whether he can ever look Leonard Rasmussen in the eye again.

FIFTY-ONE

While the evangelists face off the Scientologists outside, inside Abbuhl has pushed the disruption cleanup and a day has hardly passed before Hasschler announces the recommencement of experiments. Thad, wearing a blue brass-buttoned jacket that makes him look more a Prussian drill sergeant than ever, lifts his sabre to call for some moderate power shots, but after a few pulses the plasma becomes so unbelievably dirty, full of crap, that everyone quickly realizes that something has gone seriously wrong. Finally, Ari Socarides suggests examining the toroid's interior with one of the periscopes. They extend periscope number one and its scan reveals a molten hunk of metal hanging within the doughnut just at the bend. "Christ!" exclaims Fournier, "we forgot to retract periscope three. We fucking vaporized it!"

They try another pulse, to clean up. Then another. The same problem. Finally, they extend periscope one again, only to recognize that they forgot to retract it on the previous pulse and vaporized it along with the other.

When the realization sets in that they've just lost another day, not less, Fournier turns on Socarides. "This is your fault! You got us into—!"

"What the hell are you talking about?" Socarides replies and at once they launch into a fistfight.

Theresa absent, Krieg-Zuber does not hesitate to take charge and calls in the guardsmen. He himself grabs Fournier and wrestles him to a table, but the scientists turn on The Terminator and the militia, and within an instant a full-scale brawl has broken out. Theresa, running from upstairs, can hardly believe the scene unfolding before her, a sort of melee in molasses with rubbery arms flailing and a punch landing here or there. Her astonishment momentarily immobilizes her, but the instant she snaps to, she orders the guardsmen out and only then does the slow fury begin to evaporate, leaving more than one bloody nose and a dislocated shoulder.

From his observation post Machuzak well perceives that exhaustion is setting in, not the exhaustion relieved by coffee breaks or a good night's sleep. Here is a terminal weariness, the kind that descends when spirits begin to crumble. He phones Theresa and, like a perched angel, whispers that something must be done. A few hours later, to everyone's shock and amazement, Lise bursts through the door, not daytime Lise, the secretary, but Lise transformed into her moonlighting alter ego, Shanaz. She whirls in to a track of Bouzouki music, scarves draped across her arms, ample breasts barely constrained by her bra of jangling coins, finger cymbals clanging above her head. Machuzak suspects that the ASSET control-cast is quickly climbing the ratings, but for the moment he merely watches, transfixed, as Lise's cheering audience responds, gleefully stuffing dollar bills under her panties and bra straps until she finally dances off looking like a Christmas tree. Yes, it's getting weird, but this is the Republic of Texas. The crew is fortified and everyone returns to work.

Afterward, Nathaniel phones Theresa with congratulations but asks what the hell Krieg-Zuber is still doing there.

"He's convinced the machine is in danger. I've allowed him to remain in charge of security. Mac, after everything, it's not crazy."

By now Machuzak is convinced Zuber did know something, but Theresa is of no help. "Theresa, when you kick a king you've got to kill him," he says and abruptly signed off.

* * * *

Luckily, the damage to the machine from the vaporized scopes proves minimal and overnight they are running again. Hasschler calls for tritium pellets. The COE takes the order at sword point and programs the injection. The pulse begins. Five seconds later a high-velocity gun injects the frozen tritium pellets, developed at the MTF, deep into the torus. Across the Atlantic all eyes are on the ASSET experiment. ITER is still down and the ITERniks watch with frustration and envy as the Austin team tries experiments they hadn't anticipated for years.

Success is immediate and dramatic: three times breakeven for forty seconds. By afternoon Prometheus has achieved fifty-eight seconds at a Q of three-point-five. They've not only shattered the world's fusion record, but for the first time since this contest began, have pulled ahead of ITER. While cheers go up in Austin, Balard's team stands stunned by a never-anticipated reversal of fortune. A few Cadarache scientists applaud the Texans, but most of them make the well-known French gesture, and more than one of the Texans moon the ITERniks. Hasschler prints out the power graph for the shot and passes it around for everyone to sign. Spirits, for the moment, are on the upswing.

* * * *

The same evening Whitman puts a decisive end to his partial ceasefire. Resplendent in buckskin, surrounded by the accoutrements of his senatorial office, Big Bad Roy makes a simple move: he merely replays Shanaz's performance of yesterday, then accompanied by an expression hovering between salacity and disgust, munificently announces that only hours ago his Energy and Water subcommittee triumphantly saved taxpayers several million dollars by rescinding all CFRC funds for the remainder of the fiscal year; the subcommittee will zero funds for the next. He has carried out his threat.

"It's brilliant," mutters Machuzak to himself at the MTF. "He requires nothing more than our mistakes." Whitman overreaches then, insisting in one of his whacko moments that fusion may harm the ozone layer, but no worries—he knows this round belongs to him. Observing the ruddy face beaming from the monitor, Machuzak sees only Leonard's elegant handwriting in his mind's eye, and his conviction deepens that this battle is personal—and unfinished.

Theresa makes the best of a bad hand, pointedly returning in her webcast that the senator's ozone layer remark was simply bizarre and she stresses that the "monkey business" in the control room was a direct result of the pressure on the crew. Of far greater importance, she speaks directly to her audience, today Prometheus achieved an all-time fusion record. She offers to bet the senator that in less than three months CFRC scientists will demonstrate a self-sustaining reaction. The stakes are the senator's apology for ignition.

Machuzak gulps at her bravado and turns to see T. J. watching over his shoulder.

"You know, Doc," D'Abro announces with the satisfaction of discovery, making no comment on the broadcasts, "twenty years ago Darrell Whitman—"

"—worked at this lab."

T. J. stares at him, smile falling into something less trustful. At last she stutters, "You know?"

"I...remembered," Machuzak answers. "Did you learn anything else?"

She had. Having almost reached San Antonio, T. J. berated herself for running off half-cocked in her habitual fashion, knowing nothing more about Darrell Whitman than his cell-phone number. Turning around, she trawled public and police records in Austin to learn that two decades ago, Darrell had briefly lived in Dripping Springs. Struck by the proximity to the lab, she nosed further and was definitely surprised that on a car-loan application he'd listed ANFRL as his place of employment. She headed south again with Monteverdi's *Vespers* to keep herself company. Not a bad piece on the whole, she decided. The stakeout lasted several days until the moment when Darrell at last returned to his sprawling ranch house below Loop 410 near Van Ormy. T. J. spilled her coffee and allowed him a quarter-hour grace.

When the woman standing on his acorn-scattered porch presented her credentials, the expression on the middle-aged man, who carried himself with a corporate demeanor and bore a familial resemblance to the senator, at once clouded.

"Don't worry," she told him, realizing that she still didn't have much more than Monteverdi to go on and was, as always, winging it, "I'm investigating the events up at CFRC and I'd just like to ask a few questions."

Whitman peered at her harshly, dismissed her with an equally abrasive laugh. "What can that possibly have to do with me? I haven't worked there in twenty years."

"Well," T. J. replied diffidently, certain that it would be a grave mistake to mention the ringtone, "your name's come up in a few conversations. You've probably heard that Nathaniel Machuzak's been charged in connection with the sabotage and death of Andy Lipman and I was wondering if you had any information that might prove useful."

"I don't know either of them," he answered with an expression that continued to match his voice. "I can't do anything for you."

"Hmm," T. J. said, truly stymied as to how to proceed. Why'd she bothered? Machuzak had really given her nothing more than the Bermuda Triangle. She'd always wondered about the Bermuda Triangle...

At that moment, Whitman's wife, a classic raven-haired Texan, came up behind him and asked what all the fuss was about.

"The police are asking whether I know anything about what's going on up at CFRC. I don't."

"I'm not surprised someone wanted to blow up the machine," she put in, "the way they treat people up there. You remember Jerry Wilson, don't you, dear?"

"Not now, honey—"

The name struck T. J. as familiar. Wilson was Mac's assistant at the MTF, although he wasn't much around and she hadn't exchanged a word with him. You take luck where you find it. "What about Wilson, sir?"

"That was a long time ago."

"That's all right," T. J. returned, "the lab seems to have a long memory."

Whitman reluctantly ushered T. J. into the living room even as he began talking. He didn't offer her a chair and she didn't ask. "They're a bunch of crooks at that place. They got the contract for that rust bucket AUSTOR by promising DOE that it would be working on a certain date. They couldn't meet the deadline, they couldn't meet their own benchmarks. What did the bastards do? They cooked the data. I'd just started that year. Jerry Wilson, a nobody, was the only one who stood up to Rasmussen, who thinks he's Napoleon. Rasmussen ran him out of town." T. J. saw clearly that once Darrell got going on this topic, there was no stopping him. "That fucker ruined the kid's entire career. Jerry couldn't get work anywhere. Rasmussen told everybody he was incompetent. Who was going to believe some diagnostician without a PhD? But Jerry had guts; he fought back. He hired a lawyer and threatened to sue Rasmussen for illegally RIFing him. Rasmussen saw what was coming—yeah, if Wilson ever went public, that would be the end of the great lab—so he paid Wilson off, a couple hundred thousand."

T. J. was puzzled, held up her hand and managed to interrupt Darrell long enough to ask how he knew all this.

"Jerry and I were friends, for a year. We'd go out for beers."

"And if Rasmussen fired him and paid him off with big bucks, how come Wilson has been working at low-level positions at the lab ever since?"

Darrell laughed again, no more pleasantly. "His wife left him. He had nothin left, nada, but he kept threatening Rasmussen until the great man rehired him—"

"You mean blackmailing him."

"Rasmussen is a criminal. The man squashed anyone who stood in his way. I got out of there as soon as I could." Abruptly Whitman halted and peered at the detective. "What does this have to do with what's going on now?"

"I dunno," T. J. replied, suppressing, successfully she thought, a grin. "You tell me. You're the one who's been talkin." Confession is truly good for the soul, she learned again. At that, Whitman zipped up, only repeating that he didn't know anything about current events. "Can I ask, sir, where you work now, bein that you're no longer at the lab?"

"I've worked at Novatech for a long time. We do defense contracting for the government."

"And more than that you can't say."

"That is correct."

At hearing the word *Novatech* drop from D'Abro's lips, Machuzak jerks his head erect, but T. J. continues uninterrupted with her story.

"Hmm," she nodded at Whitman's invocation of classified matters and prepared to exit. "By the way, have you ever run into Moravec, the guy who's planning to shut down the lab?"

"GlobeTex's CEO? No, I've never run into him—her." Whitman looked her in the eye without flinching.

T. J. saluted and departed.

Finishing her story, she expects shock and awe from Machuzak, not to mention congratulations, but apart from his reaction to *Novatech*, there's been nada and now he is only nodding to himself. "What is it, Doc? you don't seem too impressed."

"Let's say scientists like independent confirmation," he answers without hint of jubilation.

"You knew all this?" T. J. asks sharply, more than surprised herself.

"Most." After a long consideration, Nathaniel slowly, slowly reveals to her his discovery of Wilson's binders, Leonard's diaries, his talk with Abbuhl. Now, unfortunately, he knows what Leonard meant by "Wilson taken care of."

"Mac!" exclaims T. J., exasperated and impressed herself, "you might've made that trip a lot easier for me."

"We haven't been on the best of terms recently," he replies simply.

D'Abro sighs. It's all too bad, all of it, really. "You do keep a lot to yourself," she shakes her head, the admonishment one less of anger than of resignation. "Whaddya you know about Novatech?"

"That it doesn't exist."

"Huh?" she abruptly halts.

"I'm glad Darrell slipped and told you he worked there. Theresa ran into a dead end with Exosystems. I'll put money down that the Whitmans never sold it. Novatech must be a shell company. If you find anything, you'll find a fake board of directors and a fake bunch of foreign employees." He's also willing to bet where that fifty million dollars went. "You didn't manage to connect Whitman and Moravec?"

"I wasn't exactly goin to tell him we'd traced his phone call." Machuzak nods and T. J. offers to look into Novatech. "Maybe it's also time for me to have a little heart-to-heart with Wilson."

Here, surprisingly, Machuzak shakes his head. "No, ask Garrett to hold a party. Tell him that…it should be a masquerade ball…and tell him to make sure *everybody* is there."

FIFTY-TWO

After D'Abro's departure, Machuzak sends a brief message to Archangelsky, checks in on the experiments, rises. The detective hadn't offered to drop charges and he didn't ask. For the time being he has chosen to continue in his liminal state, this indeterminate existence on the threshold between two planes, one of a working scientist, the other of an outcast, for he knows it is in liminal states, between dreams and wakefulness, that answers whisper their presence.

Nathaniel again stands at the door between labs, glancing left and glancing right. This time he does not take the fork leading to Wilson's lab and another night of reading notebooks. Instead he steps back into his own space and walks to the window, where he hangs his head out, staring for an infinite time at the patch he showed D'Abro weeks ago. That patch of dead grass and flowers onto which he'd been dribbling heavy water for so long. He can't understand it. Chemically, heavy water, deuterium oxide, is identical to ordinary water. Hell, it says so in the training manual, right here. That's why tritium oxide—extra-heavy water—is so dangerous. The body assumes that tritiated water is no different from the everyday stuff and puts it through the same paces. But heavy water, what's the big deal? He swigged a flask before the protestors on that fateful day and suffered no ill effects. Or did he?

It is the usual disjuncture: he is healthy; the plants are dead. He's always been a lousy gardener and can't dismiss the possibility that his black thumb just killed them. Still, he feels the scientist's persistent itch of dissatisfaction. Then there is Wilson's cold-fusion apparatus, which required heavy water to operate. Is there a connection?

Machuzak decides to perform an experiment. The flame jet on his test cylinder is a small one, unsuitable for what he has in mind, so he wanders through the machine shops across the hall until he finds a hydrogen blowtorch. Back in his lab, he spends an hour concocting from metal and glass a distillery, one with the torch at its input, which will burn a tank of deuterium to heavy water in a few hours. Of course, there is a slight danger of blowing himself to bits, but he figures he doesn't have too much to lose at this point. Nathaniel connects up a deuterium tank and an oxygen tank and begins.

The watched pot. The process can't be hurried and he'd rather not stare at heavy steam as it condenses drop by drop into a beaker. Once more he tunes into the control-cast.

* * * *

He is unprepared for what takes place within the next heartbeats. Theresa's phone rings on the captain's deck. He can hear only half the conversation, but he sees clearly the blood draining from her face and minutes later Diana Cochran runs into the control room and climbs the steps to the deck where Theresa is waiting.

"We've had a leak on one of the main helium feeder lines!" she heaves breathlessly. "We just lost a ton of helium."

Krieg-Zuber, standing below, shoots at her a glance overflowing with suspicion and alarm, but Cochran anticipates his question. "No, Cy, we lost the nitrogen insulator and then a section of pipe went, that's all."

"I demand an investigation this minute!" Krieg-Zuber insists, pointing at her.

"We'll investigate when there's time!" Diana replies angrily. They have a more immediate problem, a much more immediate problem.

"Will you have to bring the machine up?" Theresa asks with trepidation, knowing that a second three-week cooldown would mean the end.

Diana shakes her head. "We've closed the line and it can be repaired overnight, probably, but you've got to stop the experiments. We don't want to risk a quench."

Loss of superconductivity in the magnets.

Theresa at once gives the order to Larissa. As the machine is shut down until further notice, everybody throws up their arms, a sizable number of the crew storms out of the room determined to get drunk, while others begin dancing. Across the Atlantic ITERniks are already smiling, applauding, knowing that the accident has given them the chance they've been waiting for to regain the lead.

"I'll see that rupture," Zuber insists.

"This isn't the problem, Cyrus," retorts Diana with increased aggravation. "We've got to import a shitload of helium and we've got to do it now." Without losing a beat she phones the Federal Helium Reserve in Amarillo. The others watch her color drain before their eyes, and by the time she signs off she has turned as pale as Theresa was moments ago. "They're out. The whole country is fucking out." Cochran's persistent nightmare for the past years has abruptly become reality.

"Where else can you get it?" Theresa asks, refusing to throw in the towel because of a mere national shortage of a vital element.

Brain blocked, Cochran shakes her head and Machuzak simultaneously hears his wrist-set go off. Theresa: where they can get helium, fast?

"Algeria," he tells her flatly, "unless ITER has the supply locked up. Algeria's the world's largest supplier."

Theresa blanks out like Diana. How are they supposed to get helium from Algeria?

"Garrett's private jet," Machuzak answers and Theresa is at once on the phone with The Chairman, who instantly agrees to lend them his plane. The fog lifting, Cochran is out the door even as she tracks down the Algerian supplier at Azrew.

"I want you on that jet," Theresa turns to Krieg-Zuber.

For a moment he hesitates, unblinking. "My duty is to protect the integrity of the control room," he finally decides.

"Integrity of the control room?" she squints at The Terminator and puts it to him directly: "Are you expecting another attack, with the machine down, after the arrests?"

"W—we c—cannot rule out another attempt to hack in," he uncharacteristically stutters. "I have been monitoring the systems."

Theresa's stare at once becomes wrathful. "You disconnected the control-room machines from the Web. What's going on? I noticed you chatting with Mercedes before. She's defected to our archrival, Cyrus. Are you feeding her information?"

He visibly flinches, offended, puts his finger behind his collar. "To the contrary…" he says, but does not finish his thought.

Theresa does it for him. "I want you on that plane. Alert the Algerian authorities. Pay what they ask, *deputy*."

* * * *

Over the next twenty-four hours, ITER makes a full recovery from its disruption and again pulls ahead of ASSET, running close to four times breakeven. The Texans look on hopelessly, unable to do anything except watch and curse. Theresa phones Nathaniel in the morning, intending to pay him a visit, but he asks her not to. She is surprised, but accedes to the strange request. He does ask about helium.

"Cochran's team is finishing the line repairs," she tells him. "And Cyrus is returning with several tons of helium. We'll have it tomorrow. But ITER is running at nearly Q equals four."

"Soon things should start to get interesting," Nathaniel answers with a sharp, nearly sarcastic inflection to his voice.

"Are you all right, Mac? Thanks for suggesting Algeria."

"I'm fine," he says and abruptly hangs up.

Krieg-Zuber arrives angry but on schedule, bearing a shipment of helium in Garrett's jet and a promise of more by Algeria, where betting on the race has become a national pastime, and a few hours later Prometheus is up and running. Hasschler's crew stumbles back into the control room, grumpy, unshaven but more alive than seventy-two hours earlier, and they plunge in again.

Within another forty-eight hours ITER has stalled, gaining a plateau of four times breakeven, a world record, but not ignition. Though no one knows what's going on, Hasschler isn't waiting to find out. By week's end he has closed the gap and they are breathing down ITER's tail. The deadline calendar in the control room, automated by one of the engineers while the machine stood idle, stands at seventy. Days, not centuries.

* * * *

Nathaniel has rarely ventured out of the lab for the entire week and sleeps on his mattress in the corner. He tries hard to ignore the mountains of hate mail and he's killed any number of cockroaches, each big enough to drag a dead cat across the street. Late in the week Toshi puts his head in, looks askance at Machuzak's dishevelment and asks pointedly what he is doing. "Solving problems" is the only answer forthcoming, to which Matsushima shrugs. "As is said in the *Tao te Ching*, 'When the master runs into a difficulty, he stops and gives himself to it.' You are proving very unoriginal, Nathaniel." Toshi swears not to abandon the ignition campaign and departs.

Having heard nothing from Nat Edward'ich for days, Slava appears, having again hopped the fence. Entering the MTF he can hardly believe his eyes and peers at the several dozen exhausted bottles of deuterium, virtually all on hand, and half that number of empty oxygen cylinders.

"*Radi boga!*" he exclaims, glancing between the chaotic surroundings and the unshaven recluse. "What in God's name are you doing? You look like floating shit in an ice hole."

That bad, Machuzak thinks. He does his best to explain that he's produced about a dozen liters of heavy water, which he's either drunk or used to water his plants.

"Jesus, *why*?" Slava's eyes are as wide as those eyes can get.

Nathaniel clasps his head with his hands. "I don't know." He does know the geraniums are dying, that he is feeling nervous, hyperactive, intoxicated. He tells Slava of the dead plants, his nonreaction when he drank heavy water on the day of Moravec's visit, Wilson's cold-fusion apparatus.

"But this is mad, brother," Archangelsky says without amusement, "mad! Those plants could have died for any number of reasons."

"I know that, but why am I feeling these symptoms? What about those fish?" He points to two goldfish that he's moved from the pond to a beaker of heavy water; they are indisputably dead. "You know, I know that the chemical properties of two isotopes of the same element are identical. What's going on?"

"What goes on is that you've become crazy, *pazzo*."

Machuzak reminds Slava that the time he noticed a slightly unexpected behavior in particle transport in one of his tokamak models led to a new magnetic-field configuration and made his career.

"This is entirely different. Experimenting on yourself like...like I don't know what, like... Frankenstein."

Good, he has said it. In fact, Machuzak does not feel like Frankenstein. His quietude, this liminal existence, has led him to that place, the goal of all art, Toshi has said, where one flies by instinct, where one has forgotten one's training, where learning lost has been learning gained.

Wait a minute. He abruptly leads Slava into Wilson's lab, scouring the workbench while the Russian watches. Half buried amid the junk he finds a glass condensation tube: the water jacket, the inner spiral, not significantly different from the tube Machuzak has these past days been using in his own distillery. "There," he points.

"There what?" Slava peers after the finger skeptically.

At CFRC there is no particular use for heavy water except to placate environmentalists or to build a cold-fusion apparatus, which like the one he found on Wilson's desk consists merely of platinum and palladium electrodes immersed in a container of room-temperature heavy water and which does nothing.

"Why should Wilson have a cold-fusion apparatus?" Machuzak scratches the stubble on his chin. "And a whole notebook on his experiments?"

"Christ," growls Slava, "maybe he bootlegs moonshine. How the hell should I know? You are totally nuts, Edward'ich. I'm getting you out of here."

Machuzak realizes then that he has not shared with Slava the recent revelations and now takes him outside to tell him everything: Wilson's low temperature readings on AUSTOR, Leonard's diaries, Darrell Whitman, a ruined career, Novatech.

As he finishes Slava whistles, but he still doesn't see any heavy-water connection, and when he sees Nathaniel disappearing again into the building he runs after him, grabs him by the arm and drags him with full force back toward the exit. "I told you, Edward'ich, I'm getting you out of here."

Suddenly, as they pass a Right to Know information station, which he has never in living memory paid attention to, Machuzak shouts, "Hold on!"

Facing them is a poster with a medley of goggled cartoon characters, one concocting a chemical compound at a lab bench, another wheeling a gas bottle around, the usual scientific-nerd activities. Big black letters at the poster's center advise

WHEN IN DOUBT

CHECK

MSDS

OUT!

—says Bill Balustradi

Fastened to the wall below the poster is an old steel basket holding a phone-book-sized binder, safety yellow trimmed with black stripes. In ten years, Machuzak has never so much as glanced at a Material Safety Data Sheet, or known anyone who did. He frees himself from Slava, paging through it. Each sheet, headed by "US Department of Labor," is dedicated to the properties and hazards of a single chemical substance, but the book is in absolute chaos, an archaeological fragment of times gone by and forgotten, and it's impossible to find anything. They march into Machuzak's lab to check the online version.

It takes only a few moments before they have it, an MSDS on heavy water. Nathaniel is dumbfounded that such a thing even exists. The first pages are of little interest; deuterated water is an odorless, colorless liquid that doesn't explode. But on page five, the health-hazard data: "Prolonged contact may cause skin irritation. Ingestion may impair kidney function, create nervous system disturbances, hormonal imbalance, and anemia may occur when concentration in body fluids reaches 10%. Death occurs..."

Machuzak and Archangelsky blink at one another, each attempting to mind-read the other. Nathaniel's thoughts are a tumult, gyrating without control, too fast to catch, too tangled to sort out.

Slava's thoughts may be equally disordered but he recovers first. "This is impossible. Deuterium is just isotope of hydrogen. Chemically should be same as ordinary water."

That is what all physicists believe, what they all learn in high school, what is found in the manuals. Nathaniel even points it out to Archangelsky in the lab's radiation training course. Somebody is wrong, and Machuzak suspects it is not the MSDS.

Yet it is not the information that heavy water is less benign than they had always believed that has put the physicists' thoughts in such disarray. The two men stare at each other, knowing full well that the described symptoms closely resemble Leonard Rasmussen's own.

"No," Slava finally says, "this is too vague, vague enough to be coincidence. I don't believe it. They said Leonard has MS or a cousin."

"I've heard that MS is difficult to diagnose," Nathaniel answers, unsure of himself, "that it's often missed, mistaken for other things."

Borisovich wrinkles his nose. "I don't believe it. You are out of your mind to think it. Wait, Nastya is a research physician. Maybe she knows where to find more information. Nobody could have experimented with heavy water since the war. I'll call her when I get home."

Archangelsky continues to insist on taking Machuzak into town and he no longer resists. As they switch off the lights, he at least knows why a single flask of heavy water had no effect on him; it was simply not enough.

On the northward drive Nathaniel asks whether Slava or Toshi has come up with anything astounding, but Archangelsky shakes his head. "If Toshi were designing system from scratch, it would end up looking nothing like tokamak, but it is too late in the game and we are too constrained. Our ideas will be little ones, like most ideas."

Nathaniel asks whether he has received any warnings from Park.

"No," Slava replies, "I told you we would get nothing."

This worries them both. As the deadline approaches, so does the certainty of another attack. Krieg-Zuber, evidently, also knows this.

"Do you think I'm crazy?" Nathaniel says finally.

The Russian shrugs. "I don't know. Your math sucks but your intuition is astounding. I do know that if you tell anyone about this, they will lock you up."

As the city comes into view, Archangelsky is muttering, "Death by cold fusion…"

For his part, Machuzak is wondering what to do next.

FIFTY-THREE

Having dropped off Machuzak, Slava drops out of sight. For several days Nathaniel attempts to contact him, nothing. Suddenly, at week's end, his phone rings; Borisovich asks to meet at the West Mall of The University, the jammed gathering spot for every student and protest group in Austin. Attempting to trap him as he shoves through the crowds, Scientologists insist their "Thought-O-Meter" measures "thought energy fluxing from space through your mind," and when Machuzak replies that the device is an ordinary electrical resistance meter, which as a physicist he uses all the time, they scowl, "What's a physicist?" Of late the question has become a pointed one and he moves on, ignoring the reconquistas, passing the Internet stations for the homeless and refusing to confront Greenpeace, which offers a petition against the existence of CFRC. At last he spies Slava sitting at one the circular fountains; he joins him and they remain anonymous.

"I've discovered the connection between Whitman and Moravec," Slava begins abruptly, giving his companion no chance to react: "Niger."

"Huh?" is Machuzak's single, dumbfounded response.

"After you told me Darrell lives near San Antonio, I decided to pay him a visit." Before Nathaniel can get the words out, Archangelsky shrugs. "He's listed in phone book. But we didn't talk. I reprogrammed his phone—"

"What?"

Nathaniel, struggling to catch up, is met only by a second shrug. "I spoke to his wife, telling her I was friend. She gave me his cell number. So I sent service message—you know like phone company sends to update the SIM card on your phone. With freeware anybody can do it. I reprogrammed phone to include me in his calls. D'Abro would wait for Cyber Crimes Unit. We don't have time. I waited 'til he phoned Moravec."

Machuzak stares down at the fossil-impregnated limestone beneath his feet and clasps his head between his hands. "What are we becoming, Slava?"

"What circumstances demand, *brat*," Slava replies emotionlessly, "what people want us to become… So, Moravec and the Whitmans hate each other, that is confirmed. Moravec longs to be remembered as green cowboy, maybe cowgirl. She doesn't like game Roy and Thomas Whitman are playing against CFRC and has begun to protest. Listen." Slava motions for Nathaniel to put on his earpiece and phones him.

"All right," he hears Moravec say to Darrell, "you've put the squeeze on CFRC, made your point. Why don't we give them time to reach ignition. They could do it—"

"We want that lab dead, Moravec, that fucker Rasmussen dead..."

"To what end?"

"Remember Niger, Moravec, and remember your pension package." Click.

Machuzak, bewildered, needs Archangelsky to clarify. "After hearing this, I went fishing, contacted friends. You know for last fifty years there's been one coup after another in Niger. Governments change but one thing doesn't—military's control over Niger's uranium deposits. They don't do people of Niger any good, but with country supplying eight percent of world's uranium, it sure does France and the multinationals good. Before Moravec went solar she was into fission, supported—organized—more than one coup. Lots of people dead. Whitmans know this."

"They're blackmailing Moravec?"

"*Pravil'no*. Cases are pending in International Criminal Court."

Machuzak merely shakes his head, overwhelmed at once by incredulity and a greater sadness.

"Moravec, big green hero, can't rescind ignition deadline unless she wants to end life as war criminal, maybe lose retirement package. No wonder she shuns public. There's more... Never mind, we pygmies can do nothing about Great Game. I came to talk about something else." He suddenly puts in Machuzak's hand a rolled-up sheaf of paper. "Nastya sent this."

Nathaniel unfurls it to see an article from the *Journal of Pharmaceutical Sciences* concerning the toxic effects of heavy water. It dates from the Cold War, before their births, and reports studies even older, nearly a century old. Nevertheless, it is certainly the source of the MSDS they found. Nastya has done her homework.

During the days when people were concerned about the use of heavy water in fission reactors, the article informs him, someone discovered that neither plants nor animals survived in water containing high concentrations of the stuff. His grass and geraniums, Machuzak nods at the confirmation. Few tests were ever performed on humans and the data mostly concern mice, rats, dogs. Even a small amount of heavy water, 1 percent of body weight, caused signs of intoxication. Good, he's pleased that his imagination was not running into overdrive. The more laboratory mice drank, the thirstier they became; thus his addiction to his experiment. When more than about 10 percent of body fluid was replaced by heavy water, symptoms included hyperactivity, hyperirritability and infertility.

Beyond that, the data become confusing. Replacing between 15 and 30 percent of body fluid in mammals caused serious effects; at the upper level death resulted within weeks. Curiously, the ultimate cause of death by heavy water is unclear. Deuterium oxide interferes with the heart and kidneys, causes central nervous system impairment, blocks the function of enzymes, induces hormonal imbalances... Finally, the authors conclude, although harmful effects at low concentrations went unobserved in laboratory animals, they probably exist.

"Wow," whispers Machuzak, "all because of one extra neutron." Deuterium, the paper points out, is heavier than hydrogen, so the molecular components vibrate more slowly than ordinary hydrogen like heavier balls on springs. The entire chemistry is altered. Any chemistry student would have guessed. Physicists know shit about chemistry. Machuzak grants himself a moment to bask in his ignorance, but what needs not be said aloud is that many of these symptoms have been observed in Leonard Rasmussen during the past year. "Heavy-water experiments can't have been performed much since the war," Machuzak reflects.

"You mean to say until now," Slava returns.

Nathaniel remains silent, but Archangelsky does not. "I know what you are thinking," he says, "and you are jumping to conclusions. Leonard's condition has dragged on—"

"They don't know about 'effects at low concentrations.'"

"Does Leonard have kidney problems?"

"Leonard has every problem."

"In God's name, how would you feed him heavy water for so long?"

Machuzak cocks his head, thinks. "There's a water cooler in his office. It would be easy enough for Wilson to fill the bottles... A perfect weapon, indistinguishable from multiple sclerosis."

Enough. Slava stands as a group of Hari Krishnas passes by, banging cymbals and drums. "*Brat*, we're not doctors. We must be missing something. This is all big coincidence."

"Nastya's a doctor. Did she read this?" Reluctantly Slava nods. "What did she say?"

"She said it sounds like multiple sclerosis... Edward'ich, I told you to forget it. Nobody will believe this before crayfish whistles on the hill."

Machuzak's stubborn gaze is familiar. "I'm right," it says.

"And I say forget it. Nothing good can come of this." Slava's gaze is severe, his eyes resembling coals of Mephistopheles.

He may, after all, be right. "Garrett has agreed to throw a party. Be there." With that, Machuzak abandons Slava on the West Mall to be accosted from opposite sides by an evangelist and a member of the Socialist Workers Party.

FIFTY-FOUR

On the day D'Abro sought him out, The Chairman arrived at the main building to be greeted in the lobby by Rodin's Gates of Hell. Disturbing, Garrett wrinkles his nose at the famous sculpture, or its replica. Christmas tree lights twine festively around the portals, which frame the calendar, and the small replica of *The Thinker* above is plastered with Balustradi's face. The Chairman cannot fathom any of this, but as he passes through the gates no one needs to remind him of the descent.

Below he finds a filthy, littered control room, crew members sacked out on cots, crashed out at their stations, surrounded by coffee cups and Red Bull empties. For the past few days ITER has stood ahead and, though they have narrowed the gap, the Prometheus team has been unable to close it. Surveying the junkyard in disgust, Garret cannot doubt why. At that moment one of the engineers jogs up to Theresa, tripping on the steps to the captain's deck, and agitatedly reports that the filament on Brazil has broken. Theresa nods with a mortal weariness, ordering the COE to halt operations. Hasschler explains that the deuterium and tritium accelerated by the neutral beams are ionized by a large tungsten lightbulb filament, which has blown.

"Do you have replacements?" Theresa asks, barely getting out the words.

"Yes," Hasschler confirms, "this is not fatal."

Installation, though, will take several days. Worse, he tells her, the machine is now hot—that is, radioactive—and so the techs will have to work in controlled-access shifts in order not to exceed their dose limits.

Garrett, gaze sweeping the room, wonders whether in its present condition the team can safely carry out such an operation. "No problem," Hasschler declares, but The Chairman finds reasons for doubt at the entrance of the big three-hundred-meter tunnel connecting the control room to Prometheus, where he sees a technician riding full tilt toward him on a service bicycle, only to crash headlong into a wall. Others rush to carry him off, arm broken.

When D'Abro relays Machuzak's request for a masquerade ball, Garrett decides that a party for the end of the world cannot be the worst idea.

* * * *

Machuzak realized at once that if it would not be a masked ball, it would prove to be a masquerade. The Chairman announced that, things at the lab as they are, the party would be held on his yacht, the *Star-maker*, moored at Lake Travis, the man-made lake that sidewinds for a hundred kilometers northwest of Austin.

To force Archangelsky to attend has proved nearly impossible, for Slava has no more desire than he does to confront former colleagues who view him as a criminal. Machuzak himself has had second, third thoughts and only a week on their mutual racks has persuaded them. But as he at last reaches the designated marina, Nathaniel knows that the hour to get an answer to Lorenzo's question is at hand and he will not shirk from his duty. *In vino veritas.*

As he crosses the *Starmaker*'s gangplank, a whiff of a live *balalaika* band reaches his ears and he glances around. He has seen such boats only in dreams and otherworldly advertisements. No super-modern cruiser resembling a UFO, *Starmaker* is outfitted in dark woods and shining brass, which lend it the feel of a past age. Lighting everywhere is soft and recessed, the lower deck partially covered by an arched canopy, whose roof serves as the upper deck. *Starmaker*, Garrett let drop, is his little yacht, only sixty meters. Its elegance, enhanced by the setting sun, seems out of place not only in this world but on a lake dotted with the last water skiers and windsurfers of the season.

Machuzak steps aboard. Toshi, Slava and their wives are already circulating among the guests; Abbuhl and Wilson. Good. D'Abro as well. Nevertheless, as perfectly anticipated, once-familiar faces turn from him, absolute blanks, granting no hint of history or recognition. Only Theresa, dressed in her most glittering gown, approaches with a glass in one hand, lays her other hand on his shoulder and audaciously kisses him on the lips. Almost immediately, she withdraws her fingers to her long, necklaced throat, as if recoiling from her own boldness. Machuzak meets the eyes of those looking on curiously before walking to the bar to fortify himself.

Soon they are under way, tooling along the lake's placid waters, attracting the attention of other boaters, who sail up to the *Starmaker*, curious to discover what transpires on this iceberg floating above them. More than a few strangers request permission to come aboard and receive it.

Nathaniel enters the salon where Theresa, Garrett, Nastya and a few others have gathered around a big white cake trimmed with pink icing and inscribed with a message to Slava: "Yaroslav Borisovich Archangelsky—it ain't over yet." The cake and band are an obvious bid to soften up Archangelsky. When the crayfish whistles on the hill, as Slava likes to say. But Borisovich, already showing effects, puts his arm around Machuzak's shoulder while the others shout, "Speech! Speech!" and the *balalaika* players strum a fanfare.

With reluctance and embarrassment, Slava raises his hands. "Richard Garrett and Theresa are attempting to bribe me to return to lab. It won't work but I thank them anyway. As long as I am making speech, I also thank my wife, Nastya, for putting up with me…sometimes, and I raise my goblet to Nat Edward'ich, who has remained on two feet, or at least one, while he has put up with more than the human being should put up with. If he had sense of a flea he would resign too." Slava pauses, looks quizzically into his glass, says that he has been asking himself much recently what he would do if he had his life to live over. "Maybe I lack imagination, but I still choose fusion. You must beat the deadline."

Machuzak, to his surprise, finds himself brushing aside a tear. Nastya leans to him, saying that he must answer the toast with a longer one. "Slava and I have known each other six years, most of them within the last four months," he says simply. "I can always count on him to make a difficult situation worse. Most people on this boat believe we are saboteurs. Before the evening is out they will know otherwise. What you are doing is important. Regardless of what happens, do not give up. You can beat the deadline; you will beat the deadline."

The little speech is met by hesitant, melancholy applause. Machuzak nods only briefly as he sees Fred Abbuhl exit the room and he follows him to deck, where he joins the chief engineer at the rail, leaning over with a glass in his hand. Let's get this show on the road.

Abbuhl does not wait for him to speak, but instead offers in full drawl, "My liege, if you want to beat this deadline, there is a surefire tactic."

Machuzak turns his head, a question.

"Declare it beaten. We could do it this moment, sir." Fred gathers himself and glances at the dancers above, who are just revving up. "Ladies and gentlemen," he announces with arms raised and a voice loud enough to compete with the music, "I hereby declare GlobeTex's deadline beaten. Prometheus has ignited, indubitably, signed and witnessed on this day by me, Frederick Abbuhl the Third, head of ASSET Operations…"

Droll, Fred, very droll. Machuzak takes him by the shoulder. "And my good man," he whispers, "just how do you expect to get away with *that*?"

Abbuhl looks at him, puzzled, glances away, back again. "Why, sir, you merely lie. That's how Leonard beat the government contract for

AUSTOR. He told the government that we had achieved the target and that was that."

Good. Machuzak was hoping Abbuhl would talk more tonight. "Surely the data—"

Abbuhl concedes a sigh. "Yeah, *Herr Doktor* Professor, data is always troublesome, isn't it. But if you are Rasmussen, you just have it cooked..." Falling silent, he turns away fully and watches the dim, approaching form of Mansfield Dam, which towers above them. Then he goes below.

Machuzak makes to follow but collides with D'Abro. More stunning than ever, she is swathed in a gold dress cut nearly to her navel, her back bare, a coruscating necklace plunging nearly as far as her dress. Tonight she has resolved to be blatantly, ultimately sexy. She is startled too and stops short, but not short enough to prevent the wine in the glass she holds from spilling over her. "Damn!" she exclaims. Machuzak would prefer to stand and admire; instead he takes her by the wrist and leads her below.

He finds Abbuhl in one of the staterooms, dominated by a bed in a teak frame and a wall-sized screen facing it. Regarding the circles under the older man's eyes he says, "Fred, I need to know what happened when Rasmussen fired Jerry Wilson." The chief engineer starts, notices D'Abro, but Nathaniel won't relent and speaks as if she weren't present. "You've told me there were disagreements about the measurements. Were Wilson's measurements wrong? Did Leonard buy his silence?"

Abbuhl turns way, but not before Machuzak sees his face struggle against collapse. He must steady himself against the wall unit. "Mac," the chief says at long last, "you know how it was when Rasmussen put his arm around you, convincing you that victory needed to be obtained at all costs, that you were the point man in the charge. One day he came up to me and said, 'Fred, you don't really believe Wilson's measurements can be correct, do you? This is the whole program.'" Abbuhl seems to be watching his entire career dissolve before him. Fighting tears, attempting to retain some dignity, he turns back to Machuzak. "*Herr Doktor* Professor, I told you how it was. Wilson's measurements were low—very low—a few were higher, a couple absurdly high. We just sort of pushed, collectively, convinced ourselves that the high measurements were the ones to believe. They weren't. Jerry was right."

It was entirely believable, this group deception. It had happened often in the history of science. Cold fusion. Result Amplification by Stimulated Emission of Publicity. But this...this was a lack of moral fiber on the part of the profession that most loudly proclaimed its dedication to Truth.

"And Rasmussen paid Jerry off?" D'Abro puts in, speaking for the first time.

His blond-silver hair shining against the window, his body weighed with more than years, Abbuhl nods heavily. "Jerry was fired. His wife left him. He was broke, career ruined. A couple years later he suddenly showed up again. There were rumors. That's all I know."

"Thanks, Fred," says Machuzak, patting him on the shoulder, feeling that familiar, terrible pit in his stomach as he watches Fred slowly exit the stateroom.

"It's time to talk to Wilson," says T. J. flatly.

"First let's make a phone call." Machuzak pulls out his handset, throws the picture up on the big screen. It is late in Cadarache, France, but Mercedes doesn't appear to have been sleeping. Her 3-D shock, however, is plain when she sees who faces her. "Hello, Mercedes," Nathaniel says. "How is Cadarache? Or should I say, what are you doing in Cadarache?"

"Cadarache is fine. What I'm doing here is none of your business."

"It's very much my business given that you were an accomplice in framing me for a crime I had nothing to do with. In the end, what did your treachery get you? Not the assistant directorship."

"Who gives a damn about the assistant directorship?" she answers archly. "Jules and I are engaged to be married."

Nathaniel and T. J. exchange glances. *That* was unexpected. Nice work, Mercedes.

"You may have to postpone the wedding. I have evidence that you hacked into the programmable logic control of the helium factory and sabotaged it on the day Whitman and Moravec visited."

"What!" Mercedes' shock at the accusation seems genuine, but Machuzak is feeling merciless.

"I found the PLC address on your workstation and the password in your desk drawer."

"I swear I had nothing to do with that!" she shouts, hands going to her face. "Jesus, you can't believe I would do such a thing!"

"Can't I?" Nathaniel says icily. "Prepare for extradition."

Mercedes' eyes are flitting wildly, desperation plain.

"She's right, Doc," T. J. intervenes with a hand on Machuzak's arm. "I had the handwriting on the list of passwords checked. The last two entries don't match the others. It's someone else's."

For a moment, Machuzak looks at D'Abro without expression, then puckers his lips. "Good. Many happy returns, Mercedes," he says to the screen and ends the call. "Wilson."

D'Abro goes above.

FIFTY-FIVE

When Jerry Wilson appears at the stateroom door to find Machuzak waiting, he shudders, but can only guess what's up and nervously takes the chair offered by the detective.

"Well, boys," T. J. begins, "we got a situation here. As you know, Jerry, Dr. Machuzak has been charged with serious offenses. We got forensics, we know he was in that surge room the night before the dedication, the deuterium bottle came from the MTF and we have hard evidence that he was none too fond of Krieg-Zuber. We even got what appears to be a death threat. Gotta tell ya, Doc," she swivels on Machuzak, "people have been convicted on less."

"What's this have to do with me?" Wilson asks sharply. For the first time in a long time Nathaniel is aware that Jerry is older than himself, middle-aged bulge showing around his waist and hair silvering. His ruddy, puffy cheeks have begun to sag.

"Well, other information has been coming to light, which makes it possible that you, Jerry, were involved with this here capital sabotage. Now I've got to make a decision. You two broncos wanna duke it out?"

Neither man moves and Nathaniel must remind himself that he has not cleared himself yet.

"No? Well," T. J. goes on, "Jerry, maybe you can answer a few questions for me. Do you deny that Leonard Rasmussen kicked you off that old tokamak AUSTOR?"

The silence is terribly long. Machuzak cannot know what memories are stirring in Wilson's mind, whether he's debating whether to consult a lawyer or to reveal what was once public knowledge. Finally he answers, "Yes, it's true."

"And you thought Rasmussen was perpetratin fraud on the US government?"

Wilson nods.

"He sank your career, blackballing you from one lab to another. Your wife walked out. So you blackmailed him—he rehired you and was payin you off to keep quiet and you've been wanderin around from one low-level position to another ever since."

"It's true," he whispers.

"I know," affirms D'Abro, "I checked your bank deposits. But all that didn't restore your career and you decided to torpedo the demonstration to get back at Rasmussen."

"No!" Wilson suddenly shouts. "I didn't!"

"And you framed Dr. Machuzak by puttin the sulfur hexafluoride bottle in his lab—"

"No!" Wilson shouts again. "It came from his lab!"

"Why me, Jerry?" interjects Machuzak, peering hard. "What have I ever done to you?"

Wilson returns the stare, and it is not friendly. He remains silent, unreadable. T. J. tells Jerry that the silicon and carbon impurities they found in the deuterium bottle indicate that it originated in his lab, not Machuzak's.

"I-don't-know-what-the-hell-you're-talking-about!" Jerry exclaims once more, punching out each word. "I didn't do it," he hisses through his teeth.

"All right, boys," T. J. says, raising her hands. "Here's what I'm gonna do. On that SF$_6$ bottle where somebody replaced the label, it was a little sticky and I got me a hair sample." She has the attention of both men and approaches them, taking a pair of scissors out of her purse. "I got warrants for your hair too. Gentlemen, if you please." She steps up to Wilson, snips off a sample, then turns to Machuzak. "Actually, I already have a few of yours." Machuzak smiles. It's the closest thing to a joke D'Abro's made in a long while, but she takes a new sample anyway.

"Now, I'm gonna take the launch into town. I'll be back in a few hours. Before you try to leave this boat, remember the sharks in the water. By the way, I also had those handwriting samples from Mercedes' desk checked. Forensics'll settle this all by midnight."

D'Abro moves to the door, but that's as far as she gets.

"All right!" Wilson shouts, stretching out the words as he rises. "What did you expect? The goddamned bastard destroyed my life, my whole fucking life. I couldn't get work anywhere, we had no money, my wife couldn't take it. I had to leave the country for two years." The bashful Wilson everyone knew has vanished from sight, to be replaced by a bitter, hardened man, raging against the world. "You can't imagine what it's like to have your whole career, everything, trashed because of somebody's fucking ego. He was *wrong*. He was *lying*. That machine *didn't* work. Rasmussen *cooked* the data. They all did, fucking assholes…"

Wilson has more of Machuzak's sympathy than he could possibly know, but again he asks, "Why frame me, Jerry?"

"You're one of them. You never lifted a finger for me."

Machuzak feels Wilson's accusations are unjust, but he has long since ceased believing that he is a figure of universal esteem; D'Abro allots him no time for contemplation.

"How'd you do it, Jerry?" she asks levelly.

A shadow flashes furtively across Wilson's face, he wipes his forehead with the back of his hand and plunges ahead. "It's like Machuzak laid out at the press conference, pretty much…" Almost exactly. Wilson went into the surge room, late, coming through one of the old tunnels. He didn't need to badge himself in. Lipman had already departed and nobody was around. He was smart enough to wear gloves and clean-room slippers from the pentagon assembly unit, he cut the busbar with a torch, put a hose through a convenient hole in the surge-room wall. As everybody knows, it didn't go off. He was one of the first people down there after the fault light went on and in the confusion managed to remove the hose without anyone noticing. He put the deuterium bottle in the rack where Lipman and Faberman eventually found it. The hard way. He wasn't sure anyone would ever notice the tank, but later moved the SF_6 bottle into Machuzak's lab, just in case.

"I wish I could have blown the whole machine sky high," he says angrily, halts and, almost as an afterthought, looks quizzically at D'Abro and adds, "I didn't mean to kill anybody, least of all Lipman."

Machuzak believes him, actually. "And the helium factory?"

"A few years ago I was programming for Cochran. My password still works. It was easy to get into the programmable logic control from my handset. When the lightning struck…" He moves his thumb. "Simple."

T. J. and Mac glance at each other, nodding. Apparently it was, simple. Now Machuzak abruptly changes course. "Tell me, Jerry, what did you do with your cold-fusion apparatus?"

Wilson returns the question with a dull stare. "Huh? I thought I'd try to get cold fusion. Everybody tried it sooner or later. I would have cleaned up. I needed to."

"That's all?"

"What the hell are you talking about?" His anger has erupted again.

"Mac," T. J. interrupts severely. "Can it." She walks over to Wilson and tells him that he's under arrest. She cuffs him to the chair, leads Machuzak out of the stateroom, locks the door and calls for a police helicopter. Now that they are more or less alone, she smiles at him, a genuinely open smile. "I'm truly sorry about everything, Doc, but you know, it was all part of my plan."

"Huh?" *This* doesn't compute.

"Oh yeah, bein that we had a real scientific investigation on our hands and that some of this stuff wasn't exactly in the police manual, I needed a little help. I knew if I tightened the screws enough, you'd figure it out."

"Why you—"

He is cut off by her grin and an affectionate finger to his lips. The only possible response is to laugh.

"I guess no conspiracy," she sighs. "Seems I owe you a hundred."

"Balard is coming out clean," Machuzak acknowledges, "other than that we riled him up so much that he's declared all-out war. But you know, solving one scientific puzzle inevitably leads to a deeper one." He reveals his heavy-water discoveries, his belief that Wilson has been poisoning Rasmussen.

T. J. struggles to hear him out, but when he's done, she exclaims, "Doc, that's the most cockamamie story I've ever heard!"

"More cockamamie than the rest of this?"

"By a long shot. Slow poisoning by heavy water? It's not cockamamie, it's positively medieval." They're now shouting at each other, like lovers, to the amusement of passersby. Neither of them understands. "You guys are the weirdest bunch I've met in my damned life. Let me tell ya something, Doc, in my business you take what you can get. *That charge* would *never* stick. Ockham's razor, shit… The most likely explanation is that you made it yourself, in your own lab." She peers at him with a gaze balanced perfectly between jest and accusation and he is forced to laugh again, nervously. "Let it go," she says.

Machuzak takes a moment to return to equilibrium and concedes, "I guess you're right. But hold that hundred. There's still Park. I don't see where he fits yet."

"Neither do I," says T. J., "but let's drop those charges. Come on up. I've got an announcement to make."

"About those hair samples—"

"Oldest police trick in the book. Pure bluff. I never had the handwriting checked either."

She takes his hand.

FIFTY-SIX

Above: moonlight and commotion. The yacht has just turned from the dam with its great sluice gates and greater shoulders of rock while onlookers wave from the roadway above. Young women who have climbed aboard in cutoffs and halter tops kick and fall on their butts to the accelerating huff of an asthmatic accordion. Nastya intercepts Nathaniel, loops her arms around his neck and attempts to lead him in some saccharine-drenched romance. She confides that her prodigal husband has been absent much recently, drunk the remainder, that their marriage is rapidly headed toward the shoals. "Wait," Nathaniel advises.

At that moment, D'Abro seizes a microphone from the bandleader and calls for attention. The music subsides and passengers gather round. "Ladies and gentlemen," she says as a skyrocket whizzes off into nowhere, "I have an important announcement. Additional evidence connected to the sabotage has come to light, and I'm having all charges against Drs. Machuzak and Archangelsky dropped. I offer my sincerest apologies for the distress I've caused them; I wish I could offer something more. I am publicly requesting that Dr. Archangelsky rejoin the lab."

A chorus of startled gasps and murmurs follows, even unconcealed disappointment, but when a police helicopter noisily descends and Wilson is hustled aboard, those aboard the *Starmaker* must concede that the situation has seriously changed. Abbuhl offers his hand to Machuzak and Slava, while Cochran gapes and turns away from them without a word. She isn't alone.

Slava, now drunk as a nipple, his term, raises his glass and agrees to return to CFRC, then to some scattered applause says mysteriously, "To tritium."

Finally, Theresa steps forward and declares that she'd be pleased if Nathaniel Machuzak would resume his role of acting director. The general reaction her proposal evokes is tentative except for one: Krieg-Zuber immediately detaches himself from the others, tilts toward her with a curled fist and shouts, "I forbid it, Mrs. Rasmussen!" There can be no doubt that he means it. In an uncontrolled rage he advances on Theresa with hands raised. She takes a frightened step backwards; Nathaniel interposes himself, takes one look at The Terminator's sluggish arm and—decks him.

"Stay out of my control room," he warns, standing over the prostrate figure.

Despite Cyrus' fury when he finally staggers to his feet, T. J. merely answers his demands that she take in Machuzak with a shrug: "Dr. Krieg-Zuber, this is Texas."

From the bar Slava applauds with an appreciative, if shocked, grin but stows it when Nathaniel saunters over and asks, "What did you mean by that?"

"By what?" Archangelsky answers, feigning surprise.

"Tritium."

With a crook of his finger, Slava motions for the bartender to pour a couple shots of vodka. Clinking glasses and downing them, Slava offers a pickle. "Everything depends on tritium now, doesn't it?" Nathaniel searches for what is missing here, but the Russian offers nothing more except, "I have become drinking buddy with Darrell Whitman. He suggests I apply for job at Novatech."

"*What!*" Machuzak exclaims at the top of his voice, as surprised by this as by anything recently. Slava claimed he never met Whitman.

"Interesting company," the Russian remarks.

No time is granted to clarify Archangelsky's meaning, for none else but The Chairman then wedges his bulk between them, throwing his arms over their shoulders. "Well, I'm glad everything has been cleared up, boys, and with you on board again, Dr. Archangelsky, we stand a chance… I'm real sorry for everything that's happened."

"I wish you could have been sorry two months ago," Nathaniel replies, causing the fat man to flinch with a wounded expression. As hard as it is to believe, Nathaniel realizes he has hurt Richard Garrett. "I'm sorry," he says, in no apologetic mood, but recognizing that he must forgive what is human for everyone's sake, including his own.

All pardoned, Garrett asks to speak to Machuzak below. As they enter The Chairman's private stateroom, with columns supporting the ceiling, a king-size bed, three-meter screen and Jacuzzi, Nathaniel says, "Tell me, Richard, I've never been able to ask, why did you invest in CFRC? Surely you realized it would never turn a profit in your lifetime."

"It's not about profit, son. What's the point of having money if you don't do anything with it…? You know, I look at my kids and I want to be sure they don't go through what my generation has gone through. And since the government is about as useful as a cow in a bog hole, somebody should do something."

"That's it?"

Garrett shrugged. "What did ya expect? It's nice to discover life on Mars every couple years but space isn't the only frontier… I do wonder whether I did right by picking Rasmussen."

"You picked him?" Nathaniel asks with raised alertness.

"I should say he came beggin. ANFRL had collapsed. I was actually plannin to choose Balard but Leonard put it out that Jules César advocated shuttin down the US program in favor of ITER and wanted Princeton closed. I bought it, but Leonard was lying. Rasmussen himself shut down Princeton by building ASSET. He mighta suffered a cut to save both labs, but he made sure Princeton took the bullet." Machuzak listened. Some of this he had missed in the diaries, but surprise was now a thing of the past.

"Leonard had the greatest ego of anyone I ever met, myself included. One night at Sugar's he's braggin to his lap dancer, 'Darlin, I enjoy influencing Congress, especially in real time. I watch C-Span and send my recommendations direct to the floor.' He did, too, Christ. When he learned that the Whitmans had funneled off a chunk, Len took a shotgun to Big Bad Roy's house, planning to blow his brains out. I tied him up myself."

At this point, Machuzak merely nods, numb to revelations, confirmations.

"Gotta admit, though, Leonard did a lot for the Asian programs, Korea, Japan, China, collaborating with them, offering them our designs and expertise. And ya know, if we fail, if ITER fails, they'll carry on… Are we gonna fail, Mac?"

The eternal question of the damned. "I don't know, but now that the saboteur's confessed, we stand a better chance. So far Toshi hasn't come up with the stroke of genius I'd hoped. Maybe it's too late."

"What Leonard did to that man…" Garrett whispers reflectively from the edge of the sofa on which he's sitting.

"What?" Machuzak asks.

"Everything you can imagine. If I hadn't picked up the tab, Toshi'd be on the streets. Helluva thing to see talent like that wasted… If we only had more time—"

"Force it from Moravec," Nathaniel cuts him off bluntly.

"How do you intend to do that?" a Moravec avatar answers, entering the room.

Machuzak is startled, Garrett less so. "You *did* request everybody."

"I was in the area," he says via the bot. In the past few moments there had been more helicopter noises.

Nathaniel stands. Any affability the CEO once displayed is gone. Neither does Machuzak offer a greeting; instead he gathers himself and puts to Moravec all that Slava has divulged to him: Niger, uranium, murder.

Moravec listens, considers, darkens—and laughs. "Dr. Machuzak, if this is blackmail you'll have to do better. I am not the only energy baron who's turned green," he tosses a glance at Garrett. "Who in this country remembers conflicts that took place decades ago in Africa—or cares? Who will believe such preposterous allegations? The International Criminal Court? Hah. The only thing that will come out of this is movie rights."

Machuzak says he knows the Whitmans are holding him hostage.

"Whose blackmail is blacker, yours or theirs? And how are you so sure?"

"Monteverdi."

At hearing the word, Moravec on-screen noticeably pales but recovers. "Try harder, Dr. Machuzak. I *will* see you at zero hour. Good luck." With that the avatar turns and exits. Shortly, the whine of helicopter rotors is audible again.

For a few moments Garrett and Machuzak sit in silence. "Talk about sleepin with the devil… Well, son," he slaps his leg ruefully, "remind me never to hire you as a wedding planner…and get that machine to ignite in sixty-six days…" With a bite of his lip he glances up at Machuzak. "You wanna see Leonard?"

"He's here?"

The Chairman nods. "In the dining room. He wanted to say good-bye to everyone. I warn you, he doesn't look good. Nature sure is a hard mistress."

Nathaniel walks forward to the salon rimmed by Japanese screens, where he finds Leonard slumped in his wheelchair next to the table. A large, recessed portal illuminates the room from above with a soft light harsh enough to reveal that this is the last time he will see Rasmussen alive. He requests of the other guests a few moments alone and, as they depart, locks the door. Standing before Leonard, he wonders whether he can at this late juncture reverse the affliction, at least reveal his suspicions. He also considers murdering him.

"Hello, Nathaniel," Leonard mumbles, barely mobile, hardly audible. "Take my hand."

Machuzak refuses. By this huge lacquered table with its formal chairs, he stands over the dying man, weighing, struggling. Giving no notice and affording no grace, the most difficult moment of his life has descended. The hesitation wells up, the choking that thwarts confrontation, the constriction in the throat that prevents swallowing. At last, he tries—no, he cannot—he tries again, no again, he forces himself: "Every disaster of the past months has taken place because of you. None of it was necessary. Damnit, none of it! You destroyed programs and the program you built may be a dead end. You destroyed careers...you destroyed lives. That's what I can't forgive. All because of your fucking ego. And you've left it to the rest of us to pick up the pieces. It was you who warned away Slava at Cadarache with the car bomb, wasn't it? You were the only one who knew why they were there; I stupidly told you over dinner at your house and you must have called some French lackey. Why it took me so long to realize, I don't know. I've been blind. Do you deny any of this?"

He waits for Rasmussen's answer, but the only reply he receives is a stare laden with the fading embers of a lifelong rage.

"No wonder everyone in fusion would like to kill you—maybe they all have. Who have you been? No mentor of mine, no friend. Good-bye, Leonard. Rot in hell."

It seems that Rasmussen is struggling to say something, but Machuzak has finished waiting and closes the door behind him.

* * * *

Above, guests gathered at the bow clap their hands in delight as one skyrocket after another shoots into the night sky and explodes. Women giddily point to the water, which reflects the fireworks with clarity and distortion, and everyone cups an ear to the echo of the booms as they ricochet off the coastline. The commotion has certainly not gone unnoticed by the natives. Three canoes, propelled by a war party of furiously paddling Indians, are rapidly closing on *Starmaker*. Wearing full headdresses and paint, the raiders glide directly up to the port side and climb aboard. For a few moments they stand shaking their weapons and shrieking, then they accept the drinks offered them and join in the dancing.

Toshi, seeing Nathaniel alone, approaches him at the stern. "This party reminds me of the battle of Asculum," he says, surveying the wreckage. "No one remains on his feet."

"Leonard is downstairs dying," Nathaniel says.

The Japanese-Korean rarely imbibes and remains stone sober.

"I know, I overheard your conversation. You have seen too much."

Is that possible? "Have you said good-bye?"

"Never," answers Matsushima impassively but hiding nothing. "How naïve you were, Nathaniel, refusing to believe that it was not Krieg-Zuber but Rasmussen who did everything to discredit me, who banished me to Alpha Site, poisoned the federal agencies against me, shut down my computer accounts... You threatened him too. He understood the implications of your resonance heating experiment when you didn't. He knew it potentially jeopardized his own investment in neutral beams. Krieg-Zuber defended you. Oh yes, I heard the conversation. He hated you, as you did him, but he respected your abilities."

Machuzak can no longer deny anything but it remains hard.

"This was not all. The real reason Rasmussen desperately needed to get rid of me was that I knew Wilson was right about AUSTOR and was prepared to say so. Only Garrett saved me." Toshi smiles, taking a sip of juice. "Now I will have the last laugh."

Without saying a word, Nathaniel abandons Matsushima at the rails, only to cross paths with Archangelsky, who now drunk enough to stand on his eyebrows, staggers up to him and puts his arm across his friend's shoulders. "You aren't happy, *brat*."

"The betrayals I can get over. My own delusions are harder."

Archangelsky nods. "This is because you are the most idealistic idiot I've ever met. Must have been raised by wolves. Listen, maybe I told you, Lorenzo fought a duel with his own double and killed himself. Don't."

Machuzak levels a surprised stare at his companion and assures him that he harbors no such intentions.

Slava, barely upright, wags his finger at Nathaniel. "You know, this whole shitty affair is like the old story of the two Jews on a train." Machuzak shakes his head; he doesn't know it. For a moment Slava struggles through the haze to remember. "On the train, one Jew says to the other, 'Ver are you going?' and the second answers, 'To Zhitomir.' And the first says to himself, 'Vat a sly fox. He told me he's going to Zhitomir so I'll think he's going to Zhmerinka, but if I think he's going to Zhmerinka, I have fallen for his ruse. He can't fool me—he must be going to Zhitomir.'"

That about captures it, thinks Nathaniel as the *Starmaker* nears port, that about captures it. By the time the yacht docks in the early morning, most of the passengers have passed out on deck, but those yet sensible hear the whisper that Leonard Rasmussen has died.

FIFTY-SEVEN

Six hours later, as the first messages of condolence begin pouring in from around the world, Machuzak arrives at the gate. Quarantine is behind him. The protestors do not mourn and their numbers this dawn are large, mood at the boil. A small, well-dressed coterie of Christians proclaims to the cameras that the CFRC experiments herald this year's End of Days, and they intend to prove it. Greenpeace pugnaciously taunts the militia, whom the Scientologists are simultaneously attempting to recruit with copies of L. Ron Hubbard's *Way to Happiness*.

At the exact moment Machuzak steps in, one of the crowd picks up a rock. Nathaniel grabs her wrist—too late. Tear-gas canisters are flying, tumbling; they roll sputtering along the ground and in the next instant everyone is scattering pell-mell as coughs and screams rise into the air.

"Enough!" Machuzak shouts, retreating with the others. When the air has cleared he walks back choking to the gates and orders the Guard off the premises. Only the governor can make that decision, the captain replies. "Are you in charge of the lab again, sir?"

"In charge."

For once luck smiles on them: sirens wailing, T. J. pulls up and jumps out of her car, quickly appraises the situation and phones the governor. By a miraculous alignment of stars she manages to reach him. Seconds after she hands the phone to the recalcitrant officer he says, "Yes, sir," and orders his troops to stand down.

With a flourish Machuzak opens the fence and shouts, "Come on! Watch first, protest later." As always they are reluctant, but once he shoves the Tritium Kid through the gate the rest follow.

By the time the parade reaches the main building, the rifles and sandbags are coming off the roof and the Guard is packing up. The entire lab has gathered by the lake, cheering. Reporters crowd around, forcing on Machuzak their terrorist question: How do you feel? When he answers that he feels no different than he has since Detective D'Abro threatened to arrest him a month ago, they respond with incomprehension. "How is it possible?"

Machuzak, scratching his chin, invents an answer: "All experience is interesting. Anyway, someone needed to keep a cool head around here."

He has baffled the journalists. Toshi, standing nearby, adds, "The master allows things to happen. And if you want to be reborn you must die." Machuzak gently shushes him. Many of the lab hands who weren't at Garrett's shindig approach him now and slap him on the back, saying they knew he was innocent all along. Much of him wants to tell them to fuck off, but instead he answers their congratulations and good wishes with a noncommittal smile.

"Why don't you tell them to fuck off?" prompts Slava, regarding the general hypocrisy. "Spineless worms."

"Slava, the lab first... And remember, two more months."

Precisely, sixty-five days. Crowd after him, Machuzak passes through the Gates of Hell and tears off the sheet of the deadline calendar. He tells everyone to observe from the visitors' gallery and they spread out above the big glass windows.

Below, the control room's tawdriness is matched only by the somberness of its mood, the fresh news of Leonard's death casting its darker shadow over the deadline pall. Hasschler stands at his traditional place, but even with the sabre in hand appears more a zombie than a living human being. Further shocked stares greet Machuzak and Archangelsky's entrance, followed by more tentative and scattered applause. Accompanying them, T. J. repeats the announcement she made aboard the *Starmaker*, which sensibly lightens the atmosphere, then takes Nathaniel aside for a moment alone.

"Well, Doc," she tells him, "Dragonmaster's disappeared and that truly worries me—"

"For sure," Machuzak breathes.

"I'll keep on him from downtown, but there's nothing I can do here anymore. Just wanted to say thanks for a helluva ride and good-bye for now. Sorry for all the fuck-ups."

"Well, in science, you get the right answer only after you've made all possible mistakes."

"Seems to be a general rule. I'll be back for ignition, for sure."

"I hope so," he smiles.

"Do it, for me..."

"We'll give it our best shot."

"...for the world."

The two embrace lightly, kissing each other on the cheek.

"Ya know," she says as an afterthought, glancing at all the equipment. "You folks might consider a virtual tokamak—it would sure be a lot simpler than all this..."

"When the world uses virtual energy, we'll build a virtual tokamak."

"Keep in touch," she says smiling, and with her fingers trailing, disappears through the doors.

* * * *

Without ceremony Machuzak takes over. His first act is to shake Orne and Fournier awake and have everyone clean the place up. He calls for a moment of silence, which is broken by the deadline clock, and leads them in some calisthenics, which he proposes to institutionalize. He reopens access to social media for five minutes an hour.

Since the recovery from the helium leak and blown filament, the situation has not significantly changed. In his absence ASSET attained a Q of four, but ITER also inched upward, fighting something unknown but remaining ahead in power and pulse length. And so the great metallic horses continue galloping onward in their desperate race, a race in which the finish line lies at an unknown distance and in which it may never be given them to cross.

Having assessed the state of affairs, Nathaniel takes Toshi aside and confronts him. "I want your ideas, now, Matsushima, you've been stalling."

Toshi shakes his head. "No, Nathaniel, I have been trying to convince Thad to try liquid lithium. He is hesitant. It has never been attempted on this scale before."

Toshi had come up with this thought some years ago, but to get it past Krieg-Zuber—no, Rasmussen—he was forced to have it fronted by others. Nathaniel nods. "I'll speak to him."

With a glance at the ITER control screen, Hasschler clenches his teeth and agrees. Larissa passes on the order and at the base of the doughnut the door to a lithium trough slides open. Soon the element is being evaporated to coat the torus walls, effectively creating tokamak walls of liquid metal. In theory lithium should prevent dirt from being recycled into the plasma and enhance performance. In theory.

Everyone, Matsushima particularly, is pacing but the first shot goes well, the second one better. All day it is back and forth with ITER, ITER by virtue of its size, Prometheus by virtue of its design. One record after another is shattered. By midnight, ASSET has crept ahead and when Nathaniel awakes from the cot where he's crashed in a remote corner of the control room, they remain in front. The magic number five looms brightly within sight.

Every pulse/ Now is more/ Six seconds longer/ Than before/ By using Burma-Shave.

ITER lacks a lithium trough and across the Atlantic the tension on Balard's face is showing in technicolor as the huge man once again dominates his control center. An ITERnik presents him with some data and without any warning Jules César explodes, hurling the screen to the floor.

It takes a while for Machuzak to piece together what's going on in Cadarache, but from the data streaming over the Web and all the chatter between the two control rooms—oh yes, with friends and colleagues on both sides of the Pond, applause and obscenities are running a distant second to nonstop covert texts and twitter posts, and soon Nathaniel learns from Slava that ITER is having trouble with high-field pulses. They zoom in to observe Balard's mortification at being told that ITER's great magnets are not behaving as designed. With pulse after pulse, their critical temperature—the temperature above which the magnets abruptly stop superconducting—is creeping downward.

Machuzak swallows. This is unalloyed bad news for ITER. Superconducting magnets simply mustn't be allowed above their critical temperature and if that is falling, ever more effort, and helium, will be required to keep the magnets at operating temperature.

Now Jules César blanches and Machuzak can no longer doubt what has just taken place. Seconds later he hears it over the webcast: in attempting a thirteen-Tesla shot, ITER has suffered a quench. This is serious business. It means the magnet temperature has risen to roughly 18 degrees and the magnets have gone critical. They've instantly lost their superconductivity and become ordinary electromagnets. They've quenched. Nathaniel doesn't know exactly why. Maybe it was loss of helium, maybe it was stray magnetic fields that force the niobium-tin filaments in their conduits to rub against each other and heat up.

Machuzak does know that ITER, as ASSET, is designed to deal with quenches. Prometheus' magnets contain no fewer than three quench-detection mechanisms: pressure sensors to detect boiling helium, fiber optics whose properties change with a rise in temperature, ordinary wire whose resistance can be compared to the superconductor's.

It ain't overkill. When the sensors detect a quench you have a thousandth of a second, less, to fire the giant circuit breakers that shunt all the electrical energy circulating in the magnets—out. He didn't show them to Whitman and Moravec, but each breaker is the size of a small room. If they fail, you've got a backup: explosive resistors, the size of big paint cans, which—well, explode. You use them once.

If the whole system fails, the electrical energy stored in the great magnets has nowhere to go but into the magnets themselves. Then they explode with the energy of several hundred kilograms of high explosive and the machine is destroyed. That is why Diana Cochran has been worried about straining the liquid helium supply.

FIFTY-EIGHT

Weeks hurtle by. Nature, like protestors, will grant no respite for mourning, Theresa tells Nathaniel on his return, and she is right. Few at CFRC have the strength for lamentations over a director already well absent in spirit and Leonard Rasmussen, according to his last wishes, is cremated at a private ceremony long on fanfare and short on attendees. Nathaniel watches Theresa scatter his ashes over the hills above the lab but any voice for eulogy has deserted him. If he feels anything, it is utter emptiness. As the winds carry Leonard away forever, Theresa turns to him with a faint smile, takes his arm and says, "Let's get back to work."

* * * *

Both Cadarache and Austin have continued to battle the intransigence of the plasma and mysterious magnet deficiencies, but both machines have consistently been operating above a Q of four. As five comes into sight, that itself is a cause for some cheer. Slowly, quietly, around CFRC rumors begin to circulate that something has changed. Mostly the mood has changed. There is still no certainty that they can pull it off, but the uncertainty is a victory over the previous certainty and for the first time people begin to whisper about winning. Then the odds on the betting board suddenly drop to 50:1 against ignition, and the odds against the assassination of Moravec fall to 10:1 in favor. Each shift now joins in for calisthenics or Tai Chi. Crew members occasionally walk with a spring in their steps. Ever more lab personnel drop by, asking brightly, "What's up?"; protests at the gate have ceased and instead visitors, young and old, line the gallery above while vendors sell hot dogs and fajitas. Not to be left out, the *Statesman* website has begun to publish a daily Deadline Calendar at the bottom left of their homepage, summarizing the latest events: no change from yesterday.

Out of Whitman's subcommittee in Washington indistinct signals of discontent emerge. Should the rescission be put on hold? Whitman instantly quells potential mutiny, but his webcasts take on the first tinge of desperation. "These experiments are getting ever more reckless," he warns one night, resplendent in buckskin, "and cannot be allowed to continue. I am formally demanding that the governor of Texas call a halt to them."

Theresa, now officially director ex-officio, has continued her daily webcasts and loses no time in her counterattack. Within an hour, cameras pan over the octagon, Chen the armadillo in the background, to show her shaking hands with the governor. Then, casting her gaze directly at her nemesis, she says, "The senator is worried. Tell us, Senator, why should the prospect of our success worry you?"

Machuzak and the other scientists pay no attention to the politics, though. They are too busy, too determined.

* * * *

Toshi appears to be getting somewhere: the lithium wall has significantly improved performance. From day to day the goal seems to lie just beyond the touching, then it recedes with the next plasma intransigence or equipment failure. ASSET surges ahead, sometimes falls behind while ITER's intermittent magnet problems baffle the Cadarache scientists.

After the morning's runs on day t-minus-thirty Hasschler makes an announcement that elicits sudden cheers. It is one of those obscure technical things, which makes every difference—alpha heating. Helium nuclei—alpha particles—are the waste product of the deuterium-tritium reactions, but sufficient prodding can force them to collide with the tritium and deuterium circulating in the doughnut, and contribute their energy toward fusion. The theorists insist that alpha heating is necessary to achieve ignition. Now they've got it. Prometheus has crossed a watershed and Hasschler, bowing on the captain's deck to applause, calls for two bottles of champagne.

"I want to attempt alpha channeling," Toshi says.

Hasschler regards him skeptically. "That is risky, Toshi, very risky. It has never been tried."

"Some time ago we entered the territory of the untried. Archangel-sky's codes should be able to adjust the fields and rf heating."

"Do it," Machuzak says simply.

The strategy is a delicate one. Normally, much heating energy is wasted on all the electrons floating around, which don't contribute directly to fusion. By a clever injection of radio waves and twisting of the fields, alpha channeling selectively guides the energy to the alphas, increases their heating ability and catalyzes the reactions. In theory it should work.

Hasschler gives the command. They try a few shots. The initial results are negative, nothing whatsoever but a fall-off in performance.

Before the day is out Thaddeus has begun to fume in his characteristic fashion; Matsushima calls for patience. "After all, this is science."

"Is it?" Hasschler shoots back. "I call it black magic!"

Theresa, walking into the control room to relieve Nathaniel, interposes herself. "Gentlemen, get some sleep." She may not be a physicist, but she is right.

* * * *

Throughout the night experiments proceed with Archangelsky asking for adjustments. At dawn he disappears, turning over to Orne his series of planned experiments. Nathaniel wakes up from the cot in the corner, and after a cup of coffee and Ritalin, he relieves Theresa.

She briefs him on the night's progress and prepares to return home, but at t-minus ten seconds on the morning's first shot something takes place that has never occurred in the history of CFRC. Without warning Prometheus loses electrical power. At the same instant everyone's head jerks up at the sound of a faint, distant roar.

"Jesus!" shouts Larissa. "MG set number one has gone!"

No way. Machuzak, Theresa and a dozen others tear out of the control room through the big tunnel, grabbing hard hats from the racks along the way, exchanging worried—no, disbelieving—no, incredulous—glances. No way in hell a motor-generator could have failed.

Long before they surface at pentagon one, the smell of burning oil is assaulting their nostrils. By the time they are inside, the techs have opened up the pit and everyone stands watching, pygmies at the rim of those 700-ton flywheels, which cause earthquakes, which according to legend store enough momentum to roll clear to the Gulf of Mexico. Which power their experiments. The wheel is still spinning, screaming horribly as gray smoke pours out of the pit. Accompanying that banshee's wail is a torrent of water as the big tower outside floods the pit with emergency cooling water, turning it into a great fountain. Machuzak and the others stand stunned. Even if they could hear each other above the noise, no one would have the words. They cover their ears. Nearby, a tech is shitting in a hard hat.

On the way back to the bunker, Johanssen, a big, bearded tech wearing a Harley Davidson T-shirt, says with awe, "Man, I thought it was a dive bomber comin in, and all of a sudden, all this smoke pouring out of the pit. Then this incredible crashing, like…like King Kong tearing the place apart. The parts were blowing holes in the air diverters. I fuckin dove for cover." His voice lowers to a hush. "I thought it was the end of the world."

As Machuzak listens to Johanssen, he reminds himself that these monsters spin in pits for a reason.

In fact, hours go by before the flywheel has slowed enough for the brakes to stop it, and then everyone returns to the MG room to view the stricken colossus. The flywheel seems slightly cockeyed and the smell of smoke is still strong in the air. Soon after they arrive a flashlight followed by a head pokes its way up between the flywheel spokes.

"We lost oil pressure under the thrust bearing," the engineer says. "The entire assembly has fried."

The news couldn't be worse. The entire seven hundred tons rests on a single bearing and the bearing floats on a thin layer of high-pressure oil—or did. Christ almighty! To repair it, the whole assembly, the great flywheel itself will have to be removed. Machuzak glances at the crane above, knowing that it could be weeks. They don't have the time or the manpower, but they do have spares.

"Is number three ready, gentlemen?" Abbuhl asks.

The power engineers nod.

"So be it," he says. Machuzak can see that Fred is once more dreaming of retirement.

If you dislike/ MG failures/ Slow down/ Till you/ Can read these signs/ Burma-Shave.

* * * *

The collapse of motor-generator number one leaves everyone shaking for the day. Although MG-3 begins operations promptly, an air of unreality descends well before number one has stopped its futile rotation. Nobody can concentrate or talk about anything else. Fournier offers 300:1 against ignition and only Machuzak takes him up on it. The bookmakers cease taking bets on the assassination of Moravec, regarding it as a dead certainty.

Strangely, Nathaniel finds himself once again overtaken by the Schubertian calm that possessed him during his quarantine. "Come on," he says, slapping a few guys on the back, "forget the fucking deadline. Let's do this for the love of it and we will win even if we lose."

His proposal is met by incomprehension, by the zomboid stares, which have returned. He then offers another suggestion. "Why don't we call it quits for the day. Let third shift take over. We'll get a fresh start in the morning."

* * * *

Morning: Slava tweaks his software, which actively controls Prometheus' magnetic fields and radio-frequency heating. Larissa gives the word and the countdown begins.

"... zero."

A minute later the terminals around the room are lighting up with the data from this run. Archangelsky, Matsushima, Hasschler...everyone crowds around.

"*Bozhe moi*," Slava crosses himself. Not ignition, but a significant advance. They are closing in on a burning plasma.

Hasschler orders five bottles of champagne cracked.

For the next days they explore the territory that Toshi and Archangelsky have staked out; the results appear sound. But thoughts of surrender have not crossed anyone's mind in Cadarache, and the ITERniks manage to duplicate each Austin success. Both sides are simultaneously angered that their secrets have leaked to their opponents and resigned to the knowledge that it must be so. This is science, Slava has said, what remains of it.

As the two machines push each other onward and record after record falls, elation grows, spirits become more determined. By four and a half times breakeven, the ASSET magnets have quenched several times. Bad news, and an irritated Hasschler must call a huddle to decide what to do about it. Now. The fact that the problem has proved far worse at ITER, where their wayward magnets have suffered quenches on a daily basis, provides only distant consolation.

Toshi is hardly paying attention. Day t-minus-seventeen. Peering over Slava's shoulder at the latest data he lifts his head and says, "I request diamonds."

"What!" growls an already impatient Hasschler, turning with a face etched with perplexity and exasperation. Machuzak, too, can hardly believe his ears. A murmur arises from the visitors' gallery above.

"You heard me, diamonds. Crushed diamonds. Diamond powder."

"Toshi," says Machuzak approaching the Japanese physicist, "what are you talking about?"

"Diamonds reflect x-rays," answers Matsushima with the distant air of a professor who can't be bothered. "I want to coat the tokamak walls with diamonds, and I want to run diamond powder through the cooling water."

Hasschler cannot contain himself. "This is insane!" he shouts, raising his sabre.

"Remember the hydrogen bomb," Toshi replies in the same strange, detached tone. "The fission bomb produced x-rays, which were reflected by the casing to trigger the secondary."

"We believe that is how the hydrogen bomb worked," Hasschler objects, refusing to waste another second on this nonsense. He is right: the details had never been declassified.

"Diamonds," insists Toshi.

Machuzak takes Matsushima aside by the arm, gazes into his eyes and whispers severely, "Toshi, this sounds nuts. Tell me you are sure."

Toshi stares back at the younger man with narrowed eyes and umbrage. "How can I tell you that, Nathaniel? There are no certainties now, none."

"Does it stand a chance?"

The physicist nods.

"I say we try it," Machuzak announces to all those gathered in the control room.

But Hasschler fully explodes, striking the table on the captain's deck with his weapon. "How? Damnit, tell me how!"

"One can buy artificial diamonds cheaply," Matsushima shrugs. "We'd need to crush them."

"That we can do in the machine shops," puts in Abbuhl, who has been following the argument with disbelief and intrigue.

Machuzak gets on the phone and tells the purchasing officer to find a stash of diamonds. "At light speed." Hasschler storms out. Toshi isn't far behind.

FIFTY-NINE

The order goes out. To receive the diamonds, crush them, inject them will take a few days, which do not exist. With each passing hour the great spectre of the deadline has become more tangible, until now it confronts them with a hand beckoning to oblivion. The reality hits home on day seventeen when Garrett reiterates Moravec's threat to be present on Zero Hour. "Like the devil at midnight, he intends to collect." Machuzak shrugs off The Chairman's warning and the gallery remains packed, the spectators hopeful, while among them vendors hawk "Plasma Blast" T-shirts and "Fusion Swirl" coffee mugs.

Despite his threat to stay clear of the control room, Machuzak learns from security that Krieg-Zuber has been prowling about, at the helium factory, everywhere possible. Henderson's news is disturbing enough that he seeks out Cochran, but she was one of the first to have turned her back on him and the division head remains unforgiving in the way of those who have wronged others. She replies only that Krieg-Zuber still considers himself the rightful director and, certain that another attack is imminent, he is monitoring.

"Certain? How certain?"

Diana only shrugs.

"What is he monitoring?"

"Everything he can."

That night, the alarm sounds. To the commands of Henderson's voice over the PA, each and every person evacuates the bunker. Within minutes scientists and spectators alike are standing outside by the lake as the Emergency Unit roars up, reporting that someone phoned in a bomb threat. They pace in the cold, waiting for the bomb squad to arrive and sweep the control room. Hasschler, the entire team, is cursing the precious seconds lost. More than seconds; they spend half the night in the chilly, drizzly air, drinking coffee, cursing again.

"In heat of past weeks, Nat Edward'ich," Archangelsky says to Machuzak, "I have not forgotten Sangjun Park, but this is not him. I do not know what this is."

Nathaniel nods, walks through the crowd, on the lookout for Zuber, but spies neither the former deputy nor Toshi. At length, the bomb experts with their barking shepherds conclude that the whole thing has probably been a hoax, but that the control room door is locked. Machuzak orders Henderson to keep the crowd at bay while he grabs Theresa's arm and runs to the bunker. They pound on the door; no response. At length, Henderson arrives, they find a code that works—Krieg-Zuber's—but the door has been bolted by a crowbar thrust through the handles. Another twenty minutes pass before the techs bring a blowtorch and cut through. Machuzak cautions Henderson and he and Theresa enter the control room alone.

Before him Cyrus is sitting by himself, attention so riveted to one of the terminals that he doesn't notice the two people rushing toward him. Catching sight of Machuzak, he jumps but at that instant Nathaniel lunges and with every strength in his possession hurls Krieg-Zuber to the floor.

Machuzak stands back to catch his breath, and in that moment Krieg-Zuber struggles to his feet and levels a pistol with his good hand at the intruders. "I am through with you, Machuzak, old boy. Sit. You too, Mrs. Rasmussen." The ex-deputy, teeth clenched, beads of sweat rolling down his forehead, is more agitated than Machuzak has ever seen him and, with the gun waving erratically between him and Theresa, he is not to be disobeyed.

Nathaniel and Theresa sit before one of the monitors. "What are you doing here?" Machuzak finally breathes. "I barred you from this room."

"Doing what is required," Krieg-Zuber says with a strangled voice, a voice from on high but infused with desperation, "which until now all of you have failed to do, flattering yourself with the hope of impunity."

"What are you talking about, Cyrus?" Theresa says as calmly as she can.

"Machuzak," Krieg-Zuber ignores her, directing his words to Nathaniel, "can you really believe that Jerry Wilson—*Jerry Wilson*—was clever enough to have conceived of that deuterium sabotage on his own?"

The thought had, truly, never occurred to him. "He confessed," Nathaniel replies levelly.

"Oh yes, under pressure, but in cooperating with your detective his feeble story has lately crumbled. You wouldn't have noticed, absorbed as you are with the experiments that were mine to direct. Others may have been duped by your leftist tactics, Machuzak, but if the mysteries of nature have been closed to me, a solemn duty has nevertheless been placed on my shoulders and I will not shirk from it."

"I don't know what the hell you're talking about," Machuzak answers.

"Of course you don't!" cries Cyrus. Shaking, losing control and sweating profusely, he struggles to wipes the perspiration from his forehead with the sleeve of his bad arm as he keeps Machuzak at bay. "Wilson was working for Matsushima, correct?"

"Yes, part time," Nathaniel agrees cautiously, glancing briefly at the frozen countdown clock.

"Do you concede, Machuzak, that Matsushima loathed Leonard Rasmussen?"

When Nathaniel hesitates, Theresa answers. "That is true." Her reply is evidently made at some cost.

"Would it not be more believable that Matsushima could devise such a plot than Wilson?"

"Don't be absurd!" Machuzak exclaims, forgetting himself, but when Krieg-Zuber raises the barrel toward him, he lowers his voice. "Toshi has been here every day contributing his ideas."

"Ideas certain to destroy us."

One bad idea, disguised as a good one, Balard's words drift back to Machuzak. "Damnit, you're insane!" he shouts and Krieg-Zuber cocks his pistol.

Theresa takes Nathaniel's arm. "Mac, quiet," she says and addresses their captor. "What proof do you have, Cyrus?"

"Thank you, Mrs. Rasmussen," Krieg-Zuber bows slightly and backs up to the nearest monitor. A click later they are watching a video shot in Toshi's office, where a disgruntled Wilson is ranting about his treatment at the lab and Toshi suggests offhandedly several ways that the machine might be sabotaged, including a deuterium bomb.

Machuzak no longer bats an eye at the surveillance, but he is surprised at Theresa's expression, which approaches resignation rather than astonishment. "You've tried this tactic before," he says, again forgetting himself. "It didn't work the first time and it won't work now."

"You are much mistaken, *docteur*," Krieg-Zuber answers, gun still raised. "All of you turned your backs on Leonard, except me. Matsushima suggested the idea. You, Archangelsky and Wilson carried it out the night before the dedication. We know he was there, after all, and we know you were there at the same hour." For a moment Krieg-Zuber stares fixedly at his pistol.

The man may have gone mad, but there is too much here that can't be dismissed and Machuzak asks to phone the Austin sheriff's department for confirmation. He raises T. J. on her cell and she sadly tells him that it's true: Wilson, out on bail, has been fingering Toshi, claiming that the sabotage idea came from him. She is already en route to the lab to question Matsushima.

"Looks like he's not inventing this," Machuzak turns to Theresa.

"Ah!" cries Krieg-Zuber. "Repent! Don't stand in the way, *docteur*. All I have ever wanted is for the Mission to succeed. It hasn't been easy, being surrounded by idiots who sneer because they write computer codes, when what was required was someone who could steer the lab through treacherous waters. That person should have been me"—he thumps his chest, breathing heavily—"is me! Now you are going to pay the price!"

"You are fucking crazy!" Machuzak shouts at the same moment that Theresa, staying his arm again, says, "Give me the gun, Cyrus. We'll put you in charge of the ignition campaign."

Before anyone can react the crowd surges through the door past Henderson and Krieg-Zuber is surrounded. With labored breathing, he waves the gun wildly as he backs up to a control panel. His normally unflinching eyes blink uncontrollably, the internal conflict marked by tics and the twitches taking over his face. Suddenly as the circle closes in, he grabs his bad arm and, grimacing as if the devil has tapped him on the shoulder, swings around with his head turned skyward and drops like a stone to the floor.

With an infinite hesitation this time, Machuzak kneels to administer CPR with Henderson's aid, but it is no go. After some minutes Henderson puts his ear to his chest, hears nothing and Machuzak stands. "A man in his condition should take it easy," he says.

Another fifteen minutes pass before the Emergency Unit produces a gurney and carts the body away. As Machuzak gazes after the last of The Terminator, he turns to Theresa and says, "Where's Toshi?"

"I haven't seen him all day," she answers.

By this time, D'Abro has arrived on the scene. Wearily, Nathaniel explains what has just taken place. "What was Krieg-Zuber doing?" she wants to know.

Nathaniel has no good answer. Ari Socarides checks the computer Cyrus had commandeered, and after running some tests concludes that everything appears to be as it was, but Toshi is gone.

"Let's go," says T. J. with a motion of her head.

En route to Alpha Site Machuzak phones the Japanese physicist. No answer. They run into his lab, empty, office likewise, drive to his house in Austin. Abandoned. Every twenty minutes Nathaniel redials, leaves messages, texts, tweets, but by the end of the day, it has become clear that Matsushima does not want to be found.

* * * *

Work resumes the next morning. The diamonds have arrived, but with Toshi missing Hasschler puts his foot down and refuses to be party to such insanity. The team presses on, glumly, along the course they have chosen, with Archangelsky monitoring, adjusting his codes and progress is made. ITER has again stalled, dropped behind and the newscasts turn their focus to the protestors outside ITER's gate, vociferously demanding of the French authorities the cessation of tritium experiments. Within a few days, ASSET's lead is significant and spirits are once again high, determined.

Day t-minus 5, 3:00 p.m. Slava urgently strides up to Machuzak, takes him aside to the sleeping area and shows him the screen of his laptop. Dragonmaster Park has returned. The URL is no longer Cadarache but a site in China. Fusion World's DeLorean leads them past a squarish stone gate and a luxury hotel. "I've been there," Archangelsky whispers. "Hefei. He's not disguising his location."

The car flies them through the familiar tokamak. Emerging, they observe a cartoonish profile of Toshi hanging in the sky and a spoon lying on a smooth diviner's board, spinning wildly. The tour ends with the dragon and fish resting at their feet.

Machuzak has seen that spoon before. It is the lodestone compass from the Han Dynasty, the world's earliest magnetic compass. "*He's going for the magnets,*" Nathaniel breathes. "My God, he's going for the magnets." The entire control room darkens, recedes. Machuzak feels as if he is about to faint. Seconds, minutes pass and he does not know where he is. Only when he senses Archangelsky's hand shaking him does he come back to the immediate world.

"Are you all right?" Socarides calls from across the room. "We've got a shot coming up."

The countdown is well under way. "Twelve…eleven…ten…"

"No!" Machuzak shouts, running into the control room proper, flailing about. He catches sight of the nearest emergency stop button, flips open the plastic cover and punches it.

"What the hell!" exclaims Larissa as a series of emergency overrides lights up the COE's panel.

"I'm sorry," Machuzak bellows back. "Just hold everything."

The scientists gather on the captain's deck and Nathaniel tells them that the machine is in imminent danger.

"Damnit!" Hasschler explodes. "Soon we will be within the width of an ant's eyebrow of ignition and you tell us to stop?"

Nathaniel has regained enough presence of mind to realize that any explanation he might offer will be taken for the ravings of a lunatic and he bites his tongue.

"He's right," Archangelsky interjects, but also offers no explanation.

"For how long must we halt operations?" Hasschler demands.

"Long enough for Slava and I to get to China. Two days."

"You're out of your mind, Machuzak!" Thad touches Nathaniel's throat with the point of his sabre. "We cannot risk such time!"

The lunatic turns to Theresa, saying nothing, and she nods, once.

Nathaniel and Slava are half out the door when he calls out, "Raise Jikang Xiu, the director of the Chinese program. Tell him to have visas ready."

"You'll miss ignition," Theresa calls after him.

"We'll prevent ignition."

SIXTY

Since Machuzak's first admonition a lifetime ago, D'Abro's sweater and passport have never rested beyond arm's reach, and this time when his call reaches her she beats him and Slava to Bergstrom. By the time, twenty hours later, the three stagger into Hefei airport, Jikang Xiu, director of the Chinese Academy of Sciences' Institute of Plasma Physics, greets them with visas in hand and waves them through passport control. They declare nothing.

From the windows of the limo hurtling toward the lake, the large, spacious city remains a blur except for a pair of golden arches, a Hilton and a variegated stream of rickshaws, tricycles, ox carts and Mercedes. They have arrived at China's Daejeon, science city, but four times the size of its Korean rival. Halfway across the bridge to the peninsula, Xiu, an affable sixty-year-old, tells them in slightly accented but otherwise impeccable English, "Like many across the world, we have been glued to your desperate race with ITER and are sorry that the purpose of your visit is apparently not a happy one. But it was not entirely unexpected."

Before Machuzak or Archangelsky can ask for clarification, D'Abro interrupts, "Professor Xiu, someone at your institute is attempting to destroy ASSET."

"I have recently become aware of this myself," Xiu replies somberly. "Quite recently."

Moments later, the institute comes into view and with it, an immense construction site visible beyond, on the lakeshore. "What's that?" D'Abro exclaims despite herself.

"Our ITER. Participating in a project with thirty other countries has proved inauspicious and we decided to build one ourselves. After all, twenty billion dollars is hardly significant in the scheme of things, considering the potential payoff. As you know, manpower is still relatively cheap in China and it costs little to pay villagers to wind magnet coils. However, our machine is not a tokamak; we are attempting a tandem mirror device based on Toshi Matsushima's ideas."

Once D'Abro has recovered from the sight, she cannot help but comment on Xiu's English. His answer comes with a shrug. "I received my training at Princeton, Miss D'Abro."

The limo screeches to a halt, Xiu ushers them quickly across the rock garden with its pleasant ornamental boulders and into a white, multistoried building. "I believe you know each other," he says.

Neither Machuzak nor Archangelsky is surprised to see Matsushima waiting in the lobby.

"The gang's all here," remarks Nathaniel with a lack of amusement as sharp as his fatigue.

"Hello, Nathaniel," Toshi replies cautiously, extending his hand.

Taking it, Machuzak's tone remains unchanged. "Tell me you are not part of this, Toshi, I pray that you tell me."

Matsushima looks at the younger man with some surprise, which quickly however dissolves into comprehension, and he nods. "Given recent events I can understand why you suspect me, Nathaniel. I would have suspected me myself. But no, when I learned that deep shadows had been cast on my reputation, I decided my duty was to clear my name."

"How did you know? Hefei, I mean."

"Ah, that," Matsushima smiles. "Some time ago, when you showed me the dragon and fish emblems, I told you they were Korean, but Korean culture, after all, flows from China. Hefei was the only possibility."

"Come," Xiu interrupts the reunion. "This way. Quickly."

He leads them upstairs into a computer room where two others sit at a table. Archangelsky speaks first, with fatality. "Hello, Park. Since I do not carry gun, I strangle you now with my bare hands."

Sangjun Park recoils as Slava moves forward, but T. J. restrains him. "Meet Dragonmaster," he says to her, and to Park: "You have fled here?"

"A few days ago he appeared," Xiu explains, "asked for a job. He has been a visitor once before, his credentials are good, so we have let him work on magnets."

"I told you I was trying to warn you!" Park exclaims agitatedly.

"Your warnings were bullets made of shit," Slava responds with menace, "I have said before."

Even as Machuzak concedes that the bizarre breadcrumbs did lead him to Wilson, Rasmussen, Park casts a pleading gaze at the young Chinese sitting next to him.

"Tell them!" Xiu commands, revealing genuine anger, but the second fellow remains mute. "This is Longwei Zhao. He works on magnets as well. I have always thought him to be very strange, secretive. As of this morning I know why. Tell them what Park has told me!" Xiu raises his hand, preparing to strike. "I'll have you arrested, shot, if you don't speak!" The director begins shouting in Chinese, hitting him on the head.

"Sir..." T. J. holds her hand up, sits down facing Zhao, leans over and waits. Her posture lets him know that he isn't going anywhere.

At length, surrounded, Zhao begins in broken English. "Five years ago, Leonard Rasmussen gave me money to work on ITER project here. To us he was great master. He liked it here and visited often. One day he comes late to my lab and offers me more money than I could ever dream of in China. I ask why, is this for fellowship at CFRC? He tells me, maybe that too, if I prevent ITER magnets from working."

"Rasmussen wanted to sabotage ITER!" T. J. blurts out, astounded.

Zhao nods desperately. Machuzak registers not the slightest surprise.

"I came up with simple plan, but could not force myself... As much as I honor Rasmussen, no. Too much at stake. Rasmussen angers, tells me my career is finished, done. I am so upset, I tell Park, my friend."

All eyes swivel back to the Korean, who attempts to rise until Xiu forces him down. "I went to ITER for two years as post-doc..."

As we know, Archangelsky nods, seeing the damn video in his mind's eye, as we know.

"Some time Dr. Krieg-Zuber was visiting," Park continues. "He becomes friendly, takes me out to dinner at French restaurants. One night we get a bit drunk, I tell him about Rasmussen's attempt to bribe Zhao—"

"Krieg-Zuber?" Machuzak bores into Sangjun Park. "You told him that Leonard wanted to sabotage ITER?"

Very slowly, sadly, the Korean nods. "It was like story, 'Hey, did you hear that Dr. Rasmussen wants to sabotage ITER?' A joke."

Nothing, ever, was a joke to Krieg-Zuber. Suddenly things are beginning to become clear—crystal.

"Did you tell him how?" Archangelsky puts in severely, casting around for a blowtorch, but the room contains little more than terminals. "Method."

"I could only give him sketch of sketch Zhao gave me."

"Jesus," Machuzak whispers. With his natural paranoia, Krieg-Zuber must have quickly begun to expect something. No wonder he surveilled every person at the lab. "How did Wilson get involved?"

Park hangs his head, wipes his hair aside. "I was at CFRC for a while—"

"You get around," snarls Slava, "like venereal disease."

"Difficult to find permanent job in physics. I became friendly with Jerry Wilson and mentioned..."

"Jesus," Machuzak whispers again, wondering whether the posters around him are advising DO NOT TALK TO STRANGERS. "Did Krieg-Zuber find out what you told him?"

Park shrugs. How should he know?

"I doubt it," puts in Toshi, for the first time saying anything. "He seems to think only that I proposed the deuterium bottle bomb to Wilson."

"Did you?" Nathaniel suddenly asks, staring.

"We joked about such scenarios," Matsushima stares back with equal intensity, "as you and Slava did. We all hated."

Sangjun Park cannot follow the sidebar and continues. "Sometimes I receive mail from Jerry, not on lab network. Months ago, I begin to get messages from him, strange messages. I think he is up to something, not sure."

"You could have told us!" Machuzak returns with his fist at the Korean's chin.

This time Park jumps to his feet. "I was trying! I did not know exactly what he was doing. What would I tell you, anyway? All this?" He throws up his arms, glancing desperately around the room.

Machuzak's patience has ended. "What *would* Jerry he doing?" he growls, turning once more to Zhao. "How did you plan to sabotage ITER's magnets? Five years ago they were already designed, under construction."

Zhao's reply is a shake of his head. "You don't need to sabotage magnets, just quench-protection system." Through his imperfect English the young man explains his diabolically simple plan. When checking that the quench-detection system is operating properly—the fiber optics, the pressure detectors, the voltage comparators—you don't want to fire the great breakers or risk wasting the explosive resistors. You merely want to see that the quench detectors are producing the proper signals. You put the system into "test mode," which tells it to ignore the quench signals. But if the system is in test mode when the magnets do go critical, it will ignore a genuine quench.

"Very clever," Slava nods, stroking his beard.

"Shut up!" With the push of the past days, ITER's magnets have been quenching on nearly every run. Zhao might as well have planted a car bomb—

"But you never carried out your plan?" Machuzak presses.

Zhao shakes his head.

Park nods. "I think Wilson has—on ASSET."

"Wilson was arrested two months ago," D'Abro objects. "He's out on bail but hasn't been allowed at CFRC since."

"Doesn't matter," replies Sangjun Park. "It is three lines of code in the quench-detection software. Months ago he wrote to me about a surprise on Leonard Rasmussen's birthday. All he needed to do was have the bug activated on that date."

"Are you sure he did this?" Machuzak bears down harder.

"He really hated Rasmussen."

That Nathaniel knows. "When is Leonard's birthday?"

"Yesterday," Park answers without expression. "You are too late."

"No," says Toshi, glancing at his watch, "today. The deadline has just passed in Austin."

Machuzak feels his breathing stop. There is the same sensation of the room receding that he experienced yesterday, today, in Austin. Again he feels about to faint and grabs the nearest cabinet for support. Shaking off the dizziness, he takes out his handset and a few seconds later is speaking to Theresa in the bunker. He can hear the countdown clock in the background:

"Twenty-seven, twenty-six, twenty-five…"

"Theresa, this is Nat calling from China. Stop the run immediately."

"Twenty…nineteen…"

"The countdown is going, Mac."

He can hear the screeching. "Theresa, believe me, if you don't stop that countdown, the machine will blow sky high."

"Thirteen…twelve…eleven…"

She shouts the order on to Larissa. "Theresa, Machuzak hasn't been acting—"

"Larissa!"

"Damnit!"

"This instant!"

Theresa punches out the words with every bit of authority in her possession. The COE capitulates, hits the emergency stop and the countdown ends at t-minus three seconds.

They are not clear. The detection circuitry is locked in test mode, Ari Socarides confirms with horror, and the massive electrical current circulating in Prometheus' superconducting magnets will circulate quite literally forever. The energy needed to blow the machine remains stored within. They now have a live bomb that must be defused before anything causes the magnets to go critical.

Machuzak is now holding two conversations simultaneously: one with Abbuhl in the control room, the other with Zhao in China.

"Mac, sir," says Fred, "this is being caught between the proverbial rock and a deadline. We are close, so close…"

"Is there a manual override to the quench-protection system?" Nathaniel asks, flailing about. "Can you shunt the current out of the magnets before anything goes wrong?"

"Manual override? Mac, nothing in America has had a manual override for at least forty years."

Machuzak kicks the table where he is standing. "Fuck! Who designs these things?"

"We do, *Herr Doktor* Professor, sir. Maybe we could rig up a by-pass—"

Machuzak returns to Zhao. "Will the software reset to run mode if we reboot?"

Zhao makes a question mark with his shoulders. "I do not know what Wilson did. If he followed my idea, I can perhaps find the bug and remove it, but you should just reinstall the original code."

Socarides can't find the original.

"Fix it," Machuzak orders Zhao to log on as he gets a password from Ari, who must port a drive between the secure and unsecure machines.

Xiu, taking Machuzak aside, says that it is a huge risk. "I think this person is crazy."

"Compared with some others," Machuzak replies, "he has acted with great restraint."

Under their observation, Zhao scans the program. Only a few minutes go by before he points. "There."

Indeed. Jerry Wilson, the lowly diagnostician, had sabotaged ASSET, sabotaged it in a way that would utterly destroy it at the next quench.

Zhao, though, believes it should be simple to fix and within a few more minutes has made the corrections. In Austin they port the code back to the secure boxes, restart the system and a few checks confirm that everything is finally in order.

"We'll see you guys tomorrow…today," Machuzak says to Abbuhl and Socarides and signs off.

"Can we arrest these people?" Slava asks T. J.

"I'm afraid that's up to the Chinese authorities," she answers with a glance at Xiu. "Honestly, I don't know what you'd arrest them for."

They cannot afford any time and prepare to depart. In the lobby, Xiu bids them tarry just a few moments more and says something to an assistant. Shortly afterward, the young woman returns with a small tank, a miniature version of the deuterium bottles that have caused so much grief. Xiu presents it to Machuzak. "Please accept this as a token of our esteem and as an apology for all the trouble we have inadvertently caused you."

"What is it?" Nathaniel and Slava ask simultaneously.

"Helium-three."

The words shock the visitors into silence. At length, Machuzak stutters, "W-where did you get it?"

"From the moon. Our probes have been mining it. Perhaps it will bring you luck."

The Texans wish the Chinese the best with their ITER and vanish.

* * * *

On the plane, T. J. raises the sheriff's department and a few hours later, when the image of a newly corralled Wilson is full on the rear-seat screen, she engages in an in-flight interrogation. Confronted by the evidence, it isn't long before he confesses with pride to planting the bug in the quench-detection software. Machuzak has only one question: "Who gave you the password?"

"Krieg-Zuber, of course."

Why?

"He was scared shitless about an attack and wanted me to check the program against the original source code, which I then erased."

"He didn't suspect you?" Machuzak demands with disbelief.

At once Wilson lets out a sharp laugh. "None of you guys thought I was worth anything. Cyrus, oh, he was clever, urging me to seek revenge on Rasmussen with that deuterium firecracker, but the joke was on him." Now Wilson laughs even harder. "The Terminator. Hah. He didn't realize he was handing me the keys to the kingdom."

Machuzak settles back. There is not much left to understand. For another hour they argue about how to put the helium-three to use. The isotope provides more energy than deuterium-tritium, is nonradioactive, but requires a far higher ignition temperature. There's the rub.

"Perhaps in a hundred years," Toshi says, gazing fondly at the tank in his hand.

Nathaniel, sitting next to him, takes the opportunity to apologize again for his suspicions, but Toshi demurs. "In a sense you were correct. We have all been guilty of something. I have pretended that Leonard Rasmussen was beneath my contempt, but in fact I have been extremely bitter, have I not? I have ignored the opening lines of the *Dhammapada*: "'He was angry with me, he attacked me, he defeated me, he robbed me—'" those who dwell on such thoughts will never be free of hatred.'"

"It is difficult to apply teachings to oneself."

"That is true."

With that they all fall into a profound sleep.

SIXTY-ONE

Eighteen and a half hours before deadline the four land in Austin. The weather has turned, turned frighteningly bad with severe thunderstorm warnings posted for the entire region. Texas thunderstorms.

When Machuzak, Archangelsky, Matsushima and D'Abro march through the Gates of Hell, they must part the crowds that have gathered there. By now it is everyone. Secretaries, technicians, engineers, physicists, cafeteria personnel, cleaning ladies. Reporters too, living and not, have sprouted up cactuslike at each step with lights and microphones, all casting at the arrivals the same question, which they cannot decipher.

Farther on, the visitors' gallery is no less swamped. People sit atop one another's shoulders, climb over the ledges, determined to get the best possible view through the observation windows. As the quadrumvirate approaches, the spectators shower them with applause, cheering and confetti, and do their best to clear a path to the control room door. All Austin has turned out to witness the great miracle of the age or the end of a laboratory. Vendors drape over the passing shoulders "A Day Without Fusion Is a Day Without Sunshine" T-shirts, free of charge.

Below they are met by handshakes and backslapping. Practically jumping from the captain's deck, Theresa throws her arms around Nathaniel, turns to embrace Slava. Reporters lying in ambush pounce at once, and finally the arrivals understand what the journalists above were clamoring about: can they deny Senator Whitman's claim of the past hours that tritium has been stolen from the lab?

"Is this true?" a dumbfounded Nathaniel asks Theresa.

True that in their absence Whitman has intensified his assaults, insisting that tritium has been stolen. She has unequivocally denied the allegations, every five minutes.

Machuzak and Archangelsky glance at each other. Slava shrugs, while Nathaniel laughs. "This is just his last-ditch attempt to divert us. Believe me, we have other things on our minds, like ITER. Where are they? Ahead, behind?"

It is now Theresa's turn to stare with incomprehension. "You haven't checked their site?"

No, since China they've been busy.

From the nearest monitor she replays the press conference. Balard, teeth clenched, clothing soaked by his own sweat, is explaining that at the urging of environmental groups, the French authorities have forced ITER to suspend operations because the machine has accumulated more than the legal limit of tritium. "We wish our colleagues in Texas well," he growls and signs off.

Nathaniel finds himself hardly able to move for this shock above the others. ITER has thrown in the towel.

"There's something about a divertor on their website," Theresa's voice penetrates his stupor. "I didn't really understand."

Slava at once puts two and two together. "Divertor in tokamak takes brunt of exposure to plasma. They intended to replace carbon divertor with tungsten one for DT experiments, a year or two from now. But when race got out of control, they couldn't, maybe forgot." Slava shrugs. "Carbon absorbs tritium."

Theresa has already sent condolences that Cadarache could not better manage its protestors, but Balard did not expect mercy from the Austinites and neither does Theresa plan to grant any. In their absence, Hasschler is explaining, they have pushed Prometheus to within the width of a mite's eyebrow of ignition. "This is several times closer than an ant's eyebrow," he says with uncharacteristic humor. Still, no cigar.

"I want to try the diamonds," Toshi presses and this time, having no choice, Hasschler acquiesces graciously.

While they were abroad Fred Abbuhl had the gems crushed in one of the machine shops and he gives the order to inject the powder into the lithium trough. Before morning the walls of Prometheus are coated with diamond dust and performance has improved. As Toshi predicted, the powder is reflecting x-rays, helping to heat the plasma. Before sunrise, 100 million viewers worldwide witness ignition in the plasma's core, a little bit, for about one second before it sputters out. It is conceivable that they might get the whole plasma to ignite before the day is out.

Toshi proposes injecting the diamonds into the water that cools the heat shield of the vacuum vessel. Why not? The order is carried out and again performance is enhanced. Slava and his cronies go to work tweaking their codes, fine-tuning the fields.

At precisely six hours before midnight, a Moravec emerges with Garrett onto the captain's deck to observe. Even on-screen, her face cannot disguise her shock that the Austin lab has not yielded and neither can she quite comprehend what is taking place. She is equally shocked that no one pays the slightest attention to her. Nathaniel alone growls, but Slava from a nearby terminal sends him mysterious advice: "Soon enough, Nat Edward'ich."

They continue with reporters from every continent sitting at their sides, bugging them. The scientists shoo them off, but without anger. The atmosphere, if Nathaniel can describe it, if he can find the right word, has become...elevated.

With each run the audience counts. "Ten...nine...eight..." With each run the crew does a little better, more of the plasma burns for slightly longer, ten seconds, twenty, fifty. Everyone, above and below, senses that the forces of Nature are converging and that the scientists are riding them. They forget the clock. They just work. They are collectively where Nathaniel has of late sometimes been, in that rare place where they have lost what they have learned and gained what they have lost. They are in the zone.

Toshi, Slava and Nathaniel consider tossing in the helium-three for good luck, but for now Toshi demurs. "The diamonds, I think, are sufficient. Let us save the helium-three for future generations."

Finally, late in the evening, Thaddeus Hasschler announces, "I believe we can achieve ignition on the next shot." His voice betrays a mixture of solemnity and pride.

Then. The thunderstorms have been rolling in, with their torrential rains and lightning crashing all around. There hasn't been a storm like this for years. When the strike finally hits, it seems preordained: a bolt, a huge bolt. It is so close that the thunderclap seems simultaneous, a bomb exploding in their midst, as on the day of the helium incident. For a minute or two they lose the lights and everyone is left gasping until the emergency power switches on. The phones come alive and the techs begin their frantic dash into and out of the tunnel. After some moments the whispers condense: they have suffered the worst. It falls to Abbuhl to convey the news. His voice is choked, he is having a hard time getting out the words. "Ladies and gentlemen, that bolt caused a massive short in the motor-generator circuitry. I regret to say that two of our remaining generators are out. We cannot fix the problem within the half hour remaining to us, and we cannot run on one. I am sorry."

Slava rises to his feet and walks slowly through the crowded room to Nathaniel's station. "God does not want us to succeed, *brat*. This is surely a sign." He slaps Nathaniel wearily on the back and, for the second time in his life, Machuzak watches a tear fall from the eyes of Yaroslav Borisovich Archangelsky.

No one moves. The knowledge that the race is lost has not penetrated and everyone remains frozen in place, stunned. At last, Nathaniel gets up and pushes his way through to Abbuhl. "Fred," he asks, "can we take power directly off the grid?"

The chief engineer has not heard such a request in decades and the glance Machuzak receives is a strange one. "Direct from City of Austin Utilities?"

Nathaniel nods.

Fred returns the nod, slowly. "Yes, we can do that, *Herr Doktor* Professor, but we'll cause Austin to black out."

"For ten seconds Austin will forgive us."

Gradually a smile creeps onto the older man's lips. He calls over to pentagon one, the MG plant, where on Abbuhl's command the operating engineer, sitting before a huge, gray control panel of the kind that traditionally occupies a hydroelectric station, switches Prometheus directly onto the Austin utility grid.

"Ten…nine…eight…" The crowd roars the numbers so loudly that the scientists can hardly hear the exchange of instructions. "… seven… six…five…four…three…two…one…zero…"

For the next ten seconds, much of greater Austin suddenly darkens. The residents, watching their lights wink off, blame it on the thunderstorm. At the end of those ten seconds, the chief operating engineer switches off all the heating power to the machine. For about thirty seconds more, in the interior of Prometheus, a star burns on Earth, unaided. Then the plasma wins out and the star vanishes.

SIXTY-TWO

All remaining bottles of champagne explode together, enveloping the control room in spray. The exuberance sweeps through the visitors' gallery up and beyond into the lobby. No New Year's celebration, not the millennium, has witnessed such yelling and cheering. To talk is futile. Garrett descends from the deck, mobbed, and seeks Machuzak out. "That was one hell of a show, Mac," he shouts over the noise, gripping the scientist's hand. "This never would have happened without you."

"Without a lot of people."

Theresa is only a step behind. She and Nathaniel embrace silently, a space within the noise and downfalling streamers and wipe away tears. D'Abro has waited her turn patiently, then practically jumps onto Machuzak, embracing him so tightly he must fight for breath.

"See ya later, Doc," she says with a smile and disappears into the crowd.

Nathaniel turns to find himself facing Moravec. "Well?" he says, but with the grimmest of expressions GlobeTex's CEO does nothing more than extend a robotic hand and a moment later, no word having escaped his avatar's lips, vanishes as well.

By the time Nathaniel has gained the lobby, the crowd is already tearing apart the Gates of Hell, pulling down the banners, tweeting. People are content to hang around until the rain stops—which it does shortly—and once it's tapered off, they pour outside, still screaming, shouting, splashing in the lake and climbing over the fountain, all in the continual glare of TV and phone lights. The fireworks begin. #ADayWithSunshine.

Eventually, Machuzak intersects paths with Slava and his wife, who also exchanges kisses with Nathaniel, then the two men stroll together toward the far end of the lake, where revelers are few and crickets many.

"Well," Nathaniel says, putting his arm around Archangelsky's shoulder, "eighteen minutes to deadline. We've improved."

Slava nods as a cloud of bats circles overhead. "So how come you are not jumping for joy?"

The scent of clean air is truly pleasant. "As I told you weeks ago, I was prepared to walk out at midnight, satisfied, regardless of the outcome. You aren't dancing in the lake either, brother."

"True." Archangelsky takes out a cigarette, contemplates it. "For me… I don't know. The cost was too high…and anyone who thinks one event has saved the world has his head up his ass…"

Only Slava when drunk claimed that they could save the world. "How do you think history will regard this moment?" Nathaniel asks him as an explosion lights up the waters of the lake. "We seem to have fulfilled our kairos."

Borisovich snorts. "If we are lucky, we will get one line: 'At 11:42 p.m. on this date, the world's first self-sustained fusion reaction was achieved in Austin, Texas.' More likely it will read: 'In that year several research groups around the globe first achieved a self-sustained fusion reaction.' Of course, the greatest possibility is that it will be credited to ITER. No one will care."

Such a destiny does not perturb Nathaniel in the slightest. "That's as it should be," he laughs. "I hope it will be taken for granted, someday."

As another skyrocket casts its fleeting glare over them, in the form of Bill Balustradi's face, Slava glances at his watch. "How jet-lagged are you?"

"Not too bad. Adrenaline has been pumping and we didn't stay long in China."

"Good. It is time to take down Whitman. Let's go."

Skirting the celebration, they climb into Slava's old Volvo and head south. Machuzak is yet reeling from the Russian's remark, but before he can ask for his meaning, Slava reflects, "I suppose it is fitting that Rasmussen ended up sabotaging own machine."

"Yes, I suppose." The sadness and anger also linger. "Funny about Krieg-Zuber, he doesn't seem to have had any hand in this—just doing his job as he saw it. He knew that something was imminent, but not what. When we found him in the control room he was trying to check the quench detection software. He hadn't realized he'd sabotaged the machine himself by giving Wilson, a nobody, the password, and his computer expert Mercedes was gone."

"He wasn't so altruistic," says Slava and hands Mac a flash ring that he plugs into his wrist-set. "T. J. found this in The Terminator's pocket."

The point of view is a lapel camera, Zuber himself invisible, voice clear. "Leonard," he says on that day half a decade ago, with a slam of his fist on the desk. "I know what you have attempted against ITER."

Leonard feigns ignorance, to no avail.

"Don't play the innocent with me, Leonard. I've spoken to Longwei Zhao, and the lad confessed. The welfare of the human race is not on your mind. You seek power, status, historical position, and nothing will stand in your way. Except me, Leonard. I am standing in your way."

"What do you want?" Rasmussen at length replies calmly.

"You will turn over control of the lab to me, unofficially for now, officially when you step down, which shall take place as soon as ASSET is commissioned. You'll put it in writing."

That is all as the scene is abruptly cut. "Do you think Rasmussen refused and Krieg-Zuber decided to poison him with heavy water?" Nathaniel muses. Archangelsky laughs somberly and Machuzak opens another video. This time it is in Krieg-Zuber's office, a conversation between him and a disgruntled Jerry Wilson.

"Jerry, I understand completely how you feel, being exploited by the fools who surround you. I know what Rasmussen has done to your life."

"Do you?" Wilson replies bitterly and launches himself on a rant that Machuzak has heard himself.

"Oh yes, I understand what it means to have one's dreams shattered… Think of your position as an opportunity, Jerry. You are a nonperson, beneath everyone's contempt. You know the lab better than anyone and fly beneath the radar with total freedom. Do what you will. Matsushima, Archangelsky and Machuzak have already decided what needs to be done. This is your moment, Jerry."

Again the scene goes dark. For a time Archangelsky and Machuzak ride south in silence, the car splashes through a big roadside puddle. "W–where are we going?" Nathaniel asks finally. "W–what are we doing?"

"You remember the reporters when we got in?" Slava chuckles his best diabolical chuckle.

Nathaniel answers with a noncommittal noise. "Something about Whitman claiming that tritium has been stolen? Sounds pretty desperate."

"It was never stolen. Let's say borrowed."

"*Slava?*" Machuzak jumps in his seat, hitting the roof of the car.

In the moonlight, he can see only the faintest outline of a smile, but it is there, gleaming. "Tell me, *brat*," Slava asks, "how would Whitman know that tritium is missing?"

Nathaniel thinks long, hard. "He has it?" he suddenly asks.

"Ah, and how would he get it?"

That question is even harder. Nathaniel falls silent as Slava exits the main road, heading…somewhere. No, he doesn't see.

"Well, once I became drinking buddy with Darrell, he confirms that Whitmans sold Exosystems to themselves and renamed it Novatech.

They make parts for high-powered laser systems, which are used in Star Wars program and in laser-fusion devices, at home, abroad. That fifty million they siphoned off from magnetic fusion went to NIF, and from NIF back into their own pockets."

"Efficient recycling."

"*Ochen'*. They also make weapons and parts for uranium processing that they sell on international market. I say Whitmans are bigger scumbags than Rasmussen, so I borrow idea from Chekhov—you remember, if a gun is hanging on the wall during first act, it must go off in third. Everyone wants tritium to be stolen, I figure we'll oblige."

"How? The vault is guarded twenty-four hours a day. You're not badged, are you?"

"No," Slava shakes his head, "there was only one safe answer." He pauses long, waiting for Machuzak to guess, but his companion hasn't a clue. "Kettering, of course."

"No!" Nathaniel exclaims. "He's a goddamn marine for Chrissake!"

At that Slava chuckles again, shakes his head like a reproachful parent. "You have always been better at science than people, Nat. Of course Kettering is marine. That is point. You don't think ex-marine who wishes he participated in Tower shootout and carries fifteen rifles in his truck would jump at chance of covert operation to pull down goddamned senator?"

Nathaniel is forced to laugh, at his own naïveté, at Slava's perspicacity.

"With Kettering's help, it was play of child to get bottle of tritium out. Late at night, wave to guard, turn your backs to cameras, substitute empty bottle, put full one in elevator, go up to loading dock, collect, that's all. With all the tritium we've been using, wasn't even a suspicious maneuver."

"What have you done with it?" Nathaniel asks, yet confused.

Slava shrugs. "One night I met Darrell Whitman under that pavilion on top of Mt. Bonnell and—sold it to him." He taps his breast pocket.

"*Slava!*" Nathaniel shouts again, no other reaction being possible. He cannot think of how many federal laws the Russian has broken. At the same time he is amazed and impressed by how much has been going on behind his back, although knowing Archangelsky, perhaps he shouldn't be. They again fall into silence. Machuzak has lost track of where they are, on this moonlit night at 4:00 a.m., several hours south of Austin, almost to Laredo, near the uncontrollable Mexican border.

"Now," says Archangelsky, pulling over to the side of the road, "we are going to do something I have always wanted to do."

Slava takes some binoculars off the backseat and they get out. Shortly, another car pulls up and parks thirty meters down the road. A figure opens the door and approaches. It is T. J., carrying a long-focal-length camera.

"Hi, Doc," she says in a low voice, smiling.

A moment later a third car approaches and parks not far off. This one is easy to identify—Garrett's limo, complete with longhorns, and by the time The Chairman alights, Machuzak isn't surprised. But he is when the chauffeur opens the other door and a Moravec climbs out, a live one.

The gang's all here, again, thinks Machuzak.

Slava leads them through a clump of woods. They stop at the far side, remaining hidden. About fifty meters before them, behind a chain-link fence, stands a large warehouse, one of those corrugated metal jobs. Sodium lamps light the perimeter with their harsh glare. Two men are talking in front of the office. Slava hands Machuzak the night glasses.

"Who's that?" he asks.

"Darrell Whitman."

"The other?"

"He's one of mine," says T. J., indicating the fellow with a dark complexion and beard as she shoots a video.

Soon, Whitman ducks into the office and brings out the LP-18 tritium bottle. The plant hands him a briefcase from the trunk of a car sitting in front of the warehouse.

"That's it," says T. J. "You guys stay put."

She draws her gun and walks through the open gate. "Hands up! Police!" she calls, reaching them.

Whitman makes a break for it, but when T. J. fires a warning shot, he freezes and raises his hands. She frisks him against the wall, cuffs him, thanks her colleague, waves the others over.

"Hello, Darrell," Slava says familiarly.

Whitman, without doubt his uncle's nephew, glares at him, no more.

D'Abro doesn't plan on wasting any time. "Now, gentlemen, let's take a look at what we got in here."

"You have a warrant?" growls her prisoner.

"Yeah," she slaps it in his face. "Let us in."

She cocks her pistol and Whitman capitulates without further argument.

When the lights come on inside, they reveal a cavern of wooden crates stacked nearly to the ceiling, many stamped "GlobeTex." T. J. crowbars a few open. She whistles, hoists a rifle out of a box, takes aim. Rapidly the picture becomes clear. They are standing in a wonderland of machine guns, rpgs, shoulder-launched missiles. About the only thing missing is the old standby, the AK-47.

"Well, I'd say the Whitmans are gonna have a helluva lot of explainin to do," remarks T. J. "GlobeTex too." She turns to this Moravec, a live man, who has not said a word. "Where are these weapons bound?"

After a silence Slava says, "Niger, I guess. Our environmental hero has been organizing coups over Niger's considerable uranium deposits. There is also matter of Azeri oil." Now he addresses the Moravec directly. "I think even if you can explain this to your green fans, you won't be able to explain to the law."

Belatedly, as usual, Machuzak has caught on, even more amazed at Archangelsky's espionage. "Now you have a choice," he says to the Moravec. "The Whitmans have been blackmailing you to keep quiet, right, Darrell? We blackmail you too. The lab for our silence. Take your choice."

Garrett throws a glance at GlobeTex's CEO, but the Moravec replies only, "I'll think about it."

"You'd better think quick," Nathaniel interjects. "I predict the Whitmans will begin crumbling before sundown."

"The money, Slava," T. J. says, holding out her hand as Garrett and Moravec walk away.

While Archangelsky turns over the money Darrell Whitman paid for the tritium, Machuzak removes his wallet and hands her a hundred bucks.

"What's this for?" T. J. asks, surprised.

"One conspiracy, admittedly not the original."

For a moment they regard each other but D'Abro refuses to accept the money. "Ockham's razor, yes," Machuzak acknowledges, but "the world isn't always as simple as scientists have sometimes thought."

Smiling, T. J. finally takes the bills and gives him fifty in change. "Well, be seein y'all," she says, kisses Nathaniel and Slava on the cheek and leads Whitman away. A few paces on, she turns, casts a brief glance in their direction and vanishes into the night.

SIXTY-THREE

The party scheduled for Theresa's place that evening was one of many. After six months of living in a pressure cooker, the entire CFRC community understandably exploded and the planned festivities would run nonstop. By five o'clock Nathaniel had received nearly three thousand messages of congratulation from eighty-seven countries. #GodFoundInTokamak.

He arrived at the party early to help out. Theresa appeared radiant and giddy. Collapsing into each other's arms they remained there for what seemed an hour until she said, "Oh, I have something to show you," and put into his hand a message from the president, congratulating them on their historic achievement.

"Should I have it framed?" she asked playfully. Almost certainly.

At this moment, unable to contain herself, she struck him more as a little girl at Christmas than a sober adult. "And do you know what else? Garrett has asked me to become permanent director of the lab."

"Why not?" Nathaniel replied. "You did a good job—and I don't want it."

Retreating a step with a blush, Theresa confessed she was thinking of running for office and then, pointing to the wall monitor, asked whether he'd been watching the news.

Nathaniel nodded, smiled. The news of Darrell's arrest had broken within moments of daylight and, as D'Abro had predicted, the Whitmans had a helluva lot of explaining to do. By midday, calls for an investigation were loud and Whitman's offensive against CFRC abruptly turned into a battle to save his own neck. Now, as Nathaniel watched, Big Bad Roy was explaining and explaining. Although the intricacies of his and Thomas's shady dealing through their laser company were surely lost on the public, the one thing everyone comprehended was that the brothers Whitman had been engaged in illegal arms trafficking and only hours ago attempted to sell a strategic material to a foreign national.

"You look like the cat who ate the canary," Theresa said, and Nathaniel couldn't deny his satisfaction.

Not permitting him time to gloat, Theresa asked that he bring up some ice cubes from downstairs. Certainly. Turning from politics,

Nathaniel descends to the basement to get a few trays from the extra refrigerator there and opens the door. It is one of those units with the freezer compartment on top. He removes the ice-cube tray and pauses to glance over the contents of the refrigerator, to see if there is anything else they might use. Seven Up? Grabbing a bottle, he is about to shut the door when something glints in his eye. The refrigerator is absolutely normal, as far as he can tell. Bottles of wine, tonic, juice, extra stores for these occasions, and an ice cube stuck on the rack in the back corner. He hasn't dropped anything, and that is precisely what bothers him now. It's been sitting there a long time. The soda bottles, wine bottles all contain liquid, as they should at 38 degrees Fahrenheit, the reading on the thermometer. He taps it; it seems to be in working order. He lowers the stuff in his arms to the rough floor, empties out a small freezer bag, collects the cube and pockets it.

Upstairs he tells Theresa that he's forgotten something important, and will be back in a couple of hours. Kissing her, he heads down to the MTF. What he has in mind won't take five minutes. At his terminal he first accesses the same Material Safety Data Sheet that he and Slava found months ago. Yes, they'd missed it before, the melting point of deuterium oxide: 4 degrees C, 39 degrees F. To be certain, he carefully measures out ten milliliters of the cube, which has by now melted in the bag, and weighs it on one of the laboratory balances. No question remains in his mind: this water is heavy.

* * * *

Nathaniel walked through the party in a daze. Even when everyone gathered around the television to watch T. J. explain the discovery of the arms cache and the Whitman connection, he did not care, or when Whitman himself appeared for the tenth time making impotent denials about his involvement. Even when Slava said he called the senator's office, offering him stock in a cold-fusion company, Nathaniel's own laugh struck him as distant and hollow, as if it had come from someone else. When he accepted Toshi's hand and heard the words "By devotion to selfless work one achieves the supreme goal of life," they left almost no impression.

At 3:00 a.m., once everyone had departed and he and Theresa were at last alone, he bid her follow him into Leonard's study, where he asked her to sit. Standing above her he said, simply, "I found an ice cube downstairs."

For a moment Theresa's lungs appeared about to collapse under the air she expelled, but her eyes remained dry and she displayed no panic. At length she said, staring straight ahead, talking as if to herself, "I had to put an end to it."

"You read the diaries?"

She nods. "There were so many treacheries, so many. The bribes, the blackmails, the battles, the affairs… I think it was the one with Lise that finally killed me." She glanced up at him, smiling faintly. "It's always that, isn't it…? He so utterly betrayed me, everyone."

At once Machuzak felt utterly betrayed himself, but utterly incapable of passing judgment. "How did you know about the properties of heavy water? It's one of the more arcane facts I've ever stumbled upon."

Theresa shrugged, still as if elsewhere. "You can find it on Wikipedia, or in that old edition of the *Britannica* behind you. I needed to give a talk to some women's club and looked up deuterium, that's all."

"It's not easy to poison someone with heavy water," said Nathaniel, becoming analytical again.

"Oh, there was time, plenty of time."

"And where did you get it? It doesn't come out of the tap."

He's afraid to hear the answer, but as she stares up at him with limpid eyes, he cannot doubt what it will be. "From your lab. You made a lot, Mac. I would just come by sometimes and put a bottle outside your window."

Nathaniel vainly attempted to absorb the knowledge that he had been an unwitting accomplice in Leonard's death and found himself unable to react. Theresa was going on from afar about how she would just mix it in Leonard's morning coffee, or put it in his drinking cup on the exercise machine in the other room. "But I don't know that it worked," she laughed suddenly, brightly. "And you can't prove it. I think Leonard died of natural causes."

"You're right, I can't prove it. Have you been blackmailing me with this? And were you guiding us to the Whitmans' company?"

She nodded matter-of-factly. "I didn't know every detail, not at all, but I wanted you and Slava to end it…all of it. Are you going to turn me in, Mac? I think you must, you are so honest, the most honest person I know."

"God, Theresa, why did you tell me? Why?" It's the only thing he can manage. Managing no more, he leaves the study and wanders out of the house.

* * * *

A long week passed before Machuzak began thinking and when he did, he could not avoid wondering whether Theresa's behavior of the past months, what he had taken for grief, might be construed as something else. He sent her a message that he needed some time alone, but the fact was he could not decide on a course of action and hoped that time would provide the solution.

A few weeks later, Moravec announced that GlobeTex would withdraw from CFRC. That aspect of their plan had backfired. As Whitman came under increasing attack and faced imminent indictment on multiple charges, Moravec's past and radioactive present inevitably came to light and the physicists lost any leverage their paltry blackmail had given them. When he pulled the plug Moravec said, "I do not believe fusion will ever be economical."

The dominos fell rapidly and within two more weeks Garrett directed anyone not involved in the decommissioning of Prometheus to clear out his office.

"What will you do?" Machuzak asked Slava one night as they strolled down Sixth Street, pausing to glance at the gorilla.

"How long do you think gorillas live?" Slava answered.

"Probably longer than physicists."

"Longer than politicians. Did you hear Whitman's resignation today?"

Machuzak had. The opening words of the senator's resignation speech were "I have been set up," which was true. "Maybe you should become a secret agent," Nathaniel suggested.

Slava nodded approvingly as he avoided a deranged skateboarder. "Pay should be good, but I think it is inevitable that I go to work for ITER, or China. What about you?"

"You know," Machuzak said, "all of us behaved pretty stupidly at one time or another during the last months, even criminally."

Slava's response is wiped out by a blast of music as they pass one of the cafes and he needs to repeat himself. "What did we do that was so criminal?"

"Okay, suppose you were sure I committed a felony. Dead sure. Would you turn me in?"

Slava shrugs, absently accepting a tract from an evangelist. "I don't see why, unless I thought you were dangerous."

"Your internal sense of right and wrong, your duty, even your citizenship wouldn't compel you?"

"No." They stop to watch the movie playing on the screen of Fat Tuesday, which neither of them recognizes. "As usual you confuse science with life. They are two different things."

"It is easy for you to hold two truths in your head. One for science, one for life?"

"Hey man, got a cigarette?" asks a cowboy in front of one of the massage parlors.

"It is."

They walk on.

* * * *

Machuzak did not turn in Theresa, but neither could he bring himself to see her. He waited for the moment when the question would decide itself. He, Slava and Toshi all received job offers at ITER and Hefei, but only Slava swore he would go. A few times Toshi talked about starting a new religion as a tax dodge, but more often he'd say, "All things end in the Tao, as rivers flow to the sea."

On their last day at CFRC, after Nathaniel had packed away his belongings, pausing to consider the memories attached to each, the three of them ducked into the pentagon for a look at Prometheus. It stood there, as always, in the immense, dimly lit and echoic test cell. The place was deserted now, no workers scrambling over the tokamak's multifold surface. Otherwise the machine was unaltered in its appearance: gigantic, untoward, improbable. But in their minds' eye it had changed because they knew that inside that unruly beast briefly burned a star, which they had created. None of them spoke as they walked away, preferring that memory to the empty tokamak bay they would find if they ever returned.

* * * *

A few evenings later Machuzak was driving through Hyde Park and passed by T. J. D'Abro's house. On impulse he slammed on the brakes and pulled into the driveway. About to knock, he halted, as the Magnificat from Monteverdi's *Vespers* came to his ear. Aware that someone was lurking on her porch, T. J. opened the door.

"Doc!" she exclaims, face brightening. "It's about time you showed up. Why are you standing there? Come on in."

Nathaniel accepts her offer of a drink and her condolences about the fate of the lab. "What will you do now?"

"I don't know," he admits. "I haven't decided. Maybe biology…"

"You know, I quit the force again. Never could stick, and after this adventure I figured anything else would be a letdown, but I finally got me a bit of meditation in. Ever thought of becoming a private detective?" She peers at him.

No, he hadn't, Machuzak shakes his head.

"Let me tell ya, Doc, we'd make a pretty good team, you and me. I'm even getting into this music…"

She says it with such mirth, such sass, that he's tempted. They listen to music for an hour, then another until it is, as on that other occasion, very late.

"By the way," she says then, narrowing her eyes, "what were you really doing down in the power area that night at one o'clock in the morning?"

"Bedbug—!"

She kisses him gently on the lips before wrapping her arms around his neck and laying her head on his shoulder, and this time they both manage to fall asleep.

ACKNOWLEDGMENTS

In 1959, when I was six, my family relocated from the Philadelphia area to Lawrence Township, New Jersey, after my father, Milton, got a job at the Princeton Plasma Physics Laboratory. Until a year earlier PPPL had been the classified Project Matterhorn and for some time to come it was the leading fusion research center in the world. I consider myself lucky to have spent my formative years climbing around the machines there, watching the researchers perform experiments and pestering them with boy-scientist questions.

Although I eventually became a physicist, it was in the area of general relativity and cosmology and I cannot claim to be an expert in plasma physics. While writing *Firebird*, I not only relied on many friends and colleagues for technical details but am indebted to one in particular for the initial impetus to undertake the novel.

During the 1980s Bill Hooke, who had been my father's closest friend at PPPL, suggested to me a suspense novel set at a fusion lab. The idea stuck, but only a decade later were we able to get to work on it. The plot was devised in conjunction with Bill and during the initial stages I relied heavily on him for technical advice and background material. At that time, 1995–1996, I was able to spend a year at the lab as a visitor, doing research while researching the novel. The first version of *Firebird*, however, ended up lying dormant on my computer for almost a decade and between 2007 and 2012 it was completely rewritten, twice. At this stage perhaps little remains of Bill's original idea, but it is my pleasant duty to acknowledge him as the prime instigator.

Let me also express my gratitude to Rush Holt, then assistant director of the lab, now US congressman, and the entire gang at PPPL for making me feel at home during my long-ago stay there, and for giving me free run of the place even when they knew what was up. I am certain that I have forgotten many people who provided one suggestion or another, but special thanks are due to Robert Budny, Sam Cohen, Nat Fisch, Bob Gross, Paul LaMarche, Charlie Neumeyer, Howard Seliger and Patti Wieser, as well as non-PPPL folks Mijan Huq, Sharon Micinksi and the Travis County Sheriff's Department. Most of all I am indebted to my buddy Al von Halle, PPPL's chief electrical engineer, for his treasure trove of stories and technical information, who after well over a decade never seems to lack enthusiasm for the endeavor.

—Tony Rothman
Princeton, 2012